KEEP HIM CLOSE

Keep Him Close

EMILY KOCH

Harvill *Secker*

LONDON

1 3 5 7 9 10 8 6 4 2

Harvill Secker, an imprint of Vintage,
20 Vauxhall Bridge Road,
London SW1V 2SA

Harvill Secker is part of the Penguin Random House group of companies
whose addresses can be found at global.penguinrandomhouse.com

Penguin
Random House
UK

First published by Harvill Secker in 2020

penguin.co.uk/vintage

A CIP catalogue record for this book is available from the British Library

ISBN 9781787301016 (hardback)
ISBN 9781787301023 (trade paperback)

The excerpt from the poem 'The Light Gatherer' is from
Feminine Gospels © Carol Ann Duffy 2002, reproduced
with permission of the Licensor through PLSclear.

The excerpt on p.129 is from the poem 'Want' from
My Body © Joan Larkin 2007, reprinted by
permission of Hanging Loose Press.

Typeset in 10.75/15.75pt Scala by Jouve (UK), Milton Keynes
Printed and bound in Great Britain by Clays Ltd, Elcograf S.p.A.

Penguin Random House is committed to a sustainable future
for our business, our readers and our planet. This book is made
from Forest Stewardship Council® certified paper.

MIX
Paper from
responsible sources
FSC
www.fsc.org   FSC® C018179

For my parents

and as you grew,
light gathered in you

Carol Ann Duffy
'The Light Gatherer'

Never, never, never, never, never.

William Shakespeare
King Lear, Act V, Scene iii

It should have been louder.

He would think, later, about all the other people, only metres away, who must have heard it. A taxi driver on Queen Charlotte Street with his windows lowered in the August heat, picking up the post-pub crowds. A pot-washer from the Italian in Welsh Back, tossing rubbish bags out of the kitchen glow and into the dark. A double bassist with the blues band playing at the Old Duke, packing the boot of his battered Skoda.

He would wonder if it was louder for them, at ground level, or for him, ten metres above the road, too scared to lean over the edge and look as the screams and howls began, and the sirens floated closer.

That thud, when flesh connected with tarmac: he knew the truth as soon as he heard it. Still, for a few seconds, he waited for a laugh or a shout. He waited to hear his own name pitched up from the road.

But you don't survive that kind of fall.

He didn't need to look. The sound was enough. That cracking thump, heavy and hard but too short and nowhere near loud enough to measure up to the life it had marked the end of.

He had to get away from here.

I

Alice

17th August

Was there a more irritating sound than the laughter of other people's children? In the impossible heat of the loft, Alice had considered, for a moment, opening the skylight. But that would make the din louder. They were probably on their scooters – thank God those hadn't been around when her boys were small – flying down the alleyway that linked Alice's road to the allotments butting up against the bottom of her neighbours' gardens. She hadn't yet lifted the lids on more than three boxes, but already sweat pricked at the skin across her back; it pooled in the creases behind her knees as she crouched; it made her eyebrows itch. She carefully untied her hair and plaited it again, sweeping the stray strands from her face, splitting its bulk into three precise sections, and lifting the weight of it off the back of her neck. This room was an oven. But she would not open that window and intensify all those whoops and shrieks and giggles. Or, God forbid, the parents' laughter. That was always somehow worse, though she couldn't decide whether it was a mother's glee or a father's that repelled her more.

She looked up at the neat rows of boxes stacked on the shelves, scanning the typed labels: 'Plugs and electrical items', 'Bulbs and fuses', 'Vinyl (A–H)', 'Vinyl (I–Z)'. One box on the top shelf contained the old turntable she and Étienne once put to use every evening. Next to it were two more whose labels

3

had faded but she could just about make out what they said: 'Board games' and 'Christmas decorations' (neither had been touched in years). She pulled one marked 'B & L (March 2006– September 2010)' on to the floor and lifted its lid, before leafing through exercise books and school reports – this wasn't what she was looking for.

'What you doing?' Lou's deep voice behind her made her jump, and she slammed the lid down, creating a cloud of dust.

'Where did you spring from?' She coughed, turning to face her younger son. He sat on the edge of the loft hatch, legs dangling over the ladder. How long had he been watching her? She caught a glimpse of something in his eyes, something she could not quite identify.

It was quickly replaced with a grin and the mocking arch of his eyebrows. 'Got something to hide?'

She stood, reaching a hand out to the slanting beam above her head. 'The answer's no, Lou.'

The grin disappeared. She had correctly deduced why he had sought her out; it wasn't to see what she was doing.

'As in, no, you haven't got anything to hide?'

She pressed her fingers harder against the warm wood of the beam.

Lou pushed himself up from the hatch and shifted his attention to the light cord, plucking at it repeatedly to switch the bare bulb on and off, on and off. Keeping her eyes on him, Alice listened to more children racing through the alleyway. Surely it was past their bedtime? Those parents would be the same ones complaining after the school holidays that their little darlings wouldn't settle back into a reasonable night-time routine. Every September, they'd come in and moan to each other in the kids' section of the library. She'd make an excuse to take herself off to the health and well-being section upstairs, or sort through the disparate collection of leaflets (covering everything from fostering information to rambling groups, choral societies to a local chess club) by the entrance. What did they expect? Children needed discipline. Consistency.

She'd given that to both her boys, so what had gone wrong? How could one of them become Benny and the other turn into this scruffy, disrespectful dropout in front of her? Lou had not long turned eighteen, and she didn't like the man he was becoming.

He kept toying with the light cord. On. Off. On. Off.

She ran a hand across her face, shielding her eyes. 'Stop that.'

He didn't. 'Looking for the birthday cards we used to make you?'

So he had remembered, after all. She didn't care about these things; she wasn't bothered about presents and flowers. But the lack of respect from her boys got to her. She'd seen forty-five years come and go, and she'd dedicated almost half of that to them. And today, even Benny had failed to say anything.

'No,' she lied, pressing so hard against the beam now that her wrist ached. 'I didn't keep much. Hoarding is for people who can't let go of the past.' She meant it. She hadn't kept many things from the boys' childhood, and whenever the time felt right she streamlined her collection even more. Today, she was angry – both with them and with herself for caring. Today she would get rid of the few old cards she had held on to.

Lou let go of the light cord, flicking it at the wall, and gestured at a pile of boxes in the far corner. 'Over there. You saved some of the ones Benny made.'

She didn't move. It drove her mad that he knew her so well.

'You've done an inventory up here, have you?' She laughed. 'Watch it, you'll make me proud if you're not careful.'

He snorted. 'Kill me before I become as anal as you.'

She had kept some cards made by Benny at school, he was right. None from Lou, though. But that was only because his had upset her so much. Even at the age of four or five, he'd known how to hit a nerve, signing them 'from Louis and Daddy', or including his father in a crayon family portrait of the four of them, where her face would invariably be drawn into a frown.

If he knew that she hadn't kept many of his childhood drawings, then presumably he also knew she did have a box with Benny's hospital bracelet, his baby blanket, a curl of his hair, one of his tiny white vests. And that there was no box with similar mementos of Lou, born less than two years later into a home full of noisy discord and hurt silences. Alice looked at him. She couldn't imagine him caring. If pushed, she could explain it. The lack of a baby box for him had seemed appropriate, she would say. He'd never been very babyish – not with those knowing eyes he had. To this day he remained a strange mix: a wise old soul and a petulant child woven into one.

As if on cue, the childish side of him emerged. He began jumping from one side of the open hatch to the other, landing only a few inches away from the edge.

'Lou, don't. It's not safe.' She knew she was talking to herself and turned her back on him, resuming her examination of the boxes on the shelves. The boys' extensive collections of books, CDs and DVDs filled most of them. She always thought of the loft as hers, but it was their space, too, she supposed, if a room was claimed by the amount of a person's belongings contained within it. There was little of hers in here.

Lou's feet thudded behind her, followed by the creak of the floorboards under his shifting weight as he lined up his next jump across the hatch. 'Safe's boring, *Maman*,' he said.

She closed her eyes and tilted her head to one side, biting her lip. *Maman*. He did it on purpose.

'Who wants to be safe?' he continued. Thud. Creak. Thud. 'It's all about the thrill.' Thud. Creak. Thud. 'That's what makes it exciting.'

6

Alice fished out a tissue from her pocket and dabbed the sweat from her forehead. She knew Lou wanted her to watch him, that he wanted her to beg him to stop. Instead, she lifted the boxes she'd been through back into their places, matching each label with the corresponding stickers on the shelves. When Étienne had been here, the loft had been full of instruments, and a mess. He needed to keep his old guitars, just in case, he'd said, along with dozens of boxes full of records. (She should have sold them when he moved out, rather than looking after them until he was ready to take them away. She certainly could have used the cash – it might have fed the three of them for a couple of weeks.) There had been unusual drums and other percussion picked up on his travels which he claimed might be of use some day. It would all be part of Benny's musical education, he used to say. Not any more. Now, there was less of him in here than there was of her, and that took some doing.

Casting her eyes around, there were only two things she could see of hers. One was a box of old piano music her father had delivered one day, with the explanation that he didn't have space for it and she should really consider playing again. She'd ignored him, but kept it up here. It was comforting to occasionally flick through her collection of Mozart, adorned with neat pencil notes in her teacher's hand marking up the fingering for particularly tricky runs, circling tempo changes she was prone to miss, identifying moments when the music should be 'breathless' or she needed to 'toss the note away'; it was reassuring to thumb at the corners at the bottom of each page, folded ready for a quick turn mid-performance. She was struck suddenly by a mix of memories – one of playing Mozart's *Fantasia in D Minor* when she was pregnant with Lou, her first feeling of his kicks as she floated her wrists through the adagio's beautiful, tugging, 'sighs' section; the other of her teacher's voice as she played the same piece as a girl. *'Breathless'. Popcorn in her belly.*

7

'Lift your wrist, now drop it.' *Lou's tiny unborn feet, dancing.* She tore her eyes away from the box to her suitcase: plain, black, sturdy, and little used. It looked tempting, as she stared at it now, with Lou continuing to launch and land behind her. But she would never be that person. She could never abandon her responsibilities. Lou had that part of Étienne in him which meant he might up and go at any moment. Some mornings, after they'd had a row, she was surprised that he was still there and hadn't packed his bags and disappeared into the night. Benny would never do that to her, though. In a few weeks he'd be leaving for university, but that was different. Happy, carefree, intelligent and popular – he had the world at his feet, her eldest. Even through the disappointment she felt today, she was proud of him, going out into the world.

'You should watch it, though, up here on your own,' Lou said. 'You're not as sure-footed as I am.'

'I'm always careful.'

He laughed. 'You don't say.'

The tightness in her chest coiled. She studied what she could see of his face for something other than derision, something other than disappointment. But she couldn't see much behind the mess of long hair, dyed a pale green-grey a couple of days ago. Seapunk, Benny had called it, much to Lou's irritation. 'Do I look like a fucking mermaid to you?' he had snarled. Alice had left them to it. Perhaps if she showed little interest in Lou's hair, he might cut it off, tidy himself up and finally look presentable.

He was sweating now, short of breath, still jumping from one side to the other. She imagined his foot catching on something as he leapt over the gap. Imagined him falling. As though he knew what she was thinking, he stopped.

'Hot as hell up here.' He leaned back against the exposed brickwork, panting. 'Why don't you open the window?'

'I'm going downstairs, please fold the ladder when you're done.'

She swatted at a moth as it fluttered past her face. It changed direction, heading towards Lou.

With a swift snatch of his hands, he caught it, cupping it gently and peering at it through the gap between his thumbs.

'Hello, little guy.'

'Don't,' she said.

'Don't what?'

She wasn't sure what she was asking him not to do. Not to look at it? Not to taunt it? Not to kill it? Her face flushed. Was she programmed to think badly of him? To nag at him, to assume the worst, to berate him before he even acted? He would do it, though. That was the thing.

Lou let the moth go and it fluttered for a moment before it dropped to the ground. 'I think its wing is broken.'

Alice stepped over the hatch, and together they crouched above the moth until it regained its strength and took off again.

'Talking of being broke.' Lou straightened, stood, leaned back against the wall.

She had been right. 'No, Lou.' She stood too, taking a step away from him towards the skylight. She moved her hand to scratch her back, then – with what she hoped was a subtle movement – dropped her fingers to check her back pocket. Her purse was still there. She always kept it on her these days, at least when she knew he was in the house.

'A tenner. Come on.'

'I said no.'

He exhaled, flaring his nostrils, and sneered at her. 'You've got wet patches on your shirt.' He pointed at her armpits. 'It's disgusting. You know you don't have to wear that stuff all the time? Normal people have casual clothes; they get changed when they come in from work.'

Despite herself she reacted, adjusting her collar, tugging downwards on the front panels of her white shirt. 'Normal people also wash their clothes occasionally, darling,' she said, tilting her head back as she sniffed, staring at his oil-stained grey T-shirt with a faded band logo splashed across the front. 'Fresh perspiration isn't what smells. The odour comes from the bacteria—'

'How many times, *Maman*? Save your pathetic trivia for your pub quiz team. Oh, wait . . .' He laughed. He didn't need to explain why he found that funny, he'd pointed out her lack of friends enough times. 'Give me a twenty and I'll be out of your hair.'

'A twenty now, is it?'

'Don't you love me?' He threw this at her every so often and it blindsided her each time. There was no humour here, no wheedling, no messing around.

But she never answered.

He took a step towards her. 'Okay, ten quid. That's all I need. Benny'll buy the rest of my drinks. Let me get him one.'

She refused to back away. 'No. If you're so determined to throw your education out of the window and spend your life get-ting covered in oil under a car, go and do that. Earn some money of your own.'

He took another step in her direction, and this time she did move slightly – enough to feel the boxes behind her. She put a hand out to steady herself against the wall, brick dust and grit sticking to her damp palm.

'We're back to that, are we?' he laughed. Yes, they were. Back to that envelope on Thursday which he hadn't shown her the contents of. He hadn't needed to, Benny had told her: D, D, E. Why had she bothered pushing him so hard all these years? He wouldn't be getting a decent job with those grades; he wouldn't be able to support himself, let alone a family if he ever had one. He was going exactly the same way as his father, living off others, scrounging around for his next pay packet.

She felt dizzy as she moved away from the wall. The heat was getting to her. As she swayed slightly, Lou grabbed her wrist, pressing hard. She wrenched away, stumbling against him, and fell to the boards covering the floor of the loft. Before she could push herself up to stand, Benny's face appeared at the top of the ladder.

'What's going on?' he asked. She put a hand to her hair, smoothing it back in place. 'Lou?' Benny climbed into the loft and glared at his younger brother.

Her sons had always been tall, but from her position on the floor they looked enormous. Athletic, with their father's strong build; they towered over her. Benny, surely, had stopped growing by now – at nineteen he should have reached full height. But Lou wasn't showing any signs of slowing down.

'You all right, Mum?' Benny asked. 'Jesus, Lou. You're such a dick. What did you do?'

'I'm fine,' she said. 'I didn't realise you were home. Nice day at the seaside?' She managed to speak without her voice wavering, and stood up, dusting herself off.

'Good,' Benny said, not taking his eyes off Lou, who smirked back at him.

'A mysterious one, isn't he?' Lou squared up to his older brother.

'Cut it out.' Benny looked uncomfortable. 'And apologise to Mum.'

Alice looked at their feet, not far from the edge of the hatch. 'Let's all go downstairs, shall we?'

Lou smiled. 'He doesn't want to tell us what he got up to at the beach, it appears. What is it with this family and secrets?' Alice swallowed and looked at Benny. He was busy avoiding Lou's eyes, just like her. 'We all have them. Don't we, *Maman*?'

'What do you want me to say?' Benny said. 'It's Weston. We had ice cream, went in the arcades. End of.'

'Whatever.' Lou returned to his primary concern. '*Maman*

was just deciding how much money to give me to help us celebrate my A-level results.'

Benny looked at her warily, watching for a reaction, but she
wouldn't let one escape. He stepped back towards the top of the
ladder. 'I'm not so sure I'm in the mood to celebrate with you,'
he said. 'Not if you're going to be all aggro like this. Apologise to
Mum.'

'I'm fine, honestly.' Her voice sounded quiet, and she wondered for a moment if she'd actually spoken the words out loud.

Lou ignored Benny's order. 'Piss off, then. I don't need you
cramping my style. I was doing you a favour.'

Alice saw Benny's fist clench. 'You're such a dick.'

And then – as it always went with them – Lou laughed. Benny
did, too, as he dropped his hands to the floor, lowered a foot on
to the second rung of the ladder. These two could go from the
depths of an argument to being best friends within the space of
a few seconds.

Lou called after Benny, following him to the top of the ladder.
'Wait up. Are we getting the bus?'

'Can do,' Benny shouted back, already downstairs, opening
the door to the back room and slamming it shut.

Lou stopped, halfway down the ladder. 'Hey, Mum,' he said.
She met his eyes.

'*Bon anniversaire.*'

As she listened to him bound down the stairs to join his
brother, she wondered if it hadn't been intended in an entirely
unkind way. When he spoke French, she usually saw it as a
taunt, a reminder of Étienne. But maybe he meant this as more
of a shared joke? She was often left analysing their conversations like this.

She skirted around the hatch as she went to switch off the
light, and something papery and soft squashed underneath her
bare foot. She knew what it was before she stepped away to look:

the moth. She patted the back pocket of her chinos, feeling again for her tissue to wipe its remains off the ball of her foot. The tissue was there, but something else was missing. She glanced around. Her purse must have dropped out when she fell. With a sigh, she knew it was futile to search up here for it. She knew where she would find it. Downstairs in the kitchen, on the counter, twenty pounds lighter.

With no decent qualifications, Lou wasn't likely to move out any time soon, even if he wanted to. Despite the heat, the thought made her shiver. Things between them couldn't continue like this. But how could she make it better? The damage seemed irreparable. It was done so long ago.

As they had so many times before, in the darkest hours of the night, her thoughts drifted as she heard her boys rattle keys and shut the front door, laughing.

Would she ever be free of him?

Indigo

17th August

As I climb the stairs, I rehearse what I want to say to him, keeping my eyes focused on the serene face of the woman in the portrait hanging on the wall ahead of me. *There's something I wanted to chat to you about.* No, I should launch straight in. My mouth twitches in imitation of the woman in my print, immortalised by Klimt with her elegant red fan and kimono sliding off her shoulder, her lips set in a calm and self-assured smile. How would *she* have this conversation? How would Klimt himself go about it? With passion, honesty and light-heartedness, I would guess.

Those are the things I love about his work, along with the bold colours and swathes of gold. I feel like we're kindred spirits, he and I; he wouldn't stand here on my staircase, for example, and tell me I should choose one single colour to paint the walls, instead of using blue for one side and yellow for the other. He would love the small mosaics of mirrored glass I have stuck in swirling shapes above the banister. He wouldn't turn his nose up at my collections on the edge of each step – the pile of papers, the bottles full of sea glass and shells, my scraps of beautiful fabric, the postcards I plan to frame. He wouldn't call them a fire hazard, like my sister does. He'd understand that my mind needs to be surrounded on all sides by these small pockets of beauty. He'd understand my belief that a house should look lived in, and loved.

I try another line for size. *You always used to bring girlfriends home.* No, that isn't quite right, either. I avoid the creaky step – I don't want him to hear me coming and rush me into this conversation.

It's important that I don't appear to be telling him what to do. *I'd love to meet him.* Would that work? Maybe I should try reverse psychology. *I'm not sure I need to meet him. I understand you wanting to keep him to yourself.* I grip the plate I'm carrying towards his bedroom. Maybe I shouldn't say anything at all. Now isn't the time to rock the boat, I don't want him going off to London with any reason to avoid calling me. I pause on the landing, transfixed by Klimt's delicate touches of turquoise in his subject's pale skin. In a certain light, Kane's eyes are that colour.

With one more step I can see him, through his open bedroom door. At nineteen, is my son still a teenager? He's officially a man, but always a boy to me. Certainly not old enough to be going off to university in five weeks' time. I swallow hard. He's standing by his bed with his bare back to me, head bent, looking at something in his hands. I'm struck suddenly by what I really want to say to him. *Life is better without secrets, Kane.* We learned that lesson the hard way, me and my boy.

'Kane?' I nudge the door open a little wider with my foot. 'I brought you a sandwich, love.'

Kane shoves whatever is in his hands underneath his pillow. 'Just a minute, Mum,' he calls, without turning around.

I nearly knock over a slowly burning stick of incense propped up amongst a pile of pebbles on the landing as I retreat a few steps, so that he can't see me – or more precisely, so that he won't guess that I have seen him. We don't hide things from each other, Kane and I, we never have. It was a family rule we established nine years ago, and it has served us well. Only once has he broken it: I didn't find out he was smoking for a good six months after he'd started, at the age of fifteen. When I told him that, while I didn't think smoking was a great idea, it was his lungs he would ruin and his life to do with what he would, he told me he used to conceal lines of cigarettes in the deep hem of his curtain to keep them from me. Now he leaves his packs of Marlboro Reds in full view, and I prefer it that way. If he is hiding something, it's probably a gift for me – a leaving present, perhaps? He's a sweetheart.

The door swings open, and he appears, beaming at me. 'Cheese and pickle?' He lifts the sandwich off the plate and pauses before he takes a bite. 'You know this is Ash Anderson's go-to combo?'

I recognise the name of one of his film director heroes. 'Strange. Whenever I meet him for lunch he orders the coronation chicken.'

Kane laughs as he takes the plate out of my hands and wanders into his room to add it to a pile of dirty crockery on his desk. 'Another to add to the collection.' My eyes follow him in and land on the pair of navy trainers next to the plates. *Shoes on the table are an invitation to Death.* I can hear Lily's voice saying the words; sometimes my mother's sayings are a comfort, but not always.

I pick them up, trying to do it without him noticing. Not even Kane understands why I am so bothered about avoiding bad luck. People don't get it – but then they haven't been dealt the same hand in life that I have. As I move them to the wardrobe, I'm hit by the smell of barbecue smoke coming in through his open window from one of our neighbours' gardens. The student house. That'll be Kane, next summer. Enjoying life with his new friends, not wanting to come home.

'It's a perfect evening out there.' I hope the words came out as brightly as I intended. I stay at the window, looking across the patchwork of fences and gardens. Our next-door neighbours aren't alone in their al fresco dining, and several plumes of smoke are rising into the hot August sky.

'God, yeah. Life is good, isn't it?' He's in one of these moods. My son is either happy, inspired and on top of the world or quiet and entirely wrapped up in himself. Never anywhere in between. His music gets louder, and I turn to see him doing something on his mobile. The track changes. Ambient, I think he'd call this style. It's not offensive, but it's not exactly The Clash, either. That's what I listen to when life is good.

'A lot of tips today, then?' I'm stalling.

He looks at me, confusion in his beautiful blue eyes. I made those. 'What do you mean?'

'I'm wondering why you're so happy. Work went well, did it?' It is only then that I take a proper look around his bedroom, taking in more than his unmade bed. One of his walls is bare. The shelves above his bedside table are empty.

'Oh, kind of,' he says, though I barely hear him as I stare at the space where his collection of novels used to be. 'I guess it was all right.'

All is well, all is well, all is well. I repeat my silent mantra, breathing in through my nose as I bite on my knuckles. A bin bag is propped against the end of his bed, and I see rolled-up posters and books inside it. Packing, already?

'Do you want your backpack for that lot?' I ask. He's even taken the blobs of Blu-Tack off the wall. When he leaves, it'll be like he was never here.

'Sorry?'

I kick some clothes out of the way on the floor and lower myself to sit with my back to the wall, watching him get ready. 'The one you took to France. I take it you're getting ready for uni?' Our tabby, Lucian, slips into the room and curls himself around my legs.

'Oh, you mean that stuff by my bed?' Kane asks, as he pushes through shirts in his wardrobe. The hangers clink against the rail. Will he take those with him as well? I stroke Lucian's back with a little too much pressure and he jumps away from me, finding a spot on Kane's bed instead. 'That's for the charity shop; might sell some of it too. Bit early to pack yet, don't you think?' He slips a dark green short-sleeved shirt over his shoulders.

I put a hand on to the carpet and immediately regret it, jerking it back into my lap and brushing off bits of fluff, crumbs of food and strands of hair that have stuck to it. My palms are sweating – attracting anything they come into contact with. I've always let Kane take responsibility for his room, and that includes the cleaning. I'm all for deprioritising housework (life's too short), but maybe I'll leave the vacuum in the hallway tomorrow morning and see if he fancies taking it for a spin.

I catch myself and shake my head in frustration. Cleaning? If I'm thinking of domestic chores then I'm definitely procrastinating.

'I was thinking earlier how much I love the way we are able to talk to each other so openly.' I pretend to examine the allotment dirt under my fingernails from this morning's weeding but risk a stolen look at Kane.

He presses his lips flat but says nothing as he buttons his shirt.

There's no going back now. 'As you know, secrets have a habit of being incredibly toxic.'

Am I imagining it, or do his eyes dart to the bed, to the pillow and whatever he hid earlier? Whether they did or not, he's now looking back at me.

'Mum.' He flicks his nose ring with his thumb. 'I'm not like Dad.' This leap takes me by surprise, though it shouldn't. Of course, what I want to say to him is about Glyn, on some level. Kane has always been so much more at ease talking about his father than I am.

'No. I wasn't suggesting that.' I hurry away from thoughts of my husband, but then stop myself – maybe this could work to my advantage. 'Although, now that you mention him, have I ever told you about the first time I brought him home to meet my parents?'

Kane grimaces. He knows exactly where I'm going with this.

'Listen, you've done the difficult bit. You've told me. And that went well, didn't it?' I recall that conversation, before he left for Paris in March. Of all the shocks life has handed me, my son revealing his sexuality was the most welcome. 'And you've told your friends. All I'm saying is I'd really like to meet this boyfriend of yours.'

'I know.'

'I won't embarrass you.' I don't look at him, concentrating on my wrist instead, twisting the thin yellow beaded bracelet that he brought me back from France. 'Is he older, is that it? Or is he older *and* bisexual, and you're worried he might fancy a cougar like me more than you?' I look up at him, trying to keep a straight face.

'God, Mum . . .'

I laugh. 'All right, all right. Seriously, though. I don't care who he is, love, as long as you're happy.' It's not how I planned to say it, but I haven't done too badly. 'Are you seeing him tonight? Why not suggest it?'

Kane crouches, puts a hand on my knee. 'I wish you'd focus on your own life.'

'He could come over for dinner.'

'Have you brought in your brushes from the shed yet? The easel?'

'I could make that sweet potato tagine you like.'

'Stop ignoring me. Why don't you bring your easel inside?'

'Okay. Fine. I'll bring it in, if it will get you off my back.' And I will, soon. But with any luck it will be rotten after nine years in the damp.

He stands, moves over to his desk and sprays himself with

aftershave. It's not so unlike the one Glyn used to use. 'You don't like being told what to do,' he says.

I shake my head, unseen, as I watch him rolling up the right leg of his jeans and putting his trainers on.

'And neither do I,' he continues. 'You can't fix my problems and I can't fix yours. I told you about . . . everything.' He still has a problem saying the word 'gay', no matter how much I say it is nothing to be ashamed of. 'But it wasn't because I wanted solutions. Sometimes people don't want answers; they just want someone to listen.'

When had my broken little boy become this perceptive young man? I accept defeat. 'What about Dawn? Will you be telling her next week?'

'Auntie Dawn?' He wrinkles his nose, unplugging the charger from his mobile phone, and the music stops.

'No, Dawn French, obviously.' I stretch out a hand for him to help me up. 'Yes, your Auntie Dawn! No matter what you think of her, you're going to have to tell her at some point. And Nana.' Lily has voiced her suspicions before, though Kane doesn't know this. It was the nose ring, she told me. A definite indication, apparently. Plus, she had a grandmother's intuition.

He holds my shoulders. 'You know that dress is kind of see-through, Mum?'

'It's nice and cool,' I say, brushing my hands down the flowery cotton shift, and scratch at a patch of mud on it left over from the allotment this morning.

'All the same. At least, perhaps . . .' He grins, shaking his head. 'I can't believe I'm saying this to my mother.'

'What?' I punch him on the arm, laughing with him.

'Just do me a favour and consider wearing a bra, if you're going to wear it out in public.'

'I thought you wanted me to attract a new man.'

'Yeah, but . . .' He runs a hand through his blond curls as we turn to head down the stairs. 'You've got to leave a little to the imagination.'

I check my reflection in the hallway mirror while I wait for him to bring his bike in from the lean-to at the back of the house. The dress isn't that bad. My hair, though, that has seen better days. I half-heartedly drag my fingers through the tangle of it, hanging loose just above my shoulders.

'You'll meet him,' he calls out to me as he wheels his bike through my studio. 'I promise. But not this week. If I could make it happen I would, but it's not as simple as just inviting him over. All right?'

He pushes his bike towards me and props it up under the mirror. Taking my face between his hands, he kisses me on the forehead. I remember when he first did this as a chubby toddler, and the pleasure the simple gesture brings hasn't lessened over the years. Every time he does it, I think how lucky I am to have this joy in my life. I watch as he checks his reflection one final time, hooks a faded blue baseball cap over his head, picks up his house keys, wallet and two D-locks. He opens the front door and manoeuvres his bike out. 'It's all going to be fine,' he says from the doorstep. I find myself waving, too late, at the back of the door as it slams shut.

Alice

18th August

She stood in the porch and stared at the front door, tugging her dressing gown tight around her. They knocked again, louder this time, but her hand refused to move to the handle.

Alice knew she had to let them in. She knew it was the police; she could see the bright blue and yellow of their car through the window as she came downstairs. She knew Theresa at number seventy-five would be watching through her venetian blinds and Kev at number eighty-one would be out on the front doorstep. The only thing she didn't know was what these people outside were going to tell her.

She squinted into the glare of the streetlight as she pulled the door open. There were two of them – one in uniform, one not. It was the tall one in a suit who spoke first.

'Are you the mother of Louis and Benoît Durand?' He pronounced it as 'Lewis'.

'It's Louis,' she corrected him as she nodded. She pulled the dressing gown tighter, even though the night air outside was warm.

'My name is Detective Constable Grant Brailsford, and this is PC Jim Wildish. Can we come in, please?' He adjusted his tie as he spoke. 'I'm afraid we have some urgent news.'

She tried to speak but no words came, so she turned and let

them follow her into the hallway. One of them switched the light on.

'Miss Hyde.' The detective was still doing all the talking. 'It might be a good idea to take a seat.'

She sank down to sit at the bottom of the stairs.

'Wouldn't you like to go somewhere more comfortable?'

She shook her head.

'If you're sure.' He cleared his throat. 'There's been an incident in the city centre.'

The one in uniform got his notebook out and Alice watched him flick to a blank page, preferring that to having to look at the detective's ruddy face, which was full of pity. 'We believe your son, Louis, was involved and has died.'

Somehow Alice found herself in her living room, clutching a tissue the detective had given her. She must not cry in front of them.

'Whenever you are ready, we can explain a little more,' DC Brailsford said.

'What sort of incident was it?' It was the kind of question they were expecting. The sooner she could get this over with, the sooner she could get them and their sympathy out of her home.

'He fell from a car park in Queen Charlotte Street, from the third storey.'

'Fell?'

'I can't say anything more than that, yet.' DC Brailsford ran a hand through his sandy-coloured hair. She was sure she saw some dandruff fall on to the shoulders of his already grubby-looking suit, and no doubt some would also find its way on to her sofa before she managed to get him out of the house.

'What was he doing in a car park?' Alice straightened up in her armchair and smoothed her own hair. She needed to give off a good impression, for Lou's sake. They needed to see what kind of family he came from.

Brailsford coughed and looked at the PC next to him. 'It wouldn't be appropriate for me to comment at this stage. All we know for sure is that he fell.'

She closed her eyes, pressing the tissue to her lips. She saw Lou's face, the last time they had spoken. That look he gave her. 'Would he have died straight away?'

'He was pronounced dead at the scene, I believe,' Brailsford said. 'I'm afraid we don't have an awful lot of information at the moment. But we will get you set up with a family liaison officer as soon as possible, and they can explain more to you.'

Did he suffer? That's what she needed to know. Would he have had time to realise, as he fell, what was happening? She picked up the gold embroidered cushion next to her on the arm-chair, remembering that Christmas when Lou had given it to her unexpectedly (they didn't do gifts, as a rule), as she plucked at some stray strands of cotton. She'd suspected he knew she wouldn't like it ('I know how much you adore sparkly things, *Maman*'), but she refused to give him the opportunity to laugh at her expense and displayed it defiantly in the living room. Now, though, she hid it behind her back. Did it make her look frivolous to these two men? Were they looking round the room, judging her and her sons? They were a serious, respectable family – just look at how neat and clean she kept it in here. Just look at the sensible colours she had redecorated with, every four years without fail: the greys and creams. They were decent, ordinary people.

'I'm so sorry, Miss Hyde,' he said. She wished he'd cut the compassion. 'Is there anyone else you need to inform?'

Alice closed her eyes again and she was back in the delivery suite nearly eighteen years ago, bent double over the side of the bed, with the midwife asking her if she wanted them to let anyone know she was there. 'Baby's father, perhaps?' If only she could fend off this detective's questions by pretending to have another contraction.

'His father's abroad,' she said. 'We aren't together.'

'I see. Would you like us to call him?'

'I can do it.'

The other officer stood up and walked over to the mantelpiece, peering at a pile of coasters she'd bought when she was a teenager and still obsessed with becoming a professional pianist. Each was printed with an image of a vintage manuscript – a Chopin nocturne, Gershwin's 'Rhapsody in Blue', Rachmaninoff's second piano concerto. Strains of the music shown on the fourth coaster filled her head. *Mozart's Fantasia in D Minor. Popcorn in her belly.* She rubbed at her ears, trying to force the music away, and focused hard on PC Wildish. With one hand resting on the squares of wood, he looked around. She felt sure he was looking for family photos to scrutinise and she was glad she didn't go in for cluttering the shelves and walls with them, as so many people seemed to do. She didn't need photographs; the memories were firmly planted in her mind. Suddenly, uninvited, one such image of the boys came back to her. They were about eight and six. They had both managed to climb on to the roof of the small shed outside the back door, and as she came out to warn them to get down, Benny fell on to the patio. They had spent hours in accident and emergency that afternoon – Benny could have broken his arm, the doctors said.

Benny. Where was he?

'My other son . . . he . . . Do you know . . . ?' For the first time since she had allowed these strangers into her home, she started to panic. How had she not thought of him until now?

'Benny's fine. He's unharmed.' Brailsford smiled briefly. 'He's at the station, giving my colleagues a statement.'

'But when will he be home?'

'I appreciate that this is all incredibly difficult for you, Miss Hyde.' He tilted his head to one side and put his hand on his chest. 'You'll have plenty of time to talk to your son later but we need to get a full statement from him. It could take some time.'

Should she insist on being taken down there to see him? No. They had their rules for a reason. She should follow them, let the police do their job.

Brailsford shifted in his seat, pulling some keys out of his back pocket. That was all she needed – scratches on the leather of the sofa.

When she didn't respond immediately, he seemed to feel compelled to fill the silence. He leaned forward, resting his elbows on his knees. 'The thing is, Lou's death is being treated as unexplained. CID are involved. We need to do this properly.'

'Unexplained?' Should she be asking to speak to his boss? Brailsford suddenly struck her as looking very young. With his top button left undone behind the knot of his tie, he reminded her of Lou in school uniform. Was he authorised to give her what she needed to know? Had they sent along a lower-ranking detective because it was the middle of the night? 'But you told me he fell,' she said, and now she felt like she was the one who was falling.

'We'll be able to tell you more soon, I'm sure,' Brailsford said.

'And Benny – the questions you're asking him . . . he's not in trouble, is he?'

They reassured her that he wasn't, that this was standard procedure. She surveyed the DVDs under the TV as they asked her, again, if there was anyone they could call to be with her. *They're not in alphabetical order.* If there was anything else she needed to ask them before they left. *When would the boys learn to keep things tidy round here?* If it would be okay to send some officers round in the morning, at a more reasonable hour, to search Lou's bedroom. *Was she really asking so much?*

After they had gone, she wandered into the kitchen to make a coffee. It was three o'clock, but there was no point trying to go back to bed. For a long time she stood there, in the dark, staring out of the window above the sink at the twenty-foot prison wall at the end of her garden, the spirals of razor wire on top and the orange glow of light rising behind it. It shouldn't be her standing here – it should be the boys, stumbling in, making themselves toast and finishing all the orange juice left in the fridge, like they always did after a night out. When she eventually turned a light on she noticed Benny's skateboard propped up against the kitchen table. He was her only son now, she thought with a jolt. An only child, like her. What would she say to people, if they asked how many children she had? Logically, she should answer, 'One.' But that made it seem as if Lou had never existed. Was she a mother of one, or still a mother of two? Was Benny still a brother?

She wiped up a scattering of sugar, picked at some dried onion stuck to the edge of the hob. Next to a crumb-dusted plate was a tub of cream cheese that hadn't been put back in the fridge. She picked it up, but as soon as she did so she realised Benny didn't eat this stuff. It must have been left out by Lou the evening before.

She dropped it back on to the wooden counter, feeling the ghost of his hand in hers.

Indigo

18th August

I woke early with the bright morning light peeking through my bedroom curtains but went straight back to sleep. There have been so many beautiful sunny days recently that I don't feel the need to spring out from under the duvet and make the most of it, like I usually do. But after some sunbathed snoozing, it's now past ten o'clock and I need a cup of tea. I drag myself out of bed, patting a hand across the bedside table for my glasses, and pad downstairs in my slippers.

I collect the Sunday paper from the doorstep and wave at Paul from number thirteen, who is pruning the climbing rose that trails around the top of his front door.

'Another hot one,' he says.

'The allotment's gasping for some water. Kane and I are planning a little rain dance this evening, if you and Helen want to join?'

Paul laughs. 'What would you do if I said yes?'

'I don't know what makes you think I'm joking.' I grin. Lucian sprints in past my feet as I close the front door, and I follow him into the kitchen. Kane is already up – unusual for a morning after a night out – and he's sitting with his back to me at the breakfast bar. I'm going to miss this sight. It's always nice to walk into a room and find someone there.

'Morning, love.' I yawn, stepping over Lucian as he stretches out in a sunny spot on the terracotta floor tiles. 'Want a cuppa?' I pat Kane on the back as I pass him on my way to the kettle.

He doesn't answer. After I fill the kettle and flick it on, I turn around. 'Love?'

What am I seeing here? I push my glasses up the bridge of my nose.

'Your face. Kane, your . . .' I am suddenly very awake. 'What's happened?'

He's wearing the same clothes he left the house in last night, but now they are crumpled and smeared with dirt; evidently, he hasn't been to bed. His baseball cap is on the breakfast bar next to him, marked with spots of what looks like it could be blood. In the place of last night's wide smile is a bruise down the side of his face, a nasty graze and a busted lip. And he doesn't seem to have noticed I am in the room. His gaze focuses on the fallen pollen from my vase full of yellow foxtail lilies, which he is forming into a neat line on the counter with the index finger of his right hand.

'Kane?' I touch his shoulder. 'Love, what's happened? Were you mugged?'

'I wish.' The way he speaks scares me more than anything in his appearance. I step back, drawing my hand away.

'You wish you'd been mugged?'

The kettle clicks in lieu of Kane's answer.

I stare at the steam rising from it, fogging the window above the sink, then force myself to look back at him. 'Have you been to hospital?'

'I don't need to.' He looks up, spreading his arms wide. 'I'm here, aren't I? I'm alive?'

'You're scaring me, Kane.' My voice is loud and shaky. 'Where did you go last night?'

At this, his face falls, his bottom lip wobbles like it used to when he was a little boy, and he lets out an awful moan. Lucian jumps up and escapes through the catflap in the back door. 'I wish I could go back to then, Mum. What if I hadn't gone out?'

'Oh, love.' I move a stool towards him and sit down, clutching his hands. They are bruised and scratched, too. I rub the pollen from his fingertips.

'Lou's dead, Mum. He fell on to the road.'

'He was hit by a car?'

'No.' Kane sobs. 'We were in the car park, a few floors up . . .'

'What were you doing in there?'

'In the car park?' He blinks. 'I – we . . . we were getting a lift home, one of the guys was parked up there.'

I bring one hand away from his and lift it to my neck, pinching at the skin under my chin. 'How old was he?'

'Eighteen.'

So young. His poor mother. I squeeze my skin harder until I make myself wince. 'How did it happen?'

Kane pulls his hands out of my grip and brings his knees to his chest. He still has his shoes on. How many hours has he been sitting here, alone? 'We were just messing around, and Lou . . . he was . . . he was leaning over the wall, shouting stuff at people on the road.' He pauses, buries his head in his thighs. 'We were just having a bit of fun.'

'And then, what? He just fell?'

'It all happened so quickly. He slipped, I think . . . I . . . I . . .'

'It's okay, love.'

He sniffs, rubbing his forehead against his jeans.

'And what about you? Your face. Your hands.'

He lifts his head, pressing his fingers to the bruise on his cheek as if he doesn't know what he looks like; then he stretches his right hand out in front of him, examining the grazes on his knuckles.

'It must have been when I grabbed Benny, afterwards,' he

30

says. 'He went mental, and I got a hold of him . . . but he . . . he smashed me in the face.'

'Benny's Lou's brother, isn't he? He's the one you work with?' Kane nods.

'He was there, then? Benny? He saw it all?' Poor lad.

'He . . . yes. He lost it, started thrashing around.' Kane touches his cut lip.

'It's okay, love; it's okay.' I shouldn't be feeling relief, not when a boy has died. But I do. Kane was just restraining his distraught friend. I get up and hug him, hard, bringing his head to my chest and kissing his hair. The scent of sweet alcohol sweat and stale cigarette smoke fills my nostrils.

'You poor thing,' I whisper into his curls. 'Why didn't you wake me when you came home?'

'I didn't know what to say to you.' He grabs my arm.

'Have you given a statement to the police?' We need to think of the practicalities. What do I need to do in order to get him through this? 'Did they give you a lift back here?'

There is a sudden stillness in his body, a stiffening of his limbs. It's only then that I notice, as I look across the top of his head into the dining room, that his bike is there, leaning against the radiator. So, nobody brought him home. I hate it when he cycles home drunk.

He gently pushes his way out of my arms and looks me in the eyes for the first time this morning. 'The police . . .'

I don't know what it is – the whiteness of his face? The way he swallows? The rapid blink of his eyes? Something causes a shudder to ripple through me, as though my body knows how much trouble he is in moments before my brain does.

'They don't know I was there, Mum. I ran away.'

Alice

18th August

If anyone were to ask Alice Hyde what else took place in those first twenty-four hours after Lou died (which they wouldn't, because who was there to ask?), she could have told them about Benny returning home, about her conversation with Étienne, about the police searching Lou's bedroom. But she would have struggled to recall the order in which those events had taken place. Maybe it was because time was turned upside down when she got up in the middle of the night to answer the door to the police. Or maybe this was simply what happened, when your child died before you. Natural time had fled this most perverse of homes, where natural order had been defied.

She had found herself outside, hadn't she? Outside, standing in the shade of the prison wall. With the mass of bricks behind her, Alice looked around, making a mental list of tasks she could do to keep her mind from thinking. *A baby, hot, damp and white, being placed in her arms. Never enough, nothing had ever been enough.* Not much weeding to do (she was too diligent), but she could do some edging around the lawn. She could trim the lavender back. She could stake the dahlias. *Hot, damp and white.* She shook her head, shaking the image away, and walked towards the house, opened the shed, pulled out a pair of secateurs and her edging shears. She checked her blue gardening gloves for spiders, then slipped them on and got to work. *Never enough.*

That new one, the liaison officer, interrupted her. DC Garcia, that was her name. 'Can I get you a drink?'

Pudgy little fingers, reaching for a blue beaker. The sigh of satisfaction after he takes a gulp.

Alice wiped her forehead with her sleeve and carried on with her edging.

'I don't think we got off to the best of starts, did we, Alice?' DC Garcia clasped her hands together in front of the waistband of her perfectly pressed grey suit trousers. Alice refused to look up at her face. She could have said: 'I never gave you permission to call me Alice.' She could have said: 'I never asked for you to come here.' She could have said: 'No, I don't want a fucking drink.' But she didn't – she kept edging the lawn.

'I'm going to head off now. I can be here as much or as little as you want, and I'm picking up signals that you would like to go for less rather than more.'

Alice straightened up and looked at the girl. Now they were making progress.

'It's my duty to keep you informed, but I'll stay away as much as I can. Here's my number.' She handed Alice a card. 'Call me if anything comes up.'

Alice would have said thank you, really she would have done, but at that moment she heard the distant sound of the front door slamming. Benny?

'Excuse me,' she said, pushing past DC Garcia in her impeccable suit, leaving the shears to fall to the parched ground with a thud. 'Benny?'

No . . . this conversation, this time spent in the garden, it must have taken place much later than she remembered. She had spent most of that day wondering when Benny would be home, wondering if she should be doing something to help him.

*

She had gone into the garden earlier on for a reason: to speak to Étienne in private, when he finally returned her calls.

'I should take this,' she said, leaving that other policewoman in Lou's bedroom, going through his cupboards.

Alice remembered accepting his call as she descended the stairs. 'Hold on a minute,' she'd said, waiting until she was outside, with the back door closed, before she continued. 'It's Lou. You need to know about Lou.'

But what did she say next? She couldn't recall. He was in pieces, a shocked wreck on the other end of the line. She had tried to say something to soothe him, but the words wouldn't come; it was still too difficult to find tenderness in her heart for the man who had walked out on her when Louis was a few weeks old. The man who never sent his sons birthday cards. The man who transferred twenty pounds to her bank account every few months until they were sixteen and expected it to be enough. 'I'm sorry,' she said. It was the best she could do.

'No.' A cough. He was trying to pull himself together.

'Can you come back?' She screwed her face up with the effort of asking. 'I know you're on tour, but . . . For Benny.'

Étienne sighed. '*Je sais pas*. I don't know if I can . . .' He paused. 'I can't believe he's gone.'

Alice stood under the apple tree, a few feet away from the battered old Triumph Tiger motorcycle Lou had insisted on restoring on her beautiful lawn. Possibly, she thought, his determination had been because of her protests, not in spite of them. Wedging her phone between her ear and her shoulder, she pulled the tarp off the bike, laying it over the brown patches of ground where Lou's frequent little oil spills had killed the grass.

'Alice.' Once, she had loved the way Étienne said her name. *Al-eez*. When they'd just bought this place (before he left her to pay the mortgage on her own); when she was pregnant with Benny and he was excited about their big adventure in starting a family (before he got bored and began looking for the next new shiny life experience to add to his collection); when his work as a music teacher was fulfilling enough (before he'd jacked it in to allow himself 'more creative space' as a blues guitarist). Then, he used to roll over in bed in the morning and whisper, 'You're the most beautiful, *Al-eez.*' Now, it made her cringe.

'You must not blame yourself,' he said.

She pulled her mobile away from her cheek, squeezing its edges so hard her fingers hurt. She heard Étienne say 'Alice?' again as she jabbed a finger against the red cross underneath his number.

You must not blame yourself.

How did he know about all those times in the middle of the night when she had fantasised about being free? She had never wanted this. *Never this, Lou.* She thought of DC Brailsford in the early hours of that morning, asking if Lou had left a note anywhere. Asking how he had been before he went out. There was no way Lou would have jumped. Not her son. She took a step forward, towards the motorbike, and ran her palm over the handlebars. 'What happened?' she whispered.

She would have to shift it somewhere; it couldn't stay in the garden over the winter. Her father had bought it for Lou when he'd finished his exams, after watching him tinker about with the engine of the beaten-up Polo he shared with Benny. Lou had spent hours out here pulling the Tiger apart, listening to that awful music he liked on his headphones, staining the patio with drips of oil and leaving plastic bowls of petrol out for weeks on end. Having grown up around her father's repair workshop at home, the stink of the petrol didn't bother her; it was the mess Lou made of her garden that she hated. But knowing that she would never look out of her bedroom window and see him out here again? That made her chest contract with an emotion she couldn't quite name. All she knew was that she wanted to box it up, put it away, and not have to feel it again.

She'd called her father, too, before Étienne, and broken the news to him. That had been harder. He had been close to Lou, closer than he had ever been to her. He only lived up the road, but barely visited until recently, when he'd realised he had something in common with his younger grandson: a love of finding out how something works. She'd told him this morning that no, it would be best if he didn't come round – things were too busy with the police. She could hear his sadness over the phone, and she didn't know that she could cope with his grief as well as her own.

As Alice ran her hand over the Tiger's warm leather seat, picking at the edge of a strip of gaffer tape holding a seam together, she wondered if she should be allowed to grieve for Lou. She had always struggled to find that closeness with him – that same bond she'd had with Benny – from the moment he was placed, hot, damp and white, into her arms. What gave you the right to mourn somebody? Surely you had to have loved the person a certain amount; you had to have loved them *enough*. Nothing she had ever done for Lou had ever felt like enough.

Her father had ignored her, and within half an hour of her call he had appeared on the doorstep. They both knew better than to attempt a hug, but when he made her a coffee she didn't realise she was craving, she was grateful, and inexplicably she felt reassured to have him at her side when, not long afterwards, DC 'call-me-Hannah' Garcia arrived with that other one, what was her name? Hobson? Dodson?

It was still early when they showed up. The sun was hitting the privet in the front garden; it hadn't shifted round to the back yet. But in Alice's skewed memory, this visit happened much later in the day.

'Can I get you another drink?' As far as Alice could remember, this was one of the first things DC Garcia asked, as they stood in the kitchen. What was it with these police officers offering her drinks? She was forty-five, for God's sake; she could control her own hydration levels quite sufficiently. She wasn't a child. Not like Lou as a toddler, who needed to be reminded to have sips of juice. Like a slap in the face, an image hit her of his pudgy little fingers reaching out for that blue beaker of his with the red spout. A noise filled her ears – him, gulping the juice down, and copying Benny with an exaggerated sigh of satisfaction when he came up for air.

Alice rubbed the heels of her hands over her ears and eyes, half aware of her father answering for her. 'She's just had a coffee; I think she's all right for the moment.'

Alice looked DC Garcia up and down. A family liaison officer, that's what she had called herself. 'Here to help and support you.' She looked no older than Benny. What could she do to help them?

'What news do you have for me? When will Benny be allowed home?' Alice ran a finger around the rim of the fruit bowl on the breakfast bar, empty apart from the stalks of ghost grapes. She felt compelled, suddenly, never to throw these tiny twigs away – Lou had probably eaten those grapes. *Don't be ridiculous, Alice.*

'I'm afraid I don't know, Miss Hyde.'

'I don't really see why he had to be taken to the station.'

'I understand it is all very difficult.'

'Do you?'

Alice's father put a hand on her forearm, and when she looked down in shock at the touch, she realised she was gripping the edge of the fruit bowl so tightly that her own hand was shaking.

'My colleagues needed to speak to Benny and it is much easier to do that at the station.' DC Garcia leaned her elbows onto the breakfast bar. 'But I'm here if you need help understanding anything. Anything at all.'

Alice couldn't stand it. This familiarity. This girl patronising her. She let go of the fruit bowl and walked over to the French windows, looking out over her garden and Lou's bike under the apple tree, shrouded in its grubby tarpaulin.

Pudgy little hands reaching for a blue beaker. Alice screwed her eyes shut, shaking her head.

'. . . not going to ask you lots of questions today, you've had a long night.' DC Garcia was droning on. Why was she still there? 'But I will need to come back in the next couple of days to take a statement from you.'

Why did Alice need to give a statement? She hadn't been any-where near Lou when he died. She thought again of how she had wished to be free of him. She wouldn't have to mention that.

'. . . would that be all right?' The other policewoman was talk-ing now.

Alice stared at her blankly. Her father stepped in. 'DS Hob-son was wondering if you could show her Lou's room.'

When she heard Benny get home, Alice left DC Garcia in the garden. The girl said she and DS Hobson would see themselves out, but Alice didn't acknowledge her. Instead, she threw her gardening gloves on to the wooden table on the patio – the one she got out of the shed every year but had never once sat down at for a meal with her sons. All around her, there were reminders like this of the ways she had tried to pretend their family func-tioned normally.

'Benny?' She pulled off her trainers and sweaty socks as she went into the house and for a brief moment enjoyed the relief of walking across the cool linoleum kitchen floor, before she remembered she should not be enjoying anything today. She walked straight past DS Hobson and her father. 'Ben?'

He wasn't in the back room or the living room, so she headed upstairs. She had an idea where she might find him. The thought of having to go in there forced her to blink away light-headedness. When DS Hobson had searched it, Alice had stood

38

outside on the landing, giving permission to go in the wardrobe, the cupboards, under the bed – all without stepping inside.

'Benny?' She stood outside Lou's door. Perhaps he would come out, and she wouldn't have to go in there after all. She waited. Sighed. Braced herself.

As she pulled the door open, she was hit by the heat in the room. Lou would have still been asleep in here, if he'd come home last night. With the heat came the smell of her son, of deodorant and sweat and petrol, and of the rotting skins of oranges in his bin.

'Feels like he'll show up at the door any minute.' Benny was sitting on his brother's red duvet, wearing the clean T-shirt and pair of jeans she'd sent in with Brailsford this morning. What had they done with what he was wearing last night?

She looked around. The room was a tip: Haynes manuals lying half-open on the bed, T-shirts draped over the TV, the glint of discarded daily contact lenses on the floor. The walls were covered with drawings and notes about his beloved Tiger. They were beautiful, in their own disordered, scribbled way.

Her gaze returned to Benny. He looked exhausted, staring at the floor, shoulders slumped. She should go over to him, hug him, or at least put an arm around his shoulders, but they didn't do that.

'We'll get through this.' It was all she could think of to say. She knew it was inadequate. 'How did it happen, Ben?'

He didn't answer her. He wasn't staring at the floor, she realised, but at his hands, which were holding a coiled leather belt.

'Is that Lou's?'

Benny followed her gaze and nodded. 'Do you mind if I keep it? I want something . . .'

'We'll find something better than that, I'm sure.' She paused. 'Did he ever seem depressed to you?'

'What?'

'I need to know. Did he jump?'

He took a deep breath. 'I don't think he'd do that. Do you?'

'No. But then, what . . . ?'

'He was in a good mood, y'know? We'd had fun. A few drinks at the Old Duke, then the Llandoger.'

Alice nodded. She could imagine the two of them, joking around together. That brotherly bond she'd never been part of.

'After the Llandoger closed, Lou and one of our mates were climbing up the side of that car park round the corner. Just for a laugh.'

'Climbing the walls? How high?' Never in her life, no matter how much she had to drink, did she ever consider scaling the outside of a car park.

'Two, three floors maybe?' He held out a hand, gesturing for her to calm down. 'We were mucking about in there for a bit. I went off to get a drink from the shop, and when I came back . . .'

He didn't need to finish the sentence. She understood from the way he trailed off what he was saying he found on his return.

'You didn't see him fall, then?'

'No.' He looked up at her with those big, dark eyes. Étienne's eyes.

'So something must have happened while you were gone?'

He looked away.

'Let me get this straight, you were mucking about, then you left . . .' She rubbed at her temples. 'But nothing unusual had happened before that?'

'No.'

'And you two didn't row? Who did you say was out with you?'

He picked at the holes punched through the belt. Why did she get the feeling he was avoiding looking at her? 'I told you, we were having a good time. He . . . he was happy, on good form.'

She studied his face and noticed for the first time a fine red scratch down one cheek. It reminded her of the wounds the boys inflicted on her skin when she had let their fingernails grow too long as babies. 'And . . . ?'

'And what?'

'Who were you out with?'

He pulled the belt straight in his hands, then started coiling it up, even tighter this time, as she felt him closing off from her.

'Benny?'

'I'm not dragging anyone else into this. What good would it do?'

'I need to know.'

'That's the one thing I'm not going to tell you.'

She decided not to comment on his choice of words. *The one thing.* There was plenty he was choosing not to reveal to her, she was sure of it. 'Come on, Ben.'

'I won't grass up my mates.'

When the police had told her they were taking Benny's statement, she'd considered asking if she needed to get him a lawyer. But she didn't, because only guilty people needed one of those, and in the early hours of this morning, she hadn't thought Benny had done anything wrong.

Did she still believe that?

'Miss Hyde, in the next couple of days, once the post-mortem is completed, someone will need to come and identify the body.' DC Garcia had said this, in the kitchen at some point.

No. There was no way she could do that.

'Does it have to be Ali? Could I do it?' She had never been so grateful for her father than in that moment – she even immediately forgave him for shortening her name, which he knew she hated.

Pudgy little hands reaching for a blue beaker. Hot, damp and white.

*

41

That evening they sat in front of the TV together like zombies, the three of them – Alice, her father and Benny – after everyone else had gone.

Benny kept checking his phone, irritating Alice more and more each time he pulled it out of his pocket.

'If that's your friends wanting to know details,' she said, 'don't give them any. Don't fuel the gossip.' Her voice sounded harsher than she intended it to.

Benny frowned at her, putting his phone away again, as if she might somehow be able to read over his shoulder from the other side of the room. 'I'm just letting the bar know I won't be in for a few days.'

Suddenly he grabbed the remote and the voices blaring out of the TV became much louder. '. . . investigating after an eighteen-year-old man died in the city centre last night . . .' a woman was saying. Alice sank her head back against the sofa to stop a surge of giddiness.

'DC Garcia mentioned that this would be on—' her father began, but Benny cut him off.

'Quiet, Pops. I want to hear.'

Grainy CCTV images appeared, showing two different men: one with a baseball cap on, the other with a hood pulled over his face. They had been caught by two different cameras, one jogging and the other walking, on two stretches of road Alice didn't recognise.

'Police are keen to identify these two men,' the journalist said, before the camera showed her standing by a police cordon outside the Queen Charlotte Street multi-storey. Benny turned the TV off before she could say anything else.

Alice thought one of the men looked familiar, but how could she be sure when you could see so little of them? What did they have to do with what had happened to Lou?

'Benny?'

No answer.

'Come on, this is ridiculous. There's CCTV, for God's sake. Who was that?'

Even in the darkness of the room, she could see that his face had gone a few shades paler.

Her son looked scared.

Indigo

19th August

I didn't sleep last night. When I showed the police out of the door nine years ago, I didn't expect to have anything more to do with them in my life.

But now this.

My son on the local news, unrecognisable to most people, perhaps, but his gait and his clothes and that cap made it clear as day to me.

He said he didn't know who the other lad was, the one with the hood. But he had the TV on constantly, flicking between the local news bulletins as they came on through the day. He sat there on the sofa in front of the TV for hours, texting. Eating nothing, drinking little. Holding ice packs wrapped in tea towels to his face, which I kept replacing for him. He only got out of his stinking clothes from the night before and had a shower at eight o'clock, then went straight to bed.

So I haven't slept. I lay in bed wondering what I should do, staring at the brown damp mark on the ceiling. Why do the police want to speak to him? Because he didn't stick around to see that boy's body? Is that a crime?

At one o'clock this morning I decided I should take him to the police station, admit to them that he was the one in the CCTV.

At two o'clock I changed my mind. Should we get a solicitor?

At three I was downstairs, sitting at the kitchen table with a glass of water, wondering how I could find out what time the station down in the city centre opened. Was that the closest one? I didn't know, did I? Why would I need to know where the nearest police station was? *All is well. All is well. All is well.*

At four o'clock I put the BBC World Service on the radio, in a futile attempt to distract my brain and trick it into letting me sleep.

I got up and dressed at five, forced down a piece of toast and raspberry jam, and drank several cups of peppermint tea, inhaling the steam in deep breaths to calm myself down. I waited until seven, with Lucian curled around my feet instead of slippers, before I woke Kane.

Once I had tempted him out of bed with coffee and toast, I told him to get dressed.

'We're going down to that police station by Broadmead.' I was trying to be strong for him, pretending that I knew it would all be okay and that this was the right thing to do.

'I don't know . . .' He put his head in his hands, elbows on the dining table.

'That's why I'm taking charge. You need to go in and tell them how you were involved, and it needs to be of your own accord.' Did I sound calm and in control?

I walked with him into the hallway and watched him climb the stairs.

'Mum?' he paused, turning to look at me. 'I don't know if I can do it. Hand myself in.' He leaned against the wall, fear in his blue eyes, his fingers playing with his nose ring.

'You're not handing yourself in. That's what people do when they've done something wrong.'

He didn't look convinced.

Fast-forward two hours and we are outside the station. Kane goes through the two sets of sliding doors first, and I follow, putting a hand on his back to push him towards the reception desk.

45

I want to make them see that there's been a mistake, explain it all away for him, but I know I can't. He's nineteen. They aren't going to be interested in what Mum has to say.

'You saw him fall,' I say in a low voice as we approach. 'You panicked, you were upset. You say you didn't want to see the body. You say you're sorry, you realise now that you should have stayed around. You answer their questions then you come home.'

One of the men behind the desk looks up. 'How can I help?' There's a dog-eared teddy bear on the shelves behind him. I can't look away from it. Has it been left behind by a small child? Who would bring their child to a police station? Me, I realise. I have brought my only son here, to face unknown consequences.

'I'd like to speak to someone, about the ... the CCTV on the ... uh ... the news.' Kane shoves his hands into his pockets.

'Can you be more specific?'

'The kid who died in the city centre, Saturday night.'

I touch his back. *All is well. All is well.*

'Right. What's your name, son?'

I flinch. When was the last time a man called him that?

'Kane. K-A-N-E. Surname's Owen.'

'Okay, thanks. Take a seat.' The man gestures to a waiting area behind us. 'Someone will be out to see you.'

I sit on a wooden flip-up bench. The place doesn't feel like a police station. It could be an airport departure lounge or a fancy hospital waiting room. There's a jazzy pattern on the walls in green and black, light streaming in through the huge expanses of glass. Kane doesn't sit but goes to stand by the windows, watching as a woman locks her bike to the racks outside.

I bite at the jagged edge of my thumbnail.

'Kane Owen?' a female voice asks loudly, behind me.

'Yes.' He approaches the woman, a tall brunette officer in uniform. At least she looks kind.

46

'Thank you for coming in. The detective on the case is on his way. Would you mind waiting through here?' She gestures at a door on the far side of the reception desk.

'Sure.' Kane looks at me as he passes, blinks, squeezes my shoulder. 'You might as well go home. I'll call when I'm on my way back.'

'Don't be silly.' I laugh, then wish I hadn't. I sound nervous. 'I'll wait. You won't be long. He won't be long, will he?' I ask the woman. She presses her lips together in response. It's almost a smile.

For the first hour I flick through a copy of one of those local life-style magazines they have everywhere, reading the words but not taking any of it in. I fill a plastic cone of icy water from the machine, taking a few minutes to look at the blown-up photo-graphs stuck on the walls, of police in action – talking to normal people like me, riding police horses, all shiny and happy. The photographs are peeling off and chipped in places. They could have employed a local artist to do a beautiful bright mural across this wall instead, but perhaps that is more to my taste than who-ever makes that kind of decision around here.

In the second hour I start to get uncomfortably hot in my thick denim dress, and wish I'd worn a T-shirt and trousers instead. This place is like a giant greenhouse.

As I enter my third hour of waiting, I wander over to the desk.

'Hi there. My son, Kane Owen?' I point at the door the officer had taken him through. 'He's been gone quite a while. I was just wondering if you'd have any idea how much longer he might be?'

I smile. I don't want to be annoying. He shakes his head.

'Sorry, Kane Owen's mum. They don't tell us anything out here, I'm afraid. Why don't you go and get a coffee? I can let him know where you've gone, if I spot him coming out.'

'I'll just wait here. I'm sure it can't be much longer.'

He nods.

'I've been watching you. All three of you.' I glance at his two colleagues behind the reception desk. 'You're very nice to everyone.' I stop short of saying that I hadn't expected it to be like this.

'Everyone's a human being.' He shrugs, and the black epaulette on his shoulder with the words 'police staff' embroidered on to it pops up.

'Yes.' I think of Lily's favourite motto. *Be kind, always.* 'Thank you.'

I sit on my bench again.

For the fourth hour, I have a few more people to watch, at least. There is now a reasonably steady stream of people approaching the reception desk. A stressed young woman pushes a pram with a screaming newborn up to the desk and I'm tempted to go and comfort her.

'Mrs Owen?'

While I've been watching the anxious mum, I haven't noticed a young man making his way over to me. The way he wears his ill-fitting suit immediately reminds me of Glyn when he had to get dressed up for a wedding or an interview; you can tell by the shirt (unironed) and tie (askew) that he doesn't like having to look smart and doesn't intend to conform any more than he absolutely has to.

I jump up. 'Yes, thank you. I mean, yes, that's me.'

'I'm DC Brailsford.' He smiles, but there's something unsettling about his eyes.

'Have you finished with my son yet? Can I take him home?'

'Mrs Owen, I think perhaps you should sit down.'

Alice

19th August

Every so often, Alice wondered: what would other people do? Monday was one of those days.

Other people wouldn't go back to work less than two days after their son had died. Other people would have friends, and those friends would bring round lasagnes and bouquets of white lilies. Other people would accept the gifts and then burst into tears. Other people would stay in their pyjamas for several days and refuse to leave the house. In short, other people would go to pieces. But those were just words to Alice, an alien concept. *Go to pieces*. Alice Hyde had never gone to pieces. She was the mistress of catching herself, just as she was about to shatter.

The key was carrying on. So, on Monday, Alice got up at half past six, even though she hadn't slept. She couldn't stomach any food yet, but she still poured her bowl of muesli and a black coffee, and sat with them at the kitchen table for four minutes; this was all part of the routine. Then she put her trainers on to walk her loop of St Andrew's Park. She arrived at the library at eight o'clock sharp, let herself in the staff entrance – although her foggy brain caused her to input the alarm code incorrectly, twice – and started on her morning's tasks before the doors opened at eleven. With James on long-term sick leave, she couldn't possibly take a day off. They needed her here. As supervisor, it was her job to step in when there were staff shortages, to scale down her responsibilities in the two other branch libraries she oversaw. It suited her to spend most of her time at the Bishopston branch, as she had been since James had broken his hip. It was only ten minutes' walk from her house.

The news reports yesterday didn't name Lou, so she didn't have to contend with Jenna or Carolyn's sympathy. She busied herself with checking the return trolleys. She could handle customers if needed, but her teams generally knew by now not to bother her with renewals, printing queries, registering new members or tedious questions regarding recipes, housing problems or directions. It was James who had been bold enough to say to her once, 'Not much of a people person, are you?'

But no matter how hard she concentrated on the weight and reassuring smoothness of the books in her hands, no matter how determined she was to keep her mind on track, she couldn't stop it drifting. She replayed the moment in the loft, when Lou had wished her happy birthday – was there love in the way he had said it? She wondered how Benny would cope when he had to leave for university. What if all this stress affected his grades? She thought about the police, asking if Lou had left a note. And then, again, back to Benny. What was he hiding from her? Some people might call it a mother's intuition, this feeling she had. But Alice didn't need intuition; all she had to do was look at the facts. Before Lou died it was easy to talk to Benny, and now it wasn't. When she asked him about the events of that night, he clammed up.

The boys used to be fond of a stupid game when they were a couple of years younger, where one of them would propose two different undesirable situations and force the other to choose between them. For example, 'Would you rather get off with Miss Long or have Mr Richards grope your arse?' That one had generated much debate. They'd stopped laughing as soon as she had walked into the room, of course.

What would she rather? That Lou took his own life or that his brother had played a part in his death? There must be a third choice. But what could she do about it, in any case? The law was the law. She had to let the police get on and do their jobs.

'Alice?'

She snapped her head up from the trolley and was appalled to see DC Garcia standing in front of her. 'What are you doing here?' She kept her voice low but blushed as several pairs of eyes turned to watch.

'I tried the house.' DC Garcia didn't speak quietly. Everyone would be able to hear her. 'I assumed you would be there.' There was disapproval in her voice.

'I'm needed here.' Alice sniffed. The girl stood on the other side of the trolley, so close that Alice could smell her overpowering floral perfume.

'Of course. When might be a better moment for me to speak to you? I'd like to take a statement, if you could spare me a little time.'

She'd mentioned this yesterday. They wanted to stick their noses into her and Lou's lives. Alice looked around her. The library was relatively quiet and she'd had a productive morning. Better get this over with, and get DC Garcia away from her eavesdropping colleagues.

'Now is fine.' Alice neatly stacked the books still in her hands back on to the trolley. 'Can I meet you back at the house in ten minutes?'

Alice explained to Jenna that she had a family emergency, ignoring her wide eyes and attempts to ask if she was okay. She collected her rucksack from the staff room, changed back into her trainers and walked home to let DC Garcia in.

They sat in the living room because, Alice explained, it was the coolest room in the house. She could hear Benny moving around upstairs and the familiar rumble of his skateboard on the floorboards – he would often sit on his bed rolling it back and forth under his feet – but he didn't come down to see what she was doing home. Alice sat in the armchair, stuffing the gold cushion behind her back, and DC Garcia took the sofa, pulling out a pen and a pile of forms from her bag.

'That's a Swiss cheese plant, isn't it?' She pointed at the pot next to the armchair.

'*Monstera deliciosa.*' Alice reached over the side of the chair and tapped the soil. She hated common names such as the one DC Garcia had used – the Latin always sounded so much better. 'It's toxic to cats and dogs.'

DC Garcia coughed, caught Alice's eye and launched into her script. She started by saying how sorry she was, again. She asked how Alice was feeling today, whether she had slept, whether she had told family and friends. Alice answered politely but concisely. She was beginning to feel a little light-headed; it must be the combination of no sleep, no food and DC Garcia's horrible perfume. Several times she forgot what she was trying to say, mid-sentence. Several times she got lost with Lou's ghost, especially when the questions about him began – basic ones about where he had been at college, things like that. What was he interested in? That summer, it had all been about that bike. He set an alarm early every morning to get up and start work on it, and when he wasn't with it, he was thinking about it, planning it all out in his head. The sketches covering his bedroom walls had all been done at the kitchen table in the middle of the night. She had never seen him so obsessed by something.

'Alice?'

'I'm sorry, what was the question?'

'I was asking what was said, the last time you saw Lou?'

Alice patted the arm of her chair. She wasn't sure why this was relevant, but clearly there were hoops to be jumped through.

'He wished me happy birthday, told me he was going out with Benny. I gave him twenty pounds to buy a couple of drinks.' DC Garcia didn't need to know anything about the difficulties. What difference would it make now? She could remember so lucidly the first time he had told her he hated her when he was about eight years old, and she'd said, 'Good.' That had shut him up. 'I'm not here to be your friend,' she'd told him. 'So if you hate me, I'm obviously doing my job right.' But it was when he started finding ways to tell her without saying the words – that was when it really got to her.

'Would you say you had a good relationship with him?'

'Yes, I would say so.' She stared DC Garcia in the eye, daring her to doubt her answer.

'And Benny? Did he get on well with his brother?'

Alice's skin prickled. What did they think Benny had done? 'As I'm sure he told your colleagues yesterday,' she said, 'they were very close.' It was her first honest answer.

'And would you say Lou was happy?'

'Yes, I would.' Alice wasn't sure how else she could answer this, even if she wanted to be truthful. Was he?

'And his exam results, last week – would you say he was pleased with those?'

'Yes.' Alice scratched at her elbow.

DC Garcia narrowed her eyes. Before she could say anything, Alice added, 'Every child is an individual.' She parroted out what she'd heard some of the soft-touch parents saying in the library. 'Grades are not the only marker of success.'

DC Garcia nodded and made some more notes.

'I have questions for you, too,' Alice said.

'I'm sure.' DC Garcia smiled. 'But maybe we could get through this first and then have a bit more of a chat.'

Alice ignored her. 'Why are you treating Lou's death as unexplained?'

'I'm afraid the details of what took place on Saturday night aren't all that clear at the moment.' DC Garcia's features hardened a little. 'We are doing everything we can to find out, though. Shall we continue with the statement?'

Alice wanted to ask if she thought someone had pushed her son, but she was scared to hear the answer and reluctant to put the idea into the girl's mind if it wasn't already there. But it must be. That's what all this was about, wasn't it? All she could do was to deflect attention away from Benny, but it was so hard when she knew so little.

'The men in the CCTV,' Alice said. 'Have you identified them yet?' The more she replayed the clip on the police's website, the more she was sure she recognised one of them – but couldn't think from where.

'As far as I know, we've not made any progress on that. We're working on it, I assure you, but . . .'

Alice noticed that she averted her eyes as she spoke, flicking back through her notes.

'But what?'

'I'll be honest with you – resources are really stretched at the moment. We're putting absolutely everything we can into this but you may feel at times that things are moving a little slowly.'

'I see.'

'But while we're talking about the CCTV, could you tell me who your son was out with—'

DC Garcia's phone rang, and she took it out of her bag.

'Sorry, I should get this.'

Alice considered moving into the kitchen, but this was her own home and she'd sit in her armchair if she wanted to. Let DC Garcia be the one to leave if she needed privacy.

'Hi,' DC Garcia said, standing and moving away from Alice towards the window, squeezing past the coffee table and tugging at the edge of the curtain to look out into the street.

Alice pulled her own phone out of her pocket as DC Garcia answered monosyllabically. There was something about the way this girl asked her questions, and the way she watched her after she asked them. She googled 'Family liaison officer' and tapped on one of the results. A few lines jumped out at her. 'Common misconception . . . not only there to support the family . . . build trust and report anything useful back to the investigation team.' What was it she'd said yesterday? *Here to help and support you.* Not quite the full story, was it? Alice scowled at her across the room, pocketing her phone again.

'Yes,' DC Garcia was saying, 'I'm with her now. Right.' After a moment's silence she looked directly at Alice. 'No, that's fine.' She let the curtain drop. 'Yes. I'll inform her.' She pulled her phone away from her face, without breaking eye contact.

'You'll inform me of what?'

'There's been a development. We're now treating your son's death as a murder investigation.'

Indigo

19th August

'Kane couldn't kill anyone.' I'm sitting in an interview room at the station, still trying to understand what DC Brailsford has just told me: my son has been arrested on suspicion of murder.

'It must be extremely difficult for you to take in.' He seems even taller as we sit here, facing each other across a table. I feel small in comparison, but not intimidated. The awkwardness of the way he tries to find a comfortable position for his long limbs makes him appear more as an ungainly giant than an imposing threat. 'You're obviously very worried about your son. That's only natural.'

I sniff and look around. There are no windows in here. No pictures. It's a horrible, depressing little box. Is Kane in a room like this? Is he next door?

'I need to call a solicitor.'

He shakes his head, holding out another tissue towards me. His hand feels ice cold as I take it. 'We offered him one, but he refused. He could—'

'And you took no for an answer? He's nineteen!' I push my chair back and stand up, leaning on the table. 'I want to see my son. Where is he?'

'I'm afraid you can't. He's been taken to the custody suite in north Bristol.' He reaches a large hand across the table towards me. 'Mrs Owen, I know how upsetting this must be. Would you like to call anyone to be here with you? Can I get you a cup of tea?'

'You took him away?' It feels good to tower above him and shout. 'You can't do this.'

He glances down, noticing a stain on his suit jacket, and withdraws his hand to scratch at it. I assume he is trying to avoid my eye, but then he looks up at me again. 'There is something you could do for Kane. I wasn't going to ask just yet, but . . .'

I pace to the back of the room. 'Of course I want to bloody help him.'

'Okay. You could give me a statement.' He retrieves a wad of A4 forms from a shelf behind him.

'But I wasn't there. The first I knew was when I got up yesterday morning and found him in the kitchen.'

DC Brailsford clicks the end of his pen and gives me an encouraging smile. 'Sounds like a perfect place to start.'

And so I start talking. Would a killer be as upset as Kane was? Would a killer come to the police station voluntarily? DC Brailsford writes it all down, nods, asks me a few questions. Did I notice any blood on his clothes? ('A little, but it was his own.') Had there been anything unusual about him recently? ('Not at all.') Did he have a girlfriend? ('No. He's gay, actually.') As I speak, I feel my heartrate slow a little and I sit back down. This man is only doing his job. I need to cooperate, help Kane.

'There has clearly been an awful mistake, I'm sure you can see that now. Will you take this back to whoever . . . ?' I gesture at the paper and then at the door. 'Explain to them that Kane couldn't possibly have done this?'

'I promise you it will all be taken into consideration.' He adjusts his tie and it shifts from a cobalt blue to viridian green in the light. Green is calming, I tell myself, staring at it. *All is well.* 'You've done a great job, thank you.'

'Now what? Will I be able to see him?'

He puffs out his cheeks, slowly exhaling, before speaking softly. 'Mrs Owen, your son has been arrested on a very serious charge. We need to question him and find out exactly what took place on Saturday night. It's going to take some time. When he is booked in and has been read his rights, he will be allowed to make a phone call, but who he calls is down to him.'

I fumble in my bag for my mobile phone, hurrying to switch it on. What if he has already tried to call me? 'So what do I do now? Go home and wait?'

He reaches his hand across the table again, so it is only a few centimetres away from mine. 'What I'd like to do, if you'd let me, is drive you home.'

My poor boy, he must be so scared. I meant what I said to DC Brailsford, he has never been in trouble. Not with the police, not with school, not even really with me. I joke to my family about him being the perfect son. My sister is convinced I've been too laid back, but look how he's turned out – much more polite and nicer to be around than her over-disciplined brats. 'So, you never set him a curfew?' she'll say to me. (No, I'd rather teach him to take responsibility for his actions.) 'You've never grounded him? But how do you punish him?' (The key to well-behaved children isn't punishment. That only invites rebellion.) 'You went *with* him to get his nose pierced?' (He's expressing himself. And it suits him.)

No: I've brought my son up to be a decent human being, I think, as I stand here in my kitchen. That's how I can say with absolute certainty that he didn't do this. Lucian is doing figures of eight around my ankles, his smooth fur comforting against my bare skin. Upstairs, I can hear the police ransacking Kane's bedroom. Every now and then they come downstairs with things in brown paper bags and take them outside. I know what they will find; I was only in there a matter of hours ago myself when

58

I convinced him to go to the station. There's a stack of library books, that bin bag full of things to take to the charity shop, a pile of neatly folded T-shirts on the floor. I have betrayed him, but what could I do? On the way home, DC Brailsford told me that they would need to search the house, and if I'd let them in it would be a lot easier all round.

There was another unmarked car waiting for us when we arrived. DC Brailsford gave the officers inside it a nod as we approached the front door, placing his hand gently against my back and patting it. Sweat suddenly pricked on my forehead. I felt small and unimportant, unable to question them or assert my rights because I didn't know what my rights were. Could they just search the house?

As his colleagues stepped into the hallway, he looked at my portraits on the wall – my mother, Kane as a boy. Forced to stand close to him to let someone pass, I noticed the smell of garlic, a Chinese takeaway perhaps, coming from his suit. *Kane loves cooking me stir-fries*, I felt strangely compelled to confide in this man. As if it might help show what a good kid he is. *His favourite is steak and broccoli, with cashews.*

'Did you do these?' he asked, pointing at a pencil drawing of Kane. 'They're great.'

I nodded, watching the other officers move through the house. I appreciated his kindness, using small talk to take my mind off the intrusion into my home.

'Do you still paint?'

'A little. I'm an art therapist,' I said, as though that would explain why I had stopped doing my own work. 'It can be a very effective way of helping people overcome difficulties in their lives.'

He looked down at me with a sort of smirk, quickly correcting himself to look genuinely interested, nodding and forming his mouth into an 'oh'.

'Intriguing. Do you think it would be effective in helping me overcome the inordinate amount of overtime they've got me working every week?' He laughed, but I didn't join in.

A chill passed through me as I sensed, for the first time, a cold and disdainful energy about him – something at odds with the sympathetic giant I had thought I was dealing with. Why had I thought he was on my side? I replayed our earlier conversation in the police station. What had I told him about Kane? I had been stupid and naïve. I should have been more careful about what I revealed. He wasn't here to find evidence for Kane's defence. He was here to get evidence to prosecute him.

A woman shouted down from upstairs. 'Sir?'

'Ah, yes.' He turned to me. 'Where did you say his bedroom was?' he asked, resting a hand lightly on my shoulder. *I didn't*, I wanted to say. 'Top of the stairs and then . . . ?' The way he spoke, like we were friends, made the hairs on my arm stand on end.

I pointed up to the landing. 'First door on the left.' He wouldn't get another word out of me other than what was completely necessary.

'And is there anywhere else we should look?' he asked casually, as if I wouldn't guess what he was trying to do. He smiled, and I saw, very clearly now, how fake it was.

I knew what he was asking. He wanted to know if Kane has any secret places, holes under the floorboards or boxes at the back of cupboards.

I'd be damned if I told him anything that would help him pin a murder on my son.

'No,' I said.

Alice

20th August

Summer was slipping away. Alice made a mental note as she looked past the pale pink rambling rose sprawled across the fence next to the tennis courts in the park: she would soon have to prune her own *Rosa moschata*. She was watching two rather unfit men rallying while she sat on her favourite bench in the evening sun, keeping a hand on the loaded shopping bag next to her at all times in case one of the dodgy-looking lads over by the garages felt like trying their luck. She wouldn't put it past them – she'd noticed several with piercings and they were all wearing their trousers low-slung, exposing the tops of their boxer shorts.

Since she'd found out Lou had been murdered, Alice had struggled to think of anything else. Normally, dinner would be something uncomplicated like pasta with grated cheese or beans on toast, so that she could spend the evening reading, listening to the radio or watching a documentary. But, traipsing around the house in a daze, she had tried all of these usual relaxation activities last night, substituting the simple dinner with a couple of carefully poured measures of vodka. None of it had blocked her thoughts enough.

Had Lou been scared as he fell? she'd wondered repeatedly. Would he have had time to realise what was happening?

Even as she had stood in the fruit and vegetable aisle at Tesco, she had been distracted by thoughts of DC Garcia calling her earlier this evening to tell her someone had been charged for Lou's murder. 'Excuse me, can I just . . . ?' A man with dreadlocks had reached an arm across Alice to reach for a bag of carrots. 'Are you all right?' he asked, as he dropped them in his basket. 'Yes,' she'd replied, still staring blankly at the array of food. And before she could think about what she was doing – talking to a stranger, for heaven's sake – she added, 'Relieved, in a way, I suppose.' He nodded slowly, muttered something and walked away. She was, though. Relieved. Now they had charged someone, she could believe that it definitely wasn't suicide. And it wasn't anything to do with Benny. So why did something still niggle at her chest when she thought of him? *What are you hiding?* She had picked up a head of broccoli, a red pepper, a couple of onions, a bag of chillies, ginger and a bulb of garlic. Some prawns from the fish counter.

She'd felt a grim satisfaction as she walked back down through the park, towards her bench. The prawns would need deveining; the broccoli would need chopping; the creation of the curry paste would require crushing, grinding of spices and some blending. Then there would be a significant amount of washing-up to do. The curry itself wouldn't be eaten, she knew that; she hadn't managed more than a dry piece of toast since Sunday morning and Benny didn't appear to be eating anything either. But there was enough there, she hoped, to keep her hands and her mind occupied, away from Lou, for a couple of hours.

'Does the name Kane Owen mean anything to you?' DC Garcia had asked, on the phone.

It hadn't.

'He's a little older than Lou. Nineteen. They knew each other.'

Alice had been walking home from work at the time, but when DC Garcia said this she stopped still in the middle of the pavement. One of Lou's friends did this to him? A wave of dizziness passed over her and she swayed slightly, reaching out a hand but finding nothing there to hold on to. Benny must have known him, too. Why did he want to protect the identity of his brother's killer?

'We believe Lou fell following an affray,' DC Garcia had said.

An affray. So this was it. His death was not 'unexplained' any more. It was all down to a fight with a friend. *No,* she had wanted to scream down the phone, at the people overtaking her on the pavement, and up towards the sky. *What a waste of a life.*

On her bench in the park, she pulled out her phone. Her hand was shaking slightly, and she gripped the edges of the screen tighter as she opened Facebook. She had a profile but did not accept friend requests as a rule, not that many were forthcoming. Lou had once discovered her on there and found it hilarious that she would even consider it. 'Just don't add me, Mum,' he'd said, laughing. 'Let's keep our boundaries clear, yeah?' She saw the incredulous expression on his face as he'd said it, but then it shifted into bewildered horror as she imagined a hand shoving him firmly in the chest, and him falling backwards – down, down, down and away from her.

She tapped in the name Kane Owen. Several results came up. A doctor (couldn't be him), someone listed as living in Stourbridge, another whose brief profile told her he was a member of the Jaguar Enthusiasts' Club. She filtered them by city: Bristol, UK. A blank grey screen appeared, with the words, 'We couldn't find anyone to show for Kane Owen.' Perhaps he didn't have his location set. Without that, she had no way of telling which of the original results list could be him. She tried Instagram but didn't have any more luck. She needed to ask Benny about him. Now he had been charged, it wouldn't constitute the 'grassing up' her son was so reluctant to get involved with. She needed to have the conversation face to face in order to see how he reacted to the news, but he hadn't been at the house when she got back after work, and he hadn't answered any of her calls or texts imploring him to get home as soon as he could. She dropped her phone in her lap and thought back once more to what DC Garcia had said. There hadn't been anything else mentioned about this boy, had there? Any other clues as to who he was? No, not long after giving his name, she had taken the conversation on to an abruptly different tack. 'How is Benny?'

Alice had started walking again along the pavement, more slowly this time. Why was she still asking about him? They had their man now, didn't they? She thought about what she'd found out about DC Garcia's role, and imagined her feeding all these conversations back to that scruffy detective who had come to the house the night Lou died. Cautiously, she answered, 'Very upset. We thought it was an accident. To find out his brother was murdered . . . it's a lot to take in.'

'Has he mentioned anything about the CCTV?'

Surely they had asked him about that at the station? Alice could tell DC Garcia wasn't just waiting for her answer, but also listening closely to how she reacted. At least Alice didn't need to lie about this. 'Nothing.'

'And you don't recognise either of the men? One of them, we know now, was Kane Owen. But we still want to talk to the other man, the one in the hooded top.'

He was the one Alice had thought looked familiar. She hesitated.

'It may be that Owen had an accomplice.'

Alice turned on to her road. 'I don't think I've ever seen him before.'

'We know how popular Lou was,' DC Garcia had said. 'Could he be one of his friends?'

Alice pressed the phone to her ear, wondering if she had misheard. 'Lou?' It was Benny who was popular. Lou was a loner, like her.

'We've spoken to the college,' DC Garcia went on. 'Some of

64

his classmates have been down at Queen Charlotte Street, laying flowers – he was well liked. Was there anyone in particular who came by the house?'

'No. He never had anybody over.' Was she talking about the same person? An absurd thought crossed her mind – was it really Lou who had died? Had there been a huge mistake?

'You've got my number, if anyone comes to mind,' DC Garcia said. 'Owen will be appearing at Magistrates' Court tomorrow morning.'

Thankfully, she had gone on to say Alice was not expected to attend, and in fact had discouraged her.

Now, as she watched the tennis players walk towards the net and pick up their water bottles, Alice thought about what court would be like. Being the kind of person who stayed on the right side of the law, she'd never had any reason to go inside one. She pictured a young man standing in the dock of a large wood-panelled room, his hands on the barrier in front of him, like those of the skinnier tennis player holding on to the top of the net. But, not knowing what this Kane Owen looked like, the only face she could bring to mind for this figure was Benny's.

She shook her head to get rid of the unwanted picture, turning away from the tennis courts to look instead down the path towards her house. Two men were walking towards her, and one was waving.

Was that Benny? She squinted. Yes. But who was he with?

The other man was wearing a suit, a satchel slung across his shoulder. As they got closer, Alice could see that he didn't look much older than Benny, but he was smarter, with his hair slicked back.

Was he a police officer? Alice stood up. Had they told Benny about Kane Owen?

'What's going on?' she asked, leaning over the back of the bench, when they were a couple of metres away.

65

'I thought I'd find you here,' Benny said, tugging at the neck of his T-shirt – he always did that when he was agitated. 'You said in your text that you were off to Tesco, I wasn't sure how long you'd be. He says it's important. This is . . . what was your name again?'

The man's eyes were large and sad. 'My name's Jacob Prince, Mrs Durand.' She didn't correct him. 'I'm a reporter at the *Bristol Post*. I'm so sorry about your son.' He paused. 'I was happy to wait at the house, but Benny here said that if—'

Alice picked up her shopping and stood. 'What have you told my son?'

'Nothing, I just said—'

'What is there to tell me?' Benny fixed his eyes on her, dropping his hand from his neck. 'Have you heard something?'

Alice looked at her son, opened her mouth and closed it again. This was not a conversation she wanted to have in front of a journalist.

She turned to Jacob Prince. 'Leave us alone.'

How had they found out that Lou was the boy who died? How had they got her address? She didn't want his face plastered all over the papers.

Handing Benny the shopping, she started walking home. 'Come on.'

'Mum? What's going on?' Benny asked, at the same time as the reporter called after her, 'Wait, please.' She sped up.

'This is harassment,' she said loudly. 'Come *on*, Benny.'

Jacob caught up with her and held out a business card with blue and red lettering on it. She snatched it and screwed it up in her hand.

'I'm not interested. Benny?'

'Okay, okay,' the reporter said, slowing down, and calling after her. 'I'll let you get home. But call me, Mrs Durand. There's something you need to know.'

Typical sleazy press, trying to hook her in like that. What on earth could he know that she didn't?

Alice heard Benny's footsteps behind her. 'Mum,' he hissed. 'What the fuck?'

She bit her tongue to suppress a reprimand for his bad language and turned to look at him as they reached their road. In the distance she could see Jacob Prince watching them, but he was out of earshot by now.

'Keep walking with me, I want to get away from him,' she said. 'They've charged that guy with murder. They said he was one of Lou's friends . . . Kane Owen. Is he one of those precious mates of yours you wouldn't tell me were there? Why would he hurt your brother?'

Benny dropped the shopping bag and the onions rolled out along the pavement. 'No . . . I don't—Who told you?' He scrabbled around on the ground, refilling the bag.

'DC Garcia.'

'There's been a mistake.'

'I don't think so, Ben.' They were at their front door now. Alice took her eyes off him for a moment to put her key in the lock. When she looked back, his face was screwed up in disbelief.

She stood to one side as he passed her in the hallway and put the shopping down on the breakfast bar. 'Why do they think it's murder?'

Alice studied her son's face. He looked genuinely shocked and confused. But why, again, did she feel that there was something she was missing? Something not being said?

'Why didn't you say anything about a fight? About him being pushed? She says he had a fractured eye socket.'

Alice forced her mind away from unwelcome images of Lou being cut open and examined, of the mess his face must have been in even before he was pushed from the car park. 'Ben, why?'

'I told you, I didn't see anything . . .' He spoke dreamily, staring out of the window into the garden, almost as though he didn't know she was there. Alice badly wanted to believe him.

'Was this Kane Owen guy a friend of yours, too?'

Benny nodded. 'He worked at the bar with me.' He rubbed his fists against his eyes. 'They really think Kane killed Lou?'

'I'm sorry, Ben. They said they have compelling evidence. More than the fight, even.' She held his hand briefly. For a moment, she forgot to watch him for clues about what he might be keeping from her. She only saw a devastated boy, who had just found out that his friend had murdered his brother.

'Kane . . . killed Lou,' he said deliberately. 'Kane killed Lou.' Each time he said it, he sounded increasingly convinced of the words' truth.

Indigo

21st August

The whole place reeks of body odour and cigarette smoke. I'm trying my best to sit still but my legs won't do it and my heels bounce on the floor.

Someone called me last night from the police station to say they'd charged Kane, and that he'd be here at Magistrates' Court for a hearing this morning. Charged with murder. My boy. This can't be happening to us. I screamed that down the phone, but the officer had already hung up, and I was alone in my bedroom with only Lucian for company through the dark, quiet hours of the night. I didn't sleep. I couldn't cry.

I smooth my skirt and straighten my jumper. My fingers find my yellow bracelet. How many times have I twisted it around my wrist in the last couple of days? Several hundred on Monday while the police searched the house, and a few hundred more after they left as I stood in Kane's bedroom, staring at the hem of his curtain, where he'd once told me he used to hide his cigarettes. I had a feeling there would be something in there. Was I breaching his trust by looking? This was an extreme enough situation to justify snooping. I stuck a finger into the gap. I had been right – there was a piece of folded card. He must have forgotten he'd told me about his hiding place. I took a deep breath and pulled it out. On the front of the card there was a geometric pattern of black and blue shapes. On the back, written in a scrawled hand I didn't recognise, were the words, 'He wants shrimp and sweat and salt', followed by a small doodle of a heart. The words were in quotation marks, so maybe it was a line from a film that he liked. Was it a note from his boyfriend? If I could find out who he was, perhaps he would tell me something that I could use to help Kane.

So, here I am again, twirling these yellow beads. I don't feel so different now to when he gave me this bracelet, the day he returned from France: apprehensive, excited. Wondering what I will say to him when I see him. I smooth my skirt again and check the clock. Ten forty-five.

I'm sitting on one of the metal seats outside court three, where I've been told Kane will appear, when a man wearing a red tracksuit bursts out of it, storming off towards the stairs. He kicks at a wall on his way, and shouts, 'It's a set-up! It's Gaz Philips what's done it and he's got it in for me.' The other people in the waiting area are momentarily distracted from the TV screen mounted on the wall. Everyone here looks like they've been dealt a rough hand in life; I wonder what all their stories are. I'm sure they don't want my pity, but I can't help feeling it.

While the tracksuited man causes a scene, someone else walks towards me. This man is very different. He's dressed in a suit, for a start, with his grey hair cut into a smart, neat style. He has a pile of folders and papers under his arm, his face is flushed and he is out of breath.

'Mrs Owen? Excuse me.' He coughs.

'Yes?'

'Clive Parsons. I'm the duty solicitor today. I'm sorry to do this here,' he says as he sits next to me. 'But I got caught up in court two and we don't have much time. I would normally see if they had an interview room free but . . .' He looks at his watch.

'Duty solicitor?'

'Yes. I'm going to be representing your son. He said you

would probably be here, said he'd asked them to call you from the station last night?'

I could hug him. 'I thought he didn't have a solicitor. Thank you. It's such a relief to know—'

'Just doing my job. He wasn't that keen to see me, I have to say – but I explained it would be in his best interests.'

'How could they charge my boy with murder?'

'The post-mortem has shown there was some kind of fight or struggle. There was damage to the victim's eye socket.' He pauses for a moment and looks away from me, flicking through the papers in his lap. 'And Kane has admitted it.'

'What?' I must have misheard him.

'Kane has told the police he pushed the victim over the wall in the car park.'

He didn't do it. He can't have done it.

'Now, as for today . . . all that will happen is that his case will be sent to Crown Court. Magistrates don't deal with the more serious crimes.'

I nod, trying to follow what he is saying.

'Kane wants me to strike a deal with the Crown Prosecution Service. It's not what I would recommend but he is adamant that he committed this crime.'

'A deal?'

'He'll plead guilty to manslaughter. The CPS would rather take that and get the case over and done with than drag it through an expensive murder trial.'

'But he's innocent.' This isn't what I had expected, at all. At worst, I have been imagining a trial, with a jury that sees my son for who he really is and lets him go.

Clive looks at me without sympathy, which I am grateful for. 'He's admitted it, Mrs Owen.'

'Why would he do that?'

'He confessed very early on, before he was arrested. With no solicitor there. That's bad, in many ways . . . I would never have let him. But it's also good.'

'How can it be?'

'The prosecution case is shaky. Officially, they've not done anything wrong – they offered him representation and he declined. But they've not played entirely by the book and they know it. His early admission, without legal advice, could come back to bite them and they will want it all wrapped up as soon as possible. We could get a good deal.'

'But he'd still end up in prison?'

Clive adjusts his tie, avoiding looking me in the eye.

'We need to fight it,' I say. 'What can you do to build a case in Kane's defence?'

'Kane has instructed me to go after a plea deal, Mrs Owen. I'm afraid I'm acting on his behalf, not yours.'

'I see.' Clearly this man is spineless.

There's a woman in a long black gown who has been stepping in and out of court three all morning, calling names and beckoning people over. She opens the door now, holds up her clipboard and bellows: 'Anyone for Kane Owen?'

Clive waves at her, nods once at me, and we stand up to go in.

As we pass through two sets of heavy wooden doors to get into the court, Clive takes my elbow and whispers, 'Kane wants trainers, by the way. You can take some to the prison when you visit.'

Visiting him in prison? The thought hadn't occurred to me until he said it. As I find a seat in the front row of the public gallery at the back of the court, I try to remember what I was thinking before I came here. Did I think Kane would be coming home today? I look around at the other people in the gallery. Is everyone here for Kane's case?

A door opens at the end of the room and everyone in the court stops talking and stands up. I do the same. The magistrates walk in – two women and a man – and take their seats behind a long table on a raised platform at the front of the court. We all sit down too. This place isn't what I thought it would be like; it's drab and grey, devoid of colour, in contrast to the courtrooms you see on television, which are always grand and full of polished wood and men in wigs. Clive hasn't got a wig on, and neither do any of the magistrates. The three of them look like normal people in normal clothes.

The woman in the black gown who ducks in and out of the courtroom stands up. 'Our next case is Kane Owen and he is represented by Mr Parsons.'

I twist my yellow beads. A few moments later there's the sound of keys jangling, and a wooden door opens to my right. Kane steps through it, into the dock – a glass-sided box with a row of seats inside. With him are two security guards wearing blue surgical gloves, who unlock sets of handcuffs which attach their wrists to my son's, before standing either side of him in the dock. My stomach flips and I can't believe I was looking forward to seeing him just a few minutes ago. His eyes meet mine.

I love you, I mouth across the room, and he puts a hand to his lips, before scanning the rest of the public gallery. His eyes settle on someone behind me, and I'm sure I see fear flash across his face. I turn to see two police officers sitting one row back – I don't recognise either of them. What have they done to my boy?

A man sitting at a computer in front of the magistrates is the first to speak to Kane. 'Can you confirm that your name is Kane Owen?'

'Yes.' His voice is croaky, and he coughs.

'And your date of birth is the twentieth of November, 1999?' 'Yes.'

'I have an address for you of Sunnyside, Fairlawn Road, Montpelier. Is that correct?'

'Yes.'

'The matter you are here for today concerns the death of Louis

Durand in Queen Charlotte Street, Bristol, on the seventeenth of August of this year. You are charged with murder.'

Kane nods. *Why have you told them you did this?*

The magistrate sitting in the middle of the three, a woman with cropped blonde hair, smiles at him. It warms my heart. Can she see that he is innocent? 'Sit down, please, Mr Owen. We are going to work out what we need to do next.'

The rest of the hearing passes in a blur for me.

I can only stare at Kane. I thought he'd be in his orange shirt, the one he went to the police station in, but instead he is wearing what I assume are prison-issue clothes – a huge, grubby grey sweater and matching jogging bottoms. He has dark circles under his eyes. He already looks thinner.

I think of that man who stormed out of the court earlier, shouting that he had been set up. Is that what has happened to Kane? Who would have anything against my son? He gets on with everyone. The only person I ever knew him to fall out with was that boy at school, but that had all sorted itself out years ago.

Clive is saying something else to the magistrates, but I am struggling to concentrate with the blood pounding in my ears. My poor boy is rubbing the base of his neck repeatedly with one hand and fiddling with his nose ring with the other. His hair looks dirty. I think I'm going to be sick and I start to plan my exit, grabbing my pannier bag and looking for the best way out of my row. But then the lady magistrate speaks again, loudly, to Kane.

'Stand up, please, Mr Owen.'

Kane winces as he does so. Is he injured?

'We are sending your case to the Crown Court,' the magistrate says. 'We are remanding you in custody because we have serious concerns that you will fail to surrender and may interfere with witnesses, due to the nature and seriousness of the allegation.'

Kane's guards open his door, put him back in handcuffs and

usher him out. He doesn't look at me again before he goes. I want to shout out his name, but it won't help him, will it?

People start filing out of the room and more replace them. Clive walks over to me, clutching his files.

'They've set the next date, for Crown Court. It could change, though. I'll get my secretary to call you and let you know.'

'Can I see him now?' I whisper.

Clive looks at me with confusion. 'Did you think you were going to be able to?'

I sit back down heavily. My son, I just want to see my son.

'Did you not hear? He'll be in the prison up the road, in Horfield. I'll get you the details – the number you need to call to register for a visit.'

I rise to my feet and stumble as I move past other people in my row. I look up to check where I am going and I see a man in the back row of the gallery, directly behind where I had been sitting. I recognise him. He is looking straight at me with such hatred in his eyes, and I want to look away, but I can't. It's only when Clive pulls at my elbow and leads me out of the courtroom that I turn away.

Wasn't that the dead boy's brother?

Benny

17th August

The thing was, their mum had given up a lot for them. Benny probably remembered more of the early bit than Lou did: those years after Dad had left. All she did was take them to nursery, work, pick them up, feed them, get them to bed, then start again. Pops helped to look after them at the weekends so that she could work some more. Benny distinctly remembered one day at nursery – he must have been about four – when he heard a little girl talking about her daddy putting her to bed the night before, because Mummy was out 'on the white line' with her friends. Their nursery teacher had laughed, suggested maybe she had been drinking wine rather than on a line, but all Benny could think about was the fact that his friend's mother had left the house in the evening. Her mummy had *friends,* like Benny and Lou did? And her *daddy* had put her to bed? It blew his tiny mind.

Lou was oblivious to all of that. By the time Benny started school things had started to get easier. Mum was working less overtime, she was always around to help with his homework, she'd take them places at the weekend; they'd run around the woods by Blaise Castle, walk over the bridge to see the deer at Ashton Court or go on the steam train at Avon Valley.

And yeah, it was true that Lou had a bit more of a hard time from her than Benny seemed to, but they all knew Lou often deserved it.

'All I'm saying is stop making her life such hard work.' He looked out of the bus window as they passed the line of restaurants on Pigsty Hill. It was a warm evening and they all had plenty of customers sitting outside. Through the open window he heard wine glasses clink, the scratch of cutlery against plates. Benny had never eaten at any of them – a bit too pricey for his budget. Miss Millie's fried chicken, a box of which was being eaten by the bloke behind him, was about as upmarket as he ventured. He sniffed, the smell of the chicken batter making his mouth water. 'When I go off to Exeter you need to look after her. Help out around the house a bit more.'

Lou snorted, sliding down in his seat and kicking his feet up against the one in front of him. 'You do fuck all around the house.'

'That's not true. I do more than—'

Lou pretended to yawn. 'Can you just, not? Enough of the lecture.' He pulled some chewing gum out of his mouth in a long string, then popped it back in. 'Mum and I will be fine. I'll make my bed occasionally. Happy?'

'Ecstatic.' Benny paused. 'And you won't say anything to her? About, you know . . . Dad?'

'No.' Lou's face hardened. 'Look, what's more important right now is that we work out where we're starting tonight. Do we really have to meet Kane?'

This again. 'Yes, we do. What's your problem with him?' Benny slid two of his fingers along the small ledge at the bottom of the window, pretending they were on a tiny skateboard, which he then flipped and landed perfectly.

'It changes the dynamic, you know? This is meant to be a lads' night out. Remember when we used to go to gigs?' He tapped Benny's knee. 'Just you and me? They were good nights.'

'You want to go to a gig tonight?' Benny pulled his phone out of his pocket. 'We could see what's on, we could all go.'

'I've looked. Nothing decent. Can we at least go for a beer on our own? Once, before you abandon me with my number-one fan?'

'If it'll shut you up.'

Lou had always been a bit like this. Always wanting Benny's attention, his approval. He'd never forget the first time he allowed his little brother to join him on a night out, just for a few beers in town. Lou had tried to act all cool and disinterested when Benny had suggested it, but he could see the excitement in his eyes. He saw the way he kept looking over at him in the pub, checking to see if Benny was laughing at his stories. He even bought him a bag of crisps, unprompted – that's how chuffed he was to be included.

'He doesn't even bring in the girls. I thought that was meant to be the point of having a gay boy for a mate?' Lou took his gum out, reached down and stuck it under his seat.

'Don't . . .' Benny closed his eyes and exhaled. Lou made him feel like such a nag. It did his head in, but it needed saying. 'Why do you say shit like that? Gay boy? You know it's offensive, right? I know you don't mean it.'

'They're just words. Chill out.'

'You're looking for a reaction, that's all.' Benny stood up, gesturing for Lou to do the same.

He didn't move. 'Is that right?'

'Come on, Lou, this is our stop.'

'Only if we're meeting your token homosexual friend.' He slowly eased himself out of his seat. 'Is that any better? Accurate, isn't it?'

Benny bit his lip. If he said too much, Lou would keep winding him up. But if he said too little, he was letting him get away with it. They made their way down the steps to the bus's lower level, Lou swinging his bodyweight out from the handrail as he went.

Benny put a hand on his brother's shoulder as the bus slowed to a halt. 'Don't be a dick.' He squeezed slightly. 'I'm warning you.'

Lou laughed. 'Cheers, drive,' he said to the bloke behind the wheel, as they stepped off on to the pavement.

As Lou lit a cigarette, Benny gave him a playful shove towards the bus stop and attempted to lighten his tone. 'It's my job, as the father figure in this family, to keep you in line.' He wagged a finger at him. 'I'll give you a good hiding, son.'

Alice

23rd August

When Alice arrived home on Friday afternoon, she found Benny's laptop open on the kitchen table. That's what she would say if he caught her.

Because strictly speaking it *was* open, in that it wasn't closed – but actually the lid was tilted down. It was too tempting. She had to work out what was going on with him; his uncharacteristic evasiveness must be more than just grief. After the news about Kane Owen being charged, he had completely shut down. She saw him this morning before she left to do a couple of hours' extra work at the library. Normally he commented on her going in when the library was closed – he knew it wasn't open on a Friday – but this morning he made no eye contact and only grunted a few words at her. He'd been like this all week, not that she'd really seen him – he was either shut away in his room or out. If she managed to catch him when he got home and ask where he'd been he snapped at her to give him a break and fobbed her off: 'Just for a skate', he'd say (alone?), 'Quick sesh at the gym' (though she noticed he didn't have his gym bag), 'Been watching a film round a mate's house' (but he wouldn't tell her whose). She had been used to this attitude from Lou, but not from Benny. He never used to mind telling her what he'd been up to. Alice swallowed as she touched the smooth laptop lid.

Quietly dropping her rucksack on to the floor, she looked over her shoulder into the hallway. He must be upstairs; she would hear him if he came down. Just time to have a quick look. She lifted the lid and sat down, pulling the chair close in behind her. The sensation of her stomach touching the table made her catch her breath. An arching melody came into her mind. *Mozart's Fantasia and a sea breeze through the open door. Her belly pressed up against the edge of the piano. His tiny unborn feet, dancing.* She blinked hard, cutting the music off in her head, and studied the screen. Benny had Facebook open, and her eyes were immediately drawn to the name in the middle of the screen. Kane Owen's profile page. At the top was a black-and-white photograph of a quiet street, a neon hotel sign reflecting on to wet cobbles. Underneath that was a photo of a boy with dark blond hair, curls falling over his forehead, his bright blue eyes not looking at the camera. Only his head and shoulders were visible, but it was obvious that he was skinny from his slim face and the way his cheap khaki jumper hung from his frame, the collar of a tangerine-coloured shirt just visible at his neck. This must be her son's murderer. And yet, to her, he looked like a child. He looked younger than Benny; younger even than Lou. A baby-faced killer. She shook her head. She couldn't feel sorry for him. *Lou's dancing feet. Her belly pressed against the edge of the piano.* Nineteen, DC Garcia had said he was. A man – old enough to know right from wrong.

It was only when she clicked on the photo to enlarge it that she realised she had seen him before. When Benny had told her he worked at the bar, she'd assumed she didn't know him. But there had been that one time at the house, hadn't there? He'd had shorter hair then – when had it been? A couple of months ago? She recognised the ring in his nose, she thought, as she wrinkled her own in disgust. He'd been leaving one day when she arrived home, and as she approached she had heard him talking to Benny and Lou on the doorstep. What had they been discussing? She wished she could remember, but all she could recall was his faint West Country accent and the way he'd been unable to meet her eye as she slipped past him to get inside.

Had she asked his name? Possibly not – he hadn't seemed like the kind of boy she needed to show interest in, certainly not the kind of company she would like the boys to be keeping. 'Who was that?' she'd asked, after Benny had closed the door.

'Friend from work,' he'd said.

'Where's he going to university?'

Lou had laughed as he went up to his bedroom, taking the stairs two at a time, leaving Benny to answer her questions.

She fully expected to hear that the boy wasn't continuing his education, and Benny's reply did not do much to improve her opinion. Alice firmly believed in the soundness of her first impressions, and she felt she'd got a pretty good measure of that boy.

'One of the London ones,' Benny said. 'Film studies.'

'That's not a real subject.'

'What's your problem?'

'The piercing, Benny. You know how I feel about boys with piercings. And on his face, too.' It was unsanitary, for one thing, and how did the boy ever expect anyone to take him seriously in a work environment?

'I do, yes.' Benny rolled up his sleeve to expose two thin black lines on his forearm. 'The same way you do about tattoos.'

Alice looked away. 'You'll regret it, one day, I stand by that.'

'Anything else about him you decided you didn't like, in that thirty seconds?'

'His manners weren't the best, were they? And you can really tell he's from Bristol, can't you?'

Benny had laughed, shaking his head. 'Well, that's because he is. There's nothing wrong with a Bristol accent, Mum. Just because you've spent your life trying to get rid of yours . . .'

Alice frowned at the suggestion that she'd ever sounded anything like Kane.

'And as for manners, you practically pushed past him to get in the house. Where were yours?'

So that had been him. The hairs on Alice's neck stood on end as she remembered the encounter. She had met her son's killer.

She got her phone out and took a quick photo of the laptop screen, then scrolled down to see more pictures of him. There were several. Kane Owen leaning over a video camera; Kane Owen with friends in the park; Kane Owen with his arm around a woman much older than he was, with shoulder-length white hair. His mother? Alice shuddered. To be the mother of a murderer. She clicked on the photo to get a closer look at the woman. It was hard to gauge her age, but her smooth tanned skin suggested she was younger than her hair indicated, not much older than Alice – maybe it had greyed prematurely. Those round, black-rimmed glasses she wore were the kind Alice saw students wearing, not the barely there frameless type that Alice thought more appropriate for women of their age. And she was wearing a thin-strapped bright pink vest top. Alice was no expert, granted, but even she knew that clothes like that were made for teenage girls. Her head was nestled on the boy's shoulder, as if they considered themselves friends rather than mother and son. She looked like the sort of woman who would be proud of that.

But poring over every detail of a photo of Kane Owen's mother wasn't helping her work out what was going on with her own son. The fact that Benny had been looking through this man's timeline didn't tell her anything that would help her keep him safe. She swiped her finger over the tracking pad and hovered the cursor over the icon for Benny's Facebook Messenger inbox. She closed her eyes, took a deep breath, and clicked.

As she did so, she was startled by a large crashing sound from outside on the patio. She slammed the laptop shut and leaned forward to look out of the French windows, just in time to see

Benny kicking over a chair. He must have been out there all this time. Had he seen her? He wasn't looking in her direction.

'Benny?' She tapped on the glass, but he didn't seem to hear her.

He turned towards the end of the garden, threw his arms above his head and shouted, 'You happy now?'

'Jesus.' Alice ran through the utility room to the back door and flung it open. 'Benny, what are you doing?'

'What . . . you done?' Benny hadn't registered her being there, he was still shouting down the garden.

'Who are you talking to? Benny?'

He was staring at the prison wall and swaying, holding up a bottle of Peroni. Alice looked around and saw several other empties amongst the garden furniture he had kicked over.

'I told you . . . leave it,' Benny slurred, still yelling in the direction of the wall.

'Okay, it's all right.' Alice edged her way towards him. 'Come on, now. Let's go inside, shall we?' He looked at her. His face was blotchy.

'Mum?' The word came out as a rasp. He took a swig of beer as she put an arm around him and led him into the kitchen.

Alice ran the tap and poured him a glass of water. 'Here. Drink.' She removed the beer bottle from his hand.

He was still staring out of the window over the sink, down towards the foot of the garden.

'This is about Kane Owen, I take it?'

Benny closed his eyes.

'You think he might be in there?' She pointed at the brick wall and the buildings beyond it.

'I know he is.'

'What do you mean?'

'I went to court today, didn't I? Saw him. They said he was in there.' He flung his arm towards the prison.

84

Alice walked to the back door and leaned against the frame as she looked outside. In all these years, since moving into the house shortly before Benny was born, she had never been disturbed by the prison. 'Doesn't it bother you?' people would ask, but it didn't. Most of the time she couldn't hear anything to remind her of it, and you could only really see the prison buildings from the back bedrooms. But in those nineteen years or so, she'd never known anyone inside it. She shivered, despite the warm afternoon air, and thought of the face she'd just seen on Benny's laptop.

'Can you trust him?' She turned to face her son.

He took a sip of water, watching her over the rim of the glass. 'What do you mean?'

'What's he going to say to the police about you?'

Benny rubbed at his eye with the heel of his hand. 'Why would he say anything about me?'

'Come off it, Benny. I'm trying to help you.'

'How should I know what he's going to say?' He slammed his glass down on the sideboard and water spilled out on to the wood. Alice almost reached out to wipe it but stopped herself. She hoped he hadn't acted so defensively when he spoke to the police.

He leaned over the sink and rested his face on his arm.

'We will get through this.' She stepped towards him and touched his face as he looked up at her. *Her belly pressed up against the edge of the piano. Mozart's Fantasia. Lou's first kicks, during the sighs of the adagio.*

'I miss Lou, too. I know we didn't always get along.'

Her wrist, dropping on the A and floating up on the G sharp. Breathless, Alice. Breathless.

'You don't have to explain,' Benny said.

'I just wish you'd give me the full story.'

'I can't tell you who else was there.' He grabbed her hand. 'Please don't ask me to.'

85

'Give me something, though, Ben? Anything? Were they fighting when you were there?'

'Okay, okay.' He squeezed her fingers. 'Yeah. I swear I didn't see him fall, though.'

'And what was the fight about?'

'He rubbed people up the wrong way; you know what he was like.' Benny suddenly seemed much more sober. His eyes were flickering around, from her to the sink and back again. 'He said stuff without thinking.'

He was playing for time, she could see it. 'What kind of things?'

'It was about a girl, I think. Other things, too, but . . .' He trailed off.

'What girl?'

'No names, remember, Mum?'

She bit her lip. She'd never agreed to that rule. 'What did he say about her, then?'

'Kane was telling Lou he couldn't handle a relationship, that kind of thing. That he was too immature. Lou . . . Lou said he didn't want one anyway, only losers wanted to settle down before they were twenty. He was winding Kane up—'

'And that was why he pushed him? That was it?'

'I don't know, Mum. I wasn't there, remember?'

'You promise me you're telling the truth about that?'

'I swear.' He looked her in the eye, and she was relieved to find that she believed him.

'Anything else you want to say? Now's the time.'

'That's it, that's all I know.'

She studied his face, but he held firm and didn't look away.

'Right then. Come on.' She crouched to open a cupboard full of redundant cooking paraphernalia – a stick blender, casserole dishes, a sandwich toaster – and reached past them all to pull out a half-empty bottle of Żubrówka before pouring herself a double into an old, chipped tumbler.

86

She faced Benny, glass in hand. He was staring at her.

'Secret stash,' she said.

'I don't think I've ever seen you with a drink.'

Alice wasn't sure whether to be pleased that she had succeeded in fooling him or sad that he hadn't ever noticed. 'Lou discovered it last month,' she said. 'I found him using half the bottle to rinse out his carburettor.'

Benny laughed. 'But that's nice vodka, that is.'

'I don't drink cheap stuff.'

She could suddenly see Lou's face so clearly. When she found him with the bottle and the carburettor, she'd asked him what he was doing. 'Works as well as anything else,' he'd said. 'Pops' idea. He's all for hacks and alternatives. I found this in the cupboard, looks old.' (It didn't.) She'd felt she needed to offer an explanation for its existence and told him she'd used it in a stew a while ago.

Benny reached up into the cupboard and pulled out another glass. She put a hand out to close the door and stopped him. 'Not for you,' she said, lifting her own to her lips. 'I think you've had quite enough.'

'Why are you drinking, then?'

Alice walked towards the back door. 'You're angry with this guy? Me too.'

As he followed her out into the garden, she called over her shoulder. 'Bring one of your empties.' She gestured at the pile on the patio and Benny picked a bottle up before following her down the steps and on to the lawn. They walked past Lou's Tiger and the apple tree, until they were no more than four metres away from the towering wall, separated from it only by their own garden fence and the alleyway that ran between the two. Looking at the brickwork and the weeds and ferns growing in its cracks, her whole body tensed.

She downed the vodka and it burned her throat. 'Here's what we're going to do,' she said.

87

Lifting her glass above her head, she imagined that thin, evil face, those dirty blond curls. 'You took my son!' The words burned at her throat even more as she roared them. Then, more quietly, she said, 'You took away any chance I might have had to fix things.'

She swung her arm back and threw her glass up, over the fence. It smashed against the wall, shards falling into the alleyway.

She turned to Benny, who was gawping at her. 'You next.' She nodded at the empty beer bottle.

'Mum, I don't know if this is—'

'Let the neighbours talk. Let the police come knocking. And you know the prison won't care, those probably aren't even switched on.' She pointed at the CCTV camera above them.

Benny laughed nervously.

'We're having a horrendous week, Ben. We've lost our Lou, for ever. I'm telling you, this is okay.' Her voice was hoarse.

Benny shrugged and looked at the wall for a moment.

'He was my brother!' he shouted finally, and hurled his bottle against the bricks.

He held a hand out and she took it as they stood there, staring at the razor wire and the clear blue afternoon sky above it.

Driven by a strange impulse, Alice had only done this for him. But she hadn't expected it to feel so good. Her heart was pounding, and the tension she had been carrying for days had gone from her body, leaving her feeling almost weightless.

She took a firmer hold of Benny's hand.

The next morning, Alice called the number DC Garcia had left her with.

'It's been brought to my attention that the man you have charged with my son's murder is being held in the prison next door to our home,' she said when DC Garcia answered, looking at the photo of Benny she had in her hand. She'd found it when the police had asked for one of Lou last weekend. Benny was only about eleven or twelve in it, standing in the garden, grinning from ear to ear. She wanted that boy back. Kane Owen wouldn't take him away from her, not as well as Lou. 'I'd like an explanation as to how this could possibly be deemed an appropriate place to keep him.'

'Good morning, Miss Hyde. That's not a decision I have been part of, but I can certainly look into it for you. I can understand that—'

'I doubt you can, actually.' Alice rolled her shoulders, easing the sore muscles she had woken with. 'I want an explanation, in writing, but more importantly, I demand that you transfer him into another prison.'

'I can certainly put in a request.'

'I didn't make a request, though. I made a demand.' It felt good to be taking control again. Alice had a focus she'd missed since Lou died.

'I don't know if it will be possible, that's all. I don't want to promise something I can't make happen.'

Alice ground her teeth to stop herself saying something she would possibly regret.

Putting a hand to the glass of the French window, she traced the lines of bricks in the prison wall. 'DC Garcia. *Hannah*. I suggest you make it possible.' She hung up.

Indigo

24th August

I haven't been in Kane's bedroom since I found that note in his curtain a few days ago. After he was in court, I cycled out to Nailsea to clear my head and then went to bed early, determined to wake up refreshed and ready to do something to help him, but instead I woke to a migraine which wiped me out for two days. This morning I have been working up to it – to going into his room and tidying up the mess the police left it in, checking if there is anything in there I can take to him or deal with for him while he's away.

I pace outside his closed bedroom door, running my fingers along the polished-smooth banister. *All is well.*

I stop midway through one of my laps of the landing, turn the handle and I'm in there, at last. It's worse than I remembered. They turned it upside down, threw his books and DVDs across the pale grey painted floorboards. I lean against the doorframe. Of the one wall of film posters he hadn't taken down yet, each has had its bottom edges lifted, and there's a tear in the bottom left-hand corner of *Vertigo*, stopping just beneath the V of the title. I'll have to repair it for him. It's not just the rip that draws my eye to it – it's the violence of the red background, and the mesmerising spirals of the image on it, the way the characters look like they are falling, spinning out of control, sinking into oblivion.

A peal of bells rings through the house. As I walk down the stairs to answer the door, Kane fills my mind as he has done all week. In the last two days all I have thought of is him in prison. What is he doing at this moment? Is he being treated well? The doorbell rings again. Does anyone knock before coming into his cell? Does he have any privacy? Is he safe? *It's going to be okay, Kane. We'll get you out.*

I stop by the mirror in the hallway to straighten my glasses and pull my cardigan closer around me. I sweep my hand over my hair but it's beyond looking presentable, it feels greasy under my fingertips. I shrug and turn the handle.

I smell her before I see her – the sickly lily of the valley scent that fits her so perfectly. My sister: beautiful, delicate and popular, yet poisonous. The smell is being carried in by the morning's fine-drizzle humidity, which Dawn is protecting herself from with her umbrella.

She tilts her head of perfectly cropped hair and her pearl earrings dangle against her shoulder. 'Are you going to make me stand out here in the rain?'

Lucian's claws clack against the floor behind me. He takes one look at our visitor and runs out of the front door, straight past her. I don't want her in this house either. Not right now. 'It was sunny when I last looked out of the window.'

Dawn shakes her head and turns her mouth into that patronising smile of hers. 'It certainly isn't any more. Come on, Indy. Let me in.' She closes her umbrella and shakes it on my doormat as she pushes past me, before using it to point back at the empty school playground over the road. 'Those banners on the railings are too big. You should complain to your councillor.'

'It doesn't bother me.' I shut the door and step in a puddle of cold umbrella water as I follow her back through the hallway.

'It should. It's an eyesore. The kind of thing my constituents get very hot under the collar about.' It took me a decade of living away from the Midlands to notice the Brummie twang in my sister and mother's voices, but ever since it sticks out to me as starkly as if I had never lived there. It grates on me when Dawn speaks, but not when Lily does.

It suddenly hits me why she is here. 'It's Saturday.' I rub the sole of my wet foot against the other leg of my pyjamas. If I could find my diary, lying somewhere in the house with my discarded bike pannier bag, wherever I threw it when I returned from court, I know it would say 'Dawn visiting' next to today's date. 'You've come all the way from Stafford,' I say to her back, as she disappears into my kitchen.

'Of course I've come from effing Stafford. That's where I live.'

She knows nothing about Kane. I haven't told her. 'I'm so sorry, I totally forgot. I've had the worst migraine.'

'I'll make you soup or something.' Dawn looks around. 'Don't tell me you still don't own a microwave? I don't know why you're so worried about the radiation, it can't get out.' She wafts a damp folded newspaper in front of my face before slamming it down on to the counter with her expensive-looking patent-leather handbag, then opens her umbrella back up, showering me with more tiny drops of water. I flinch but don't say anything. 'I'll leave this here to dry out a bit,' she says, balancing it against a cold radiator, and looks me in the eye, challenging me to ask her not to, so that she can call me a superstitious fool and say I am 'just as bad as Mother'.

I ignore her and fill the kettle. 'Tea?'

'Where's Kane?'

I close my eyes and see the dizzying spirals on his *Vertigo* poster again.

'Kane?' she shouts in the vague direction of the stairs. 'Get down here and say hello to your favourite auntie.' She steps towards the counter as I open my eyes to watch the steam starting to escape from the kettle. There's a brown cardboard box next to the sink, held together with gaffer tape, and she lets out a horrified cry as she takes a look inside.

'What in God's name is that?'

I presume she's found Kane's taxidermy pigeon. 'Some of Kane's props. Film stuff.'

Dawn pushes the box away. 'Where is he?'

I spin the beads on my yellow bracelet – something about the way she is acting isn't right. She's never normally this eager to see him. What can I say to get rid of her? *The thing is, it's not a great time right now.*

I force myself to face her. Now that she has taken off her mackintosh and slung it over a chair in the dining room, I see that she is wearing her silk scarf printed with Van Gogh's *Starry Night*. Kane bought it for her as a joke Christmas present one year when she asked him for 'something arty, like you and your dear mother', but she didn't get the joke. She loved it, and every other hideous one he has bought her since. 'Wearable art,' she'd said, her eyes lighting up when she saw the blue and yellow swirls. 'Just the thing.' Just the thing for what, we'd never understood.

'He isn't here.' I reach past her head and pull a box of teabags out of the cupboard to find the Earl Grey I know she will want.

'Visiting friends, is he?' Her beady eyes are on me, even as I turn my back to her again.

I pour hot water into two cups, drop her Earl Grey teabag into one, and a red berry and hibiscus mix into mine.

'Out with his camera somewhere. You know what he's like.'

All I want is to be left to get on with Kane's room. *I've not been well. It might not be a migraine. I wouldn't want you to catch it.*

I spoon the teabags out, set her cup down and take a sip from my own, as she picks up her damp newspaper and unfolds it, holding it in front of my face. 'When were you going to mention this to me?'

It's the *Bristol Post*. The front page has a mugshot of Kane on it, his face sallow and scared. It's about his court appearance. I put my cup on the counter and grab the newspaper out of her hands. It has yesterday's date.

'Where did you get this?' My voice emerges as a whisper.

'The shop round the corner, where do you think? I went in to get my nephew his favourite chocolate and was confronted with this.' Dawn prods a finger at Kane's photograph.

I realise to my horror that it's the weekend edition – the one they put in shops on Friday and leave on sale for the next couple of days. How many people will see it? I read the short report quickly. 'Can they print this?' Our neighbours will have seen it, as well as my clients and my friends. My cheeks burn. I can't stand to think of them all assuming he is guilty.

'When were you going to tell me?'

'Soon.' I flick through, looking for more.

'You can't say anything to Mother.' I look up at my sister. Her face is set hard. Even with our mum approaching her eightieth birthday, Dawn still refuses to follow her wishes and call her Lily. She had insisted when we were girls. 'I see us as sisters, not mother and daughters, don't you?' But from the moment Dawn hit puberty she had recoiled as far from that idea as she could, towards the coldest, most austere and least fitting name possible. 'She doesn't need this.'

I look towards the window and focus on the tumbling vine from the devil's ivy hanging from the shelf above me. Green is calming. Green is the colour of balance. Yet all I can see is red.

'I wasn't going to.'

'She has enough on her plate. You know they've moved her again? The woman in the room next to her snores so loudly she says it's like she's in the bed with her.'

Oh, Lily. Lily, with her long hair, which she loved me to plait when I was sad, and her fingernails, which would trace intricate mandalas across the skin of my arm. *Be kind, always.* I know

94

Dawn's right, and I can't burden her with this. But if I could, I know she would know what to say to make it all okay.

At some point, Dawn will ask me how I'm doing. She's in shock, that's all. I follow the devil's ivy vine from leaf to leaf, right down to the lowest one, which is covered in small pin-pricks of moisture from the kettle steam.

'You've not asked me what happened,' I say, but my quiet words are lost under hers.

'You simply cannot,' she continues. 'No one can know about this. I'm a councillor.'

In Stafford, I want to scream at her. That's all she's worried about. Her reputation. Not her nephew. Not me. Certainly not Lily, who she's dumped in an expensive care home, paying away the guilt she should be feeling. But instead, I find myself saying: 'He's innocent.'

She ignores me. 'You need to distance yourself. Are you worried about your business? I don't blame you.' Dawn spins me round and clutches at my upper arms. 'You need to start firefighting.'

'I've cancelled my clients for the next week. I said it was a family emergency.'

'Take down any photos of the pair of you together on Facebook, Twitter. Ask the police to put out a statement on your behalf expressing your sadness, saying this isn't the son you know.'

'It *isn't* the son I know.' I look up at her.

'Exactly, say that.'

I pull away from her, taking in the new lines that have appeared on her face since I last saw her, across her forehead and around her eyes.

'Stop it,' she says. 'I hate it when you do that.'

'Do what?'

'Look at me like you're sizing me up for one of your portraits.' She reaches out to touch my shoulder. 'I know this must be dif-ficult for you, but you mustn't blame yourself. It wouldn't be a surprise if he was predisposed to a mental disorder of some sort, would it?'

If she is referring to Glyn, I will not give her the satisfaction of rising to it. I shrug off her hand, suddenly feeling hot enough to remove my cardigan. How dare she? And what was that charade earlier? Shouting upstairs to Kane? She knew all along, from the moment she'd walked through the door. If anyone was likely to develop psychological issues, it was her poor children, not mine.

'It's what you do about it that matters, I always say.' She scoops up her handbag and pulls out a lipstick and pocket mirror, taking a moment to reapply her vermilion sneer.

I pick up my cup and throw its contents into the sink with such force it sprays up the white ceramic sides, like splashes of watercolour when I rinse my palette. Swirls of cerise make for the plughole. 'You should go back to Stafford.'

She looks up from her mirror. 'I was going to make you soup.'

'It wouldn't be good for you to be seen here. You don't want that association. Go up to Cribbs, do some shopping on your way home. Stop at the nice services at Gloucester for lunch. All those things you like to do.' All those vapid, superficial things.

'You're probably right.' She stands up, hugs me and air-kisses my cheek. 'I'd better be going. You take care of yourself, darling.'

I put a hand on her back, pick her umbrella up off the floor and flick the catch so it collapses. 'Safe trip,' I say, as I gently guide her towards the front door.

I don't bother to watch her walk to her car – I run straight upstairs to his room, my determination to help him renewed.

How dare she suggest that I disown my son?

She'll have to eat her spiteful words when I clear his name.

Alice

27th August

In the days that had passed since Alice found out Kane Owen was so close, her time at home had been shadowed and heavy. She couldn't stop staring at the prison wall. It was taking more measures of Żubrówka to ease her into sleep each night, so much that she'd already opened the Black Cow that she'd bought herself for her birthday, and she blamed that for the headaches she was now waking up with. As soon as she opened her eyes, she felt the wall's presence out of the window behind her. She had rolled down the blind above the sink so that she didn't have to look out of the window as she made her coffee in the mornings. The fabric had a stain on it she had never noticed before – Bolognese or soup or God knows what – probably splashed there by one of the boys before they swiftly rolled it back up to hide it. Probably Lou. She ate her meals on the sofa in the living room (something she had always reprimanded the boys for), to get away from the French windows; they framed that red brick beyond the fence too neatly, begging her to look. She couldn't bring herself to step out into the garden, and she hadn't done so since that afternoon with Benny four days ago, even though the lawn was badly in need of a mow. What was that saying? Keep your friends close and your enemies closer. Whoever coined it couldn't ever have been in this situation.

She didn't need another looming presence haunting her. Not right now.

Over the ten days since Lou had died, she had been shocked by the tricks her mind could play on her. Rationally (and she had always prided herself on her loyalty to logic), she knew he was never coming back. So why, when Benny moved about upstairs, did she think it was Lou? Why, when she walked into the kitchen to scrape the uneaten food off her dinner plate and put it in the dishwasher, did she think she saw the flash of his head torch in the darkness outside and the outline of his body hunched over the Tiger? Why, when she got up in the night to go to the toilet, did she tiptoe past his room? Yesterday evening she had switched on the kitchen radio, automatically reaching for the volume dial to turn it down as soon as it came on. But when the music started, it was already at an acceptable level. Of course. It was Lou who always turned it up and changed stations from Radio 3 to one of his favourites playing 'indie' rock, though she had never been sure what that meant. This was ridiculous. Of all the things to miss about him, her mind was taking her to this?

It had become a relief to arrive at work in the morning.

She was at the Bishopston branch again today, a short distance to add to her usual morning walk. As she trod the pavements, she noticed things she didn't remember seeing or hearing before. Turning off her road, she heard the prison clock chime and saw two prison officers parking their cars outside the new flats. A secure van transporting inmates down Cambridge Road to the prison gates forced her to stop and wait to cross. And when she arrived at the library and tidied the leaflet rack by the front doors, the first ones she touched were pamphlets about restorative just-ice. She had never properly read them – why would she? She preferred her life the way it was before, when the prison and the city's criminal class were quiet, unobtrusive and very much in the background.

But even here, at work, it seemed she wouldn't be able to escape. There was an email in her inbox from her manager down at Central Library, asking how she was doing and if she needed to take some compassionate leave. Julie was 'so sorry' for her 'terrible loss'. How had she found out? Alice could hear her saying the words with her droning voice, and imagined Julie coming here to see her, sitting her down in the office they occasionally shared and clasping her hands on the table between them, her many rings clattering together. Alice had to make sure that didn't happen. Then, a couple of hours after they opened up, Carolyn, one of the library assistants, put her hand on Alice's shoulder, which would have been irritating enough – Alice didn't believe there was ever any need for colleagues to make physical contact. But then she asked, 'How are you coping?', with a nauseating emphasis on 'coping', dropping and drawing out the second syllable of the word in a manner that enraged Alice even further.

Alice spun around. 'What are you referring to?'

Carolyn blushed. 'We were all so, well, we were very shocked to . . . to hear about your son.'

'And where exactly did you hear about my son? This is a private family matter, not gossip for the library staff.'

'It was in the newspaper. Jenna saw it. Friday's *Post*.'

Alice thought of the reporter. How could they print something without her permission? Was that legal?

'Did it name me?'

'No, but . . . your boys have a different surname, don't they? Durand?'

'How does Jenna know that? How do you know that?'

Carolyn's eyes widened. 'Their library cards. They have, I mean, had, oh, I . . .'

'Lou had a library card.' Alice nodded, exhaling.

'And . . .' Carolyn bit her lip. 'It's in today's paper, too. I thought you would have known about it.'

Carolyn kept talking but Alice didn't wait to hear any more. She carefully set down the pile of books in her hands and walked over to the sitting area by the front windows. There, laid out on one of the small round tables, was a huge photograph of Lou. His photo took up most of the paper's front page, under the headline, 'He had the biggest smile: Family pays tribute to tragic teenager Lou Durand'.

She licked her finger, pressed down firmly on the edge of the front page and swept it aside, only to find more photos of Lou. She dragged her eyes away from them, reading the report they were illustrating. It transpired that the 'family' paying tribute was just Étienne, speaking as if he was representing them all. Apparently her son was 'charming and full of energy', 'embarking on a promising career in engineering' and 'loved nothing more than getting his hands dirty pulling things apart and then putting them back together again, a little better than they were before'. She thought of the Tiger, sitting neglected under the tarp on her lawn, destined never to be finished, never to be that little bit better than it had been before Lou got his hands on it. As she read, the newspaper shook in her hands. She folded it and tucked it under her arm.

She returned to the bank of computers at the helpdesk, where Carolyn still stood, watching her.

'I didn't mean to upset you.'

'It's not you that's upset me, Carolyn.' Alice picked up her books again. 'Although, it might have been nice to know about that article before . . .' She looked at her watch. 'One thirty-five in the afternoon.'

'I'm so very sorry about your son.'

This was exactly why Alice hadn't wanted to mention it to anyone at work. 'Let's get on with our jobs, shall we? Have you finished putting all the new books on to the system?'

'Not quite, we've – we've run out of stickers.' Carolyn looked a little confused. It was a simple question, Alice thought with a silent sigh. 'I was going to pull out the requests from children's non-fiction instead.' Carolyn held up a list of book titles.

'Excellent.' Alice clapped her hands together. 'Back to it, then. I'll man the desk and—'

The appearance of a white-haired woman with round, black-rimmed glasses made her lose her way, mid-sentence. The woman stood at one of the self-service kiosks, returning a stack of books, and Alice immediately recognised her.

It was the woman in Kane Owen's Facebook photo.

Alice turned away and put a hand over her face, as she sometimes did if she had a headache. She grabbed the mouse for the computer nearest her and pulled up the screen showing current activity at the library's kiosks. Books had just been returned for Kane Owen. The screen changed as she looked at it – another book was being returned under the name Indigo Owen. What kind of a name was that? Kane was unusual enough, but *Indigo*?

'Alice?'

She jumped before realising the voice was only Carolyn's.

'I . . . yes.' Alice took the list of requests from Carolyn's hands, putting the copy of the *Post* on top of them. 'Change of plan. You stay here at the desk and I'll sort these out. There's a . . . I just remembered I have something I need to check.'

Carolyn tilted her head to one side, giving Alice a funny look. 'Okay . . .'

Alice quickly checked where Indigo Owen was – still standing at the kiosk. Good. In children's non-fiction, Alice could keep an eye on the rest of the floor from behind a section of shelves that woman was unlikely to want to browse. She took a couple of deep breaths as she walked into the children's area, tidied up a few chewed toy cars scattered across the *Cat in the Hat* rug, tried to ignore the aroma undoubtedly emanating from a nappy belonging to one of the crawling babies who had been slobbering on the stacking bricks, and set down her papers on top of a low set of shelves. She did, for a moment, consider retreating to the staff room until this woman left. But why should she? Alice had done nothing wrong; she would not be forced into hiding. Besides, she wanted to keep an eye on her.

Kane Owen's mother was now hovering by the computers, which were all out of order today, meaning Alice had to deal with a never-ending stream of complaints, despite the very clear notices on each and every one of them. If she had to explain that the network was down (and that it absolutely wasn't her fault) one more time she was going to smash her head through one of the monitors. Indigo Owen was gawping dumbly at the screens.

And then she turned around, scanning the room. She looked at Carolyn, by the helpdesk, but she was with a customer. Before Alice could look away, Indigo Owen's gaze fell on her.

Alice's skin immediately felt extremely hot. Why hadn't she removed her lanyard and security pass? But while she was repelled by the idea of Kane Owen being close to her in the prison, Alice experienced something different as his mother approached. She could walk away, retreat to the toilets, pretend to take a call, but she didn't. Something was drawing her to this woman. What kind of family did a killer grow up in?

'Sorry to bother you, but I really need to use a computer. Are there any more available? Or are they all out of action?' Indigo Owen was standing just the other side of the half-height book- shelves full of children's encyclopaedias and guides to computer coding. She was looking straight at Alice – she evidently didn't know who she was. Pretending to concentrate on the spine of a world atlas, Alice peered through the gaps in the shelves to see Indigo Owen's bare legs and scruffy denim skirt down to her knees, as well as what looked like hiking boots, with fluorescent bands around each ankle. When she looked up to the woman's face, her eyes passed over a bright yellow cycling jacket splattered with grey muddy stains.

'No.' Alice couldn't think what else she would usually say, in a situation with a normal customer. Her mouth had gone dry. 'There are no more computers.' She sounded like a computer herself.

'Oh . . . okay. Thanks.' Indigo looked like she might burst into tears. It was only a computer, for God's sake. Before Alice could think what to say next, she began to walk away, her boots thudding on the floor.

This was one of those moments, Alice could tell, that people talked about. Now or never. She picked up her pile of papers and went after her. 'Wait.'

Indigo turned.

'The network should be up and running by tomorrow morning.' Alice even attempted a smile. She never smiled at customers if she could help it.

'I can't, not tomorrow morning,' Indigo's face fell again. 'Are you open in the afternoon?'

Alice shook her head.

'Okay, I guess I'll try somewhere else.'

Alice realised that this meant Indigo probably wouldn't be coming back. And for some reason, she wanted her to. What did people say to get someone to talk to them? It had been a long time since she had wanted to engage in a conversation with anyone other than her sons.

Alice was at a loss. But just as she thought Indigo was about to walk out, her eyes locked on to the papers in Alice's hands – or, more precisely, the newspaper on top. Her face went white.

'Have you heard about this?' Her heart racing, Alice lifted the *Post* and unfolded it, exposing the full photo and headline.

'Can I . . . ?' Indigo reached out for it. Her fingernails were painted purple but bitten and ragged, the polish chipped at the edges. It astounded Alice that grown adults let themselves out of the house in such a state.

'Go ahead.'

She opened the paper to the first double-page spread, the interview with Étienne. Again, Alice wondered, what did people say in these situations? How did you start a conversation about something like this? How could someone like Alice talk to someone like *her*?

'It's awful, isn't it?' Alice said tentatively. That was it, she thought. Adopt a chatty tone, ask lots of questions. And then, heat rising in her face, she took a risk. 'I feel just as sorry for the guy they say has done it, if I'm honest. Just a kid, by all accounts.' The inside of her mouth tasted sour as she said the words. *Sorry, Lou.*

'That's kind of you. Not many people would think like that.' Indigo started to cry now, drops falling off the end of her nose and darkening the newspaper, wrinkling it in steadily growing circles as the liquid soaked in.

'Awful, isn't it? Two lives ruined.' Alice couldn't stop now she had started. Was it wrong to enjoy making this woman cry?

'He's my son,' Indigo said, still staring at the newspaper article. 'The one they've charged.'

Alice didn't know what to say to this. She hadn't been expecting her to admit to being a murderer's mother.

'He didn't do it, though.' Indigo let the paper drop to her side and looked at Alice.

Alice opened and shut her mouth. An image of Benny suddenly came to her mind, sitting on his brother's bed, a fine scratch down the side of his face. Sweat pricked under her arms.

'I've spoken to him.' Indigo grabbed Alice's arm and lowered her voice to a whisper. 'He told me it was someone else who pushed this boy. His solicitor has uncovered some evidence to prove it.'

'New evidence?' It was taking everything Alice had not to

pull her arm away from this bitch's grip. How could she come in here, making up these lies? They had to be lies.

'There's a witness.' Indigo pulled her hand away and looked over her shoulder.

'I'm so . . .' Alice swallowed. 'Sorry.' That sour taste again. 'This must be a nightmare for you.'

'It's that all right. But no, I'm the one who should be sorry, what am I like, bothering you with all of this?' She wiped her face with her sleeve. 'I don't even know you.'

She really was desperate. To think that her son didn't do it, when the police had evidence stacked up against him. To reveal all of this to a complete stranger. To cry in public so readily.

'He's the reason I wanted to use the computers. I thought I could check a few things out. Not that I know how to use them, Kane always had to help me . . .' The tears kept flowing.

The woman disgusted her. But Alice's mind kept going back to Benny, sitting in Lou's bedroom with Lou's belt. Benny, his face paling as he watched the CCTV clips on the news. Benny, acting so out of character. Benny, definitely hiding something from her. And she thought of this woman's claim to have new evidence – what was it? She'd be damned if she let Kane Owen get off scot-free after killing her son in cold blood.

'Why don't you go home, have a cup of tea? Come back Thursday morning, eleven o'clock. I will personally ensure that a computer is reserved for you. And I'll give you a hand getting started.' This was not a service the library offered. But Alice needed to find out what this woman knew, or thought she knew.

'Would that be possible?'

'No trouble.'

'Thank you.' Indigo leaned forward to read the ID card around her neck, 'Alice. I appreciate it.'

Alice wished, again, that she had removed her lanyard. But at least her surname wouldn't be ringing any alarm bells with

Indigo. 'You take care of yourself.' Alice had heard Carolyn say that to someone the other day. It sounded about right in this context.

'Wait, don't you need my name or anything? To reserve the computer?'

'Oh – yes, of course.' Alice hoped she wouldn't see her blushing. 'Go on, I'll write it down.' She took a biro out of her pocket.

'Indigo Owen.'

Alice wrote it down. 'Great, well we'll see you Thursday.'

Indigo left, and Alice slumped into a chair in the children's area next to a large, tatty stuffed rabbit. What was she doing? Lying didn't come naturally to her. She was shocked how easily she had been able to, recently – to the police, to this woman. She prided herself in playing by the rules. But, strictly speaking, she hadn't lied, had she? She had merely omitted to tell the truth. If this was what it was going to take to help Benny, and to stop this woman getting away with the lies she was telling, then so be it.

She thrust a hand in her pocket for her mobile phone, and the small rectangle of creased card she had been carrying around. Pulling them both out, she examined the name on the card: Jacob Prince. It was his name at the top of the interview with Étienne. She tapped the card against her phone, pushed herself up and out of the chair and walked out the side door into the library car park, ignoring Carolyn's voice calling after her.

Standing in the shadows behind Carolyn's Ford Focus, she dialled the number on the card.

'It's Lou Durand's mother,' she said when Jacob Prince picked up. 'What do you know about my son?'

Indigo

28th August

We've never gone this long without talking, even when he was away in the spring.

As I cycled up Gloucester Road this morning, the nervous nausea with which I had woken intensified. But it is much worse, now that I've locked my bike up outside The Golden Lion and taken my helmet off. The smell of fresh bread from the bakery nearly makes me gag. People are looking at me differently as I walk down the road to the prison entrance. Nobody meets my eye. They all know where I am going. 'This isn't who I am, not really,' I want to explain. 'It's a mistake.' I clutch my pannier bag to my chest, feeling Kane's trainers inside it.

Everything has been different since the weekend, since that first newspaper report. I didn't think many people round us would be *Post* readers but Sally from number four definitely ignored me the other day when I passed her on my way back from the shop. And Paul at number thirteen stared at me as I wheeled my bike out this morning, although he was pretending to sort his recycling. He didn't say hello.

The news spread fast. I've had some messages; Petra texted, Kim has tried calling. I replied saying I'm fine, he's innocent, and I don't feel up for talking, sorry – when, in truth, *all* I want to do is talk, talk, talk. Normally I am the first to open up to my friends, and the first to encourage someone else to talk, to share, to halve the problem. But they've got their own problems to deal with. Petra still isn't well, and Kim's husband hasn't found a job yet. They don't need my drama in their lives. The only person I've spoken to other than Dawn and Clive the solicitor is that woman in the library yesterday. I'm going to have to do this on my own.

Other people walk straight past me, mostly women, some with children. I squeeze at the soft spot between my thumb and index finger for a few seconds on each hand to calm myself down, pretending to admire the hydrangea to one side of the door. I lean in for a sniff of its pink flowers, then straighten up and join the other visitors filing inside.

Everything that occurs in the next half-hour feels like it is happening to somebody else, not me. A group of friendly volunteers meets her, this other version of me – the one who is the mother of a boy in prison. In the visitor centre they show her the lockers and she leaves her bike helmet, her keys, her phone. In the winter, you'll also have to stuff your coat in there, so try not to bring something too bulky, they say. She wants to explain to them that she won't be still visiting come winter. She has to leave her purse but can take twenty pounds in, if she wants, they say. In coins, not notes. To buy her son a snack or a cup of tea. They show her where to leave Kane's trainers. She listens to all the other women talking, saying that their sons or husbands shouldn't be in prison – it's a mistake, he's not a bad lad, he fell in with the wrong crowd. To go through to the visitor hall, she has to give her fingerprints, show her driving licence. She has to put her shoes and coins in a shallow tray and walk through a security scanner, as if she's embarking on an exotic holiday. She has to be patted down by a prison officer, while dogs sniff around her.

But when she walks into the visitor hall and is met by the sea of expectant, hopeful faces looking up, trying to spot their loved ones amongst the stream of incoming visitors, 'she' disappears. The fog that shrouded me vanishes and I am painfully me again.

Dozens of round white tables, each with four chairs attached to them, are pinned to the dirty linoleum floor. It is brighter in here than the waiting area; there are large frosted-glass windows all along one side of the room. Colourful children's toys are strewn in a corner and one little girl has already made her way over there to play with some stacking cups. I was once the mother of a child like that, a child who I took to playgroup; not a child I visited in prison. My legs suddenly feel like they won't support my weight, as if the bones have crumbled inside them. I grab at the wall.

Before I have a chance to find Kane's face above one of the bright green bibs they are all wearing, I turn around and step outside the hall again, supporting myself against the wall as I go. I can't do this. I press my hands to my eyes. What if we can't get him out of here? Clive was useless when I phoned him and now isn't returning my calls. What if my son has to grow old in a place like this?

The door to the visitor hall swings open as someone else goes in and the hum of conversation filters out. Kane will be sitting in there, wondering where I am – or worse, he saw me come in and then leave. I lift my chin and walk back in.

Now that most of the other families have taken their seats, he is easier to spot, next to a vending machine on the far side of the room. He isn't looking for me. His shoulders are hunched, his eyes fixed on the table. He's in one of the green bibs, like the ones he used to wear as a kid playing football. But he isn't on this team, not my son. He shouldn't be lumped together with these people.

'Kane?'

He stands, but doesn't reach out to me and doesn't lift his head. I throw my arms around him, kiss him on the cheek. He pulls away. Since when was my son embarrassed of being hugged by his mum?

We sit down on opposite sides of the table.

'You came,' he says, staring at his feet. He's wearing striped plastic flip-flops.

'I managed to fit you into my busy social schedule.' A woman brushes against my back to use the vending machine and I can smell stale sweat on her. I pinch my nose and lean forward. 'I've left your trainers with them; they said you should get them later. Do you want me to bring anything else? Clive said maybe some pants?'

He blinks and shakes his head, still not looking up. The bruises on his face have yellowed and spread since I last saw him. I want to touch them. Can I? I glance at the two prison officers sitting on raised platforms at either end of the room. I don't know the rules. My eyes trail back to Kane, over the walls, painted the same deep blue as our living room. The realisation appals me. This place is so unlike home. I can feel the spotted texture of the chair leaving marks on my thighs, and the hard edge is digging into the backs of my knees. Everyone in here is watching each other, keeping an eye on what is going on. Nothing about this place feels safe.

'Nice outfit.' I point at his thin blue T-shirt.

He shrugs.

'I bet the food isn't great.' I can't stop these ridiculous words coming out.

'Not been that hungry.'

I'm struck by a memory of him as a toddler in his highchair, refusing to eat what was on his plate. I'd let him come round to it in his own time, or eat something in front of him and see if he asked for some of mine.

'I might get a sandwich.' I point at the table to my left where the volunteers are selling snacks and drinks. 'Looks like they've got cheese and ham.'

'Go for it.' He forces a smile but still doesn't look at me.

'Do you have to share a room?'

A nod.

'Are they . . . nice?'

'He prays a lot.' He puts his head in his hands, resting his elbows on the table.

I try to think of other things to say. 'Is there anything you need me to do, at home?'

He mutters something I don't hear, his quiet voice drowned out by laughter from another table. I thought it might be noisy, but I didn't expect the laughing.

'What was that?' I ask.

'Go on to my computer, find a PDF on the desktop called "Welcome pack".'

'Even if I did understand anything you just said, I couldn't do it.' Usually he loves to make fun of my ineptitude with computers, but he doesn't bite this time. 'They took your laptop.'

He looks up at me for the first time today. His eyes are red-rimmed and so full of sadness that it takes all my effort to keep looking at them. 'The police? What about my camera?'

'That too.'

He groans as he drops his chin back down to his chest. 'Well, you'll have to find a number some other way then, and make a call for me.'

'Sorry, love, I'm not following. Call the police?'

'No. You need to cancel my place.'

'Place?'

'At Brunel.'

I think of his excitement when he got the offer to go to film school. I think of the way I panicked when I saw him packing away things from his bedroom into that bin bag. I think of my ridiculous worries about being left alone after he went.

'I fancy a hot chocolate.' I stand. 'I need warming up.'

Kane doesn't move or say anything. I go over to the snack table and hand over three pound coins, watching Kane as the woman fills two foam cups with tea – they're out of hot choc-olate, she explains. Kane is even worse than I was expecting. Should I tell someone here about his dad? Explain that they need to look after him? Or will that make things worse for him?

When I put the cup in front of him, he holds it but doesn't drink.

'Your Auntie Dawn was asking after you.' I take a sip of the tea and nearly spit it straight back out – it has a horrible taste, almost as if it is coffee and tea combined. I wipe my mouth. 'I don't think there's any need to tell your gran, though. Not until we know for sure what is happening.'

'We know what's happening, Mum. I'm staying here.'

'I'm sorry I made you go to the station. I had no idea they would do this.'

'It's not your fault.'

I can't hold back the questions any more. 'Why did you say that you pushed that boy?' I lean forward to try to catch his eye. 'Kane, what happened?'

He looks over his shoulder at the prison guards, then back at the table.

'It doesn't make sense to me, love.'

He picks at his nails. I try to imagine him pushing someone with enough force that they'd fall over a wall like that. Even in his most difficult teenage years, he barely ever shouted. He never did anything violent, not my Kane.

'We're going to get you out,' I say, lowering my voice. 'Clive is working really hard on your case. He's going to prove . . .' I try to think of something that will sound convincing. 'He's going to prove wrongful arrest.'

Kane doesn't move.

'I know you didn't do it.'

His head snaps up at this and the look he gives me makes me recoil, tipping some of the tea into my lap. With my free hand

I grab the legs of my chair, the metal cold against my palm. He leans forward. 'You want to know what I did?' He hisses the words at me. 'He was digging at me all evening. But then he started on Dad.'

'What?'

' "He didn't care about you enough to stick around long, did he?" That's what he said . . .'

And this upsets me, it does – how could someone be so cruel to my boy? – but not as much as Kane's retaliation.

'I said at least my family don't think I'm a loser. I told him he was a waste of space . . . I said . . .'

He won't stop talking. I shut my eyes, trying to block it out. I lean as far back in my chair as I can, stunned, and I let that other woman take my place again, as I try to believe this is someone else in front of me. Not my son. This woman, she can't believe he said all of this, did all of this. '. . . we'd all had too many shots, we were off our faces. Things got out of hand . . .' he's saying. 'I hit him. I smacked him hard in the face . . .' It's not the boy she knows. She doesn't know what they've done with him, but this isn't her son. This boy in front of her is telling her things to hurt her, to make her hate him. She can see it in his eyes, the flash of a challenge. He's pushing her. He's saying, *Can you still love me, even after this?*

The answer will always be yes.

Alice

28th August

When the library closed at lunchtime on Wednesdays, Alice would usually work at her desk until at least five o'clock. Today, though, rattled by Indigo Owen's appearance the day before, she couldn't concentrate.

Logging into Facebook, she searched Indigo's name. Two profiles came up, both were for men. She shouldn't be doing this on a work computer, she suddenly realised, and closed the browser. Picking up her phone instead, she opened up her Instagram app. As usual, the welcome screen flashed up with a notification asking if she wanted to follow anyone, making suggestions for people she didn't know who posted pretty pictures of their homes, children, and holidays. No – Alice preferred to stay anonymous, only using these platforms enough so that she knew how to handle them.

She searched again. This time, several more results came up – Indigo Owens, Owen.Francis.Windigo, a few others. None was for anyone called Indigo Owen. Alice tapped the edge of the phone against her lips. It seemed this woman didn't have much of an online footprint. Did she have something to hide? Trying a different approach, Alice typed 'Kane Owen' into the search bar.

Now she was getting somewhere. When she'd looked on Instagram last time, there had been several Kane Owens in the list – how could she possibly know which one was him? But that had been before she'd realised she had met him that day at their house, and before she had remembered he was going to London to do film studies. Film_Kid_Kane was tenth in the list – it had to be him. She tapped. The screen that opened up had a photo of a video camera as the profile image, and underneath it were the words: 'Kane Owen. Aspiring film director. "If you truly love cinema with all your heart and with enough passion, you can't help but make a good movie."' Alice rolled her eyes.

The few photos on his grid seemed to be stills from films, with Kane explaining in the captions why he rated them. Alice looked through a few and was about to give up when a black-and-white image of Gregory Peck as Atticus Finch caught her eye. It had been posted on the sixteenth of June. The caption read, '*To Kill a Mockingbird*. A classic. Atticus is the kind of dad every father should try to be. Scout and Jem always know he will be there when they need him. This one is for anyone who, like me, finds this day difficult. #fathersday.'

So, his father wasn't around. Alice looked through the rest of the posts but none had such personal comments as that one. What did that tell her about him? About Indigo? She couldn't feel much pity for him. Her own boys hadn't had their father around, and yet they hadn't gone out and killed anyone.

She shut down her computer, picked up her bag and locked up her office. She'd need to think about other ways to find out more about Indigo Owen. In the meantime, her appetite for detective work whetted, Alice decided it was time she tackled Lou's bedroom. She'd been avoiding it for the last ten days, keeping the door closed, afraid of what might be inside. But what if there were clues that would help her work out what exactly happened the night he died?

*

When she arrived home, her father was hanging around outside the front door, peering in through the living-room window.

'Dad?'

'Sorry.' He stepped back on the path to let her pass. 'I was hoping to catch Benny at home.'

'Is he not answering the door?' Alice put her key in the lock. 'No.'

'Probably out, then.' She held the door wide and waved him into the house.

'Oh no, I won't stop, I don't want to impose.'

'Just come in, Dad.' She kicked off her trainers. 'Why aren't you at work?'

'Took the day off.'

She didn't see much of him, but this, she knew, was unusual. David Hyde and his daughter were cut from the same work-aholic cloth and both hated taking time off.

'How is he, anyway?' He knelt down to untie the laces on his boots.

'Benny?' She thought of her son leaving the house every evening and returning in the early hours of the morning. He'd grudgingly tell her he was going to a friend's house, but on the rare occasion that he gave her a name she was sure he was lying. 'Fine. As well as you could expect.'

'I thought I'd see if he wanted to, you know . . .' Her father stood up, his knees clicking. 'Chat.'

'Thanks, Dad.'

They stood together, awkwardly, in the hallway. Alice wanted to go upstairs to Lou's room, but her plan had not involved her father. She nervously ran her finger along the ironed edge of her shirt. One thing was certain – she wasn't about to sit down and have a coffee with him. He may not be able to 'chat' to Benny right now, but she wouldn't be giving him the opportunity to try it with her instead.

'I was going to sort out Lou's room,' she said. 'You could help with all his bike stuff. I wouldn't know what any of it was.' Without waiting for him to respond, she started climbing the stairs.

'I don't believe that for a minute,' her father said. 'Best workshop assistant I ever had.'

Alice paused for a second, looking down at him over the banister, then carried on upwards.

'Have you been out to take a look at her lately?' he asked, trailing behind. 'She really is a beauty. He did a good job.'

Alice hated this habit her father had of referring to bikes he worked on as feminine entities. They were mechanical, not human. 'I haven't.' And she wasn't planning to set foot out there any time soon.

They stepped through the door into Lou's bedroom together. Her father went straight to Lou's duffel bag on the floor. He crouched and started pulling out wrenches, sockets, pliers and screwdrivers, laying them neatly on the floor. Alice opened the wardrobe, unsure what she was looking for or where she would find it. She should have known the smell that would hit her – a mix of oil, petrol and cigarettes. There were no clothes hanging up, just empty hangers and a pile of dirty T-shirts and jeans crumpled at the bottom on top of a few pairs of shoes.

'What I don't understand,' she said, 'is why he never wore overalls. Why did he have to ruin all these perfectly good clothes that I paid for?' She picked up a T-shirt and dropped it on to the floor.

Her father laughed. 'Because then you're not always ready. You don't want to have to get changed every time you have a spare minute to work on her.'

Alice pursed her lips.

'Now let me ask *you* a question,' he said, as Alice piled more dirty clothes on to the floor. 'How do you feel about seeing Étienne?'

Alice couldn't think when her father had last mentioned his

name to her. Quite possibly not since he'd stepped in to help her pay the mortgage, after Étienne had left. She leaned further into the wardrobe, despite the stench, so he couldn't see her cheeks flush. 'Why do I have to see him?'

'The funeral? Court? Don't you think—'

'I don't think about him, no.'

'I don't want to see you getting upset. I could help, if you want?'

'Help?' Alice felt something hard beneath the final few items of clothing at the very back of the wardrobe. She rummaged around to pull whatever it was out, and it made a clinking sound.

'I could make sure he doesn't talk to you. Only deals with me.'

'Dad, there's no need. Really. We're both—' She looked at what she held in her hands. A bottle of Żubrówka, almost full. *Her* Żubrówka. 'We're both adults.'

She glanced at her father's back. He shrugged as he pulled a couple of hammers out of the bag.

'You were different, before him, you know.'

She reached into the wardrobe and pulled out another bottle, again with only a little of the liquid missing. 'Naïve, you mean.'

'That's not how I'd put it.' He paused. 'You weren't so hard on yourself, so closed off to everyone. You used to talk to me if you were upset about something – do you remember all our chats, in the workshop? I'll never forgive him for the way he hurt you.'

Of course she remembered those conversations with her father. But she couldn't go back to that. She couldn't even answer him, now. She had opened up to Étienne like she had never done to anyone else before – with him she was herself for the first time. When he'd abandoned them, he'd left her feeling like a fool.

Unable to find the words to reply, she focused on the bottles in her hands instead. What was Lou doing with them? She'd noticed, over the last six months, that a few had gone missing. She suspected him but couldn't confront him, because that would mean admitting she had them in the first place. But if he wasn't drinking it, why was he stealing it from her?

She set the bottles down on the floor and continued to investigate the depths of Lou's wardrobe. She found a half-full box of condoms and threw them back in. She didn't want to take her mind there. But what was it that Benny had said about the fight? *It was about a girl.* Who was she? Alice kept looking. Stuffed into one of his trainers was a small plastic bag of something that looked suspiciously like cannabis. Had drugs played a part in his death? Was Kane Lou's dealer? Or the other way round?

Her father laughed again.

'What have you got?' she asked, stepping back.

'A postcard of Bob Dylan.' He was shaking his head, still chuckling. But as she got closer and knelt down next to him, she saw a tear rolling down his cheek.

She reached out to take the postcard from him. In it, a young Dylan squatted in front of a white wall, dressed all in black, looking bored and disappointed. That expression – and his unbrushed mop of hair – reminded her of Lou. She pushed the card back into her father's hands.

'You know why he's got this?' he asked, wiping his eyes.

She shook her head.

'When I gave him the Tiger, I told him Dylan had one.' He turned the card over. 'That got his attention.'

'Did he know that you used to have one, too?'

'So, you do remember.' He looked sideways at her. 'Of course he did. That's my owner's manual he's got.' He pointed at the stack of books next to Lou's bag.

'Why didn't he do all the work round at your house?' Alice asked. 'You've got the workshop, the tools. He wouldn't have had to mess up my lawn.' She picked up a thin piece of metal about the length of a pen from her father's pile on the floor and turned it over in her hands. It felt surprisingly heavy and cool to the touch. 'I thought you were militant about looking after your "ladies". Keeping them dry and secure.'

'Why do you think?'

She ran her thumb over the metal's rough surface. It was a needle file – but a tiny one. Smaller than any she'd ever seen in her father's workshop as a child. She stood up and leaned against the bed. 'I've no idea. Do enlighten me.'

'Well, you're right. I said we should work at my place, nice and dry and with everything we needed to hand. But Lou . . .' He sighed. 'Lou was adamant. "If we do it at your house," he said to me, "she'll never see it." '

'I don't understand.' Alice frowned, still twisting the needle file in her fingers. 'She? The bike?'

'Not the Tiger, no. What other women were there in his life?'

'Are you saying he had a girlfriend?' Alice's eyes flickered to the wardrobe.

'No, Alice. You. He wanted you to see him fix it up.'

Alice cocked her head. 'No, he didn't. Why would he want me to see it?' Now it was her turn to laugh.

Her father shrugged, glancing at her like he was going to say something else, but then turned back to the bag. Alice looked down at the needle file. *Is this true?* She slipped it into her pocket.

Suddenly, Indigo Owen came into her mind. What was she doing? Would she be searching her son's room, just as Alice was? What other lies was she concocting? Alice's suspicions about Indigo's insistence that her son was innocent had been confirmed when she spoke to Jacob Prince, the reporter from the *Post*. It turned out the reason he had wanted to talk to her was merely to warn her that Étienne was doing an interview, and ask her to contribute – it was a little late for that now. But he did have some information for her: the police's case hinged on Kane's confession and the post-mortem revealing that Lou had been punched in the face before he fell. The only witness statement they had was Benny's, and Jacob said they'd given up looking for anyone else.

'What about the other man in the CCTV?' she had asked.

'Either they know who he is and have eliminated him as a potential witness or they've decided they don't need to find him,' Jacob said. 'I've prodded for more but they won't expand.'

What he'd told her was interesting, but she wasn't getting any closer to answering the question that burned away, keeping her awake at night.

Why did Kane Owen push Lou?

She knelt and pulled out a box from under the bed with two old iPods in it. She was going to have to work out what music Lou had liked, but perhaps she could leave that to Benny. What songs would they play at his funeral? What readings would there be? She wished they could at least get on with organising it, but DC Garcia said it would be some weeks before Lou's body would be released. Where was he, now? No, no, no – she couldn't think about it. Had her father been to identify the body? He must have done, but nobody had mentioned it to her. Alice looked at her father's back, shuddered, and moved her mind on from thoughts of what he had been forced to see.

'Mum?'

She jumped up. 'Jesus, Benny. You scared me. When did you get back?'

Benny looked at the pile of clothes. 'You're not throwing this stuff away? It's only been ten days.'

'We'll need to do it one day.'

'What's wrong with you?'

She wanted to say: my son died, and my other son won't tell me what happened. Instead, she turned back to the wardrobe.

'Benny.' She heard the click of her father's knees as he stood. 'We're just having a look through. Nothing's been decided yet.'

But Benny ignored him. 'You're back at work. You're chucking his stuff.' Benny picked up the clothes and threw them on to the bed. 'You're carrying on as if nothing's happened.'

'That isn't fair, Benny,' her father said. Alice shot him a look. She wasn't used to having someone helping her raise her boys.

There was another box at the top of the wardrobe, full of scraps of paper. She set it on the bed, aware that Benny was towering over her, scowling. She thought about how she fell asleep every night not long before daylight and woke up a couple of hours later. She put a hand to her stomach, which was empty, and a thumb in between her waistband and her skin – a gap had opened up where there wasn't one before. 'I may be "carrying on",' she said, leafing through the papers in the box. 'That is my way. People handle . . .' She searched for the right words. 'People handle difficult situations in different ways.'

'Difficult situations?' Benny threw his arms in the air. 'What the fuck, Mum? Difficult situations are things like losing your job, or not getting good enough GCSEs, or getting dumped.'

'Benny!' Her father put a hand on his shoulder.

'No, Pops. I want her to show me something. Like the other day, shouting at the wall. That felt good, didn't it, Mum?'

Even if she wanted to tell him everything she was feeling, she didn't know how to. That was not her, and it never would be. Would he rather have a mother like Indigo, crying to a stranger?

'We all want things in life, Benny. I want to know who else was in that car park, but it seems you don't wish to enlighten me.'

He turned, walked out of the room and slammed the door. Her father squeezed her hand, then followed him.

She heard him call down the stairs: 'Benny, wait!' The back door crashed shut.

Alice picked out the first couple of sheets of paper from the box in front of her – a magazine feature about restoring vintage Triumphs and a review of a film she hadn't heard of. She flicked through the rest. Nothing that would explain last weekend to her. What was she expecting? She threw the box across the room and it landed upside down on top of the tools on the floor, its contents strewn across the bed.

She shut the door on the mess she had made and went into her own bedroom. Her window was open and she could hear a couple of the prisoners shouting to each other. She wanted to scream at the wall again, ask 'Why Lou?', but her bravado from the other night had gone. Maybe she would never know why Kane Owen pushed her son. She heard Benny's voice, too, and looked out of the window to see him sitting on the lawn with her father, next to the Tiger.

Putting her hand in her pocket, Alice pulled out a leaflet she had stuffed in there yesterday at work, after Indigo had left. On the front it said: 'Have you been the victim of a crime?' She started reading the inside pages and one particular phrase jumped out at her: 'Get answers.'

A few months ago, a young woman had come to the library to drop these leaflets off and talk to a small group of library users about her work. Priya, her name was.

Alice took her phone out of her other pocket and Lou's needle file fell on to the floor. She picked it up with one hand and scrolled through her contacts with the other. Priya was listed as 'restorative justice Priya'. Alice tapped her phone against her chest and touched the file to her lips.

She slid her finger across the phone screen, and put it to her ear.

Just as she thought it was going to ring out, Priya picked up. 'Hi, Alice.'

She must have saved her number. Alice had been prepared to explain who she was, and this flustered her. 'Oh, hello. Yes. I . . .' She hated making phone calls. She squeezed the file in her palm. 'I'm sorry to bother you.' She tried to think of the words to explain what had happened.

'Not at all. I've been thinking of you actually.'

'You have?'

'I'm so terribly sorry about your son.'

Was there anyone who didn't know about Lou?

'He came into the library that evening, do you remember?' Priya said. 'When I was giving my talk?' Alice did remember, now that she mentioned it. Lou had been after money. 'I was struck by how similar the two of you looked. Then I saw his face in the paper this week.'

'Did you see that they've got the man who killed him?'

'Yes.' Priya paused. 'I can't imagine what you're going through.'

Alice pressed the file to her lips again and looked out of the window, down the length of the garden to the wall. 'I was hoping you could arrange for me to meet him.'

Indigo

29th August

I dreamed last night that I had painted my life on to a canvas. Every little bit of it, from my childhood, to my wedding to Glyn, to Kane's early years toddling around and his whole life up to this day. And then a man, who never let me see his face, walked into my studio with a knife, slashed the canvas to pieces, and left again. The part of the dream I can't stop thinking about is how I stood, looking at that painting, in the moments before the knifeman came in. How I was dissatisfied with some of the tiny details in it – the way I had painted Kane's face as a child, the way the light played on my wedding dress. It was beautiful, but I wasn't happy with it.

That Saturday, the day before the night when Kane went out with Lou Durand, I spent the morning at the allotment, harvesting runner beans. I wasn't pleased with the courgette crop, because it hadn't been as good as last year's. That Saturday, I sat outside in our back garden to have my boiled egg in the sunshine but found myself thinking of Dawn's glamorous lifestyle and how she would probably be having a posh lunch out at a restaurant. When had I last been taken to a restaurant? That Saturday, I used the afternoon to deal with my urgent invoices, but longed to be lying on a blanket on the lawn, reading my book.

What I would give for that Saturday now.

Today, I have spent the morning going through my phone

contacts, looking for mothers of Kane's friends, calling them, leaving answerphone messages and sending texts, getting hung up on several times. Now, I'm standing outside the library entrance, waiting for it to open. Kane's Crown Court hearing is only five days away and he will plead guilty unless I can come up with something to help him. I need to find out who was with him that night. The idea came to me when I saw the computers in here, a couple of days ago. Dawn's voice came into my head: *Take down any photos of the pair of you together on Facebook, Twitter.*

At last, someone is opening the doors, but not Alice, the woman I spoke to before. I don't really want to have to deal with her again, but I don't have much choice; I'm not sure I can do this on my own. She was helpful. She didn't say anything rude to me. But there was something about her. She was so stern-looking. Striking, with that long dark hair and those huge eyes – but she hardly smiled. She said kind things to me, yes, but in such a stilted way, as though it was causing her great pain. It gave me the creeps.

I approach the computers and there's a piece of paper stuck to one of them. As I go to look what it says – it must be mine – someone says my name.

It's her.

'Thanks so much for this . . . is that one for me?'

'All yours. Just give me a minute.'

I didn't notice it on Tuesday, maybe it is the light today – the greyness of the sky outside – but she looks exhausted. Worse than me, and that takes some doing at the moment. I think about asking if she's okay. I normally would. *Always be kind.*

I sit down in front of the screen and pull the paper away. I rest my fingers on the keyboard. I hate these things. I'm sure I can feel the electromagnetic radiation penetrating my flesh as I sit here. But Kane needs my help.

'Right then.' She sits down next to me. 'Where are we up to?'

'Just getting my bearings.' What is that smell on her? She's so

Now that I am alone, I can do the other thing I came here for. I manage to open Google and type that line into the box on the screen – those words written on the card I found in Kane's curtain.

He wants shrimp and sweat and salt.

It's not from a film, or so the list of results seems to suggest. It's a line from a poem. Can it tell me anything about his boyfriend? I click on one of the results, but I can't see that particular line. This poem is about two women, two lovers who want different things. In this poem, the 'he' from Kane's card is replaced with 'she'.

> *She wants shrimp and sweat and salt;*
> *she wants chocolate. I want a raku bowl,*
> *steam rising from rice.*

I scroll down the page. A short analysis at the foot of the poem explains that it's about long-distance love. I sit back in my chair. Who is this boy, or this man, writing my son love notes, quoting poetry? Perhaps they met while Kane was away in Paris and he is still over there, pining across the Channel. That would explain why Kane couldn't easily bring him round for dinner.

Is Kane calling him from prison, instead of me?

I reread the final lines of the poem:

> *We've kissed all weekend; we want*
> *to drive the hundred miles and try it again.*

I feel like a voyeur, prying into the passion of my son's love life. But what other option do I have? What if this boyfriend of his could help me find a way to get Kane out of prison?

Alice

31st August

It had been two weeks, already. How was that possible? Alice rolled Lou's needle file between her thumb and forefinger in her pocket, the steel warm from several hours against her body. She was walking straight up the hill after shutting the library at midday; she had no need to stop off for any provisions and no time, either. She needed to tidy up the house ready for her guests arriving in – she looked at her watch as she let herself into the house – twenty-three minutes.

She left her shoes on – always better to meet visitors fully dressed – and went straight into the living room. As she expected, the curtains were drawn, a sign of Benny's night-time occupation of the sofa. She flung them open and the room was filled with light, exposing dust on the coffee table. She wiped her shirtsleeve over it, piled up the coasters and put the TV remote back in its place on top of the DVD player. As she picked up a half-empty glass of orange squash to take through to the kitchen, she heard the creak of a wardrobe door close upstairs.

She stopped still.

Footsteps, now. In Lou's bedroom, right above her.

Padding out into the hallway, she gently set down the glass on the table at the bottom of the stairs, looking around her for something to defend herself with. An umbrella and a shoe horn would be no use. She pulled Lou's needle file out of her pocket.

Benny and Lou were the only other people with a key for the house. Her dad had texted her shortly before she left work, saying that Benny was at his place, in case she was worrying where he was, so that ruled him out. Not even her dad had a spare. She didn't like the thought of anyone being able to let themselves in when she didn't know about it.

Slowly, keeping to the side of the stairs where she knew it would be quietest, she made her way upstairs. As she climbed, a smell of stale cigarette smoke got stronger and the noises in Lou's bedroom became clearer – metal against the floorboards, the tools her father had unpacked from the duffel bag earlier in the week. They'd not been back in to finish the job, not after Benny's outburst. 'Leave it for a while,' her father had suggested. They should have at least tidied it all away. Now someone was in there, going through Lou's things. Had they not heard her slam the front door? Should she be going up here on her own, or call the police?

She paused on the top step, blood rushing in her ears. Lou's bedroom door was half-closed, obscuring whoever it was from her view. As she stepped on to the landing, she pocketed the file again and instead picked up the pole hook for the loft hatch. Pushing open the bedroom door with one hand, she lifted the pole hook with the other, ready to strike it against the intruder's head if she needed to.

But as she stepped into the bedroom, she saw two bags on the floor: a scuffed leather holdall and a guitar case. She dropped the pole hook to her side and looked up at the back of a tall, broad-shouldered man. Black jeans and a blazer – smarter than she had ever seen him dressed. Dark hair cut neatly at the back, and shorter than usual. A few greys creeping in. A bitter taste filled her mouth as she remembered another time she had this same view, many years ago. *Looking at his back, then turning and walking away. Driving without knowing where she was going. Mozart's Fantasia and a sea breeze through the open door.*

Étienne was wearing earphones, and she reached forward to pull the wire hanging down past his shoulder.

'How did you get in here?' she asked.

He shot a hand up to his ear as he turned to face her. 'Was that necessary?'

'Did Benny let you in?'

'Alice.' He smiled in the way he always used to when he wanted to get away with something. The way he had when he tried to get her to waive his fine for a Miles Davis biography, when he'd first come into Eastville Library. The way he had every time he had asked her out, on each subsequent visit. Black lashes over glinting dark eyes. His head tilted to the side, hands reaching towards her, palms up. For a moment – a second, no more – Alice wanted to step into his arms and let someone else take this weight.

She looked away from him. 'I want to know how you got in.'

He pulled a set of keys from his back pocket and waved them at her.

She tried to grab them, but he was too quick. 'Have you done this before? Broken in?'

'It's not breaking in if I have the keys.'

How did he still have a set, for a house he hadn't lived in for eighteen years? Particularly as he was the most disorganised person she had ever met and while he lived there he would regularly lose them.

Étienne sat down on Lou's bed, picking up a few of the magazine articles she had left strewn across it on Wednesday. She stared at him. *Looking at his back, then turning. Driving without knowing. Towards the sea, the baby forcing her on towards the coast. Mozart's Fantasia and a sea breeze through the open door.*

'Don't touch them.' She should ask him to leave. He shouldn't be in their home, uninvited.

'It doesn't feel real.' His voice cracked. 'Louis. Dead.'

Alice shut her eyes. She couldn't do this. She couldn't comfort him as well as keeping herself and Benny together.

'And on your birthday.'

Étienne had always spoiled her on the seventeenth of August when they were together. Breakfast in bed, beautiful gifts, surprise day trips. Alice was filled with a sudden and violent desire never to have anyone mention her birthday again.

'I thought you were touring.'

'I called it off. Flew into Bristol this morning.' He leaned back against the headboard. 'I came to help.'

'I shouldn't have asked you to come. There's really nothing we need.' She thought of Benny going out until late every night. The way his life orbited in different circles to hers and they rarely crossed. How they barely spoke.

'I only saw Louis a few weeks ago,' Étienne said. 'He was telling me how successful you are, all the awards you have been winning at work.'

Alice rubbed her temples. What awards? What was he talking about? And they'd met up? 'You saw him?'

'And Benoît.'

Alice nodded, trying to hide her surprise. 'Oh yes. I remember. At . . .' She clicked her fingers, hoping he'd fill the gap.

'My Bristol gig. The Louisiana.'

Why hadn't the boys told her they were seeing their father?

Étienne stood up suddenly. 'I really want to help. Benoît, he must be in bits. *Laisse-moi rester, juste quelques jours.*' He put a hand on her arm. 'I won't be any trouble.'

The warmth of his skin through her thin shirtsleeve, the gentle pressure of his thumb against her wrist, made Alice wish she could say yes. But she couldn't stand to have him in the house. Not since that morning when she'd woken up to two-month-old Lou crying for milk, Étienne gone, and a note on the kitchen table: 'I fell in love again. I'm sorry. I must follow my heart.'

She pulled her arm away. 'We don't have a spare bed. We don't have space.'

'*S'il te plaît.*'

'That wasn't what I was offering, when I asked you to come—'

There was a sharp rhythm of knocks against the front door. She looked at her watch. 'I have a meeting. You need to go.'

'Let me stay tonight, at least.'

'Can't you go to a friend's? Book into a hotel?'

'I'll keep out of your way. How long will the meeting last? Who is it?'

'I don't know. Just some people, I—'

Another knock on the door.

'Go and let them in. I'll stay up here. *On parlera plus tard.*'

They certainly would talk later. She clenched her jaw, walked out of Lou's room and shut the door.

As she ran down the stairs, she caught sight of the living room: the cushions she hadn't plumped on the sofa, the carpet she hadn't vacuumed. Too late now.

She opened the front door to see two women – one she recognised and one she didn't. The new one stepped forward.

'Alice? Margaret Simms, here to talk to you about restorative justice?'

The three of them sat in the living room clutching glasses of water. Priya was as Alice remembered her – young and calm, with long dark hair in a plait down her back. Alice thought of Étienne upstairs, and how he would probably think she was beautiful. He wouldn't have quite the same opinion of Priya's manager, Margaret.

Stop it, Alice. Why was she wasting her time wondering what Étienne thought? She was struggling not to think about him, struggling to listen to what Priya and Margaret were saying.

'Organising a conference with the offender is very unusual

pre-sentence,' Margaret said, 'especially with a serious and complex case like this. Are you absolutely sure that you want to meet him?'

'I'm sure.'

'The option will still be there in a few months – years, even.'

'I need to talk to him. I don't want to wait for months to do this. Ask me anything you need to, make your decision, but I am aware of what I am letting myself in for.'

She was trying to be focused, matter-of-fact. To impress them with her togetherness so they'd let her do what she wanted. But unbidden, the salty scent of a phantom sea breeze filled her nostrils. *Driving without knowing. Towards the sea, the baby forcing her on towards the coast. Mozart's Fantasia.*

Alice pulled herself back into the room as Margaret looked at Priya, who nodded and pulled a notepad out of her handbag.

'All right,' Margaret said. 'When did you first find out that Lou had died?'

Alice repeated Margaret's words in her head but was only able to respond with the answer to a question she hadn't asked: 'When did you first know that Lou would live?' *Lou's tiny unborn feet, dancing. Driving without knowing.*

There was a crash upstairs and Margaret looked up at the ceiling. What on earth was Étienne up to? Alice didn't like to think of him going through Lou's belongings. Maybe hers, too?

'I'm sorry, could you repeat the question?'

'Of course. Take your time. When did you first hear that Lou had died?'

Alice methodically worked through her version of events, pausing to make sure Priya had enough time to make notes. Margaret kept interrupting gently to ask her what a certain event had made Alice 'feel'. Alice couldn't help but think about Indigo Owen. She would know how to answer these types of questions; she was that kind of person. It took a huge amount of effort for

Alice to come up with things that Margaret might want to hear. The words 'sad', 'angry' and 'emotional' had each been used a couple of times each.

Eventually, they got on to talking about Kane Owen.

'Normally, victims of crime want to ask questions when they meet the offender.'

Margaret took a sip of water and Alice realised her own mouth was dry, too – she hadn't spoken this much to anyone for a long time. Not only the last couple of weeks since Lou's death, but years, probably. She was telling them more than she had told any of the police officers who'd questioned her. Margaret had something Alice wanted and she was determined to do whatever she could to get it. She downed half of her glass.

'They want to know if they have done something to . . .' Margaret paused as the front door slammed.

'Sorry,' Alice said. 'That'll be my other son, Benny.' His footsteps thudded up the stairs. She should go and intercept him, warn him about Étienne.

'I was saying, victims of crime want to know if they have done something to deserve this.' Margaret held her hand out, gesturing towards Alice. 'They want to give the offender a piece of their mind.'

Alice discreetly wiped her mouth. Upstairs, she could hear their voices. He'd found him, then.

Margaret was looking at her.

'I'm sorry. Did you ask me something?'

Margaret glanced at Priya, then back to Alice. 'If you had the opportunity to talk to Kane, what would you want to say to him?'

All Alice could think about at that precise moment was that she would like to put her hands around the man's throat until he told her why. What had Lou ever done to him?

She stood up. 'Excuse me, I need to quickly check on my son.'

Alice could hear them talking as she climbed the stairs. She pushed open Lou's bedroom door and found them both sitting on his bed. Benny smiled at her – she couldn't remember the last time he had done that. 'You didn't mention that Dad was coming back.'

'I didn't know.'

'And he's staying for a while.'

'Apparently so.' She caught Étienne's eye over Benny's head. No matter what she thought of him, no matter what he had done to her, he had made Benny smile. He had made Benny talk. 'I'm just having a meeting, Ben. You two okay up here for a bit?'

'No probs. I was saying, Dad can sleep on the floor in my room.'

Étienne lifted himself off the bed, looking at Alice. 'And I was saying, it's your mother's decision.'

Alice met his eyes. 'One week. On the sofa.'

Back downstairs, she left the living-room door ajar and apologised again to Margaret and Priya. 'There's a lot to be thinking about, right now. His brother's death has hit him hard.'

'It's okay, we understand.'

'So, where were we?'

'What would you say to Kane, if you could meet him?'

Alice heaved up her shoulders as she took a deep breath. 'I would like to understand. That's the main thing.'

Margaret nodded and waited, glancing at Priya. They wanted more than that.

'I would make sure he knew how upset I have been.' Was this what they were after? 'How upset Benny has been.'

'Anything else?'

'I can't think of anything. Is that a problem?'

'Take some time. You can always tell us more if you think of it.' Margaret clasped her hands together. 'That's it for today. Would you like us to see if we can make this happen?'

'Yes, I would.'

'You realise that he could say no? And even if he says yes, I can't guarantee you a face-to-face meeting?'

'Yes, Priya explained.' Alice looked at Priya, who was putting her notepad back into her bag and standing up. 'Thank you for coming out here.'

Margaret stood too and Alice saw them both into the hallway, taking their water glasses from them.

'Not at all,' Margaret said. 'Let us see what we can do – oh, hello.' She was looking behind Alice, towards the stairs.

Alice turned. Benny was sitting there, halfway up the staircase.

'You must be Benny,' Margaret said. 'I'm so sorry about your brother.'

'Thank you.' Benny looked at Alice pointedly.

'We'll be in touch,' Priya said as they left.

Alice closed the door behind them and turned to face Benny.

'You're unbelievable.' He scowled at her. 'This isn't helping.'

'I take it you heard our conversation?'

'What do you want to meet him for?'

'I need to find out the truth.'

'What is wrong with you? Why can't you be a normal mother? Take some time off work, look at some old photos of him. For fuck's sake, at least cry about it! Even Dad has cried.'

Alice knew she was losing control of this. Of him. But she couldn't say the things he wanted her to, and she couldn't do these things he was asking of her. Benny had always been more like Étienne, more passionate and able to talk about his emotions. Perhaps that was why she always felt so much more drawn to him than she had to Lou. *Tiny unborn feet, dancing. A sea breeze through the open door.*

'Where's your dad?'

'Having a shower.' He leaned his head against the wall. 'I don't get why you want to meet Kane.'

'You don't have to get it. It's something I need to do. Like you, meeting up with your dad behind my back.'

'He told you.'

'Why didn't you?'

He pulled himself up to stand and climbed the stairs two at a time. 'There was nothing to tell. We went for a drink.'

So why did his voice waver as he said it?

Benny slammed his bedroom door, and the bass of his awful dance music started thumping through the house, reverberating through the walls.

Indigo

3rd September

I find her upstairs, reshelving books. She hasn't seen me yet, so I could easily go back down and attempt to do this without her. I wouldn't have to talk to her.

But I need her help.

'Alice?'

She turns around.

'I've found my Facebook password.' I wave my piece of paper at her. 'Had to ransack the house for it.'

'Excellent.'

'If you say I need something else or that the computers aren't working or anything like that, I swear I'll scream.'

'We try to keep volume levels down in here.'

I look at her. There's a glint in her eye – is this her way of making a joke?

'I could use your help. Have you got a minute?' I'd rather spend as little time close to these machines as possible, and if I attempt to navigate Facebook on my own, I'll be here for hours.

Alice puts a couple of books back on her trolley. 'I'd be happy to.'

Downstairs, she talks me through how to get on to the computer this time, rather than doing it for me.

As I open the internet up, she asks, 'Have you been to court this morning?'

How does she know about that? 'I hadn't realised that I'd

mentioned it. Honestly, my brain is all over the place at the moment.'

Alice's lips twitch. 'No, you . . . I don't think you did. I saw it in the paper.'

'My son's life there in black-and-white print for everyone to see. You can't imagine what it's like.'

'No. It must be . . . unnerving.' Alice's face looks softer. 'It's hard enough to deal with it as it is, without the world knowing about it.'

'Exactly.' Maybe she is human, after all.

'So, it went okay?'

'He pleaded guilty to manslaughter. Good-for-nothing solicitor.'

'I thought he was fighting your son's corner? What about the witness?'

My big mouth. 'I thought he was doing a good job.' I'm sure she can see my face flushing red. 'But it turns out he's useless. How can it be a good idea to have Kane admit it to get a better deal?' A man sitting at a computer a few desks away looks up and I lower my voice again. 'They're going to sentence him in four weeks' time.'

'And they aren't looking for anyone else?'

'Doesn't appear so. If you ask me, the police just want to pin it on someone. They don't care who. They've got Kane and they can't be bothered to do any more work to find out who really did it.'

Alice nods.

I turn towards the computer screen. 'I put "Facebook" in, up here?' I start typing.

'Yes, that's it.' She talks me through how to log in, and – thank you, Universe – the password I found works. 'What is it that you want to look for?'

'Will it show me who his . . . if he is dating anyone?'

'It might do. Do you think he has a girlfriend?'

'I'm not sure.' Why don't I say that he is gay? I'm not embarrassed about it.

'Type his name up here.' She points at a white box. 'That's it. You might be lucky. For some reason these days people broadcast their entire lives on here, they even announce to the world when a relationship ends. I certainly wouldn't have wanted to do that when—' She stops abruptly. 'Never mind.' She looks flustered.

Kane's face has appeared on the screen. 'And then I click on his photo?'

'Yes.'

'I'd have to actually be in a relationship first,' I say, 'before I could tell everyone about it.' I laugh. 'Too busy being a mum, that's the problem. Not easy, doing it all on your own.'

'Always having to be the one to take days off when the kids are sick, always having to be the one to go into school for appointments with their teachers.'

I look at her. 'Chief cook, chief cleaner, good cop *and* bad cop rolled into one.' I could go on for hours. 'You're a single mum too?'

Alice nods, but quickly points at the screen. 'Okay, now this is his profile.'

The page in front of me shows one of Kane's beautiful photos of Paris across the top, the one I wanted to get framed. It starts to blur, and I wipe my eyes. There's also a photo of his face. My gorgeous boy. My arms ache with wanting to hold him close.

'Indigo?' Alice has been talking as I stared at Kane.

'Sorry. What do I do next?'

'Click where it says "About". And then scroll down.' I do as she says. 'Dammit. No details on his relationship status.' She looks genuinely disappointed.

I bite my thumbnail.

'Could you ask him?'

'I have a feeling he has been deliberately keeping me in the dark about it.' I think of the poem I found online the last time I was here. I used to think he told me everything.

'Or one of his friends?'

'I went to the bar where he works but they didn't want to talk to me. What about being innocent until proven guilty? I don't know where to find his other friends. I've tried the parents, but they're not returning my calls.'

'And you want to look on here?'

'Yes, I was wondering if I . . . can I do that?'

'It depends on his privacy settings. We can try.'

'How do you know so much about this, anyway? Computers baffle me.'

'It's not that difficult.' Alice looks over her shoulder at a customer talking loudly to another member of staff at the main desk. 'I try to keep up with things like Facebook, but I don't use it.'

'It's more for kids, isn't it?'

'I wouldn't say that. It's more that it is for people who, well . . . They aren't like me.'

It seems an odd thing to say, even for her. 'Like you?'

'People use it to reveal everything about themselves to their friends. Everything they are feeling. The way I see it, things happen, then you move on. What's the point in attention-seeking?' This is the most she has said since we've met. 'What I've learned in life is that people don't want to know your problems, and prattling on about them makes you look weak.'

'So it's better to keep it all bottled up?' I can't help but think she is criticising me.

'I don't think it's good to dwell.'

'But then don't you risk ending up not feeling *anything*?' I know it is cruel as I say it, but she's wound me up. 'If you don't let yourself feel sadness, you don't feel joy, either.'

The words bounce off her. She is oblivious to what I'm saying. 'Shall we look for your son's friends?'

I clench my teeth. 'Yes, that would be good.' I have other things I would like to say to her, but perhaps it is better that I don't.

'You can try scrolling through his timeline, see if anyone comes up that way.' Alice reaches for the mouse. 'May I?' She takes over, and we look through pictures and links to articles and short messages from other people. Where do I start? What am I even looking for?

Then something catches my eye. 'Stop. There. What's that?'

'This? A post from his friend, Dan Kent. Does that name ring any bells?'

'No, no. It's what he's written.' I mutter as I read the post out loud. 'Great lash last night with the lads. Top drawer.' Then there's a list of names. Kane's is in there. But it's another name that catches my eye. 'I know the name Wilko.'

'You do?'

'I heard Kane mention him on the phone the evening before this all happened. I'd forgotten all about it. Maybe this Wilko lad was out with them, too?'

'Okay, let's see if we can look . . .' Alice moves the mouse over the names in the list. 'No . . . He's not tagged them . . .'

I have no idea what she is talking about.

'But we could search Kane's friends list. See what comes out of that.'

She clicks a few times and a new page opens. She tuts.

'No. Dead end. Kane must have his privacy settings ramped up.'

'What does that mean?' I ask.

'We can't see who his friends are on here.'

'Back to square one, then.' I lean back in my chair and rub my hands over my face. 'I was really hoping this would turn something up.'

'We've got that name.' Alice clicks away again, and the page with Kane's photos on it reappears.

'Wilko doesn't even sound like a real name, though, does it? I can hardly go to the police with that.'

Alice looks at me, clearly uncomfortable. She looks like she is about to say something when one of her colleagues appears next to us.

'I'm sorry to interrupt,' she says.

Alice jumps up, taking the woman's elbow and moving her away from me. She's obviously glad to have an excuse to escape. 'Not at all,' I hear her say, her voice hushed. 'Is there a problem?'

Her colleague pulls a face, as though she's confused by what Alice said. 'Not a problem as such, but would you mind . . . ?' She gestures at a customer standing by the main desk. It's the gentleman who was raising his voice earlier.

Alice steps back towards me. 'Indigo, I'm really sorry, I should deal with this. I'll be as quick as I can.'

I pick up my bag. 'No, don't worry. I'm done here.'

Alice

6th September

Alice knew who Wilko was and she knew where he lived.
She pulled up outside his flat, her windscreen wipers squeaking across the glass.

'You're sure this is it?' Étienne had insisted on coming with her. He'd been sleeping on their sofa and she couldn't bring herself to kick him out. Benny liked him being around, that much was obvious from the amount of time they spent together listening to music in his room. Their son was still going out every night. But Étienne, who tried each evening to get Alice to join him in the living room to watch a film, told her not to worry. 'He's just off out with his friends,' he'd said. 'So what if he doesn't want to tell you who? He's an adult now.' But Étienne hadn't been there, that night, when both boys had 'just' gone out with friends, and only one had returned.

She turned off the engine. 'I'm sure.' She remembered thinking it was a grubby part of town when she'd picked Benny up from here once before, and it hadn't got any better. She'd walked down here a couple of evenings ago, but had doubled back soon after turning on to the road – it didn't feel like a safe place to be. A group of shifty-looking men were hanging around on the doorstep of one of the houses, and several doors in the street looked like they'd been kicked in. The bins were overflowing and there was a distinct smell of cannabis in the air. How had one of Benny's college friends ended up in a dump like this? She'd resolved to return on her day off – reasoning that it would feel safer in the daytime, though now she wasn't so sure it did.

Étienne unclipped his seatbelt. 'I'm coming in with you.'

'That wasn't the deal.' Alice hadn't intended to tell anyone she was coming here, but when she opened the back door that morning to ask Étienne not to smoke on the patio, he'd spotted the car keys in her hand. 'Going somewhere?' he'd asked. 'Out,' she'd replied. And then, somehow – he had always had this ability to get information out of her – she had ended up telling him. '*Je viens*,' Étienne had said, dropping his cigarette to the ground and crushing it with his foot. There was something in the way he did it that had made her simultaneously furious and . . . what? What was it that had made her look away and sweep a piece of hair away from her face, tucking it behind her ear? Whatever it was, she'd given in. 'Fine,' she'd said. 'But you stay in the car. I want to talk to him alone.'

'Number eighty-three, I think it was.' She reached into the back seat and took her mobile out of her rucksack. She scrolled through her message history with Benny. Here it was: a text from him in May: *Flat 2, number 83*. She looked up the road at the line of Victorian houses. Number eighty-three was painted cream, with the stonework around the window an unpleasant pastel orange. Filthy net curtains were drawn across the window in the downstairs flat.

She dropped her phone back into her bag and tapped her hands on the steering wheel in a simple 3/4 rhythm. Étienne leaned over and held her left hand against the wheel. She tried to pull away, but his grip was strong – or was it because she liked the warmth of his skin against hers that she let him hold it there?

'You're nervous.' He squeezed her hand and she felt the stitching in the leather of the wheel against her fingers.

'No.'

'You always do your rhythms. When you're agitated.'

She slid her left hand out from under his. She wished he would forget all of these things about her. There had been other moments like this, through the week, when he'd remembered these parts of her that nobody else had ever known or taken the time to notice. On Monday it had been an offhand remark about how she hated driving over bridges (a truly irrational fear, to her great embarrassment); on Wednesday he'd bought her a bar of her favourite Valrhona Ivoire white chocolate, the kind he used to bring her back from France when they first met.

'You're not coming with me.' She picked up her rucksack, stepped out on to the pavement and folder her wing mirror in. *Don't follow me*, she mouthed through the window.

There was still the memory of that year's hot summer in the air, and in the warmth, the fine rain felt good against her skin. She tipped her chin up and marched over to the front door of number eighty-three. As she climbed the steps, she could see that it was ajar, but she rang the buzzer for flat two anyway. As she waited for a response, she looked back over her shoulder to the car. Étienne blew her a kiss, then gave her a thumbs-up. She had to get him out of their house. When she rang a second time and got no answer, she pushed on the door and stepped inside. Trying to close it behind her, it became clear why it had been open – the lock didn't work.

The carpet was in need of a good clean, but other than that she was surprised at the state of the communal stairwell. There was a little rubbish lying about but nothing that smelled too offensive. On the first floor, Harry Wilkinson's flat was easily identifiable – there was no chrome number attached to the door like there had been for number one, but in its place someone had scrawled '2' with permanent marker.

The TV was on inside, with the volume turned up high; it could have been a film or a video game, she couldn't be sure.

Whatever it was, it sounded violent. Screams and grunts were interspersed with booming thuds and cracks.

'Yeah, get him,' a man shouted at the TV. 'Fuck, yeah. That's like the move I pulled on that kid last week, Si. He never saw it coming.'

'Should have paid me on time, then, shouldn't he?' A smoother voice.

'Bosh. Right hook, yeah. Look at those teeth – look at the state of his mouth.' Laughter. How many of them were in there? 'Next time you need me to have a word with someone, I'm going to go for the teeth. Mix it up a bit.'

A third voice chipped in. 'And that's why we employ you, Chris. Nothing if not creative, are you, mate?'

Was this really a good idea? What if Harry Wilkinson had been involved in Lou's death, along with Kane? He was the one in the CCTV, she was sure of that now. Why hadn't he come forward? She could turn around now and go home. Lie to Étienne that nobody was in. But then she would still not be any the wiser as to what had happened to her son. She would still have no idea what part Benny may or may not have played. She would still be left with no way of knowing how to protect her only remaining son.

She knocked.

'You expecting anyone?' one of them said, inside.

She waited. The TV went silent.

'Who is it?'

She put her palm against the slick gloss of the painted door and leaned towards it. 'I'm here to speak to Harry Wilkinson.'

'What about?'

'Lou Durand.'

The door opened a crack and Alice could make out a face in the darkness. 'Who's asking?'

'His mother. I just want to talk to you, Harry. I know you were there.'

The door opened wider and a young man stepped out, shutting it behind him. She looked him up and down, took in his T-shirt and shorts, the dishevelled hair and stubble.

'I've got nothing to say to you,' he said. 'Does Benny know you're here?'

'No. I don't want to involve him. Five minutes. Please.'

'Wilko?' That smooth voice again, inside the flat. 'What's going on?'

Harry looked over his shoulder at the closed door, then back at her. 'Just go,' he said. There was an urgent look in his eyes.

'How much will it take? Twenty quid? Thirty?'

Harry was about to reply when, from inside the flat, there came another shout. 'Get the fuck in here, Wilko. Bring your friend with you.'

Reluctantly, Harry pushed open the door, and the stench of alcohol fumes, body odour, smoke and fried food wafted out of the darkened room and on to the landing. Alice tried not to breathe in through her nose.

Inside, a short, stocky man stood by the TV, watching them, and a third was sitting on the sofa with his back to her, counting out money into a shoebox.

'I don't know what Benny's told you,' Harry said.

'I know you didn't do anything,' she lied. 'But I still have some questions. I'll make it worth your while.'

'I don't know anything.' Harry's eyes flickered towards the man on the sofa, who hadn't turned away from his shoebox. 'You're wasting your time.'

'Take her money, mate,' the sofa man said. 'If you don't know the answers to her questions, it's easy cash, isn't it?'

Harry glared at her. 'Fine.'

'So what's it going to be? Twenty?'

'You're flash with your cash, as well, are you?' He smirked. 'I see where he got it from. Always buying rounds, your Lou.'

With my money, Alice thought, with that peculiar mix of irritation and fondness she'd felt a lot in the last two weeks when she'd thought about her son.

'Always just a half for himself, though. Strange one, he was.'

'How much do you want?'

He lit a cigarette and took a drag. 'Fifty pounds for five minutes.' He was surprisingly well spoken. Not what she had imagined, walking into a building like this, in an area like this.

Alice pulled her purse out of her rucksack and counted out a pile of tens into his waiting hands.

'Lou's mum. Famous, you are, you know that?'

'Famous?'

'He was always on about you.'

They couldn't be talking about the same person. There was no version of this world where Alice could imagine Lou talking about her to his friends.

'. . . Benny not so much,' Harry went on. 'But Lou – it was always, "Yeah, my mum could have been a famous pianist, that's how she met my dad."'

Alice shook her head. She had played as a girl, sitting at her mother's upright piano in her parents' sitting room (where it still stood, even though her mother had died and Alice had moved out years ago), but she had stopped long before she met Étienne, when she realised she could never be as good as the performers in the records her mother would play in the evenings. There had only been one time, since then, when she had played. *Popcorn in her belly. A sea breeze through the open door.*

'He meant his father,' she said, trying to bring her attention back to Harry, and away from bitter-sweet memories of her unborn son. 'He's the professional musician.'

'No, he was definitely on about you.'

If his aim was to throw her, he'd succeeded. As she tried to gather her thoughts again, she glanced around the room, briefly meeting the eye of the man standing next to the TV. He may have been short but he was muscular, standing with his hands in his pockets and his chin slightly raised. He was eyeing her, unsmiling, but it was the blond one on the sofa who was making her feel more uneasy – the way he was clearly paying close attention to what was being said without ever looking at her. The space around them doubled as a kitchen and living room, and it was like standing in an insipid, milky cup of tea; the kitchen cupboards were pale brown, the splashback behind the sink was made up of cream tiles decorated with daisies, and the carpet was beige, matching the leather of the sofa. The only bit of colour in the room came from the navy curtains, adorned with large white flowers. Her sons would rather have died than have her decorate their rooms in such a way. The incongruity of Harry – this chain-smoking, scruffy young man – living in a flat that would be more suited to his grandmother disarmed her even more. Then she saw a skateboard by the TV stand and she started to pull herself together. So that was why he was friends with Benny.

Benny and Lou, she reminded herself. That's why she was here.

Harry opened the curtains and shed light on stacks of pizza boxes, empty bottles of beer and spirits, dirty clothes everywhere, small plastic bags and cigarette papers and . . . God knows what else she was looking at here. How could anyone exist like this?

Even being back in that car with Étienne was preferable to standing here for any longer than she had to. 'Why did you run off, Harry?'

He held up a hand. 'Let me stop you there. My name's Wilko. If you call me Harry I think my mother is here.'

The man on the sofa laughed.

'I don't do nicknames.' Alice meant it. Lou and Benny were exceptions, because that way she could occasionally have a hope of forgetting Étienne, who had insisted on their French names, 'to make sure they knew their *provenance*'. But call this boy in front of her Wilko? Not a chance. 'Why didn't you stay to help Benny? I thought you were friends.'

Harry fixed her eyes with his and slowly blew out a stream of smoke. 'I left while they were all still fighting. I didn't run away, all right? I left. Got bored of the drama.'

'You didn't see Lou fall?'

'No. Like I say, I'd left well before then.'

'So why didn't you come forward when the police put out that CCTV?'

He looked out of the window. 'What CCTV's that then?'

'Don't bullshit me.'

The man by the TV stepped forward and Harry turned to face her, cigarette hanging out of his mouth. 'Look, I just don't see what help it is to them, speaking to me. I didn't see anything.'

Alice scanned the room again, remembering suddenly something Benny had told her about him. He'd moved out of his parents' house, or they'd moved away and he'd been left homeless – something like that. He had a bad relationship with them, she remembered Benny telling her that, and they didn't want anything to do with him. How was he affording this place? Even a grotty flat like this would be too much for the kind of wage Benny was on at the bar.

'It wasn't because you're in trouble with the police for something else, then?'

'What has Benny told you, exactly?' It was the one on the sofa who said this, still without looking round at her.

She was getting somewhere, she could feel it. 'Enough.' She held Harry's gaze. 'What was the fight about? Why did it get boring?'

'I don't know. Some shit they were all involved in. Your boys and that Kane kid.'

'Come off it. You must remember. What "shit" were they all

involved in? Benny said it was about a girl?' She thrust her hands into her pockets and felt Lou's needle file against the fingers of her right hand. *I'm doing this for you, Lou.* She squeezed it.

'Now that you mention it, yeah . . . Lou had been trying his luck with some bird in the pub, I think. But I didn't get her name. Swear on my mother's life.'

The one on the sofa laughed again, pushed his shoebox full of notes to one side and leaned over the back of the sofa to look at her. Alice got a glimpse of his face for the first time: underneath the neat blond hair was tanned skin, a bit of a beard, a small circular scar on his cheek. She'd seen that face before – that scar – but couldn't quite place him. Another of Benny's college friends?

'Five minutes is nearly up, Wilko.' The beefy one in front of the TV crossed his arms over his chest.

'We're almost done,' Harry said. 'Look, I wasn't listening when it all started. I was on the phone to my brother.'

'Show her the video.' The blond one on the sofa spoke quietly, but with authority.

Something in the way he said it made her realise who he was. 'You're Yvonne's son, aren't you?' He had the same assertive tone as his mother. It was Yvonne who had taken Alice on as a library assistant all those years ago, before she met Étienne, and Yvonne who had helped get her a promotion when she was a single mother of two and struggling to put food on the table with her meagre salary. She hadn't seen her for years.

He narrowed his eyes but didn't say anything. She was sure it was him – he'd always looked just like his mum. He used to come in to see Yvonne when Alice was working in the old East-ville Library. What was his name? What were the names she'd heard through the door? Chris was one of them. And the other—

'You two know each other?' Wilko asked.

Simon, that was it. 'I used to work with your mum. You probably don't remember.'

He nodded once but gave no indication that he recognised her. 'Show her the fucking video, Wilko. Then she can piss off and we can crack on.' Simon turned away, giving her another look at the scar on his cheek as he did so. She remembered him coming into the library a few days after that had happened, when he was about ten years old and had fallen on to a garden cane while playing football at home.

Next to her, Wilko was scrolling through his phone, his face red. He clearly didn't like being told what to do. So, Simon was in charge? He looked too clean-cut to be a drug dealer. Yvonne was certainly not the kind of woman she imagined would let her son go off the rails like that. She was always saying how bright he was, how he was destined for big things.

'Look, it's like this,' Simon said. 'We're really sorry about Lou, it's tragic – isn't it, Chris?' He looked at the silent, stocky one, who nodded without taking his eyes off her. 'He was a good guy, and any friend of Wilko's is a friend of mine. But Wilko says he doesn't know what happened to him, and that's it, all right? End of story. He's got a nice little movie there on his phone that might give you some, what's the word . . . ?' He pinched the bridge of his nose. 'Context. That's the best we can do for you.'

'Were you there?' Alice asked.

'Me? No. I was in Marbella with some mates from uni.'

Simon the university student fitted more with the image Yvonne had always painted of him.

'Okay, got it,' Wilko said, waving his phone. 'If I show you, you can't mention it to the police.' He looked at Simon as he spoke. 'I don't want them showing up here.'

'That wouldn't be good for Benny,' Simon said.

Was he threatening her? Alice stared at the back of his head, then turned back to Harry. 'What is it?'

'Do I have your word or not?'

She needed to know. 'Yes.'

155

'Right then. Here you go.' He handed her the phone, and it took her eyes a couple of seconds to adjust to what she was seeing.

It was filmed somewhere dark. She could hear grunting noises, and just about see people moving about. 'What am I looking at? What is this?' She didn't take her eyes off the screen.

'The fight.'

As Alice tilted her head to one side to try to work out what she could see, a face appeared.

Her hand flew to her mouth. 'Lou.'

The video showed him stepping into the light, then swung abruptly away from him for a moment. The sound wasn't good enough for her to make out what anyone was saying, but Lou was shouting. When the camera focused once more on him, she could see that there were clearly at least two other people there.

Lou lunged forward, his arm swung back and he punched someone, over and over again, knocking him to the ground. 'Who is he hitting?' She looked away from the wobbly footage and up at Harry.

'Kane.'

Did Indigo know about this? Was Alice ever going to see her again to find out? She had left the library a couple of days ago, after using the computer, without saying goodbye. This – these shadowy few seconds of footage on Harry's phone – was not what Alice thought had happened. But what *had* she imagined? She couldn't think now. She focused on the screen in front of her as someone she could only just recognise as Benny grabbed hold of Lou, pulling him back, shouting at him. All the while, the loudest part of the video was a series of whoops and cheers from the person filming.

Then the images on the screen stopped moving.

Alice stumbled back against the sofa, still holding the phone.

'Hey.' Harry reached out. 'Careful with my phone.' He took it from her.

She was stunned. That had been her son a matter of minutes before he died, if Harry was to be believed. Her son, laying into the man who killed him. Had Lou started it? And Benny looked to have been involved too, even though he was pulling Lou away.

'I'm not showing the police, though, okay?' Harry put the phone back in his pocket.

'I . . . I wouldn't want them to see it anyway.' Alice's voice sounded quiet in her ears.

'No, didn't think you would. Doesn't make your boys look great, does it?'

'Can I see it again?'

He passed the phone to her, after bringing the video back up. She pressed a couple of buttons as she watched the opening images.

'What you doing?' he asked, reaching for the phone. She held it behind her back.

'Taking a screenshot. Can you send it to me?'

'That wasn't part of the deal.'

She looked at him. He wasn't going to shift on this, she could see it in his eyes. 'Okay, fine. Let me just watch it one more time.' He nodded.

She saw it more easily now. Lou and Kane were scuffling, presumably in the darkened car park, and then Lou stepped away and—

What was that? As Lou pulled back to punch Kane, she noticed something she hadn't seen the first time round.

She tapped the screen to pause it and looked more closely.

There was a light on in what must have been a building across the street from the car park. And there was a figure in the window.

Indigo

7th September

I have specific things I need to ask Kane about. Wilko. His boyfriend. He hasn't called me since I last came here, so the questions have mounted up. Having this purpose makes today's visit feel different. I lived through that first one, I can do it again. This time, I don't skulk about, convinced that people are watching and judging me. I stride towards the prison gates. Yesterday's drizzle has been replaced by clear skies and I lift my face to feel the sun on my skin. Why should I be ashamed?

Before I reach the gates, a man on the other side of the road sneezes loudly. I look his way as he hurries on, head bowed, clutching a small paper package in his hands. It's only when he turns his head, looking each way before he crosses to my side of the road, that I recognise him.

The short dark hair. Tall frame, strong build. The skateboard strapped on to the back of his rucksack. It's Benny Durand.

He's walking alongside the wall of the prison. I look at the gates, which he has just walked past, and the relatives filing in. I check the time – I have thirty minutes before my visit officially starts at eleven. I follow him.

Where's he going? Should I talk to him?

He's sticking with the prison's perimeter wall on his right, occasionally looking up at it. I look up, too, and see plants growing in cracks in the red brick – even large, purple-flowered buddleia springing out near the top. I think of my Kane, like these shoots of green: somewhere he shouldn't be, somewhere you wouldn't expect to find him. A sliver of beauty amongst a swathe of ugliness.

Ahead of us it looks like there is a dead end. My heart races. Do I want to be in a dead-end road with this boy? I slow my pace. If Kane didn't kill Lou Durand, someone else did. The only other person I know for sure was with them is Benny. I look over my shoulder. There's nobody behind me – we are alone. I should go back.

When I look back towards Benny, he's turning the corner, taking a track I hadn't seen that bends round to the right. Keeping a few metres between us I follow him, half jogging, half walking, as the track narrows into an alleyway leading to a residential road.

I've never been here before. The houses ahead of me seem to have their gardens backing on to the prison, whose wall I still have within touching distance of my right hand. I never realised how ensconced the prison was in the area. From the main road you'd barely know it was here, and I had never really noticed it until it bullied its way into my life just over a week ago.

Benny turns at the end of the alleyway, and I do the same, slowing to a walk as I do so, glad for the chance to catch my breath. A little way down the road he steps on to the front path of a house and takes keys out of his pocket.

If he has keys . . . then he lives here? So close to my son?

'Benny?' I call out to him from the pavement. One more step would take me into his front garden.

I shouldn't be doing this.

He spins around, regards me with a frown, not recognising me at first. When he does, his eyes widen and his face reddens. 'What are you doing here?' He clutches at the package in his hands, which I now see is a paper bag with some kind of greasy food inside – the oil is spreading into patterns on the paper. 'Did he send you?'

'Kane doesn't know where I am.' I want to move towards him, but my feet remain rooted to the pavement. 'I'm so sorry about your brother.'

He unlocks the door and it swings open. But, instead of walking into the house, he stands on the doorstep. My breathing sounds loud. This is a bad idea. What if his parents are home?

'I'll go.' I look down at the ground, at the paving, at his trainers on the doorstep. The toe of each shoe is shiny, covered in some kind of clear glue.

'What's he told you?' Benny asks quietly.

'He . . .' I don't know what to say. I force myself to look up at him again. 'He's told me that he pushed your brother. But I can't believe him. He's not himself.'

The door to his neighbour's house opens and a man emerges, his arms full of collapsed cardboard boxes.

'All right, Steve.' Benny nods a hello.

'How you holding up, mate?'

'We're doing okay. Thanks.'

Steve looks at me, then back to Benny. 'Well, you know where we are.'

Benny watches him stuff the cardboard into his recycling box, then drops his voice to speak to me. 'Let's go inside.' He holds the door open.

I hesitate. 'Are your mum and dad—'

He shouts into the house: 'Dad? Are you home?'

No reply comes.

'Mum's at work,' he says. 'Dad must be out.'

When I still don't move, he steps into the house and I follow.

Once inside, my whole body tenses. Benny has walked through into the back room. I push the door to, but don't fully shut it. I glance around me. Should I be looking out for clues? Will there be anything in this house that could help my boy?

The first thing that strikes me is how bare and simple it is. There is beautiful red and green stained glass in the porch door, and black-and-white diamond tiles on the hallway floor. There are keys on a rack by the door, neatly labelled. Front door. Back door. Mum's car. Benny's car. Each of the car keys has a small novelty keyring – one has a little leaf attached to it, the other has a tiny skateboard. A botanical print of different leaf types hangs on the wall. But other than that, the place is plain. It feels cold and sad. I can't help but think it must have been like this long before Lou died.

Benny is standing by the kitchen table, which is covered with papers and boxes. There's a half-filled bin bag on the floor. He clears a small space on the edge of the table and puts his food down.

'Are these Lou's?' It looks like he's sorting through his brother's belongings. It's a heart-breaking scene.

'Yeah.'

'I really am sorry.' The words sound inadequate. But what else can I say?

'Did Kane tell you about the fight?' He is looking at the table as he says it.

'Yes.' I close my eyes and swallow, hoping Benny isn't going to repeat the words that Kane told me were said.

'Then you know what he did.' I'm not fooled by the calm of his voice. I remember that anger I saw on his face at court last week; it is still there, lying in wait.

'Yes, but—'

'And he told you himself that he pushed him.' He speaks more loudly as he interrupts me, his resentment breaking through. Only now, a matter of feet away from him, do I notice his appearance. He looks almost as bad as Kane did last week.

His skin is grey and blotchy, his chin stubbled. I shouldn't be here, intruding. This is wrong.

There's a small cracking noise upstairs and my hand flies to my chest.

'You're sure your parents aren't home?'

Benny sighs. 'Like I said, I'm on my own.' The words come out deliberately, with undisguised impatience. 'What exactly do you want?'

'I thought—'

'I don't want to believe it any more than you do.' Benny picks up some newspaper cuttings from the table and flicks through them. 'But Kane killed Lou.'

No, no, no. This isn't what I came here to listen to.

'Who's Wilko?' I ask.

I think I hoped to catch him off guard, but it doesn't work. Benny throws the cuttings back on to the table with such force that it makes me jump. He picks up a box of small notecards. 'I don't know who you're talking about.' He doesn't look at me.

'He was out with you that night, wasn't he?'

'Kane killed my brother,' he repeats slowly, rotating the box of cards in his hands.

I ignore the rage that is causing his voice to shake. I have to do this for Kane. 'Who really pushed Lou? You know, don't you?' I have risked so much by talking to him. And all to come away with nothing – I see that now. He won't help me.

'I think it would be best if you left now.' Benny looks up and I back away. There it is – that look again, the same one I saw in court. 'You're wasting your time.'

Time. Time. I look at my watch. Eleven fifteen. I groan. 'No . . . I've got to go.'

I smack my hip on the door frame as I rush into the hallway.

Benny follows and reaches past me to pull the front door open. As I step outside on to the path, I say, 'If you remember anything else . . .' I don't finish my sentence. His face is hard. He isn't going to help us. 'Thank you,' I say, though I don't know what I am thanking him for.

He closes the door, still clutching Lou's box of notecards at his waist, in his other hand. There's something about them. Something about those cards.

I stand there, staring at the dark blue paint on the door, trying to make sense of what I've just seen.

I replay the images in my head: Benny's large hands, spinning the flimsy plastic box. A sticker on its lid. Benny, clutching hold of it, only partly obscuring the cards inside. The pattern on the cards.

I grab hold of the fence separating Benny's front garden from his neighbour's to steady myself.

Those cards of Lou's were patterned with interlocking blue and black geometric shapes, just like the one I found hidden in Kane's curtain.

Alice

7th September

In the couple of hours of broken sleep she'd had last night, Alice's dreams had been full of a silhouetted figure in a window. Sometimes it was a man, sometimes a woman; sometimes they tried to warn her about something but she couldn't hear what they were saying through the glass. She had climbed out of bed at two o'clock to give herself a break from them – it was a good opportunity to put the rubbish out, she thought as she deposited an empty bottle of Żubrówka in one of her neighbour's recycling bins, checking nobody was watching from nearby bedroom windows as she did so. She didn't have time to go into town, Alice told herself as she crept back into the house – no time to find out what that building was in Harry Wilkinson's video, or track down the person she'd seen in it. What with work and looking after the house and Benny, she simply didn't have a moment to spare. She ignored the ringing in her ears when she thought about the building, when she pictured the road outside it where her son's body had been found. She dismissed the tight feeling in her chest when she considered approaching total strangers and trying to get information out of them. No. Those were merely feelings. The salient point was that she did not have the time.

But she did have a few spare minutes to do research from her office. She took a cup of coffee into her office and tilted the blinds open so that she could see out of the large windows overlooking the upper floor of the library. Sitting at her desk, she took a chocolate biscuit from the packet in her drawer and absent-mindedly picked at it while she logged into her computer. Her first stop was to look at the street on a map. She looked at photos of it using Street View, before going back to the normal map mode and clicking on the buildings opposite the car park. A name came up: Frasier House. A search on that name spewed out a few unhelpful results, and then a real estate agency website boasting about a deal brokered to move a supply teaching specialist into the building's second floor. Alice made a note of the company name. The article went on to say that the building had recently been refurbished and had attracted several new tenants to its six floors of office space. Six floors. How would she work out which company rented the office she had seen in the video?

She pressed the knuckles of her hands together.

Quickly, she opened up the Street View image showing the car park and Frasier House. She took a bite of her biscuit to stave off the dizziness that hit her as she looked at the screen. *They're only buildings,* she told herself, staring at the neat lines of brown brickwork making up each level of the car park. Swallowing hard, she counted to the third storey, rested her finger lightly on the screen and then slid it across to Frasier House. It landed in between the windows on the building's fourth and fifth floors.

Alice logged off her computer and sat back in her chair, blowing out a long, slow breath. She'd narrowed it down to two floors, but that wasn't much help.

A face appeared on the other side of her office window, peering through the blinds: Carolyn. She waved.

'Just a moment,' Alice called out.

Carolyn backed away from the glass. Alice wiped her hands over her face and brushed a crumb from her cheek, then smoothed down her shirt, sat up straight and lifted her chin. 'Come in.'

'Sorry to interrupt.'

'And yet, here you are.'

'The thing is, there's a lady asking for you by name. I have tried to help her, but she says she needs to speak to you.'

'What I would do, Carolyn, in this situation, is ask her to wait ten minutes while the person she was requesting to see had finished their only break of the day.'

'I did that.' Carolyn's face flushed. 'But this woman, she's quite worked up. I've left her sitting in the window; I told her you'd be out at about quarter to, but I thought I should let you know. She's fairly upset.'

Carolyn pointed towards the seating area over by the front windows. The woman's back was to them but Alice immediately knew who it was from the shoulder-length white hair and the fluorescent yellow jacket. She'd come back.

'What else did you say about me?' Alice stood up.

'About you?'

'You didn't mention my son, did you?'

'No. Why?'

'Thank you, Carolyn. In this instance it happens you were right to curtail my break.'

Carolyn opened her mouth as if to say something, then clearly thought better of it. If only she would do that more often, thought Alice. She scuttled off towards the staff-room door and Alice made her way over to the front windows.

As she got closer, she could see that Indigo's legs were bouncing up and down, her hands clasped in her lap then gesturing at her side, as if she was talking to someone. As she got closer still, she could hear her muttering. This behaviour verged on being described as unhinged, in Alice's book.

She considered returning to her office, but before she could do so, Indigo spun around in the chair.

'Alice.' She jumped up. 'I didn't know where else to go. I feel terrible, I had to talk—'

'Slow down, for a start.' Alice gestured at the chairs. 'Shall we?'

They both sat, but a matter of seconds later Indigo got back up again. The woman seemed possessed – looking around the place wildly, her breathing shallow and fast.

'I feel awful,' she said. 'Absolutely terrible!'

She shouted the final words and a couple of students nearby looked up from their laptops.

'Calm down.' Alice tried to employ her 'kind' voice, but it came out as more of a bark. 'Tell me what's happened.'

'I feel so guilty . . .'

Here was something Alice could get to grips with. Understand, even. 'You mustn't let yourself go down that road.' She paused. The self-help jargon felt ridiculous coming out of her mouth. She must have read it somewhere, but she'd sure as hell never deliberately employed it. 'It would only be natural to blame yourself for what has happened. We all think we are bad mothers.'

'What?' Indigo looked at Alice like she was the one who was mad. 'No, no. That's not what I'm saying.' She sat down again but stayed right on the edge of the chair. 'It's the opposite. That's why I feel so bad, don't you see? Just for a moment, I blamed *him*.' She looked up, past Alice's shoulder.

Alice turned to see Carolyn approaching with a mug in her hands.

She set it on the table between Indigo and Alice. 'There you go.' She smiled at Indigo. 'I didn't know if you'd take sugar, but I put one in. Good when you're shaken up, I always find.'

'Thank you.' Indigo lifted the mug and rested it on her lap.

Alice nodded at Carolyn. She had seen certain library assistants – Carolyn was a repeat offender – making customers cups of tea. She strongly suspected they did it frequently at the Redland branch when she wasn't there, for the homeless men and women who came in after a trip to the drop-in centre over the road. Alice had repeatedly mentioned in staff meetings that they were running a library, not a café, but her words fell on deaf ears.

'You're blaming him, you were saying?'

Indigo brought the mug to her lips and blew across the surface of her tea. 'For the first time, I let myself think he might have done it. I feel so guilty for even letting the thought cross my mind.'

Finally. Alice felt a brief wave of pity for the woman, like a cramp across her stomach. It was for the best, though. She needed to accept the truth.

'He's gay, you see.' Indigo took a sip of tea.

'I'm not following your reasoning.'

'A crime of passion would make more sense, that's what made me think it.'

'Could you start again? I'm not with you.' She spoke slowly and clearly. 'What are you saying?'

'I think . . .' Indigo paused. 'I think Kane was in a relationship with the boy who died.'

'I see.' But she didn't. Not quite.

'I found a note, written by that boy Lou to Kane. A love note.'

Alice's head began to swim. She rubbed her temples.

'I thought a boy in Paris had sent it, but it must have been about Kane leaving for university . . .'

Alice tried to listen as Indigo kept talking but she also had to understand what she was hearing. Lou and Kane? Her son was gay?

'. . . can't even ask him about it because I missed . . .'

But what about the girl Benny said they were arguing about? Had he misunderstood? Alice slowly stood up, grabbing the back of her chair. He'd said they'd been arguing about relationships, could they have been talking about their own?

'. . . they wouldn't let me in, but I wasn't that late—'

'I'm sorry,' Alice cut in. 'My phone. I can hear my phone

ringing. I'll see who it is.' Alice pointed at her office, backing away from Indigo as she spoke.

Once inside, she closed the blinds and locked the door. She collapsed into her chair and stared at the second drawer of her desk.

With shaking hands, she unlocked it and pulled out two piles of photos. Each was meticulously ordered by date and carefully enclosed in paper, tied up with string. One bundle was made up of Benny's school photos through the years – the individual headshots of him from reception class through to his GCSE year. The other bundle was Lou's. Other people might have a couple of these framed on their desk. Alice didn't want them on display, but she did like to know they were there, just in case she was having a particularly tedious day and needed to remind herself why she worked as hard as she did. She had always made the boys get the photos done, even though they were optional. She'd told them it was important to mark their progressing education, but that wasn't quite the reason.

She untied Lou's photographs and laid them out on her desk, one by one, touching each iteration of his face gently as she did so. The gap-toothed grin in year three. The too-short haircut in year six. His first year of secondary school – and the last of the photos with a smile. Year nine, with a black eye. The final one, from year eleven, with the dark scowl she had come to know so well – the one she sometimes saw in her own face when she passed a mirror.

Lou. Her boy.

Someone knocked softly on her door. 'Alice?' It was Indigo. Alice remained silent. What was she doing, trying to get information from this broken woman? She shouldn't be doing it. It was duplicitous, but more than that, it wasn't her. Alice Hyde didn't do things like this. Games were for other people – the Étiennes of this world.

'I'm sorry for bothering you. I'm going now,' Indigo said quietly.

Alice didn't try to stop her, but if she'd had the backbone to go after her, she would have said two words: 'Thank you.'

Indigo's theory could explain everything, and even the possibility of it gave Alice a feeling of lightness and relief. It could account for Lou's difficult nature, his anger. No wonder he was like that, if he was struggling with his sexuality and hiding it from her and, she assumed, from everyone he knew. Maybe it hadn't all been about hating her, after all.

But, hand in hand with this lightness, came its flip side. Darkness she had been too afraid to look into, which she had been resolutely avoiding and denying could even be there. He was gone, and she hadn't had a chance to hold him one last time and let him know – what? That she loved him? They didn't talk like that. Not Lou and Alice. She didn't know what she wanted to say to him, but she desperately wished she could have had a chance.

A tear rolled off her nose on to Lou's year-eleven face, and she quickly rubbed it off with the cuff of her shirtsleeve. She tilted her head back to stop any more falling. Wiping at her cheeks with the back of her hand, she sat down at her desk. She cleared her throat, dialled Julie's number on her office phone and picked up the handset.

'Julie?' She coughed again. 'Hi, it's Alice. No, everything's fine. But I think I need to take you up on your offer. I'd like some time off.'

Indigo

8th September

There is only one person in here that I want to talk to, but so does everybody else. While I wait to wish Lily a happy eightieth birthday, I am forced to make small talk with extended family and my mother's friends, where the answer to every question should be 'my son is in prison and I'm spending every waking hour trying to get him out', but of course I can't say that. Certainly not within earshot of Dawn, wafting around in another one of the scarves Kane gave her – Monet's water lilies this time. 'How's business?' Fine, thank you (I've cancelled all my appointments). 'How's that lovely son of yours?' He's well, thank you, so sorry he has to work today and miss the party (I haven't spoken to him for over a week and I spend every second of every day worrying that he's being beaten up in prison). 'He must be excited about starting film school?' Yes, he can't wait. It will be a wonderful challenge for him (how much longer am I going to be able to keep pretending like this?).

I look over at Lily, sitting in an armchair surrounded by flowers and balloons, beaming with pleasure as her party guests take it in turns to inform her that she doesn't look a day over sixty. She is still oblivious to what's going on with Kane. Dawn whispered sweetly into my ear as I arrived, 'We're effing lucky it hasn't gone national, aren't we?' I want to tell Lily so badly. I know I must do it, before she finds out from someone else, but today is not the day.

Dawn tried to stop me coming. 'Don't worry if you don't feel up to it,' she said on the phone when we last spoke. 'We could say you and Kane have been struck down by norovirus. They're terrified of stomach bugs in care homes, won't let you anywhere near.' When I said I wouldn't miss it for the world, I'm sure I heard my sister's face fall.

'But how will you get there without Kane to drive you?' she asked.

'A train. Or a bus.'

'It's never too late to learn to drive, you know.'

Oh, do fuck off, Dawn. I should have said it out loud. 'Probably not going to happen in the next five days, though, is it?'

She laughed. 'That's what you need. Humour. That'll get you through all of this.'

I check my phone again, as I have done at least every five minutes since I got on the train up to Cannock this morning. I still have service, I still have battery, and I've not missed a call. I never used to keep it on me, before all of this. When I was at home I'd leave it in a corner of the house as far away from me as possible, and if I had to take it out, it would sit at the bottom of my bag. But today it's in my pocket – sod the radiation. I need to get to it quickly if it rings. I know he will call today – he has to. I thought he would phone yesterday afternoon, but he didn't. I doubt the prison staff will have told him that I did show up for the visit in the morning, but that they wouldn't let me in because I was five minutes late. Five minutes.

I've been trying to work out what I'll say to him. I don't want to come on too strong with questions about Lou, but at the same time, I need to know if I'm right.

I spot my cousin Ava about to finish her chat with Lily and decide it has to be my turn by now. I hover behind her as she wishes Lily 'another happy and healthy year'. Another one? This year has hardly been kind to Lily, and I can see, now that I am closer to her, that she looks older than she did only a couple of months ago, when Kane and I last drove up here to visit her. She shouldn't be in here. When she had her fall a year ago, I wanted her to move into our spare room. But Lily said she would be a burden, and anyway, Dawn had offered to pay for her to move in here.

'You look beautiful,' I say, sitting on the arm of her chair and squeezing her shoulder. It feels much more fragile than I was expecting it to, as if it is all bone beneath her cardigan and blouse, and no flesh. 'As always. You've got a lovely healthy glow.'

'I'd be a lot lovelier and healthier if you could get hold of some marijuana for me,' she says loudly, without caring who hears. She waves at someone across the room. 'Dawn won't hear of it, you know what she's like.'

'Are you allowed it in here?'

'What do you think?'

'I'd love to help, Lily—'

'That's settled, then.' She widens her eyes and sticks out her bottom lip, a silent plea to accentuate her louder ones.

'I'll see what I can do next time I come up.'

'Ask Kane to get some. Maybe the three of us can share a spliff again when he next visits.'

I laugh, despite myself. When Kane told her that he and I sometimes smoke together, she demanded to be included and we'd spent a beautiful evening in her garden, convinced the stars were falling on our heads and eating five bags of tortilla chips. But that had been back when she was still in her own place.

I wish I didn't have to lie to you.

'It's a shame he can't be here today. Dawn says he's working?'

I nod, checking my phone again. No missed call.

'Give him a big cuddle from old Lil, won't you?'

'I'll bring him up to see you soon.' I can't look at her as I say it.

'Are you all right, Indy? You don't seem quite yourself.'

'I—'

'Everything okay over here?' Dawn appears at the other side of Lily's chair. 'Having a nice time, Mother?'

'Wonderful, darling. And it's so special to have both my girls here together with me.' She reaches out for our hands. 'My Indigo blue, my new Dawn.'

Dawn glowers at me over the top of her: it could well be because she hates the peace-and-love sentiment behind our name choices, but I suspect it's because she doesn't trust me to be on my own with Lily, not even for two minutes. 'Can I borrow you for a moment, Indy?'

I kiss my mother's head, inhaling the familiar scent of her shampoo.

'We're bringing the birthday cake out,' Dawn whispers as she pulls me away. 'You're in charge of the lights, if you think you can manage that?'

'Sounds a bit complicated.'

'I don't have time for your sarcasm today.' She flaps her hands by her face. 'Do you have any idea how stressful it's been to organise this?'

It's the first time I've felt like laughing in two weeks. She storms out of the room and I watch through the window in the door, switching the lights off as she approaches with the cake in her hands.

Everybody starts singing 'Happy Birthday' and Dawn walks over to Lily. As we sing her name, my phone starts to ring. 'Withheld number' flashes on the screen – it has to be him. I slip out of the room, glancing at Lily as I do so, but she hasn't noticed me. Dawn has, though, and is shaking her head at me over the Victoria sponge as she sets it on a table, her lips moving frantically and silently. *The lights*, she seems to be mouthing, as the door closes, and I answer my phone in the brightness of the corridor.

Someone else can turn the damn lights back on, Dawn. My son is more important right now.

'Hi, Mum.' His voice sounds so small and sad.

'Hello, love. I'm really sorry about yesterday.'

'Where were you? I was sitting there on my own for ages.'

'I know, love. I'm sorry. I got held up and they wouldn't let me in. They didn't explain?'

'I had to sit there until one of the guards came to get me, said no one had come for me.'

I can imagine him, at one of those tables, all alone. Watching all the other families arriving. I rest my forehead against the lemon-coloured wall.

'There's something I need to talk to you about,' I say. Clive has warned me that any phone calls I'll get with Kane will be short, and to say what I want to at the start of the conversation.

'We could have talked about it yesterday.'

'I wish we could have done, love. I do. But I can't come in now until next week and I need to ask you something. I really hate to pry.'

'Fire away.'

'The boy who died. Lou. He was your boyfriend, wasn't he?'

There's a click on the line and I think he's hung up, but when I pull the phone away from my ear to look at the screen, I hear his voice again.

'Who told you that?' he asks.

'Does it matter?'

'It does to me.'

'Is it true?'

His voice drops. 'Who I'm seeing – who I *was* seeing . . .' He pauses, and I know I'm right about him and Lou. I remember correcting myself like that, after Glyn died, when I talked about him and our relationship in the present tense. 'It's none of your business, all right?'

I'm not used to him talking to me like this. I've heard the stories from friends about their stroppy kids. When they told me, I would shake my head, thinking how lucky I was that my son was nothing like theirs. He's never once told me that anything in his life was none of my business.

But I don't have time to get upset right now. I can't give in to my doubts about him, and I can't take his behaviour personally. Who knows how I'd act if I was in prison? I walk further down the corridor, away from my mother's party, and plough on. 'And that other lad you were all out with, Wilko. Why didn't you tell me about him?'

'Who have you been talking to?'

'I can't help you unless you give me something. Anything.'

'Don't do anything stupid, Mum. Promise me? Do not try to find him.' His tone is softer, all of a sudden – he's begging me.

'Who, Wilko?'

'Please. He . . .' Kane's voice drops to a whisper. 'He knows people. In here. He was Lou and Benny's friend, not mine.'

'But—'

'I've never been mates with him. Not since all the trouble at school.'

It clicks into place, at last. Wilko was that kid I thought of the other week. The one who bullied Kane.

'He deals, all right? He's got this mate at Bristol Uni, they sell to students.'

I see him, now. A tall, mean-looking boy. But why can't I remember his real name? Kane didn't call him Wilko back then. What was it – Jamie? Freddy? That kid was a little scumbag when he was picking on my son; pouring Coke in his sports bag and ketchup in his pencil case, stealing his clothes after swimming, sending him home with bruises after getting him in a chokehold or twisting his arm behind his back. I'd seen enough bullies come through my studio door to know that they deserved as much sympathy as the kids they intimidated, but when it happened to my own son it was hard to see it that way.

'You still there?'

'Yes, love, sorry.'

'Promise me you're not going to try and find him or anything. If he gets spooked, then I'm fucked.'

Everything seems much clearer suddenly. Kane's fear, his paranoia. Why he's saying he pushed Lou.

'It was him, wasn't it? It was Wilko who did it?'

Kane sighs. 'No.' He doesn't elaborate. I'm right, I know I am.

But clearly Kane isn't going to snitch. I'll have to come at it a different way.

A beep starts sounding on the line. Clive warned me about this, too.

'Mum, sorry, I've got to go.'

'If you don't want to talk to me, at least speak to—'

'Time's up, Mum. I love you.'

'I'm not giving up.' I'm shouting now, and a nurse looks up at me as she leaves one of the other rooms on the corridor. 'I'm going to do a better job than those police jobsworths. I'll find witnesses. I'll do anything I have to. Kane? Kane?'

The line is dead, and he's gone.

Kane

17th August

What was he playing at?

As Kane got closer to the bar with Benny, it became clear why Lou had been AWOL for the last half an hour. Here he was, deep in conversation with a pretty blonde, leaning against the bar like he owned the place. And not just any pretty blonde: it was Jess.

'Interesting . . .' Benny winked at Kane and grinned, before pushing his way through the crowds and heading straight for his brother.

Kane tried to pull him back. 'Do we have to?' His words were lost in the din.

'I'm getting another round in,' Benny shouted at Lou, when he reached him. He asked Jess if she wanted one, too, but she made a face and said something into Lou's ear, before smiling briefly at Kane and walking off.

Lou looked at Kane like he'd won the lottery and knew Kane didn't have a quid to his name. Smug fucker. *Don't rise to it, Kane.*

Benny threw half his body over the bar to get the barmaid's attention and Kane stood silently next to Lou, trying to ignore his smirk. But there was only so much of this he could take.

'What's got into you tonight?' he hissed into his ear, nodding towards where Jess was now standing with some friends. 'Why were you doing that?' He looked over his shoulder to check Benny was out of earshot.

Lou didn't say anything, just swept his long grey-green hair out of his face. They were standing so close Kane couldn't help but inhale its scent as he flicked it back – a musky sweetness mixed with lingering cigarette smoke.

'You're just doing it to wind me up. Is that why you're drinking so much tonight, to show off to her?'

Without looking at him, Lou leaned towards Kane, bumping against his shoulder. 'So you're good enough to go out with her, but I'm not?'

'That was a long time ago.' Why was he being such a twat tonight?

'Just keeping my options open.' He looked over at his brother, who was still busy sorting out their drinks order.

'Fine,' Kane said. 'You know what? Do what you want. But don't mess her about. She's a nice girl.'

Lou stumbled against him. How much had he had, exactly? It wasn't even that late. Putting an arm around Kane's shoulder, he pressed his lips against his ear to whisper. 'That's not what I heard . . .' He laughed.

Kane pushed him away. Why did he bother? 'You should take yourself home, before—'

'Before what? What do you care?'

Benny suddenly appeared back at their side, flanked by Wilko – each precariously clutching two pint glasses and two shots.

'Benny,' Kane shouted, as the drinks were handed out. 'You should put your baby brother in a taxi. He's had a skinful.'

'Don't be a fucking killjoy,' Wilko said, lifting his pint above his head. 'The night is young, my friends. Shots!' They all tipped back the contents of their smaller glasses, and Kane grimaced as the tequila slid down his throat.

Lou turned, smashing his pint glass into Kane's so that beer spilled on to his shirt. 'Cheers, mate,' he said, with a twattish emphasis on the second word. 'How about a cheeky competition?' He looked at Benny, and Kane got the feeling he'd had so many times before: that all Lou cared about was impressing him.

Kane shook his head. 'Count me out, Lou.' He took a sip and let the liquid sit on his tongue for a moment before swallowing: it was cool, bitter, and the bubbles tingled in his throat and nose. *Focus on your senses,* his mum always said. *Focus on your senses when you need to calm down.*

'Ah, come on,' Lou slurred. 'You and me – first to down their drink wins. Loser goes home.' And he looked at Kane, his eyes full of contempt. Like he wished he'd never met him.

Alice

9th September

Alice caught the seventy-five into town. The bus was packed with Monday-morning commuters and she could feel their bodies against hers, smell their cheap perfume, hear the awful music they played through their headphones and the stupid conversations they were having on their phones. As the bus stop-started its way along Gloucester Road, she watched the library through the rain streaming down the window; it was odd to be a passer-by and not be going in there. But it was only one week off. She could survive a few days without work.

A crime of passion. Unbidden, thoughts of her shift on Saturday surfaced. The last time she had seen the library building she had been locking up shortly after midday – every part of her body aching, every part of her mind raging with information and questions. Even the process of turning the key in the staff door had exhausted her, and the incline of the road back to her house had felt much more arduous than usual. *I found a note, written by that boy Lou.* The pieces were falling into place, but there was still so much more Alice needed to know. In some ways she felt like she had more questions now than she did before Indigo had told her Lou was gay. Was this what Benny was being so secretive about? Did he know?

Étienne had been there when she got home from work,

181

sitting in the kitchen playing his guitar. She couldn't look him in the eye. She should tell him, but she couldn't – not yet.

'Don't you have people to go and see?' she'd asked, as he played a blues riff she didn't recognise. 'Can't you go and visit Joe and Lianne? Jackson?' Alice didn't see any of their old friends, but she knew a few were still in Bristol. 'You don't seem to leave the house much.'

Without stopping what he was playing, he said, 'How do you know what I do while you're at work?'

'Hidden cameras.'

He rested his hand on the strings. 'You want some space, is that it?'

She looked away, wiping her hand across the counter, collecting crumbs against her palm. 'How long are you staying, Étienne? It's been a week.' She heard the dull twang of strings vibrating as he placed his guitar carefully on the table. He walked round the end of the breakfast bar, towards her, but she didn't turn around.

'Alice.'

She tensed her body, expecting a hand on her shoulder. But he reached around her, gently took hold of her jaw and turned her face towards his. Her lips were touching his finger. She looked him in the eye for the first time since she'd got home, and suddenly felt very aware of every part of herself, the way her chest was rising with each breath, every blink of her eyelids, the softness of her tongue against the roof of her mouth.

'Stop.' She twisted her chin out of his grip, but didn't step backwards.

'You don't mean that.'

She had never been more grateful for a knock at the door.

'I have visitors.' She walked away from him to answer it. 'Just – think about finding somewhere else to stay, okay?'

'*Bien sûr*,' came the response behind her.

As she let Priya and Margaret in, he greeted each of them. 'Ladies.' He looked at Alice, 'À plus.' He picked up his leather jacket from a hook by the door and slipped out before Alice shut it, brushing his hand against hers as he did so.

Alice sat down at the kitchen table with Priya and Margaret, rubbing at her jaw and right hand, where he had touched her. What was she doing? Trying to rub him away, out of her life? She struggled to focus as they told her Kane had agreed to meet with her, that she would go into the prison and sit down in a room with him.

When they talked about ground rules she'd have to follow, all she could think about were all the rules Étienne had broken. All the rules he continued to break. You don't leave the mother of your children when one of them is no more than a few months old. You don't reappear eighteen years later in the home you once shared with your family and act as though none of it ever happened.

You don't touch someone the way he had touched her only minutes before – not when you know they don't want you to.

Stepping off the bus, Alice opened her umbrella and looked down the street to her left. It was only a five-minute walk from the bus stop to the building she wanted to visit, but she had to go the long way round to avoid Lou's car park. She turned right and made her way along the cobbles of King Street, past the theatre, until she came to the intersection with Queen Charlotte Street. She looked ahead, across the road, and gritted her teeth as she realised her mistake. How could she have been so stupid? There was no way of getting to Frasier House without taking a hideous tour of Lou's last movements.

A few drinks at the Old Duke, then the Llandoger.

She heard Benny's voice, and suddenly felt light-headed. She leaned against a bike rack, brushing water droplets from the cold metal with her finger.

Benny's voice came to her again, this time a memory replayed from yesterday.

Getting rid of those, too, are you?

The hatred in his face as he said it was what made her shudder now, remembering; it bothered her more than anything he had said to her in the last couple of weeks.

You going to fix the Tiger?

She closed her eyes against the images and words, but they wouldn't shift. She crossed the road and wandered slowly past the empty benches on the cobbles between the two pubs the boys had been to that night, and she suddenly felt weary again, as if she could sit down right here and sleep for days. She hadn't been able to drag herself out of bed yesterday morning – or this morning, for that matter – not in time for her usual morning walk. Maybe she was coming down with something. Yesterday, she had only got up when the prisoners came out at lunchtime to play football in their exercise yard. Even through her closed window she could hear them shouting and cheering. Was Kane Owen amongst them? She couldn't sleep in this room any longer. She needed to get away from him.

She had gathered her orthopaedic pillow, her radio, alarm clock, and the half-empty bottle of Black Cow from her bedside table. She unhooked her two framed prints from the wall, took some clean sheets from her wardrobe and carried the whole lot into Lou's room. She stood by his bed, with a hand on the duvet, for several minutes. Then, in a flash of energy and motion, she stripped it, remade it with the clean sheets, and set up her radio and clock. She propped up her prints – a sheet of piano music from Liszt's *La Campanella*, and a scientific illustration of the flowers and seed heads in the life cycle of *Tragopogon pratensis* – on top of Lou's desk, then sat on the edge of the mattress, looking around the room. The memories of Lou ran so deep in her; how much worse could it be, sleeping surrounded by his things? She doubled forward and reached down, stashing her bottle under the bed.

It clinked against something. She got down on to the floor and dragged out Lou's duffel bag full of tools – Étienne must have kicked it under there. One by one, she pulled out a set of spanners. She was laying them on top of the duvet when Benny walked in.

'Getting rid of those, too, are you?' He folded his arms, looking at her from the doorway.

'No.'

'You going to fix the Tiger, then?' His face was a sneer.

She could have told him that she hadn't given any of Lou's belongings away; that she didn't plan to for some time.

She could have told him that she had taken compassionate leave, like he'd wanted her to.

'I don't plan to.'

Should she tell him about Lou and Kane? Perhaps he already knew. At the very least, maybe he wouldn't be shocked. She hadn't been. She had been surprised, in fact, at how readily she had accepted the news. Lou being gay had never occurred to her; true, he'd never brought a girl home, but she'd just assumed that was because he didn't want her to know who he was seeing.

Benny must have known. That's why there had been all the secrecy about the night Lou died. But just as Lou hadn't been able to strike up a conversation with her about it, Alice could not find the words to discuss it with her eldest son.

She pulled out a hammer from the bag.

'You've changed his bed.' Benny pointed at the pillows.

'Yes.'

'Why?'

'We can't leave this room as a shrine, Benny. It's not going to remain untouched.'

He swore under his breath. 'I'm going out.'

'See you later.'

He didn't move. 'That's all? "See you later"?'

'Yes,' she had said, failing to hide her irritation. 'I assume I will be seeing you, later? Or will I not?'

Benny had laughed. 'That's the first time you've not given me the third degree in two weeks. You don't want to know where I'm going? Who I'll be with?'

The conversation had ended with him stomping down the stairs and slamming the front door. Could he blame her for being suspicious? For worrying about him?

Now Alice looked around her, at the hanging baskets outside the Old Duke, full of bright pink petunias. At the colourful streamers visible behind net curtains in an upstairs window of the pub. Did either of her boys see these things that night they were here?

She stepped forward away from the pubs, crossing the road and beginning the walk to Frasier House, along Queen Charlotte Street. It felt like she was jumping off a cliff – her heartrate rapidly increased, she was suddenly hot and sweaty, but she was drawn forwards, now that she had set off.

Keeping her eyes resolutely to the left to avoid seeing the car park, she focused on the graffiti tags on the walls, the soggy cigarette butts in the gutter, the tree bursting out of cracked concrete in the pavement. When she glimpsed a reflection of the bright yellow car park sign in a grubby window on her side of the road, she quickly looked at her feet, but not fast enough to prevent her from seeing a flash of colour at the foot of the car park wall, which she immediately knew must be the floral tributes left by Lou's friends. She rubbed at her temples and kept her eyes pointing down now, counting the number of bottles (two), shoelaces (one, brown), puddles (four) and patches of trodden chewing gum (nine).

When she came to a side road, she looked up to check for traffic and saw a set of limestone steps on the other side leading to some glass doors, with a sign above them: Frasier House.

DC Garcia had asked if Alice wanted to come down here and see where Lou had died, but Alice had no desire to do so and couldn't understand why anyone would want to. Indigo would probably be that kind of woman, on a grim pilgrimage to leave teddy bears and stick photographs to the wall of the car park. What good would it do?

She climbed the steps – she could already see the receptionist. Trying to ignore the way her heart skipped beats whenever she had to initiate conversation with a stranger, she pushed open the door. This was for Lou.

The receptionist looked up. 'Can I help you?'

Alice folded away her umbrella. 'Yes. I would like to know what businesses are based on the fourth and fifth floors.'

'There are several. Are you after a certain company?'

'Can you provide me with a list?'

'May I ask what you need it for?'

'It's a personal matter.' Was it such a difficult request? Alice's face was growing hotter.

'I will need to refer you to our buildings manager; let me just get you his contact details.' The receptionist leaned down to open a drawer. 'He'll be able to get you a list, but you may need to explain what you need it for.'

'The one I want to know the name of is in use during the night. At weekends, even. There can't be many like that.'

Holding a slip of paper in her hands, the receptionist slowly returned to an upright position and glared levelly at Alice. 'Frasier House is closed overnight.' She pushed the paper across the counter.

Alice was on to something, she could see it in this woman's face. 'I am investigating a crime that took place outside here a couple of weeks ago.' She pointed out of the building, towards the road. 'A boy died.'

'You're with the police?' The woman's eyes narrowed.

'I'm the boy's mother.'

Her mouth gaped open. 'Oh, I'm so sorry, I thought . . .'

'You clearly know the office I am talking about. Someone in there saw what happened to my son. I wish to speak with them.'

'I'd love to be able to help you. Really, I would.'

'Fine.' Alice slammed her hand down on to the slip of paper on the counter with the buildings manager's details. 'I need to contact this man?'

'Actually, given what you've just said, I'm not sure he will be able to help you after all. I'm sorry. I wish I could explain. I'm not trying to be difficult. If the police were to contact the buildings manager, I'm sure something . . .'

What was this company? Why was this woman being so cagey about it? 'The police are not interested. I am.' She wasn't about to explain to her why she couldn't go to the police about Wilko's video. 'Perhaps you could pass a message on, if you happen to remember which company on the fourth or fifth floor has staff in on a Saturday night.'

The receptionist said nothing.

'Explain to them that I am trying to understand how my son died, anything that could make sense of why he was pushed. Let me give you my details.' She flipped the slip of paper over on the counter, and pulled a pen out of her rucksack to write down her number. She pushed it back towards the receptionist, but she didn't take it. 'Or, I will be working in Bishopston Library this Saturday and all of next week.' She wrote that on the piece of paper, too.

'I can't promise anything.' The receptionist slid the paper off the counter and folded it in half.

'Do you have children?' Alice asked.

The receptionist nodded, her face blanching.

'Then please, just pass the message on.'

As soon as Alice got down the entrance steps, she leaned back against the wall of Frasier House, not caring that the brickwork was wet, and not bothering to open her umbrella.

She kept her head turned to one side, gaze aimed at the pavement, still refusing to look at the car park. But she suddenly felt aware of something out of the corner of her eye. Someone. Standing on the other side of the street. Alice had the unnerving feeling that she was being watched.

Alice pulled herself away from the wall and opened her umbrella. The person was still there, she could see their bright yellow form against the darkness of the car park wall.

She should walk away. She was imagining it.

As she turned to head back towards King Street, she pulled the umbrella down to cover her face from view, and from this protected position she let herself look over the road. Desperately trying not to pay any attention to the line of rotting, cellophane-wrapped bouquets, she focused on the other person. Her umbrella was obscuring the top half of their body, but she could see their legs. Two fluorescent straps were wrapped around their calves, just above the ankles.

She tilted the umbrella up an inch, enough to see Indigo's face.

Indigo

9th September

It *is* her.

I wave, now that she's seen me, and she raises her hand unenthusiastically in response. I wait for a gap in the traffic and cross the road.

'What are you doing here?' I'm nearly shouting to be heard over the rain, which has suddenly intensified.

'Day off.' Alice steps back away from the road to let another pedestrian get past her huge golf umbrella, and I move with her.

'Are you okay? You looked a little upset when you came out of there.'

Alice looks over her shoulder at the building she just left.

'I had an appointment.'

I pull the hood of my coat closer, drops falling off its edges on to my face, and hug my helmet to my chest. 'Doctor's appointment? Sorry, no, you don't have to tell me.'

She doesn't say anything. Maybe it's because she's not at work, but something seems different about her. She is standing less tall, somehow. Part of me wants to get on with what I came down here to do, but I don't think I should be leaving her alone.

I point up at the umbrella. 'Would you mind if I hop under? Just until it stops a bit?'

She nods, I duck underneath, and we stand, shoulder to

shoulder, watching the cars pass through what is now a shallow river on the road.

'About the other day. I'm sorry for unloading everything on you like that. I don't know what came over me.'

'You were distressed.' The way she says it is so matter-of-fact, it takes me back a little. I've never spent time with someone as robotic as her. It's fascinating, if a little unnerving. I'm not sure she's even made direct eye contact with me yet. I appreciate it is a little difficult, standing next to each other under an umbrella. But there's something about her that makes me want to hug her, shake her, shock her into a show of humanity.

'Well, yes. But I'm sorry, nonetheless. You were busy. At work. It wasn't appropriate.'

'There's no need to apologise.'

I've now said sorry twice. You'd think in return she might say something to account for the way she disappeared into her office so abruptly.

Over the road, several people have taken cover from the rain in the ground floor of the NCP. 'It's the first time I've been down here,' I say. 'I was just looking at the flowers . . . can you see, over there? Friends of the dead boy have left them. There're some lovely messages . . .'

I glance at her. She isn't looking at the car park; instead, she is staring off down the road again. Her free hand is nervously tapping at her thigh. Whatever that appointment was, it's obviously shaken her up.

Whenever I feel like that, I need a bit of distraction to get me back on track. 'What are you up to now? I could use some moral support if you've got a few minutes.'

'I'm meant to be getting back.' She looks at me, and to my surprise there is a hint of an apologetic expression on her face. 'What do you need to do?'

'I wanted to ask them about CCTV.' I tilt my head towards the car park.

'Won't the police have done that already?'

'Yes, but that doesn't help Kane, does it? They're hardly going to reveal anything that supports his case.'

'His lawyers should have access to it, though?'

I'm starting to wish I'd never crossed the road to see her. 'I want to see it for myself.'

Alice looks at her watch and up the street again, nervously. 'I suppose another ten minutes won't hurt.'

I clap my hands together. 'Great.'

We cross the road under her umbrella, and I head over to the kiosk where I spotted the security guard sitting just before I saw Alice.

'Wait,' she says, grabbing my arm. 'What are you going to say?'

'I'll explain who I am. Ask to see any CCTV that could help Kane's case. He'll feel sorry for me.'

'It won't work.'

'I don't see what other options I have.'

'Tell him you're a journalist. Say you're doing a backgrounder on the events of that night. That's what they call those in-depth pieces.'

'I'm impressed.' I mean it. I didn't think she had it in her to be so devious.

Alice shrugs, but I can see a smile at the corners of her mouth.

'Okay. I'm a reporter for . . .' I pause. 'Where shall I say I'm from?'

'The local paper.'

'Right. Okay.' I can feel the adrenalin starting to work its way through my body.

Just as I'm peering through the door, the security guard opens it. 'Yes?'

'I'm a reporter, from the local paper, the *Bristol Post*, where I am a journalist. For the paper.' I wince. Maybe it's not such a good idea.

He doesn't seem to notice my inauthenticity. He points at Alice.

'And your friend?'

'Photographer.' Alice doesn't even blink as she lies.

'What's this about?'

'What it is, you see, we want to – or would like to, if at all possible – see some CCTV from a couple of weeks ago. The night the boy fell into the road?'

'He was pushed.'

'Yes, well. Yes. Possibly. I am writing a . . . a backgrounder. About the incident. Can I see the CCTV?'

'I'm not being funny or nothing but no. You can't.' He steps back into the kiosk and starts to close the door.

'Please?'

'Oh, well, if you'd said *please* before . . .' He grins momentarily, then resets his face to a scowl. 'No. Can. Do. There are no cameras above ground level. Like I told the police.'

I can't hide my disappointment. I don't know what to say to him.

'It's an important story, we're under a lot of pressure,' Alice says, glancing at me. 'From the editor. Is there anything you can do to help us?'

He looks at her, then back at me, sighs, then closes and locks his kiosk door. 'The best I can do is show you the bit the police cordoned off.'

He leads the way up the stairs. The stairwell smells of urine and cigarettes and the walls are grimy. The security guard whistles the theme to *Star Wars* all the way up. As we climb, the lights flicker on and off, and he swears.

When we get to the third storey, he holds the door to let

Alice and me through into the car park. 'Over there, by that red Honda Civic. They pushed him over that blue bar, where the wall drops down a bit, and the poor bloke fell on to the road.' He points past a line of parked cars to a section of the brown brick wall that was lower than the rest of it. 'Now, if you ladies will excuse me, I've got to get someone to come and sort these electrics. It's the rain that does it.' The lights flicker off and on again.

He disappears back through the door. Alice is standing next to me, staring at the corner of the car park that he had pointed at. Her face is very pale, but I'm struck – not for the first time – by how beautiful she is, in a severe way. It's an interesting face; solid yet delicate, angular but soft. The kind of face I used to like to draw.

'Are you sure you're okay?' I put a hand on her shoulder. 'Do you need to sit down?' I wish I knew what she'd been up to earlier. What if she had a serious medical condition? Is she about to collapse on me?

'I'm fine,' she mutters. 'Shall we get this over with?'

What's the rush? I leave her by the door to the stairwell and go to investigate the scene of my son's so-called crime. I'm running a hand along the peeling paint on the blue railing, at chest height, when she approaches slowly.

'Kane wouldn't have been able to push him over this.' I step back and look at the wall. 'How could he have pushed him hard enough to topple him over the edge? He's not tall enough.'

Alice touches the wall gingerly, keeping it at arm's length. Maybe she is afraid of heights?

'I'll tell you who is tall,' I say. 'That Wilko kid. He always towered over Kane.'

My phone rings in my coat pocket. I fumble with the zip in a rush to get it out.

'Hello?' I pick up just in time.

'Is that Indigo Owen?' a woman's voice asks. 'I'm calling from HMP Bristol.'

'Thank you for getting back to me, I was hoping I might be able to rearrange a visit. I missed—'

'Hold on, Mrs Owen. That's not why I'm calling.'

A sharp pain spikes in my chest. I grab hold of the nearest car's wing mirror. 'Has something happened?'

Alice

10th September

*I*s this Alice?
The first text had arrived shortly after two in the morning, when she'd been asleep. Her phone didn't recognise the number. She'd replied as soon as she woke up, still rubbing the sleep from her eyes.

Who's asking?

It was several hours before an answer came. *Wilko. Is this Alice?*

She had left her number with him the other day. 'Just in case you remember anything else,' she'd said.

She texted back immediately. *Do you have information about Lou?*

Meet me on the bridge over M32, off Gatton Rd. 9 p.m.

She had tried calling him, but he didn't pick up.

So here she was, sitting in her car, half an hour early for a clandestine meeting with a drug dealer. She looked up at the bridge, a quiet pedestrian crossing that descended towards a row of tall pines on the other side of the motorway. She hadn't seen another person cross it since she'd got here – presumably that was why Harry had chosen this location. The road she was parked in seemed safe enough, although there were also several grubby caravans that looked like they had been here for years and were being lived in. She'd never been here, though she'd

196

lived in Bristol all of her life. This was not the kind of place Alice Hyde was used to visiting; this was not the kind of thing she was used to doing.

It was obviously a week for new things: she was also not used to driving other people around, but that's what she'd be doing the day after tomorrow. When Indigo had taken that call in the car park from the prison, they'd told her Kane had been moved to Long Lartin. It must have been because of Alice's complaint. Indigo's reaction had seemed disproportionate at first. Yes, Long Lartin was further away, but it was only an hour or so up the motorway. Alice couldn't understand why she was acting as if the world had ended. But, with much effort, she had made sense of Indigo's rage-fuelled rambling. Indigo didn't drive.

How was she going to visit her son?

When Alice had offered to drive her up there, she hadn't been thinking. It was a terrible idea. But there was something about this woman, bent over, distraught. For one very short moment, Alice saw her simply as another mother who had lost her son. She recognised something of herself. Now, she realised how stupid this was. Indigo's plight was nothing compared to Alice's. Indigo's son had brought this upon them all. Lou and Alice were innocent.

But in that moment of madness, she had said, 'I can take you.' And Alice Hyde didn't go back on a promise, no matter who it was to. Duty was hardwired into her DNA.

Which was also why she had to meet Harry Wilkinson, no matter how risky it was. She had a duty to her sons.

As the time edged closer to nine o'clock and the dark blue of the evening sky deepened, she considered again whether she should tell someone she was here. Étienne was the obvious choice – he knew she'd already met with Harry Wilkinson once. She'd had the chance, earlier, when, as she was leaving, he'd handed her an envelope containing fifty pounds in cash. When she'd pushed it away, he'd held her hands around it. 'Accept it as rent or use it for the funeral.' Too little too late, she'd wanted to reply. She could have told him then, when he asked her where she was going, but he'd have insisted on coming with her, and she wanted to do this alone.

When she opened the car door, she suddenly felt extremely sensitive to every sound. It wasn't just the roar of the motorway next to her; it was the rustle of the trees, the sudden sharp bark of a dog in a nearby garden. She swallowed as she stepped out of the car into the deserted street and shoved her hands into her pockets.

In her right pocket, there was Lou's needle file. She wrapped her hand around it. In her left, she wedged her house keys through her fingers. Nobody was on the bridge yet, but she was sure Harry was watching her from somewhere nearby. She walked past a wall covered with unintelligible, unimaginative graffiti tags and climbed the steps in the darkness. There was a streetlight at either end of the bridge, but the one at her end wasn't working.

She'd tried to find out a bit more about him before she drove over here, but searches were unforthcoming. There was just one short news article about him being caught with a few bags of cannabis, but somehow he'd been spared a jail sentence when the case came to court.

Alice stood in the middle of the bridge, looking north out of the city, watching the blurred headlights of the cars racing past underneath her. She felt the urge to grab hold of the railings, but didn't want to take her hands out of her pockets. It was a cool evening, and the wind rustled through the pines. *A sea breeze through the open door.* This, again. For nearly eighteen years she'd not been able to feel air rush past her face like this, without remembering that day in Clevedon. *Pulling her cardigan around her to keep him warm. The smell of salt in her nostrils.* She shook her head to keep the hair out of her eyes.

Then she saw him. He was heading towards her from the other side, in a hoody and jeans, a black baseball cap pulled down low over his face, his shoulders hunched. When he reached the middle, he didn't look at her. He leaned his elbows on the railings, standing about a metre away. Even in the limited light from the motorway below, she could see enough of his face to recognise that he seemed different, less confident than before.

'Don't look at me.' He had to shout slightly over the noise of the traffic. 'If anyone comes past, I'll walk away.'

She stared straight ahead again, down over the central reservation and the three lanes of traffic either side of it.

'And don't say anything unless I ask you a question.'

Alice clutched at the needle file.

'Benny says you've been digging around a lot. He says you're going to meet with Kane.'

Alice flinched. Why was Benny telling him these things?

'You don't want to be doing that.' He picked at a cable tie that was secured around the railings.

'The digging or the meeting Kane?'

'Either,' he said, checking over his shoulder to see if anyone was approaching. 'How well do you know Simon's mum?'

The change in direction threw her. 'Yvonne?'

'You said you knew her. Are you friends still?'

'No.' Why the hell was he asking about her?

'I'm sure she's, like, a lovely woman, or whatever. But Simon – he's not someone you want to mess with, okay?'

'Okay.' Was this a threat? She thought of Simon's words, back in Harry's flat: *That wouldn't be good for Benny.*

'I'm telling you for your own safety. I'm doing you a favour. He's not a nice guy. I've seen what he does to people, you know? Who don't pay up or whatever.'

He checked over his shoulder again. 'Benny's a mate.'

'Are you saying he's in danger?'

Harry looked like he was going to say something else, but suddenly he pushed away from the railings and walked off, kicking at some broken glass as he went, back over to the far side of the bridge.

Alice shouted after him. 'Are you threatening my family?'

Indigo

12th September

I've misjudged her, clearly.

There are not many people who would offer to drive you more than a hundred miles to visit your son in prison. She's even taken the day off to do it. If I think about it too much, I get quite emotional. In a world that has been so unkind to me in the past few weeks, Alice has restored my faith in people.

'I'm on to something with this Wilko lad.' I lean my elbow on the inside of the car door, looking at my reflection in the wing mirror. I don't look so tired today. There's something in my eyes: a glint of energy.

Alice doesn't say anything. I thought, perhaps, that the offer of a lift was a breakthrough of some kind. That she might suddenly become a different person, one with social skills. I was wrong.

I run a hand through my hair as I look in the mirror. 'There were loads of bullying incidents when he and Kane were kids. You have children, don't you?'

Nothing, although her face does twitch slightly. It's like she has tuned me out completely.

'Earth to Alice?'

'I heard you. Yes. Two.'

'Sons?'

'Daughters.'

'It's probably different with girls.'

'What is?'

'Bullying.'

'Yes, I'd imagine so.'

'Have you ever thought, though – would you rather have a child who is bullied or one who is the bully themselves?'

'It's not really down to me.'

This woman, honestly. 'But if you could choose. Bully or bullied?'

'Neither.'

I sigh.

She is probably the type of person who likes a lot of silence. Normally, in a situation such as this, I would try to go with that – it is her car, after all. But if I don't talk or do something, I'll have to think about going into this prison to see Kane, and I'm not looking forward to it. I'm not looking forward to seeing my own son. I'm worried about what has happened to him. They wouldn't tell me anything on the phone on Monday, and he hasn't called me since he was moved. Why is he here?

'Question is, should I say something to the police?' I bite at my fingernails.

'What about?'

'Wilko. All the evidence I have against him.'

'Which is?'

'He was there. He's a drug dealer. He bullied Kane. He's tall enough to have pushed that poor boy over the edge of the wall.'

'Is any of that evidence?'

'Yes. I . . .'

She's right. I move on to the fingernails of my other hand.

'I'm sure he's okay,' Alice says. Another surprising glimpse of her kinder side.

I take a couple of deep breaths. 'Do you want me to give you directions?' I need some sort of distraction. I lean around my seat to look in the back-seat pockets. 'Do you have a map or anything?'

'No.' Alice gently taps her hand against the steering wheel. 'I'm good at memorising routes.'

I check my watch. We've only been on the road for half an hour; still another hour to go. 'So, daughters?'

'Yes.'

'Age?'

'Late teens. Let me . . . concentrate. This car here is . . .'

Alice doesn't finish her sentence. I look at the cars around us, trying to look for an explanation as to why she suddenly needs to focus harder on the road.

'I always imagined girls would be harder work than boys,' I say.

'What's this idiot doing?' Alice is looking in her wing mirror.

'Do you get on well with them?'

I'm about to ask another question when she says, 'One more than the other.'

'I've always wondered about that.'

'About what?'

'If I could ever have loved a second child as much as I love Kane.'

'Hmm.'

She never volunteers anything, never opens up, never—

'I wouldn't say I loved her less. Love her less.' Her voice is quiet.

'No?'

'Even when she was a baby . . .' She shakes her head. 'Forget it.'

'Go on.'

Alice shakes her head again. 'I should concentrate on the road.'

Neither of us says anything for a few minutes. I'm thinking about her as a younger woman, as a mother, with two little girls. I can't see it.

To my surprise, it is Alice who starts the conversation again, speaking with a very slow and considered voice. 'I didn't enjoy being around her. And it was as if she knew that.' She pauses. 'I didn't feel like she was my child, not like I did with my first. I could never work out why she was crying – was it hunger or tiredness or boredom or something else? – but with my first I did.' By the time she finishes speaking, her voice has loosened.

'Hardest job in the world.'

'I suppose so.'

'Was their father still around at that point?'

'Not for long.'

'Sounds like you . . .' It sounds like she might have had postnatal depression. But should I say that? 'Did you ever get counselling?'

'No.' She laughs, eyes still on the road ahead of us.

'Why not?'

'I'm not that kind of person.'

'What kind of person is that?' I can't help it, there is an edge to my voice as I say it.

She doesn't reply.

I decide to shift the direction of the conversation before I say something I'll regret. 'I wasn't on my own until a lot later. Kane was nine. Those early years must be especially tough. And with two of them . . .' I whistle.

'I didn't really know any different. You had nine years of getting used to having someone else there to share the load – I'd imagine that was difficult, suddenly having to go it alone.'

'Is this a competition? Who had it hardest?' I laugh. 'What do we win?'

A smile crosses Alice's lips as she checks the rear-view mirror.

'It was always the evenings that got me,' I say. 'You plough on through all the chores, the exhaustion of having to make dinner every night and wash up and get them to bed. Then you finally sit down and there's no one there to talk to.'

'I quite liked that. The peace and quiet. I can see that it would be a struggle for you, though. Not talking.' She coughs, and I'm sure she is doing it to disguise a laugh.

'Now look, there's nothing wrong with being a conversationalist,' I say. 'Okay then . . .' I look out of the window for inspiration. There must be some aspect of the trials of single parenthood that we agree on. 'What about . . . do you not feel an intense pressure to stay alive? Because they need you more than they would if they had two parents there?'

'Of course. But you work out contingency plans, don't you? I've saved up money for them. My father would take them in if anything happened to me.'

I shudder. If anything awful had happened to me before Kane turned eighteen, he would have had to move in with Dawn. Alice obviously hadn't had the motivation of a hideous sister to make her quite as determined as I have been to stick around for Kane.

'But you're right,' she says. 'I do remember suddenly taking extra care crossing the road, after Et – after the girls' father left. And I avoided driving on motorways for a while.'

Satisfied that we see eye to eye on something, I sink back in my seat, attempting to sit in silence for a while, just to show her that I can do it. But before too long I get that familiar itchy feeling across my body – I need to say something. Anything. 'Your car is so tidy.' I cast my eyes around. 'It's like a hire car.'

'I just cleaned it.' She shoots a quick look at me. Have I offended her?

'I'm sure if I had one it would be a tip. Tidy is . . . good.'

She arches her eyebrows.

'I think I'd get one of those nodding dogs.' I laugh. 'And have a photo of Kane stuck up here.' I tap the dashboard.

'It's not devoid of personal touches.' She points to the keyring dangling from the ignition just above her knee, which has a fern leaf attached to it, cut out of green leather.

'I know someone else with one like that.' I pause to think who. 'This is going to annoy me now. Who is it?'

It is Alice who breaks the silence that follows.

'Would you mind me enquiring,' she says, so formally I feel like I'm in a job interview, 'what was Kane fighting about, with the boy who died? You've never said.'

I twist my bracelet around my wrist as I remember what Kane told me that first time I visited him. How could he and Lou Durand have said such nasty things to each other, that night? *You're a waste of space. Your dad didn't care about you enough to stick around long, did he?* I think of the contrast with that sweet card Lou had written to my son, of the others lying on the table when I was with Benny.

And that's when I remember where I have seen that keyring before – the one only a couple of feet away from me now.

It was in Benny's house.

Alice

12th September

Alice checked the passenger-side wing mirror and stole a glance at Indigo as she did so. She struggled to read expressions at the best of times, and such a hurried look did not reveal much about what was on the other woman's mind. She suspected, though, from Indigo's uncharacteristic silence, that her question had offended her and therefore blown her chance of finding out what the boys had been fighting about.

But Alice needed to know. It couldn't just be about a girl. Margaret had called her yesterday to say that Kane had been moved, so their meeting would now be taking place at Long Lartin. Then, just as Alice had thought the conversation was going to finish, Margaret had asked if she was aware of anything that Kane had said about her on the night Lou died.

'About me?' Alice had asked.

'He told us that he wants to apologise to you for what he said. That he said something about you.'

'What else did he tell you?'

Margaret paused, then spoke slowly. 'Kane seemed to be saying that the fight he had with Lou was about you.'

Alice had been replaying the conversation ever since. *The fight he had with Lou was about you.* If Indigo wouldn't fill her in, she would have to wait until she met Kane – and she'd rather have the information before that encounter took place. Benny hadn't been any help. He was still annoyed with her for telling him he should steer clear of Harry Wilkinson the day before. She hadn't wanted to frighten him with Harry's threats, and she didn't want to tell him she'd met him, but she needed her son to stay away. So she had lied, saying that Lou had mentioned that they'd been spending time with him. 'He's not the kind of person you should be hanging around with. I know about his brush with the law,' she had said. 'Give it a rest, Mum,' was Benny's reply. 'You don't get to dictate who I can be friends with.' So when she had asked him about the fight, after hanging up on her call to Margaret, he'd not been in the mood to help. 'I find it hard to believe it was all a row over a girl,' she'd said, thinking: *Especially when they were both gay.* 'There's got to be more to it.' *You knew they were together, didn't you?* Eventually, he'd replied, after she had insisted he answer her. 'It's just a bit awkward,' he'd said. 'It's not like you and I talk about . . . girls and stuff. But Lou was basically slagging off this particular girl, saying she puts out. You know? That she was . . . easy. Kane was friends with her and he kind of took offence, so . . .' Alice still found it hard to believe that something so petty had led to her son's death. But then, she'd only met Kane once, and they'd barely spoken. Was it any more believable that the boys had been fighting about her?

Alice had been wishing for some peace and quiet since she had picked Indigo up from her house, but now she had it she found herself willing Indigo to start talking again. Maybe she hadn't heard Alice's question?

She didn't have anything to lose. 'There was a fight, wasn't there?'

'Yes.'

Something was definitely up. Indigo didn't do one-word sentences.

Alice kept her eyes on the quiet country road ahead of them, but was still aware of Indigo turning her whole body in the seat to stare at her.

In a strangely light voice, Indigo asked, 'Did I never mention it?'

Alice would have remembered if she had.

'It started with a tasteless joke Kane made, from what he tells me. I'm not particularly proud of what he did, let me be clear about that. I've tried to forget about it, if I'm honest.' There was an edge to her voice, which Alice had never heard before.

'Tasteless?'

'It was about Lou's mother not wanting him.'

Alice gripped the steering wheel tighter. *Driving without knowing. Pulling her cardigan tight to keep him warm.*

'. . . isn't the boy I raised,' Indigo was saying. 'What he said was awful. But it doesn't make him a murderer, does it?'

Alice shook her head. She couldn't speak. *Towards the sea, the baby forcing her on to the coast. The smell of salt in her nostrils.*

'Apparently, Lou was told – a few weeks before all of this mess – that his mother had come close to aborting him. Got to the clinic, turned around. They must've talked about it that night; then when Lou was winding Kane up, he lashed out, taunted him with it.'

Alice took some short, shallow breaths: in through her nose, out through her mouth. *Her belly pressed up against the edge of the piano. Lou's first kicks, during the sighs of the adagio. Her wrist dropping on the A and floating up on the G sharp.* How had Lou found out? Who had told him about this thing she nearly did, this thing she had almost managed to convince herself never happened?

What had he been thinking? Why hadn't he come to her? She would have expected him to challenge her, to have been angry. She could have explained. *Looking at Étienne's back in the clinic, then turning. Driving without knowing.*

She opened her window and the breeze cooled her hot cheeks.

'I wonder if his mother is aware that he found out.' Indigo

shifted in her seat now, turning to face forwards. She didn't realise that she was making comments and observations that were incredibly painful for Alice to hear. She had tormented herself with the idea that he somehow knew, from the moment she had left the clinic. That he had held it against her, had hated her for not wanting him as much as she'd wanted Benny; that the knowledge he was born with infected their relationship – even from that first day she'd decided he would live, after she'd walked out of the clinic, driven to Clevedon and felt him kick for the first time. *Lou's tiny unborn feet, dancing.* She'd always been plagued with those thoughts, but they were absurd and illogical.

What could Alice say to sound normal, disinterested and not involved? Her brain drew a blank. 'It can't have been easy for him.'

'Wait, slow down!' Indigo pointed ahead of them at a sign for the prison. 'You were going to drive straight past.'

Driving without knowing. Alice braked, indicated and turned into the small side road leading to the prison entrance.

Indigo

12th September

As we park up underneath a frayed Union Jack flapping in the breeze, I can see that this place is different.

I take it all in, as I rack my brains for information about Alice. There is no welcoming committee here. Nobody is friendly. *How exactly did I meet her?* None of the other visiting friends and relatives looks at me, let alone speaks to me. The grim boxy buildings are nothing like HMP Bristol's Victorian red brick, which seem quite beautiful in comparison. *Did I approach her or did she come over to me in the library?* Despite the late-summer warmth outside, it's chilly in here. The whole place reeks of disinfectant, and yet it still looks dirty. *Can I even be sure that she works in the library?* I feel a different kind of fear here for Kane. I thought the last place was bad enough, but this is so much worse.

'Have you ever met Lou and Benny's mother?' I ask, before I've even sat down opposite him.

'I'm fine, Mum, thanks for asking.' He looks at me as though I've lost my mind.

'Have you?'

'Yes, once. Why?'

'Is she involved in whatever happened?'

He nods. 'Yeah, I told you what I said about her, didn't I?'

'But she's not involved in any other way? She wasn't there that night?'

'Their *mum?*'

I'm floundering around for an explanation, I know. None of it makes sense. Is Alice, sitting outside in the car ready to take me home, Lou and Benny's mother? If she is, why has she been doing this to me, pretending to be someone other than she really is, lying to me repeatedly? Why would she want to spend any time with me, unless she had some kind of ulterior motive?

Maybe she isn't who I think she is. Could there be another explanation for the keyring in the car? Maybe it isn't so unusual. Anyone could have one. They're probably sold in a shop on Gloucester Road. I try to remember everything I know about her. Do I know her surname? I'm sure it's on the ID she wears around her neck at the library. I would have noticed if it was Durand, wouldn't I?

'What does she look like?' I ask.

'What's this fixation with their mother?'

'Just answer me.'

'Tall, long dark hair. Kind of aloof, like she's looking down her nose at you.'

That describes her perfectly. 'Do you know anything else about her? What car she drives? What she does for a living?'

'Jeez, Mum. Chill out with the questions.' When I don't say anything else, he sighs. 'I think she works at a library.'

So it is her.

'No offence,' Kane continues, 'but we don't exactly spend all our time talking about our parents.' He glances at the people on the next table, before turning back to me. 'What's going on? Have you seen her or something?'

'Maybe. I . . . I don't know.' Suddenly my body freezes, like it used to when I realised I'd been going about a painting in completely the wrong way and I'd have to step back and bite down on the handle of my brush in frustration. What am I doing, talking to him about her like this? I can't tell him what's been going on.

What if I've done something to harm his case? What if I've said something I shouldn't? 'I was just wondering if I'd ever met her, that's all. I was curious.'

'Okay, well, I don't think you have.'

'Forget it. I'm just . . . stressed.' I look at his face properly for the first time since I got here. It's a relief to see that there are no new bruises. 'Why did they move you?'

'No idea.' He shrugs.

'It's got nothing to do with Wilko? You weren't getting threats?'

His eyes darken. 'Seriously, Mum, you need to drop this.'

'Drop what?' I say it slightly too loudly, and a woman at the table next to us looks over. I lower my voice. 'I've had enough of this. You're going to tell me who really pushed Lou. Okay?'

He glares at me across the table. 'Whatever happened to "the more you nag, the less they hear"? Wasn't that what you used to say? You're doing my head in with all these questions. Every time you visit, every time we speak.'

'It was Wilko, wasn't it?'

'You're obsessed. You think this is helping me when I get back to my cell? You think this makes me feel good the rest of the day?'

'I've been there, to the car park. I know it would be impossible for you to push him over the wall. You're too short. You couldn't have got him up and over—'

'What are you talking about?' He's looking at me with confusion, hands upturned in front of him. 'What do you mean, "up and over"?'

'You and Lou, standing there, in the car park. You couldn't have shoved him with enough force to lift him up over the wall and push him hard enough that he fell. Someone taller could have done, but not you.'

'But he wasn't standing in the car park.' Kane shakes his head and sighs. 'I thought you knew all of this.'

'I know bugger all, Kane, because you have barely told me a thing.' My voice wobbles and I have to remind myself not to shout. 'How could he not have been in the car park?'

'Lou was standing *on* the wall.'

I close my eyes and tap the bridge of my nose, trying to visualise what he is describing. If Lou was standing on the wall, then yes, I can see why the police would believe Kane could have pushed him over the edge. But they don't know him like I do. 'You didn't do it, though.'

I feel his hand on mine and open my eyes. 'Benny had gone to get ice for my face,' he says. 'Remember how bashed up it was? Lou had landed this one really hard punch. And Wilko, he left when we were still fighting, like ... I don't know, twenty minutes earlier. He wasn't there, Mum. And Benny wasn't there. It was just me and Lou. You need to face the facts. I'm not getting out of here.'

Wilko

17th August

He saw them as soon as he stepped out of the car.

Kane and Lou, smoking together round the corner from the pub, Lou with his back against the wall. They were both looking his way – they'd definitely clocked him. Shit.

As he slammed the door of the car, it pulled out of its parking space in the shadows of Welsh Back. It accelerated towards the harbourside, and Wilko felt his heart skip a beat.

He had no choice. He couldn't pretend it wasn't him, and he couldn't pretend they hadn't spotted him either, so he walked over. Kane still looked pissed off with Lou. Wilko wasn't usually interested in friendship dramas but he did wonder what the hell was going on with these two tonight. As Wilko got closer, Kane dropped his fag and extinguished it under his foot, handed Lou a plastic cup full of water and strode off, back round into King Street and into the Llandoger.

'Kane, mate – wait . . .' Wilko shouted after him but he either didn't hear or was ignoring him. Fucking hell. He'd have to go and talk to him in a minute. What did they think they'd seen? Maybe he was overreacting, maybe they were too drunk to have noticed, or too clueless to work out what he'd been up to.

Turning back to Lou, he saw he'd pulled his mobile out and was typing something, swaying slightly as he stepped away from the wall. Wilko's heart skipped another beat.

He covered the ground between them quickly and snatched the phone out of his friend's hand. 'Who you texting?'

Lou took a swig of water and shrugged.

Wilko looked down at the screen. There was no number, no name – but a draft message. He felt tension ease in his shoulders as he read it: *I'm a twat, too much to drink. Sorry. You look hot tonight.*

He deleted it and shoved the phone back against Lou's chest.

'Hey . . .' Lou mumbled as he slid it back into his pocket.

This damp, dark part of the street stank of vomit, and Wilko looked down to check he wasn't standing near any. Had Lou thrown up? What was he, fifteen? 'For fuck's sake, you're such an amateur,' he said, laughing. 'You realise you're never going to get a blowjob off her if you send messages like that?'

Lou shrugged again, took a puff on his fag and then lifted the cup, pointing in the direction of where Wilko had come from. 'Nice wheels.' As Wilko turned to look at him, Lou deliberately made eye contact and held it. 'Since when did you do business with Audi drivers?'

And suddenly he didn't look so drunk any more. He looked like he knew exactly what had been going on.

Wilko looked away first and pulled his T-shirt away from his chest, sticky with sweat. 'Since always, mate. Some of these students, they're right rich twats. Too much money. That guy, he wanted to know if he could pay on Daddy's credit card.' He laughed, but even as he did so he knew it made him sound nervous.

Lou wasn't smiling. The music in the Llandoger changed, or they turned the volume up a few notches, and the bass of the track filled the silence between them.

'It's not what it looks like.' He had to do something. He had to stop Lou running his mouth off to the wrong people.

'Oh, right,' Lou said, his voice heavy with sarcasm. 'Not an unmarked police car, then. My mistake.'

Lou was bigger than him but Wilko could take him if he needed to. And in this moment, he needed to get the message across. He grabbed him by the neck of his T-shirt and slammed his back up against the wall. Lou's cigarette and cup fell to the ground, the cool water splashing at Wilko's ankles. Lou turned his head away as Wilko pinned him there with his forearm against his chest. He didn't look scared – Wilko had hoped he would look scared.

'You say a word to anyone – and I mean anyone – and you're dead.' Some of his spittle landed on Lou's face, and Lou reached a hand up to wipe it away. Wilko let him go and stepped back. He felt better, his heartrate was slowing, his lungs felt like they were filling more easily. 'I don't have a choice, mate. It's this or prison.'

Lou hadn't moved from the wall, but he shifted his head now, just enough to shake it slightly. He scowled at Wilko.

'You know I got a suspended sentence last time?' Wilko stamped on Lou's plastic cup and it cracked under his foot. 'You know that, right?'

'Then go to prison, you idiot.' Lou stepped away from the wall and started walking back towards the pub. As he got to the corner of King Street, he turned back. 'What the fuck are you playing at? Simon's going to find out, you realise that?'

Wilko knew he was right. Simon was going to kill him. He was going to end up in the docks, or thrown over the suspension bridge. They'd said it would be over in a few months, but it had been five already. He was in deep and had nowhere to go.

He called out after Lou. 'Not if you don't tell him.'

Alice

12th September

Alice needed to speak to Benny.

The drive back to Bristol from Long Lartin had been awkward. She couldn't wait to get home and away from Indigo. For the second time in the space of a week, this woman had delivered a bombshell piece of information about her son. A piece of information that she, his mother, should have known about him.

What would she have told him, if she'd had the chance?

That she struggled to bond with him when she found out she was pregnant? That he was a mistake? By the time he had been growing inside her for nine weeks – when she found out she wasn't just tired because Benny was sleeping badly, that she wasn't just off her food because of a nasty stomach bug – Étienne had already threatened to move out, twice. She couldn't see how she would be able to love a child born out of that mess. And she had been right, hadn't she? Even once he was placed in her arms, it hadn't been as easy to find a space in her heart for him as it had been with Benny.

But when she'd driven to that clinic to meet Étienne and walked in to see him there waiting for her, his back turned, she had felt a change. She didn't even give her name at the reception. She just ran back out of the door, got in her car and drove. She drove, without knowing where she was going, but something was telling her to make for the seaside. It was like Lou, tiny nineteen-week-old Lou, was pushing her on and on to the water's edge. She drove all the way to Clevedon and wandered along the seafront, pulling her thick cardigan around her stomach to keep the baby warm; even in the spring sunshine it was chilly with the sea breeze, its saltiness filling her nostrils.

And then she saw it. The piano shop. The door was open, and she couldn't help herself. She'd not touched the keys of a piano since long before Étienne arrived in her life, and when she saw the beautiful upright standing against the wall by the window, she turned to the shop owner. 'Do you mind if I . . . ?'

He must have known she wasn't going to be spending any money that day. She had no bag with her, no purse that he would have been able to see. But she'd always remember his face, those kind eyes under thin grey eyebrows. He saw that she needed to play, and he let her.

She pulled the seat up to the keys, her round belly pressing against them, and started playing by heart. Mozart's *Fantasia in D Minor*. She began slowly, unsure that she would remember it, but her fingers hadn't forgotten. A lightness had filled her head, a total sense of calm. When she got to the sighs in the *adagio*, she remembered the way she'd been taught to play them – her wrist dropping on the A and floating up on the G sharp. But as soon as she started that section, Lou's tiny unborn feet started dancing, like popcorn bursting in her belly. It was the first time she had felt him kick. She pulled her fingers away from the keys and felt the shop owner's eyes on her, a gust on her face from the sea breeze through the open door. She held her hands to her stomach.

That was the moment she saw as the start of Lou. The moment she knew he had lived, that he would live, and she would do her best to love him – whatever it took.

But she'd had no idea how hard that would be.

*

When she got back to the house after dropping Indigo off, Benny wasn't there. It was only six o'clock – had he gone out for the evening already? He couldn't go on doing this. Étienne was nowhere to be found, either – luckily for him.

She didn't have the stomach for any food so changed into her pyjamas and climbed into bed in Lou's room, clutching his needle file in one hand and her tumbler in the other, taking a sip of its cool, clear contents. She switched the radio on and waited. It could be hours before Benny got home, but she would be ready to speak with him when he did.

Shortly before ten she heard coughs outside in the front garden and keys dropping on to the path. She got up and looked out of the window. Étienne. She closed her eyes. She couldn't speak to him, not until she'd had a chance to talk to Benny. She crept back into bed and listened as he let himself in and switched the TV on in the room below her. He'd be climbing under Lou's old sleeping bag on the sofa, settling in for the night. Why had she let him stay?

Turning the volume up on the radio to drown out any hint of Étienne, she focused – as she often did, when in search of calm – on her beloved prints, propped up on Lou's desk. The visual beauty of the first twenty bars of *La Campanella* never failed to make her smile – a bit of a musical joke with herself. She favoured listening to intricate, fiendish arrangements (none of the romantic arching melodies that were so popular) and this was one of the most technically challenging pieces of piano music that existed. The opening section, in her print, looked innocent enough, but turn the page and it was quite a different story. She had only ever managed to master small sections of it, her head bent for hours over the keys in her parents' sitting room. Next to the Liszt, the illustrated flowers of *Tragopogon pratensis* shone out like small yellow firework bursts. It used to grow in her parents' garden, and Alice would marvel at the way its flower heads opened at dawn only to twist closed again at noon, until her mother would rip them out of the ground. 'Blasted meadow salsify,' she would mutter. 'Plague of my garden.' As a shy child, Alice had wished she could shut herself away – no questions asked – every lunchtime, like these yellow blooms. They had never self-seeded into her own garden, and she'd never been able to bring herself to plant them. It felt like a betrayal; even considering it made her mother's words echo in her ears.

She closed her eyes, remembering the rest of her childhood garden. The rose arch tended with such care, and the tiny purple stars of *Crocus tommasinianus* naturalised in the lawn. The golden flowers on the *Forsythia x intermedia*, which appeared long before winter had even considered giving way to spring.

She woke up, her fingers still curled around Lou's needle file, to a commotion outside the front of the house, but wasn't quick enough to get there before Étienne did. She looked at the bathroom clock before she went downstairs, pulling her dressing gown on and slipping the file into her pocket: it was twelve thirty.

Étienne had already opened the door before she reached the bottom of the stairs, but she couldn't see who was there. He was speaking in a lowered voice to another man. Was that her father?

Étienne stepped to one side and Pops dragged Benny in, their arms wrapped around each other's shoulders, Benny mumbling that he was sorry. He stank of alcohol and was clutching his skateboard to his chest.

'What's going on?' Alice looked from her father to her son. 'Where have you two been?'

Étienne spoke first. 'David was driving through town—'

'I didn't ask you,' she snapped. '*David* is perfectly capable of telling me himself, aren't you, Dad?'

Her father looked from one of them to the other. 'Like Étienne said, I was driving through town and I saw Benny, almost passed out, sitting outside the car park.' Her father patted the side of Benny's head, resting on his shoulder. 'Queen Charlotte Street.'

'*C'est complètement inacceptable.*' Étienne wagged a finger in Benny's face. 'This is not the time for being out at all hours, drinking, whatever.'

Alice glared at him. 'You have no right to boss my son around. Leave this to me.' She took the skateboard out of Benny's hands and stroked the side of his cheek. It was rough with stubble – he hadn't shaved for days.

'*Ton fils?*'

'My son.'

Her father set Benny down on the bottom step and he slumped forward, his head in his hands.

'He is *our* son.'

'Leave this to me, Étienne.'

With an angry laugh, he went back into the living room, slamming the door.

'What is he doing here?' her father whispered, his eyes searching hers in the dark of the hallway. 'I didn't know he was staying. Are you . . . ?'

'Thanks, Dad. I've got it from here.' She looked away from him, to Benny, who was swaying slightly and groaning. 'Thank you for bringing him home.'

'Why won't you let me help you? Alice?' He put a hand on her arm.

'I've got it from here.' She turned and kissed him on the cheek. 'You get home. It's late.'

He shook his head and let himself out.

'Drink this.'

Alice handed Benny a strong black coffee. She had managed to lift him to his feet and walk him through to the back room, setting him back down again on one of the rattan chairs around the kitchen table.

Benny screwed up his face but took a sip.

Slowly, mouthful by mouthful, he drank the whole cup, eyes clearing as he did so. They sat in silence for at least ten minutes before Alice spoke to him again.

'You've been going there every night.'

He nodded.

'How do you get there?'

He shrugged. 'Skate. Bus.'

She pulled her dressing gown around her.

'Sorry, Mum.'

She had to do it now, before she lost her nerve. While he had the alcohol in his blood, the truth was within reach. She played with the belt of her gown.

'Lou found out something about me.'

He lifted his head.

'When I was pregnant with him, I nearly . . .' She pinned her arms against her stomach. *Tiny unborn feet, dancing.* 'I came quite close to having an abortion.' She studied the stitching around the pocket of her gown, beyond her folded arms. A thread was coming loose. 'It was a difficult time, with your dad. I didn't know if bringing another child into the family was a fair thing to do.'

That was only half of the reason, but she wasn't ready to explain it all to him.

She uncrossed her arms. 'That was why he was fighting with Kane.'

'Yes.' Benny put his mug down on the table.

'You knew, too.'

Neither of the boys had said anything. They'd known and not said anything.

'How did you find out?' Benny's words were only slightly slurred.

'That doesn't matter.'

'Has Kane told the police all of this?'

'I don't know.' It hadn't occurred to her that more people than her sons and Kane knew the secret she was most ashamed to share. 'Who told you?'

There was only one person, really, who could have done. But she was holding on to a shred of hope that he hadn't betrayed her in this unthinkable way.

For the first time in the conversation, she looked straight at Benny.

He twisted his hands in his lap, meeting her gaze. 'Dad.'

She pursed her lips. 'Why?' She wanted to ask, *What gave him the right?* And, *How could he do that to me?* She wanted to scream. Had he told them that he'd wanted to get rid of the baby, too?

'We went to see him, back in July. You were at work. He was over for a few days gigging in Bristol and said we should meet up.'

She nodded. Finally, he was telling her about this secret get-together.

'Lou was gunning for him.'

She curled her feet against the cold lino. 'After he told you?'

'No, before. That's why he wanted to see him. He had a huge go at him about not being around for us.'

'Oh.' This was not what she had expected. The boys always idolised Étienne. Especially Lou.

'He was going on about everything Dad never did. No birthday cards, not showing up to take us out when he'd promised. And then Dad got really pissed off and said, out of nowhere, "And your mother's perfect, is she?" Then he goes, "Well, let me tell you the truth. Your mother didn't want you."'

'I didn't think I did. I was wrong.' Alice stood, pushed her chair under the table, picked up Benny's mug and took it over to the sink.

'That's what I told Lou. I told him you wouldn't have kept him if you didn't want to. I told him you must have had a good reason to even consider it in the first place.'

'You did?' Her heart felt a little lighter to hear him say so. 'How did he take it all?'

'He was . . . he was angry.' Benny's diction was getting clearer by the second as the caffeine hit home. 'At first. He said . . . Do you really want to hear this?'

'Yes.' She kept her back to him, rinsing the mug out in the sink. The water against her skin was a welcome warmth and she let it run longer than she needed to.

'He said it made sense. That he had always known something wasn't right between you two, and he never felt like you really wanted him around. Dad said . . . he told Lou . . .'

She waited, but he didn't continue. 'What? What else did your father say?'

'He said you never bonded with him when he was a baby. And that had started before he was born, back before you changed your mind about the abortion. He said you called Lou a – a parasite.'

Alice closed her eyes. Why would Étienne tell him that? What good could it possibly do? She *had* felt like Lou was a parasite; she'd felt her body wasn't her own, she'd felt heavier than she had done with Benny, more tired, more drained. But after that day in Clevedon she'd felt better, even if just a little. Even if just for a while. 'I see.'

'Is that all you've got to say about it?'

She turned around to face him. 'What do you mean?'

'I've just told you something that . . . Well, most people would be pretty upset to find that out. And look at you.' He held his hand out towards her.

What did he want her to say?

'I don't get you, Mum. I used to think everyone's parents were like this. But it's just you. You never talk to us about how we're feeling, you never hug us.'

'You don't like being hugged.'

'You never say you're sad, you never laugh, you never say you're happy, you never get really angry. I want to shake you.' Benny stood and smacked his hand against the doorframe as he walked into the hallway. 'And then, the way you've been since Lou died . . .'

Alice left the mug in the sink and followed him.

'Pops says you weren't like this when you were younger.' He started climbing the stairs. 'I wish I'd got a chance to know you then.'

'Benny, wait,' she whispered, glancing at the living-room door. The last thing she needed was Étienne getting involved right now. Benny turned at the top of the stairs and looked down at her.

'I do feel things,' she said. 'Is that what you're suggesting? That I don't get emotional like you?'

'Then show me.'

'That's not what I do. It doesn't mean I don't feel anything.'

'I haven't seen you sit down and cry about it. Not once. Do you even care that—'

She climbed a few stairs. 'Look at me, Benny.' Was this what he wanted? She plucked at her pyjama top, lifted clumps of her dishevelled hair. 'There isn't a minute I am not thinking about him. Or you. I want to know what went on in that car park because you won't tell me, and I want to make sure you're not in any kind of trouble.'

'I'm not in trouble.' He pushed the door open into his room and paused, lowering his head. 'Look, forget I said anything. You can't change how you are.'

'Exactly. I . . .' She looked past him and saw a couple of hold-alls and a small suitcase, packed with clothes and books. His shelves looked emptier. Her chest tightened. 'You're all ready to go, then?'

It wasn't that she had forgotten he was going to university, but this moment had crept up on her.

'Pops is driving me up on Monday afternoon.'

'You don't want me to take you?'

'No. Thanks. Pops said he's happy to.' He wouldn't look at her. He may have told her to forget he'd said anything, but he wasn't forgetting it himself.

Everything she had ever done, it was for those boys. Did he not know that? The evening of her first day surviving as a single mother, she had stood over their two cots, one either side of the bedroom they shared, watching them sleep. Benny, sucking his thumb until it slid out of his mouth. Tiny Lou, on his back with one arm raised on either side of his head, as if in surrender. She had promised them she would make sure they became better men than their father. And then, later, each infrequent time she saw Étienne in those early years after he left, growing increasingly scruffier from a life on the road, the effects of nightly drinking sessions taking their toll, she would repeat her vow. Every time he asked her for money because he was 'struggling'. Every time he informed her of a change of address because he'd been kicked out for not paying his rent on time. Every time (more recently, when he'd finally started to get his life together) he cancelled last minute on weekends he was due to spend with them. She had promised them silently, again and again: *You'll be better men.* They wouldn't be shirkers or spongers or deadbeats. They might be unlucky enough to have his nature, but they had her nurture.

'I'm going to crash.' Benny had his back to her, dragging his curtains closed. 'Night, Mum.'

She backed away, on to the landing, and nearly tripped over Étienne's bag, which he had been keeping outside the bathroom door. That bastard. How could he have done this to her, and to Lou?

Benny shut his bedroom door and she was alone.

Crouching on the floor, she emptied Étienne's bag with shaking hands. Bastard, bastard, bastard. She took one of his shirts and, using the needle file from her pocket, ripped it down both the front panels. The smooth tear of the fabric soothed her, and she ripped it a third time down the back. Looking for something else to destroy, she found his passport, tucked into a leather pouch full of papers and receipts. She leafed through them. Food receipts, bar tabs, hostel bills from across Europe. Then: his touring schedule for the summer. She ran a finger down it, past a series of dates across France. San Sebastian on the fifth of August. Barcelona, a couple of days later. Avilés, Maliano, Madrid, then a couple in the Netherlands, all within the next week. Then, across the bottom, underneath the final date on the fifteenth of August: *END OF TOUR*. She turned the paper over. That couldn't be right. He had still been touring when Lou died, hadn't he? That's why he hadn't been able to come straight to Bristol? He'd been abroad.

Frantically, she started sifting through the rest of the receipts, looking for proof of the tour continuing or a new one beginning.

All she found was a booking confirmation for an Airbnb, only a few miles away. He had requested to check in from the sixteenth of August, the day before Lou died.

Indigo

13th September

My feet are getting cold on the damp grass, my backside has gone numb. The musky fox spray smell seems to be getting more intense rather than fading the longer I sit here on this wobbly wooden chair I found down the road.

But I'm not moving, not until I see that bitch come out of the house. I will sit here all night if I have to, until she emerges to buy a pint of milk for her breakfast. She won't see me, hidden away in this little alleyway across the road. Nobody has noticed me so far, though several people have walked past my hiding place.

When she dropped me off at home I paced around the house for an hour, Lucian trotting around at my heels, as I tried to piece everything together. I wrote down everything I could remember about our encounters.

There were all the times at the library.

Then I'd seen her by the car park, in town.

What had she really been doing in that building across the road? Now, her behaviour started to make sense: she was hiding something, but it wasn't an embarrassing medical appointment. It must have been something to do with Kane's case.

But what? And why was she doing anything at all? Kane had been charged and had admitted to killing her son. What more did she want?

And why would she have offered me a lift, the mother of the boy she thought had killed Lou? Why had she talked to me at all in the library, if she knew who I was? She could have asked a colleague to deal with me.

By eleven it was clear I wasn't going to be able to sleep. I have to confirm that I'm not going crazy, that she is really *her*. So I cycled up here. I wasn't sure, at first, what I was going to do when I arrived. Scrawl abuse across her door? Scream at her from the street? No. I'm not ready for her to know I'm on to her yet. I rode around the block a few times – up to Kellaway, down Bishop Road – slowing down when I passed the house where I spoke to Benny. Her car is parked up the road, but not outside that house, even though there are spaces. It's not enough to count as proof – I need to see her there.

Then I spotted this little lane, leading up to the garages round the back of the houses opposite hers. I left my bike propped up against the fence a few metres down and went back on to the street to retrieve this chair, which someone had left outside their house with a sign taped to it saying, in black letters now running blue in the evening damp, *Free to a good home*.

And for the last hour I have sat here, in the shadows. Waiting. Something tells me she is a night bird, nocturnal and creeping, and I will see her open that blue door before the morning. The dark circles I've seen under her eyes tell me she doesn't sleep much, like me. Good.

A car pulls up and parks in one of the spaces outside the house. A grey-haired man gets out of the driver's side, goes round to the passenger door and pulls out another, younger man. I straighten in my chair and hold my breath. That's Benny.

What's going on?

Benny slumps in the older man's arms, and he has to half drag him to the front door. *Don't have keys. Make her come to the door.*

Benny groans and stumbles, crashing against a flower pot,

and the grey-haired man picks him up, saying, 'Woah, you're okay, you're okay.' Slouching against him once more, Benny starts singing, incoherently but loudly.

The door opens and another man appears on the other side of it. Older than Benny, but younger than the man who drove the car. About my age. Alice's age. There's still no sign of her. He beckons Benny and the grey-haired man inside. That must be Benny and Lou's dad. Who else could it be? Her brother? Something tells me no. She's been lying about being a single mother, too. The door closes softly, and I'm left alone out here once again.

A few minutes later the older man re-emerges, closes the door behind him, and stands on the doorstep for a moment, as if considering going back inside. Who is he? Alice's father? What has happened here? Benny looked wasted. Had the two of them been out drinking? No. This man looked sober, and he was driving.

He gets back into his car, sitting for several minutes without turning on the engine. I could just about make out his shadowy shape, looking up at the house. He's uneasy, he wants to go back in. But eventually he does drive off, and the road is silent again, until the rain starts.

I came out in my fluoro cycling jacket, but I can't exactly sit here spying on her house in that, so all I have on is a T-shirt, fleece and jeans. It doesn't take long for them all to get soaked through. I start shivering. This is miserable. What am I doing here? She's not going to come out tonight. And I'm sure it is her, anyway. I don't need to see her here.

But now that I'm here, I can't bring myself to go. I'm cold and exhausted, but I think of my Kane. My reason for doing this. I think of the sketches I did of him before I came here tonight. I went to the shed and dragged the easel out, back into my studio. I clipped several pieces of thick A2 paper on to a board and opened up a new pack of charcoal. I sketched with a fever, with the kind of speed and heat I get when I know I am doing good work. I caught the beauty of his eyes but the fear in his features, the way prison has sucked the youth out of him. Then I tossed that portrait to one side and was faced with a new sheet of blank paper.

And I started drawing her, from memory. Her dark hair always drawn back into a ponytail or plait. Her wide-set almond eyes, high cheekbones. Straight nose. The lips that never smile. I drew her once, twice, three times, screwing up each sketch and throwing it to the floor. I couldn't get her right; I couldn't draw someone I didn't understand. I couldn't capture the deceit or the coldness.

So, leaving the fourth attempt clipped to the board, I grabbed my jacket and wheeled my bike out of the door. I needed to see her face again, to work out what I was missing.

I look at my watch. Nearly an hour has passed since the man drove away. The rain is lighter now, but I can't feel my nose or my fingertips. This is stupid. I stand up, lift my jacket off the saddle of my bike and shake off the water. Behind me, I hear a quiet click. I turn, hiding the bright yellow of my coat behind my back.

It's her.

In the orange streetlight I can see her face. She's in pyjamas and a dressing gown, no shoes. She has a large dark holdall in her hands and throws it out on to her front path, followed by what looks like a guitar case. She crouches down to unzip both of them. I press my back into the fence, but I needn't worry – she isn't looking around. She doesn't care who is watching her.

She disappears back into the house, then comes out again, this time with what looks like a watering can. It's that kind of size and shape. But there's no spout on it. What is she doing?

She unscrews something on it and lifts up one end, letting liquid run freely from it into the bags. She coughs and puts her forearm over her face.

As she screws the cap back on and goes back inside, the smell wafts over the road towards me.

The sweet, intoxicating and unmistakable smell of petrol.

Alice

13th September

A lice opened the living-room door without making a sound and tiptoed across the rug to the window. She pulled back the curtain slightly, the streetlight outside throwing a wedge of orange across the room, lifted the handle on the window and pushed it open.

The room smelled of him. Of skin and sweat and his after-shave. Once, this combination would have made the hairs on the back of her neck stand on end.

She stood, looking down at him as he slept on the sofa. She clenched her back teeth so hard her jaw ached and lifted the unzipped sleeping bag covering him, climbing underneath. There was just enough space for the two of them on the sofa – her body pressed up against his, their faces so close their noses almost touched. He shifted, opened his eyes.

'You?' Étienne spoke groggily.

'Were you expecting someone else?' She put her hand on his cheek, the stubble rough under her palm. She wanted to press down harder, leave an imprint.

'I thought you weren't interested.'

'I wasn't.'

She could feel his breath hot against her lips, his hand sliding down her back. 'It's been good to have you back here,' she said, moving her fingers to his neck, the way he'd always liked her to.

Étienne moaned.

'It was so good of you to call off the tour.'

He pushed forward his chin, trying to find her lips with his, but she pressed a finger on to them. A few seconds longer. She could already smell it; it wouldn't be long before he would, too.

She looked into his eyes as he moved his hand to her thigh, drawing her leg over the top of his.

Any minute now.

She stroked her bare foot up his calf, and he groaned again.

Then he sniffed. In the darkness, she smiled.

His wandering hand paused above her knee. 'Can you smell that?'

'Don't stop.'

'Is that petrol?'

'There was an accident. It doesn't matter. Don't stop.'

He laughed and resumed stroking her thigh. 'I knew you'd come round. *Comme au bon vieux temps.*'

She recoiled at his expression. She didn't remember their time together as the good old days. 'I spilled some of Lou's petrol over your bag, that's all.'

His hand stopped again. 'My bag?' Even in the dark she could see his eyes widen. 'Which bag?'

His hand gripped her leg, a little too hard.

'Which bag, Alice?'

'Mostly just your guitar case. Some on your holdall. It's okay. I left it outside the front door, to get rid of the smell from the house.'

His body was stiffening. 'The petrol? Or my bag?'

'Don't let that spoil . . . this.' Alice moved her fingers on to his chest. 'I'm sure it won't be too bad.'

'How much did you spill?' He sat up now, squinting down at her as she lay on the edge of the sofa. 'Do you know how much that guitar cost me?'

'Come back. It won't damage it, will it? There might just be a smell for a while.' She couldn't help but smile again.

She could see the conflict in his face – he was not one to turn down what he thought she was offering.

'*Je vais jeter un coup d'oeil.*' He let the sleeping bag fall down on to her and left the room, wearing only his boxer shorts. She lay there for a moment, listening.

The porch door opened, followed by the front door. She got up and closed the window to Étienne's muttered swearing outside.

When she got to the front door, he was crouched outside in the damp, holding his guitar up as liquid dripped off it.

'This wasn't a little spill, Alice. How did this happen?' He looked up, just in time to see the front door slam in his face.

He pummelled it with his fist. 'Alice!'

She returned to her viewing point at the window in the living room and watched as he turned away from the door and rummaged into the depths of his holdall.

She tapped on the glass and held up his keys. 'Looking for these?'

Even though he spoke under his breath, Alice recognised the French word for 'bitch'. He'd said it to her enough times before.

'Let me back in. What the hell are you doing? Look at me.' He gestured at his underdressed body. 'It's cold.'

'Never come back here again.'

'Alice, you can't do this.'

'Where were you when Lou died?'

He looked down at his guitar.

'Why did you let me believe you were still touring?' Steve's bedroom curtains twitched, next door. Let him look, let him hear what a bastard Étienne was. She didn't care if the whole street woke up. 'Were you even planning to see the boys while you were here?'

'I was catching up with Joe and Lianne. And I intended to see the boys, that's why I stayed in Bristol, but I didn't think Lou would want to see me,' he said, almost too quietly for her to hear. 'The last time didn't go well. Lou was so rude to me. I didn't get round to calling them, and then . . .' He lay the guitar back in its case. 'Alice, *s'il te plaît*. Let me in. *On peut pas parler comme ça.*'

'Two weeks, Étienne. It took you nearly two weeks to show up here after your son died.'

'*J'ai foiré*, okay? *J'ai complètement foiré*. Like I do all the time.'

Messed up? He'd done more than mess up. Was she meant to feel sorry for him? She started to close the curtain, but he put a palm up against the glass. The pink skin pressed flat into patches of yellow-white.

'I didn't think I'd be any use to you, if I came here,' he said.

'So why did you come back at all?'

'At least open this window, so we can talk more easily.' He tilted his head, his eyes pleading. She looked away. 'Joe talked me into it. He said I could help you. Even a loser like me.' He tapped the glass, and when she looked back at him, he smiled.

'Is that meant to be funny?'

The smile dropped. 'I'm just going to get a T-shirt on. Okay? Don't go anywhere.' He turned and crouched down, searching through his bag.

'You shouldn't have told him, Étienne,' she said to his back. *Looking at his back, then turning and walking away. Driving without knowing where she was going.*

Pulling a light-coloured T-shirt over his head, he turned towards her slowly. She could see from the look on his face that he knew exactly what she was talking about. He nodded, unable to look her in the eye. 'I didn't mean to. I was so angry with him; he was saying he hated me, what a bad father I'd been . . .'

She shouted through the glass, smacking her hand against the window frame. 'Kids say those things all the time! If you'd stuck around to see them grow up, you'd know that.'

'I'm sorry. Look, I'll go. We can talk tomorrow.'

'I never want to see you again.'

'Alice.'

'You're not invited to Lou's funeral.'

'*Arrête, Alice. Tu ne peux pas faire ça.* You shouldn't stop a father—'

'You shouldn't have told him,' she repeated.

She closed the curtain, sat down on the far end of the sofa, avoiding the warmth at the other end left by their bodies, ignoring Étienne tapping on the window and calling her name. She pulled her mobile phone out of her dressing-gown pocket and wrote a message to her father.

Étienne's gone.

Indigo

13th September

I'm cradling a cup of mint tea, inhaling the steam and telling myself it will wake me up just as well as a coffee would. I was all right on the cycle into town; the skies have cleared and the air is fresh and clean, that after-rain smell is rising up from the roads and the trees look a little greener than they did yesterday. But as soon as I sat down in this café and started reading through my bundle of notes about Alice, my eyelids got heavy. I can't stop blinking. I stayed a while outside her house last night after she poured petrol over the bags – long enough to see the man I assume to be the boys' father emerge in his underwear and start banging on the door after she closed it behind him. I wanted to help him, but I couldn't be seen there. While his back was turned, his fists slamming on the door, I abandoned my chair and wheeled my bike out on to the road as quietly as I could, then cycled home. Had she just kicked him out? Why? I pull the article about Lou to the top of my pile of papers and read it through again to see if there's something I've missed. Or at least, that's what I tell myself I am doing. I'm not procrastinating. I'm not putting off walking round into Queen Charlotte Street and into the office block I saw Alice leaving on Monday.

Picking up my helmet from the seat next to me, I drain my cup and emerge into blazing sunshine. As I pass the car park, I'm glad to have my pile of papers to clench my hand around.

Seeing the place where I waved at her, I remember her lies and it makes me want to punch something. There was me, thinking that despite her peculiarities, we could maybe, just maybe, be friends.

Lost in my anger with her, I'm halfway up the steps into the building before I realise it, looking up at a sign above the glass doors: Frasier House.

I repeat the lines in my head as I push open the door.

'Can I help you, madam?' the receptionist asks.

'Oh yes, I do hope so. I have an appointment at midday, but I can't for the life of me remember the name of the company. I'm sure this was the address. What companies are based here? Maybe I can work it out if we do it that way round.' I laugh nervously.

The receptionist frowns. 'There are several. Samson Recruitment, Cable Education, Aspect . . . What kind of business was it exactly?' The electric fan on her desk turns slowly towards her, blowing her fringe across her forehead.

'Oh well, it was a complicated one . . .' I should have thought this through more. 'Let me just check I definitely don't have the appointment details written down in my diary.'

I put my papers and helmet on the counter in between us and pull my pannier bag off my back, to make a show of looking for my diary, which I know is on the dining table at home. I haven't got much of a schedule to keep at the moment.

'It's really very silly of me to have forgotten. It was an appointment for a kind of medical thing, a counselling session, you know?'

I'm not going to get the information I want this way, I can see that now, but I feel the need to not be exposed as a liar by this woman.

She taps her fingers on her desk. 'We don't really have anything along those lines – not that I can think of.' There's the flickering sound of paper falling, and she says, 'Oh dear! Oh, let me . . .'

I look up. The receptionist has disappeared and I peer over the counter to see her crouching on the floor by her desk, scrabbling around to pick up pieces of paper. My pieces of paper.

'I don't know what I'd do without that fan, but it does have a habit of doing things like this.'

'You don't have to do that, please, let me.' I try, but I can't get round behind her desk.

She slowly sits up again, looking at the top of the pile. When she passes it all back to me, she is looking at me with a very different expression.

'Tell me more about this appointment.'

I look down at my papers. The article about Lou is on top. 'Yes, I . . . it must be somewhere else, as you say, if you don't have a counselling service here.' I pick up my helmet, and stuff my notes into my bag. 'I'm so sorry for bothering you.'

'Are you a friend of that boy's mother?' The receptionist stands up now and is pointing at me angrily. 'She was in here a few days ago. I told her—'

I back towards the door. 'No, I'm not friends with her. I'm . . . I'm just interested in the case, that's all. Is this about the article? Honestly, I'm just interested.'

'You all need to leave poor Cassie alone, all right? Stop this harassment. That's what it is. Harassment.'

'Cassie?'

'I'm calling the police.'

'No, please.' The last thing Kane needs is his mother getting arrested. 'I'm going, I'm going. I didn't want to cause any trouble. I'm sorry.'

I stumble out of the door and down the steps, then half-walk, half-run down the road, looking over my shoulder every few steps.

I'm even more confused than I was before I went in there. Who has Alice been harassing, and what does it have to do with our sons?

Desperate to get away from that building, I ram my helmet on to my head and grapple with my bike lock. As I put it in my bag, my phone starts to ring. The name flashing on the screen is Clive Parsons. He hasn't called me with any updates about Kane's case for over a week. I fumble with it to press the button to accept the call.

'Hello? Clive? What's happened?'

His voice is calm and cool. 'Mrs Owen. How are you?'

'I'm fine. Absolutely fine.' I swing my pannier bag on to my back, only realising when it is too late that I didn't zip it back up again. My notes, purse and bottle spew out on to the pavement around the bike rack, and I drop to my knees to pick it all up.

'Are you sure? You sound a little flustered.'

'What's happened to Kane? Is there news? Why are you calling?'

'Everything is okay, Mrs Owen. I'm just calling to let you know that Kane's sentencing date has been brought forward by a week.'

'A week?' I stuff everything back into my bag, but stay crouching on the pavement, dropping my head into my hands.

'Yes. It'll be a week Tuesday.'

I pull my helmet off my head and throw it to the ground.

'We're running out of time, that's what you're saying?'

'Running out of time?'

'To prove he is innocent.'

He sighs. 'Mrs Owen.'

'I have information for you. I know who one of the other people was. One of the others there that night. Can that help Kane's case?'

'He's already pleaded guilty, Mrs Owen.'

'He's called Wilko. I don't know his real name. But it can't be that hard to find out.'

'Mrs Owen, your son has admitted the crime. A new witness is not going to help matters, not now. I'm sorry, but—'

'I'll talk to him, when I next see him. I will make him see sense.'

'About that.' His tone has changed abruptly. He sounds less calming, less patronising. More awkward – as if he is squirming in his seat.

'What?'

'Kane's asked me to pass a message on to you.'

'Yes?'

'He's finding your feelings about this all a little . . .' He pauses. 'Stressful to deal with. With that in mind, he's—'

'Why couldn't he tell me that himself?' I run my hand through my hair, massaging my scalp with my fingertips, pressing just hard enough to make myself wince.

'He has taken you off his visitor list.'

Alice

14th September

This was why Alice hated taking time off. One week away from work and her inbox was full of emails. When she'd requested compassionate leave, she'd told Julie she'd be back in on Saturday, when she knew they were particularly short-staffed, but she'd ended up having to be holed up in her office all morning. She really needed to get out to help her colleagues deal with customers, but she couldn't possibly do that without dealing with this backlog first.

Her efficiency levels were not helped by her mind wandering off every few minutes. Benny had hardly spoken to her since the early hours of yesterday morning. He must have passed out in his room, because he didn't respond to Étienne's banging on the front door. She'd left him a note on the breakfast bar, telling him that his dad had gone to stay with friends, but he hadn't come to find her to ask why.

Her mobile phone buzzed on her desk. It was a text message telling her she had a voicemail. Why did her phone do this? Why hadn't it rung? She had full signal and yet no missed call. She hated picking up the phone, but if there was one thing she resented more than that, it was voicemail. You never knew what the person was going to be saying, and there was always the assumption that you would call them back. It was probably Étienne, again, leaving a message telling her that she couldn't stop him coming to the funeral. That would be the fifth one since yesterday morning.

She could ignore it. But what if it wasn't Étienne? Screwing her eyes shut, she held the phone to her ear. 'Hi Alice, it's Margaret. Just letting you know we're all set for Thursday next week for you to meet with Kane, if that is still okay with you. Call me or text me if you've got any questions.'

Alice sat back in her chair. Meeting Kane had seemed like such a good idea. But the more time she spent with Indigo, the more uneasy she felt about it. Should she come clean with her and call the meeting off? There had been too many close calls. And this person was not her. Alice Hyde did not lie. Alice Hyde was an honest, dependable, law-abiding citizen. Not a fraud. But then again, did she have to admit to Indigo who she was in order to fix this? She could just stop seeing her, spend time in her other libraries for a while, refuse to answer if Indigo called asking for another lift.

But then there was Harry Wilkinson. Why was he so against her meeting Kane? Was he serious with his threats? For Benny's sake, she should at least consider calling it off.

Carolyn poked her head around the door. 'There's a lady here to see you.'

Alice immediately thought of Indigo. 'Can you tell her I'm not here?'

'I've already said you're in your office.' Carolyn grimaced. 'I could say that you're busy, but . . .'

'But what?'

'She did say you were expecting her. She's got a piece of paper with your name on, and the address of the library, and today's date.'

'I'm not expecting anyone. She's definitely asking for me?' Alice opened up her online calendar. Had someone booked her an appointment without telling her? 'There's nothing here.'

'Shall I ask her to come back later?'

Alice sighed and stood up. 'No, I'll just have to finish these later.' She followed Carolyn downstairs.

Carolyn pointed at a woman standing with her back to Alice, by the crime fiction section. She was tall and skinny. As Alice approached her, she spun around. Her clear, line-free skin told Alice she was young, maybe in her early thirties – but she had a haunted look about her which made her seem older.

Alice was certain she had never seen her before. 'Can I help you?' she asked.

The woman rubbed her arm, looking around her. 'Can we talk somewhere?' She had a soft Northern Irish lilt to her voice which confused Alice even more as she tried to place her. Did she know anyone with this accent?

'Can I ask what this is about?'

'Is there somewhere . . . ?'

Alice sighed. 'Yes, okay. Over here.'

She gestured towards the comfortable chairs by the front windows and they sat down. The woman was still looking around her every few seconds and seemed poised to run out of the library at any moment. She clasped her hands together and turned to Alice. 'I'm sorry about your son.'

Alice stared at her. 'What did you say your name was?'

'I can't tell you.'

'What's this all about?'

The other woman stood up. 'I shouldn't have come.'

It was then that Alice saw the piece of paper she was holding. It had Alice's handwriting on it. Her name and the name of the library.

'Wait. Is that . . . ?' She pointed at it. 'She passed on my message?'

'Yes.'

'Please, sit back down.' Alice felt the blood draining from her cheeks. 'Thank you, so much. Thank you for coming. I'm sorry if I was rude, I was confused, I didn't know . . .'

The woman lowered herself into the chair.

'You work in Frasier House?' Alice asked.

'I've only come down here to stop people showing up at our front desk, okay? Do you promise me there'll be nobody else?'

'I won't come back, you have my word.'

'Okay.' She smoothed her skirt and crossed her legs. 'I was working that night . . . when was it . . . August the . . . ?'

'Seventeenth.' Alice couldn't help feeling jealous as she finished the woman's sentence. Alice would never have the luxury of forgetting that date, or the chance of experiencing it as a happy day, ever again. Every time those words – *the seventeenth of August* – came into her mind or rolled off her tongue, she felt the cogs shift strangely inside her head. Each time, her mind tried anew to shift the connotations of that day from the breathless excitement of waking up as a little girl or of buying herself her favourite apple Danish as a birthday treat on the way back from work – to her son, falling and afraid, to his body lying in the road, to that knock on the door in the middle of the night. She would welcome the disappointment she had felt on that day last month, she would gladly live through the same every year for the rest of her life, if it meant that the seventeenth of August could return to its rightful place, etched in her mind as the day she came into the world, rather than the day Lou left it; if it meant that he could still be here, the cause of her disappointment, but alive. 'It was the seventeenth of August.'

'Yes. I was standing by the window. And I saw these lads. I mean, I heard them first. Our window was open, and they were yelling. Over in the car park.'

'And one of them was—Hang on . . .' Alice took her phone out of her back pocket and found a photo of Kane, the shot she had taken of his Facebook page. 'One of them was this man, yes?'

The woman nodded. 'I think so. I couldn't see that clearly.'

'And you saw him push my son over the wall?'

She started biting at her nails. 'That's not what I saw.'

The walls of the library drew closer, pressing in around them.

'I wanted to tell you, so you knew the truth. Your son, he wasn't pushed.'

'What?' Alice rubbed the back of her neck. 'Are you saying he jumped?'

'No. Maybe. I don't know.'

Alice stood, tapping out a frantic triplet beat against the knuckles of her left hand.

'I've upset you.' The woman picked up her handbag again. 'I shouldn't have come here.'

Alice put her hand out. 'I'm not upset, it's all right. Stay, please. I'm just not sure I follow. What are you saying happened?'

'I've said enough already. I was several metres away; I wasn't close enough to see properly.' She stood up, clutching her bag to her chest.

'But you're sure this man . . .' That word suddenly felt wrong. 'This *boy*. He didn't push my son?' Alice held up her mobile phone again to show the photo.

'Yes. Nobody pushed him.'

'You need to go to the police. This is important information.'

'No.' The woman started backing away from Alice.

'You have to. There's a boy about to be sent to prison for this.'

Alice's colleagues and other library users were watching them now; they were talking loudly enough for the whole ground floor to hear. She didn't care.

'I don't trust the police, okay? They didn't keep me safe before and they'll screw this up, too. I don't want my name in the press.' She kept backing away, towards the main doors.

'Your name won't be in the press, it's fine, I'm sure they won't need to—'

248

'You can't promise me that.'

She was right, Alice had no idea what would happen.

'I don't want anything to do with the police.' With that, she walked out of the doors.

Alice stood there, rooted to the ground, staring at the mystery woman's back as she left. She looked at the phone in her hand, Kane's photo still on the screen – at the piercing blue of his eyes, the childishness of the curls falling over his face. He was just a kid.

A kid about to go to prison for a crime he had not committed.

She ran out of the library on to the street and chased after the woman.

Indigo

15th September

I'm pathetic. I've been over to that liar's house three times since Friday, and I stood outside the library yesterday morning for half an hour, trying to find the courage to go in.

I bottled it every single time.

I wish I could believe it when I tell myself that it is because I am too angry, and that I'm worried what I would do to her, what I would say to her. The reality is that I'm more scared what she will say to me.

I came home yesterday and sat in the living room, curtains drawn, looking through photo albums of Kane through the years, the yellowed cellophane covering each page crackling against my fingertips. Then I sat at the dining table to write him a letter, begging him to call or let me visit again. I drank a bottle of wine as I wrote, crossing lines out and screwing up dozens of attempts, throwing them on the floor. I woke at two this morning with my head on the table, the final version of my letter stuck to my cheek.

This afternoon I have been trying to clean the place up a bit while I get my head straight. I'm stacking dirty plates in the kitchen, with Lucian hovering at my ankles hoping to be fed, when he suddenly stops rubbing against my legs and stands stock-still. He's staring towards the hallway. 'What is it?' I ask. 'Have you heard something?' He sprints off towards the front door. As

I follow him, I hear a shuffling sound outside. I'm not expecting anybody, so I open the door ready to turn away whichever charity rep or local political canvasser is making their way down our street.

Instead, it is Alice I see on the doorstep, holding my Sunday paper out towards me.

I take it from her and throw it behind me on to the hallway floor, where there is already a pile of unopened post and take-away flyers.

'It was on the step,' she says. 'I haven't seen you for a few days; I wanted to check you were okay.'

I laugh. 'Sure you did.'

Confusion flashes across her face, but she continues. 'Can I come in?'

'No.' I say it louder than I mean to. Mr Daniels down the road is cleaning his car and looks over at us. I don't care. I've given up caring what everyone thinks of me. Let them look. Let them think what they want.

Her face goes pale now. 'You know.' She takes a step backwards.

'I trusted you. I thought you were my friend.' I feel more alive than I have in weeks as I pick up the pace and volume. 'I've lost my son, too. No matter what you think he has done, I am not to blame. I didn't deserve this from you.'

She stands there, staring at the path. 'I was coming here to tell you.'

'Do you even have any friends?' I spit the words. 'How can anyone stand you? Let me tell you a few truths. You understand that word? Truth?'

She nods.

'You've got the emotional capacity of a fly. You're rude. You're cold. You're bloody hard work. Please pass on my sympathies to your son. Having you as a mother must be hell.'

She flinches at this, but instead of satisfaction I feel as bad as if someone has just said those words to me. This isn't the person I want to be. I'm shaking, and my whole body is hot. Alice looks up at me, but I can't hold her gaze.

'I came to say sorry.' It's the softest I've ever heard her voice. 'I have no excuses.'

I nod. I have no more bile left to fling at her.

'But I also have something more important to talk to you about.'

'More lies?'

'Kane is innocent.' The rest of my street, my garden, Mr Daniels – everything fades behind her. All I can see is her face. Those big dark eyes staring at me. Her lips moving, as an eerie, slow-motion voice emerges from behind them. 'Indigo, are you listening to me? He definitely didn't do it.'

When I topple forwards, it is Alice's arms that catch me. It is her who hugs me, in an awkward sprawl on the grubby patio tiles of my front path. It is Alice who picks me up and takes me into the house, clears all the photo albums off the sofa and sits me down. It is Alice who opens the curtains, picks up a couple of dirty bowls from the coffee table, takes them through into the kitchen and returns with a cup of tea for me.

It is only then, clutching my cup with both hands, that I ask her, 'How can you be so sure?' I hadn't realised how much tension I was holding in my body. With the relief of what she's said, all my muscles feel like liquid.

'There's a lot I need to tell you.' She picks up a pile of my books from the armchair on the other side of the living room and puts them on the floor before sitting down. 'I don't know why I did it. At first it didn't feel like lying.'

I want to be able to forgive her. Really, I do. I've told enough of my clients over the years that forgiving someone is the best thing you can do for yourself. 'Did you know all along?'

'Yesterday. I only found out yesterday. I swear.' She puts a hand to her chest.

Can I believe her?

'I've been trying to find out the truth about how he died. It was a distraction.'

I can see the effort it is taking her to talk like this. Her face is pained, and the words come out disjointedly.

'When I saw you that day outside the car park, I hadn't had an appointment.'

'I know. I went there on Friday.'

'Was that when you realised?'

'No. It was in the car, on the way to Long Lartin. That keyring . . . I saw it in your house . . .' I pause. We have both done things we perhaps shouldn't have done.

She raises an eyebrow but says nothing. Lucian trots into the room and heads straight for her, weaving his way around her legs, headbutting her shins and purring. He doesn't usually like strangers. Alice lifts her hands from her lap, freezing them in mid-air as she watches him.

'Lucian.' I click my fingers at him. He ignores me. 'Lucian. I'm not sure Alice—'

'It's all right.' She slowly drops her hands back down to her thighs, but her body looks rigid. She doesn't take her eyes off him.

Some time passes as we both watch him in silence, then I speak again. 'I was in your house because I . . . I saw Benny.' I don't want to tell her I followed him. 'I spoke to him about Lou. I was desperate.'

Alice nods slowly, still watching Lucian, who is now rolling around on top of her feet. 'What did you find out when you went to Frasier House? You know that someone in that building saw it all?' She looks at me.

I sit up straight.

'Are you sure?'

She nods.

I have to put my tea down on the floor, my hands are shaking hard again. 'Who did it?'

'This woman, the one who saw, she came to the library yesterday.' Alice reaches down tentatively and scratches Lucian's belly. He stretches out to show how much he likes it.

'And . . . ?'

'Nobody pushed Lou.' Alice pulls her hand away and looks at the ceiling, blinking. 'She is sure of that. But I don't know if . . . I don't know if he jumped.'

The room is silent but for our breathing and Lucian scratching at the base of Alice's chair. My heart is beating uncontrollably with excitement for my own son, but Alice crumples back into the armchair, a corner of the yellow throw covering it falling over her shoulder. She is gripping her right hand around her other wrist, twisting it rhythmically and with such force it makes me wince. It must hurt. Every so often she looks up again, blinks a few times, then glances back at me.

I see now what I've never seen in her before. There is love, and fear, and doubt – just as much as I feel. But she's damn good at hiding it.

'Alice.'

'He died hating me.' She speaks with a shrug: quietly and matter-of-factly. 'He died thinking I didn't want him. But that wasn't how it was.' She drops her wrist from the grip of her twisting hand, exposing the red-raw skin underneath it.

And in that moment, I see a way to make this a tiny bit better for her. I can help. 'I'm sorry for the way I told you. About the argument, you know? The abortion. I was, I don't know, incensed. I wanted to get a reaction.'

Alice picks at a loose thread on the throw. I don't think she is listening to me; she certainly isn't looking at me.

'You know who told him? His dad.'

I shake my head. 'You once told me you were a single mum. Was that true?'

'Yes. He left, after Lou was born.'

Then who did I see at her house, on Thursday night? 'Has he been in touch recently?'

'He's been staying. Showed up after Lou died. I let him hang around, until I found out about this.' She looks up at the ceiling again.

The scene I witnessed on her doorstep suddenly makes a bit more sense.

'How could he tell them? He has no idea what harm it caused. I can't believe . . . I don't know why I ever—'

'Alice?'

She ignores me. 'I can't believe I ever loved that man. That bastard.'

'Alice, you need to hear this. Alice?'

She looks up, and I cross the room, crouching at her feet, gently nudging Lucian out of the way. He sits up, licking his paws while eyeing me with disdain.

I reach for Alice's hand and squeeze it. 'I didn't tell you the full story about their argument. Kane told me that when they were fighting, Lou stuck up for you. He seemed to take the view that what mattered – what he actually cared about – was the fact that you hadn't gone through with it. You'd kept him.'

Alice's free hand flies to her mouth.

'However he died . . .' I squeeze harder, as much to help steady her as myself. A lump has formed in my throat and I try to swallow it down. 'He didn't die hating you, he died defending you.'

255

Alice

15th September

A lice could hear Lou's voice for the first time since he had died. She could hear him, saying those exact words, with passion and conviction. She could see his face, set in a scowl as he said them. *What matters is that she kept me.*

Indigo looked at her with confusion when Alice smiled instead of crying.

'That was Lou,' Alice said.

Indigo smiled too. 'You must miss him so much.'

'We're going to find a way to get Kane out.'

'How quickly do you think it will happen? Once the police get a witness statement and it gets to the court? Do you think he'll be home this week?' Indigo's eyes were bright and optimistic. She rocked back on to her heels and sat on the multicoloured rug covering the living-room floor.

Alice sighed. She had meant to explain sooner, but the conversation had taken an unexpected turn and she had been thrown off course. 'She won't go to the police.'

'But she has to.'

'I tried to persuade her.'

Indigo got to her feet and began pacing the small room, from the sofa to the fireplace and back again.

'She answers phones for a domestic abuse helpline – that's where she was working when she saw them. It's manned by survivors. She's adamant; she doesn't want to deal with the police or the courts ever again after what she went through with her ex.'

'Did you tell her how long they're going to send him down for?'

'Yes. I tried, I really did. She ran off after she came to see me, and I went after her, I was trying to convince her in the middle of the street.'

'What am I going to tell him?'

'She wouldn't even give me her name.'

With a sweep of her hand, Indigo knocked everything from the mantelpiece above the fireplace to the floor.

Alice jumped up and put a hand on her back, looking down at the mess. A framed picture of Indigo and Kane lay on the rug, the glass cracked. Next to it, a strange lamp which looked like a large lump of rock was on its side, still plugged in and glowing orange.

'Why has he told them he's guilty?' Indigo asked.

Alice had been wondering the same thing. 'We'll get to the bottom of it all.'

Indigo sniffed and knelt down to pick up the photo in one hand and some of the larger shards of glass in her other. Alice got to her knees to help, picking up the lamp and putting it back on the mantelpiece. It felt warm, and left a slightly oily residue on her hands.

'This is . . . unusual.' She examined her palms.

'Himalayan salt lamp,' Indigo said, as though Alice would know what that was. 'Kane—' Her voice broke. 'Kane bought it for me.'

Alice wiped her hands on her trousers.

'It releases negative ions into the atmosphere, cancels out any radiation that's around. Meant to reduce stress, too,' Indigo said. 'And I need every bit of help I can get with that right now.' She reached past Alice's feet to pick up another piece of glass. 'Do you think it's my fault that she won't go to the police?'

'Why would you think that?'

'When I went there, they said I was harassing her. I shouldn't have gone. I . . .' She put the frame down and turned to look at Alice. 'You said she wouldn't tell you her name?' Her eyes were brighter suddenly.

'No.'

'I think I know it. The receptionist, she told me to stop harassing "Cassie".'

'But if she won't talk to the police, I'm not sure her name is going to help us.'

'It might. Let me think about it.' Indigo got to her feet. 'I should do something with this.' She looked at the pieces of glass in her hand. 'Let me just . . .'

She walked out of the room and Alice stood by the fireplace, kicking at a few other smaller bits of glass at her feet. It was the first chance she'd had to look around without Indigo right next to her. It wasn't an unpleasant place. A bit colourful and too packed with junk for Alice's liking, but it seemed clean. It didn't smell, apart from that 'other people' smell you get in someone else's house. Alice hadn't smelled that for a while.

She called after Indigo: 'Is there anything else you've found out that could help Kane?'

'Not really,' came the reply, along with the sound of the glass being dropped into a bin.

Alice followed the voice out into the hallway. She paused at the next open door, looking through into what looked like a studio. Paintings and sketches were pinned to the walls, and there was a table covered with small bottles, pots of brushes, jars of murky-looking liquid. When Indigo had said she was an art therapist, Alice hadn't considered that this might mean she also did her own artwork. Some of it wasn't bad. She looked down the hallway to check where Indigo was, but couldn't see her, and stepped into the room. Strewn across the floor were sketches – dozens of them. Alice recognised Kane's face in the top few, and another man, older and with less hair, in others. Quietly, she backed out and called after Indigo again.

'Anything at all? Even something small?'

'Only that you should never trust the police,' Indigo shouted out, her voice coming from the kitchen, further down the hall. 'Or librarians.'

Alice walked through the dining room, noticing, as she had earlier when she came through to make Indigo a cup of tea, that the table was covered with screwed-up pieces of paper. She wanted to know what they were. More sketches? She also felt the urge to sweep them off the table into a bin.

'We could try to find that Wilko lad?' Indigo emerged from the kitchen, holding a dustpan and brush. 'Remember I was telling you about him?'

'Did you say he went to school with Kane?'

'Yes.'

'Benny knew him, too – from sixth-form college, though, I think. Kane wasn't at the same school as Benny, was he? He didn't go to Fairfield?'

'No.'

Alice thought about that strange encounter on the bridge a few days ago. Wilko may not have pushed her son from the car park, but he was no good. She hadn't heard from him since and had somehow managed to resist messaging him to tell him to stay away from her son. It would only make things worse, she reasoned.

'I already spoke to him,' she said. 'That's how I knew about Cassie. He has a video of Lou and Kane fighting, and I saw her watching from a window over the road.'

'Do you have the video?'

'Don't get your hopes up. It doesn't show Lou falling, and Wilko wasn't there when he did. It might help Kane slightly but only to show that Lou was giving as good as he got. It won't prove Kane didn't push him over that wall.'

'Off the wall.' Indigo spoke quietly, running her fingers across the bristles of the brush in her hand, picking out some grey fluff.

'What?'

'It won't prove that Kane didn't push him *off* the wall.' She looked up at Alice. 'Lou was standing up on the wall before he fell.'

Had DC Garcia told her this? She couldn't remember the exact words she had used. Had she said something about him being pushed 'over the edge'? Had Alice misunderstood? She screwed her eyes shut and saw Lou standing on the edge of the wall, then stepping off. No. She snapped her eyes open and turned her face towards the bright mural next to her – layers of vivid green leaves hand-painted into a jungle that covered one whole wall of the dining room. Earlier she had thought it brash and too loud, but now she was glad for the way it forced those other, unwanted images out of her mind. She couldn't believe that Lou would do that. 'Did you paint this?'

'Yes,' Indigo said, stroking a hand across it. 'Glyn loved it.'

Glyn? Alice tried to remember if Indigo had mentioned that name before. Had she had another child? Or was he Kane's father?

Indigo set the dustpan and brush down on a chair and started collecting up the balls of paper from the table, tossing them one by one into a wicker basket near the door. 'Do you know if Wilko has spoken to the police?'

Alice picked a couple of the balls up and walked over to the bin. Looking down at them in her hands she could see that they had writing on them, not drawings. She dropped them in the bin. 'No, and I don't think he will, either,' she said. 'I think that's a dead end.'

'How can people be willing to stand back and let an innocent boy go to prison?'

Alice looked out of the window and on to the patio running along the side of the house. There was a raised bed of chaotic wildflowers just outside the window, basking in the afternoon sun. They'd grown too long and were falling over the edges of the wooden sleepers holding their roots. 'The one thing I know that could be helpful,' she said, as she mentally listed the bed's contents (*Vicia cracca, Lychnis flos-cuculi*), 'is that the only evidence the police have is Kane's confession.'

'But if he won't change his story, what can we do?' Indigo was still throwing the balls of paper into the bin at Alice's feet. They hit their target with a series of soft rustles.

Alice shrugged, squinting as she tried to see what else Indigo was growing. 'There're two of us thinking about this now, not just you. There's got to be something we've missed.'

'It's a bit of a mess.'

Alice looked over her shoulder, to see Indigo pointing out of the window.

'You should see my lawn.' She nodded her head towards the wildflower bed. 'Is that . . .' She paused, wanting to say *Tragopogon pratensis*, but guessing that Indigo didn't go in for the scientific names like she did. 'Do you have meadow salsify out there?'

'That's the one that closes up at midday?'

Alice nodded.

'Yes, I think that was in the mix. Beautiful yellow flowers, am I right? There's all sorts in that bed. I had a packet of seed.'

Tragopogon pratensis was sold in a packet? Alice thought of her mother. *Plague of my garden.*

Indigo brought her hand to her mouth and chewed at her thumb. Alice cringed at the sight of her nails, now with only small chips of purple polish remaining on them. 'Look. The only other thing . . .'

'Go on.' What would her mother make of Indigo? And her messy garden? There was a phrase her mother had adapted and liked to say every time she came in from a long afternoon on the kneeling pad, as she rinsed the soil from under her fingernails and rubbed in a meticulously measured squirt of magnolia hand cream: 'Tidy garden, tidy mind.'

Indigo fidgeted with her dress. 'This isn't easy to ask.'

Alice blinked, trying to take her thoughts away from her mother and focus on the woman in front of her, who needed her help. 'I'll do anything I can.'

'You were saying that you didn't know if Lou . . . if he'd, you know. Fallen, or . . .'

Alice nodded. 'Jumped. No. Cassie couldn't say for sure.'

'So we don't have much, by the sounds of it.' Indigo slumped on to one of the dining chairs and groaned. 'It was one thing knowing he was going to prison *thinking* he was innocent. But now that I know for sure? It's impossible.'

Alice ran her thumb along the edge of Lou's file in her pocket. 'Benny.'

'What about him?'

'You need to talk to him again.'

'I already tried, I told you. He wouldn't tell me anything.'

'But now, with what we know from Cassie . . .'

'You think he knows how Lou fell?'

'He's definitely hiding something.'

Indigo

16th September

When I was last standing outside this blue front door, talking to Benny, I didn't notice how impeccably tidy the garden was. There are no weeds in the cracks of the paving. There are no dead plants in the beds waiting to be dug up and binned. The bins themselves have perfectly aligned stickers showing the house number. There is no hint of mud or woodlice lurking underneath the doormat, which looks like it is beaten clean regularly. I didn't notice that the brass letter box was polished within an inch of its life. I didn't notice any of these things, not until this afternoon when I find myself standing here again – this time, knowing that it is Alice's house.

Now I see all these things and they make perfect sense. Nothing is out of place here; the only hint that this household is anything but perfect is the faint whiff of petrol lingering around the doorstep.

I press the doorbell and roll my shoulders back. What will Benny have to say?

It is Alice who opens the door. 'Come in,' she says, holding it wide. She drops her voice as I pass her. 'He's in the kitchen, go straight through. I haven't told him anything yet.'

I squeeze past a stack of boxes and bags in the hallway. Alice told me yesterday, when we formulated our plan at my house, that Benny was going down to Exeter this evening. I think of

Kane; he should be at his freshers' week, too, getting to know other students in his halls of residence – not sharing a cell with a criminal.

I hear Benny before I see him: the fridge door being opened, the tap running. When he turns to leave the kitchen, a plate in his hand, Alice is by my side in the doorway. He looks from her to me, and back.

'I think you've already met Mrs Owen,' she says.

His eyes widen, his cheeks flush a deep red.

'Hi, Benny.'

'You two know each other?' He puts his plate down on the breakfast bar, food forgotten about. 'Mum?'

'Why don't we go through into the other room?' Alice backs into the hallway. 'You can bring your toast.'

I follow her, pausing before I step into the living room. I smile at Benny, trying to let him know it's okay, he isn't in trouble; we just want to talk to him. It's hard to convey that much in a look.

It does the trick, though – he picks up his plate and joins us. I sit next to Alice on the grey leather sofa, while Benny sits on the floor next to the TV. He takes a bite of his toast but doesn't move his narrowed eyes from us.

'Why aren't you at work, Mum?'

She'd warned me they hadn't been talking much, but I would have known something was up even if she hadn't. The hostile tension in the room makes me shift uncomfortably in my seat.

'Half-days this week,' Alice says, with a brusque tone that confuses me. I get the sense that this is part of a bigger argument I don't know about and look away, wishing I could leave. 'Compassionate leave.'

I scan the room. Cream walls, dark grey sofa, light grey rug. One splash of colour in the gold-embroidered cushion on the armchair, which is also grey.

'I wanted to be here to see you off today,' Alice says after we have sat there in silence for several seconds, her voice softening a little.

'You didn't need to.'

I remember what she said, about him asking her father to drive him. Squirming next to her, I gaze at the print on the wall – one of Monet's paintings of his garden at Giverny. Its colour and the looseness of the brushstrokes are at odds with everything else in this room and, indeed, with what I have seen of this house. Weeping willows droop over a bed of vibrant purple irises, bathed in sunshine – while we sit surrounded by ashen upholstery, squinting in the cold, dreary light of this September day.

'Sorry, but what the hell's going on here? Are you going to explain what she . . . ?' He pauses, and I look at him. He is glaring at me with eyes full of rage. 'What she is doing in our house?'

'There's a great deal to explain,' Alice says. 'But all you need to know right now is that Mrs Owen and I have been investigating your brother's death. We have discovered that Kane did not push him.' I turn my head slightly towards her, looking at her long fingers resting on her thighs. How can she break it to him, like this – so matter-of-factly?

Benny puts his plate on the floor. 'What?' He looks at me, then back to her. 'Is that what *she* told you?'

'A witness has come forward.' Alice sighs, and her voice softens again. 'Your brother wasn't murdered.'

'What the fuck? Someone saw?' Benny leans back against the TV stand, his face contorting in bewilderment. 'What did happen, then?'

'We don't know for sure.' Alice's body follows his, and she leans forward to rest her elbows on her knees.

'So Kane's getting out?' Benny looks at me again.

'It's not going to be that simple,' I say. 'The witness won't go to the police.'

'But they have to. Don't they?'

'Not necessarily.' Alice lowers her chin on to her clasped hands. 'This is why we need to talk to you.'

'I didn't see, I told you. I wish I had.'

Alice nods. 'I know. I believe you.'

He's shaking his head now.

'Benny, I believe you.' Alice says it more firmly this time, and his eyes meet hers. 'But is there anything else you know? Even something that might seem totally inconsequential. We need to find out as much as possible so we can go to Kane's solicitor with something he can really use.'

Benny drops his head into his hands. 'How many times do I have to tell you . . . ?'

'I know there's something you're hiding from me. I'm not going to be angry, if that's what you're worried about. Are you trying to protect Lou?'

Alice looks at me. We talked about this yesterday. Could Benny be trying to keep his brother's secret?

'Protect him?' Benny looks up. 'From who?'

I glance at Alice for her approval and she nods. 'Did you know about your brother's relationship with my son?' I ask.

This gets his attention, as I'd expected. He sits forward. 'What?'

'Lou and Kane were together,' Alice says. 'You had no idea?'

Benny stands up, now. 'Wait . . . wait. Kane and Lou?'

'We thought perhaps they were having a bit of a lovers' tiff and you didn't want to let on to your mum because you'd have to break Lou's confidence.'

As I speak, he stares at me incredulously. Then he laughs. 'Kane and *Lou*?'

'It's a lot to take in,' Alice says. 'But think about it, it explains how Lou had been acting—'

'Stop, stop. Did Kane tell you that?' He points down at me.

'Yes, he did. But I worked it out first – remember that day I

266

was here, and you were going through Lou's things? I saw some cards on the table and I recognised them. Kane has one at home, with a . . . Well, it's a love note, really, written on it.'

'That wasn't . . . they weren't . . .' Benny shakes his head, turning to face the fireplace and shoving his hands into his pockets.

'If it wasn't this, what is it that you're hiding from me about that night?' Alice isn't letting him off that easily.

'This isn't . . .'

'Finish a sentence, Benny!' Alice thumps her thigh. 'This isn't what?'

He looks up at the ceiling and exhales. 'This *is*, kind of, what I didn't want to tell you.'

Alice cuts in. 'So you did know?'

'No. Yes. Just . . . let me explain. This isn't how I had planned to do this.'

He is still staring up at the ceiling, back to us, and as I look at his fingers nervously fumbling with loose stitching on the pocket of his denim shorts, it starts to dawn on me. Alice's face is still screwed up with impatience and misunderstanding. How did I get this so wrong?

'Let's put it this way, Mum,' he laughs nervously, 'you have a gay son, but it wasn't Lou.' In the moments of silence that follow, Benny looks anywhere but at her. Out of the window, at the wall above the fireplace, at his hands.

I move to the edge of the sofa. 'I should leave you two.'

Alice puts a hand on to my leg. 'Stay.' Her voice is barely more than a whisper.

Benny turns to me. 'Those cards you saw, they're mine. I was sorting through my own things, ready for uni.'

'Why did Kane say he'd been seeing Lou, then?'

'He definitely said that? In so many words?'

'I thought he did, but . . .' I try to remember our exact conversation, but I can't recall who said what. Not for sure.

'This is what you've been keeping from me?' Alice asks, eyes cast down to the rug.

Benny puts his hands back in his pockets and shrugs awkwardly, scuffing his shoe against the tiles surrounding the hearth. 'I should have told you sooner. But you know, we don't . . . it's not like we talk about . . .'

Tell him it's okay; tell him you support him whatever he does, whatever he chooses. I can't stand to watch this – Benny standing in front of Alice, both of them staring at the floor to avoid making eye contact with each other. *Tell him you love him no matter what.*

Instead, she asks, 'Lou wasn't gay?'

'No.' Benny kneels next to her. 'It's okay, though. Mum?' He looks at her face for the first time since his revelation. 'I'm still me, nothing changes.'

She grabs his shoulders, lifting her eyes to his. 'How did I not know?'

'You don't need to worry about me, please. You look so sad.'

'It's not you I'm upset about. I thought if Lou was struggling with being gay it would explain why it's always been so difficult. Now you're saying that's not what it was . . . so what was it?'

'It was just Lou.' Benny smiles sadly. 'Not every son can be as perfect as me.'

Alice laughs, almost silently, shaking her head.

'I'll run through everything I can remember, okay? I don't think there's anything that will help, but I'll try.' Benny turns to me. 'How is he?'

'Bearing up,' I say. 'Long Lartin's not great.'

He tilts his head. 'Long Lartin?'

Alice coughs. 'I tried to tell you, but with everything the last few days . . .'

'He's not in there?' He points at the wall above the armchair, towards the back of the house and the prison.

'He got moved.'

Benny runs a hand across his shaved scalp, back and forth. 'It never made any sense. I should have known it wasn't true. What kind of a boyfriend am I? Please, Mrs Owen, you've got to let him know I'm sorry. Can I see him?'

'They probably won't let you, love.' I shrug. 'But you don't need to apologise. I'm sure the two of you can get it all cleared up when we get him out of there.'

'What has he told the police? Why did he say he did it?'

'That's why we need to know everything you know,' Alice says. 'We're up against it.'

'Okay. That night, when we were in the pub, Kane was going on at me about coming out. He thought we should talk to Lou, but I wasn't ready. Lou had been getting funny about us spending so much time together; I don't think he liked Kane much. We argued about it, and in the end I did tell Lou.'

My cheeks start to feel hot. Was this because of me? Wanting Kane to bring his boyfriend over for dinner?

'Lou started making comments about us. He didn't mean it, I don't think he gave a shit, but we hadn't had a chance to—' Benny's voice breaks and he swallows. 'I never got the chance to chat to him properly about it.' He swallows again at the memory. 'Then he makes this comment about Kane's dad. Kane took it badly, but Lou didn't know what he was saying.' Benny looks at me. 'He didn't know the full story; he assumed he'd walked out on you both, like our dad did. Then Kane says, "At least my mother wanted me." I was so pissed off with him, because he *did* know what he was saying and I'd told him to keep it to himself. It was totally out of order, and so unlike Kane, but Lou had got under his skin, I guess. That's when Lou threw the first punch.'

'So they weren't fighting over a girl?' Alice asks. 'I thought you said . . .'

'They were,' he says. 'I mean, that wasn't the main problem, but it was part of what got it started. Kane thought Lou was messing this girl around, someone Kane used to go out with.' He looks at me. 'Jess?'

I nod, remembering her; she used to stay over a lot. That was years ago, though, he would have been fourteen, maybe fifteen? 'What did you do next, then, after the fight? You went off to get ice?'

'Yeah, that's it. I'd got them to break it up, but they were both in such a state. I left them up there and I went to get a cup of ice from the pub down the road. As I walked back, I . . .' Benny shuffles on the floor, over towards the coffee table in the bay window, and leans against it. 'I never told you this, Mum. You sure you want to hear it?'

Alice nods.

'As I walked back, I heard this scream. It didn't sound like Lou. And this awful noise – a really loud bang. I just started running. I knew it was one of them.'

None of us says anything for several minutes.

It's Benny who, leaning forwards away from the coffee table, speaks first. 'So if Kane didn't push him, what went on up there? Did he . . . ?'

'I don't know.'

I look at the pair of them, and it crosses my mind that I am the lucky one in this room, although it often doesn't feel that way. My son is still alive. Lou's dead, and they don't know why.

'I don't get it. What is Kane saying happened?' Benny looks at me.

'He says he pushed him.' As I say it, the enormity of the situation hits me again.

'. . . this witness that saw it all?' Benny is asking.

'A woman, in one of the offices over the road,' Alice says. 'There's a video, your friend Harry Wilkinson showed me. And I saw this woman—'

'You went to see Wilko? Christ, Mum.'

'He's a charming young man.'

I'm finding it hard to stay with their conversation. Who's to blame for all of this? Me, by the sound of what Benny is saying. Kane would never have made Benny tell Lou he was gay that night if I hadn't kept on at him. They'd never have had this fight.

'. . . we should see if he still has it,' Benny is saying. 'He'll probably have deleted it; he really doesn't want anything tying him to being there that night. Something else went on that evening, I don't know what. Not related to what happened to Lou. I think Lou saw Wilko do something dodgy, he made a cryptic comment to me about Wilko being in big trouble.'

'Trouble?' Alice asks.

'And then Wilko's been on at me, wanting to know everything Lou said to me. I think I've convinced him I don't know anything but he's worried Kane does.'

'I think I should speak to him again. Try to get the video,' Alice says.

'You're not going alone this time.' The way Benny is speaking to her has changed totally from the surliness of earlier.

'I'll be fine,' Alice says.

'No, listen. I'll come with you. I don't need to leave tonight.'

'But you've already missed the start.'

'Uni will still be there in a few days' time. It can wait. If you'll take me down there? The weekend, maybe?'

A smile spreads across Alice's lips and she nods. Faced with her relief, my desperation at the impossibility of our task intensifies. We can't do this. *I'm sorry, Kane. I don't know if I can help you.*

'. . . settled then,' Alice says, clapping her hands together. 'Let's pay Harry a visit.'

'There's no point.' I lean back into the sofa. 'We're not going to get Kane out of there.'

Who are we fooling? Unless Kane changes his story, nothing is going to be any different. This is hopeless. I have spent the last nine years worrying about how Glyn's actions might affect him. Now, sure enough, here he is; for some unfathomable reason pressing the self-destruct button on his life and refusing to take his finger off.

Lou

17th August

L ou reached up and pulled himself over the wall of the third
storey. He could still hear Kane, grunting away below him.
This was a clear victory. He wiped the sweat from his forehead
with the bottom of his T-shirt.

Benny and Wilko were already up there, waiting. Wilko was
standing a few metres away, talking on his phone; Benny
was leaning out, watching Kane. Had he even seen how fast and
smoothly Lou had done it? 'Easiest kebab I've ever won,' Lou
said, but Benny didn't acknowledge him, so he leaned over the
wall and shouted down, 'You're too slow, Kane! Need to do some
more shoulder days in the gym.'

Lou turned to rest his elbows on the wall and looked into the
half-empty car park. It was spinning slightly, and he blinked
hard. 'Hey, Ben. Did you see that? Did you time me?'

But Benny didn't answer – he was too busy helping Kane up
and over the wall.

'That's it, bro. Help Princess Kane.' Lou wiped at his forehead
again. 'I notice you didn't offer me a hand.'

'Enough, Lou,' Benny said, without looking at him. Jeez. He
was really pissed about something. 'What's wrong with you?
Give Kane a break.'

Give Kane a break or give you a break? That's what Lou wanted
to say. He saw the way Benny looked at Kane as he handed him

back his phone and wallet. There was definitely something there. 'I don't see why I have to be nice to him,' he said, looking from one to the other, following them as they slipped between the parked cars and made towards the stairwell. When were they going to let him in on their little secret?

Benny stopped and looked back over his shoulder at him. 'Because he's my boyfriend, okay?'

'Halle-fucking-lujah.' Lou clasped his hands together and tipped his head back. He shouldn't have done that; the ceiling started spinning even more vigorously and he stumbled against a red Mini. 'Why'd you take so long to tell me? It's been going on for a while, am I right?'

Benny came over to help him back to his feet, but Lou wasn't ready to stand just yet. He rested against the car's bonnet. It was warm against his legs – nothing was cool this evening. Kane was skulking around by the door to the stairwell, but Benny at least had the decency to make eye contact with Lou and look a bit sheepish.

'I've known for ages,' Lou said. 'You're always together. And I saw the way you put your hand on Kane's arm tonight when you thought I wasn't watching.' He tapped a finger against his eye. 'I'm always watching.' He belched and tasted his last pint of beer making a reappearance. What he thought, but didn't say, was that when he saw that tender moment between them, that was when he'd decided it was not a night to only have a couple of halves as he usually did. How could Benny have kept it from him all this time?

Kane walked over to join them. 'Why did we take so long? Why'd you think? Because you hate me. Because you're a massive homophobe.' He glared at Lou, his nostrils flared wide. It made his nose ring look well weird, Lou thought, and he bit his lip to stop himself giggling.

'Lads, lads,' Wilko shouted across to them. 'Keep it down,

yeah? I'm trying to have a conversation here.' He pointed to his phone.

Lou held up his hands in a mock apology and pushed himself away from the Mini. Something came over him then – was it the rush of adrenalin from the climb, still kicking in? He couldn't help himself. He didn't know why he started saying it but once he did, he couldn't stop.

He jabbed Kane in the arm. Just with his finger. A gentle tap, really. 'So what, have you two been going up to Old Market and stuff? To all the *gay* bars?'

He saw Kane's chest rise and fall, saw his hands twitch at his side, but he carried on.

'How does it work? Which one of you is the man in the relationship?' All the time he couldn't bring himself to look at Benny's face. He was thinking to himself, *Stop it, Lou. Stop being a bellend.*

He screwed his eyes shut in an effort to keep the floor from rolling around beneath him, and heard Kane mutter to Benny. 'Deal with him. I don't care if he's your brother . . .'

'What does it matter if I've got my eye on Jess, then?' Lou looked up at him. 'If you two are at it?'

Kane cast his eyes up and down Lou's body. 'Because you can't handle a relationship. You're too immature. Look at the state of you tonight.'

'Who said . . . who said I wanted a relationship?' He threw his arms up in the air. 'Only losers want to settle down before they've even turned twenty. I'm not looking for a girlfriend until I'm at least thirty-five.'

'Are you sleeping with her?' Kane asked.

Lou laughed. 'What does it matter to you?'

'Yeah, Kane.' Benny stepped away from them, leaning against the boot of a dark-coloured people carrier. 'What does it matter to you?'

275

'It matters because I care about her. She's a nice girl, all right?'

'Ooh,' Lou said. He shouted over to Wilko. 'The lovebirds are fighting; maybe they won't be skipping off into the sunset after all.'

'Piss off, Lou. Seriously, go home.' Kane pointed towards the door.

'I had all these happy images.' Lou rubbed at his temples. 'You two growing old together, two little old men holding hands, wearing matching pink suits.'

Benny wasn't paying him any attention, though. His eyes were fixed on Kane. 'How *much* do you still care about Jess—'

'But then, I guess,' Lou interrupted, speaking loudly over the top of his brother. 'Neither of you exactly have the best examples of happy couples to look up to. Your dad didn't care about you enough to stick around long, did he, Kane?'

'You know nothing about my father.' Kane stepped towards him.

'Drop it, Lou,' Benny said. 'Kane, I didn't tell him . . . he doesn't know . . .'

'Ah, mate, I'm only messing,' Lou laughed. He couldn't quite focus on Kane's face, but he could see it well enough to know it was time to give it a rest.

'You're not,' Kane said, still coming closer. 'You want to talk about families? At least mine don't think I'm a loser. You know what Benny says about you? That you're going nowhere. You're a waste of space.' He smiled at Lou for the first time all evening. 'You're a parasite.'

Benny pushed away from the people carrier. Lou couldn't bring himself to look at him. 'Hang on a minute, Kane . . .' his brother said.

But Kane was on one. He was in some sort of nasty flow. 'At least my mother wanted me.'

For a moment, they looked at each other. Eyes locked together, daring the other to make the next move. Both oblivious to Benny approaching, to Wilko hanging up on his phone call. To a car alarm going off in the distance.

Then Lou swung his arm back, and felt his fist crunch against the side of Kane's face.

Alice

17th September

Alice had wanted to go straight to Harry Wilkinson's yesterday evening, but Benny insisted they shouldn't turn up unexpected. 'Not again,' he'd said, looking at her over the top of his skateboard, which he had brought into the living room to clean while they made plans. Indigo hadn't been any use in helping her persuade him. She had retreated into a quiet despondency – giving up, that's what it looked like to Alice, and she'd told her so. 'We've not come this far to let Kane stay in prison for the best part of his life,' she'd said. Perhaps she should have tried a softer approach, but Indigo needed someone to help her pull herself together, not pat her on the back and lie that it would all be okay.

So they had spent the rest of the afternoon drinking tea and coffee and waiting for Benny to draft the perfect text message to Harry, which he'd claimed to be doing in his head while he scrubbed along the length of the sandpaper-like top of his board with what looked to Alice like a bar of soap. When he'd finally started typing on to his phone, Alice came close to ripping it out of his hands, but after an hour of deleting, redrafting, sighing and reading versions out to them, he'd been happy with what he had on the screen and sent it. It read: *PS4 later/tomoz? Your place?*

Harry hadn't replied when Alice drove Indigo home at six

o'clock. He hadn't replied by eight, when Benny went out to get fish and chips for dinner. He hadn't replied by ten, when Alice climbed into bed and lay there with her eyes wide open. But at midnight, Benny put his head round her door. 'We're on,' he whispered, the neon glare from his phone lighting up that small section of the bedroom. 'Tomorrow lunchtime.'

Benny picked Alice up from work at midday, and together they stopped by at Indigo's on their way to Harry's flat. She was quiet, withdrawn and glassy-eyed, and sat in the back seat, staring out of the window, barely answering any of Alice's questions. It was an unusual feeling, caring about someone other than her sons. But that was, quite unmistakably, what was going on here. She, Alice Hyde, cared about cheering Indigo Owen up. She wanted to help her.

Here she was again, standing on the pavement outside Harry Wilkinson's flat. She and Benny had argued last night about the best way to approach this, and her plan had won out. They agreed (at first) that they needed to get the video to the police, but differed on how to achieve that. Benny thought it would be simpler to ask Harry to WhatsApp him the video, which he would then present to the police, saying that someone had anonymously sent it to him. 'There's no such thing as anonymous, these days,' Alice said. 'But I'll delete his message, and store the video on my phone,' Benny replied. Alice grimaced at his naivety. 'There is no way to keep him out of it, if we want the police to see this video.' Benny wasn't backing down easily – quite transparently because he was nervous of dragging his friend into it. Now, on his doorstep, they disagreed about how to go into the building. Benny wanted to ring the buzzer, but Alice wanted an element of surprise. 'And, besides,' she said, 'the door is wide open.' Indigo didn't express an opinion; instead, she stared off into the middle distance.

Alice decided matters by stepping forward through the front

door and leading the way up the stairs, Benny following her, hissing, 'Mum, stop!' But when she reached Harry Wilkinson's flat, she stood to one side and nodded her head towards the door, mouthing to Benny, *Go on*. Sweat beaded on his forehead. Why on earth had her sons been friends with this reprobate? He wiped his hands down his T-shirt before lifting a hand up to knock.

'Wilko?' Benny called through the door when he didn't open it straight away.

A muffled answer came back. 'Mate, chill. Give me a minute.' His voice was almost drowned out by the bass of some atrocious dance music – a track Alice recognised hearing in Benny's room.

More than a minute passed, with the three of them waiting on the landing. Indigo kicked at bits of chewing gum ingrained in the carpet. Benny stood rigidly in front of the door, hardly blinking. Alice checked her watch every few seconds and chewed her tongue. Why should they have to be on Harry Wilkinson time?

She was about to reach past Benny and knock again, when the door opened. Harry wasn't there to greet Benny – he let the door swing wide as he walked away from it. Benny looked at Alice. She nodded, grabbed Indigo's arm and followed Benny into the stench of the flat, leaving the door open behind them.

'What do you want to play?' Harry asked, lifting up the bottom of his drawn curtains and retrieving a games controller from the windowsill. 'I've got the new—'

He turned to see the three of them, then scowled at Benny. 'What the fuck?'

'Hello, Harry.' Alice pulled Indigo forward. 'May I introduce Mrs Owen, Kane's mother?'

Harry lifted a finger to his mouth, picking at something in his teeth. 'Thought you and I had an agreement?'

'Things have changed somewhat.' Alice wasn't having this.

Not from a teenage drug dealer. 'We have discovered that Kane has been wrongfully arrested and charged. You are going to have to show the police that video of yours.'

He laughed.

'What else happened, Harry? The night my son died?' Alice didn't want to drop Benny in it by asking what it was that he was so afraid Kane knew. But questions needed to be asked.

'Nothing.'

Benny shot her a look, which she took to mean: *Don't ask him about that again.* 'Have you still got the video, mate?'

'Yeah, but you're not having it.'

'You didn't delete it, then?'

'Thought I could sell it to the press, get a bit of . . .' Harry rubbed his fingers together. 'But they wanted me to hand it over for free, so I told them to fuck off.' He stepped towards her. 'Benny, mate, I'm sorry, I just remembered I have something else to be getting on with. We'll have to do this another time.' He spoke without taking his eyes off Alice.

She thought again about what he'd said on the bridge. *I've seen what he does to people.* Should she cancel the meeting with Kane? She looked at Benny, then at Indigo, standing next to her like a limp doll. Alice meeting with Kane might be the only way they were going to find out the truth.

'Your video shows a woman watching the fight unfold,' Alice continued, walking into the kitchen and opening the fridge. She wasn't going to let him think she was scared, or that she'd put up with him threatening her and her son. 'She also saw Lou fall. Your video forms part of the evidence to show that she is a witness.'

'What video?'

'Mum, I told you this was a bad idea.' Benny started towards the door. 'Let's go.'

Alice pulled out a loaf of white sliced bread – the only item in the fridge other than a few cans of beer. 'You're better off keeping this at room temperature, Harry.' She tossed it on to the counter. 'So that's option one: you go to the police yourself.'

From the kitchen she moved behind Harry to the window and pulled the curtains open. The material felt grimy under her fingertips and she wiped her hands down her trousers, peering out on to the street. 'Option two would be us informing the police, not only that you were there, but that you were dealing to my sons.'

'Mum!'

Alice hadn't discussed this part of her plan with Benny. She didn't know if Harry Wilkinson had ever sold Lou or Benny anything, but she wouldn't be surprised; particularly if those little plastic bags in Lou's wardrobe were anything to go by.

'Suspended sentence – that was what you got last time, wasn't it?' Alice tilted her head to one side. 'I wonder what will happen when they hear about this.'

Harry tossed the games controller on to the sofa, where it landed amongst a pile of crisp packets. 'What's it worth, me handing the video in?'

'We're not paying you to do this.' Alice gave him the hardest look she could muster.

'Not even another fifty?' He smirked. 'You seemed pretty flush last time.'

Benny grabbed her arm, forcing her to look at him. 'You gave him money?'

'That was different.'

'How much do you want?' It was the first time Indigo had spoken since they arrived at the flat. They all turned to look at her, sitting on Harry's beige leather armchair.

Harry flashed a smarmy smile at Alice that made her shiver. 'A grand should cover it.'

'Not a chance.' Alice looked at Indigo. 'We're not doing that.'

But Indigo's eyes were fixed on Harry. 'It might take me a couple of days to get that kind of money.'

'You've got twenty-four hours.'

'No.' Alice stepped in between them, facing Indigo. 'If you pay him, it won't stand up—'

'I've got to get him out of that place.'

A lighter clicked behind Alice, and the smell of weed wafted towards her. She spun around.

'Toke?' Harry offered her the joint, still with that smirk on his face.

'We're leaving. You've got until this time tomorrow to go to the police with that video, otherwise we will be speaking to them ourselves.'

'Whatever.' Harry blew smoke into her face.

'Oh, and I forgot to mention – we'll mention to them what Lou saw you doing that night.'

He laughed again.

'The police?' He took another puff on his joint. 'I'm really scared.' He was looking unnervingly pleased with himself. 'You know fuck all about what Lou saw.' He clapped his hands slowly.

'Let's go.' Alice grabbed Indigo's elbow, pulling her up off the chair, and beckoned to Benny.

But Harry kept talking. 'If Kane is so keen to take the hit for this, let him. He's a grown man. He's obviously got his reasons. How do you even know this witness of yours isn't lying? Why would he admit to something he hasn't done?'

They were at the door now, but Indigo turned back to look at him.

'Has he asked you to do any of this?' Harry asked, exhaling another puff of smoke.

None of them replied.

'Didn't think so.'

He pulled his mobile out of his pocket and moved his finger

around on the screen. 'I'm done with this. Go to the police if you want, I'm not saying anything.' He held his phone up in front of them. 'This is your little video, isn't it?'

The footage of the fight was playing on the screen, with a line of icons superimposed over it. Before Alice realised what he was about to do, he'd pressed delete.

Indigo

17th September

Everything I look at appears washed out to me and unreal. Sounds fade in and out. I can't look Alice or Benny in the eye. I have a constant dull pain in my stomach. I know all these feelings; I have been here before, but this time nobody has died. And yet this thing that grips my heart is definitely grief. I know it too well.

I can't see what we are going to do to get Kane back. His life is ruined. How many years will we be apart, and what will he return to? So much will have changed. He'll have no degree, no job. It is all too much for me to make sense of. It was just about manageable, keeping those thoughts at bay, before. When I had those stupid, naïve hopes that I could change this.

After our disastrous visit to Wilko's flat, Alice dropped Benny off at their house and brought me home. 'You need some company,' she said. For the first time since we met, she has been talking far more than me. It's as if someone has flicked a switch in her robot console and she is in a different mode.

Back at home, we sit at my dining table. She found a bottle of pinot gris in the fridge and poured two glasses, even though I didn't respond when she asked me if I wanted some. I want to talk, but what could I say? Everything seems so pointless.

'I normally only drink spirits.' Alice is already on to her second glass. 'But this isn't bad.'

I'm only halfway through my first, but already I can feel my cheeks getting hotter, and I know if I look in the mirror I will see a red patch of skin at the base of my neck – I always get it when I drink. But Alice looks totally unaffected, the same as she always does. I should eat something.

'If we don't have that video, we need to move on to the next part of the plan.' Alice carefully replaces her glass on the coaster, which she found in a drawer in the kitchen. I didn't even realise we had any in this house. 'My suggestion would be to call Cassie now. If she isn't there, we try to find out when she will be working.'

She looks at me, waiting for me to say something. When I don't, she says, 'Good; well, I'm glad you agree.'

I lift my own glass to my lips. A few days ago, that might have made me laugh, but now I wonder if I will ever find anything funny again.

'I looked the number up earlier. Cassie told me the name of the charity.' Alice gets her phone out of her rucksack. 'Here.' She puts it on the table in between us, the number ready on the screen. 'Are you doing this or shall I?'

I grip the stem of my glass. It should be me that calls. I should be doing *something*. And yet I can't make my hands move towards the phone.

I open my mouth and a small, rasping sound comes out. I cough.

'Try again,' Alice says gently.

I look up at her now and focus on the darkness of her eyes. I hold on to that as I try to speak again. 'How are you . . . ?' I whisper, my voice hoarse and my throat dry. 'How are you not a mess?'

'About Lou?' Alice clasps her hands together on the table top.

I nod. 'How are you holding it together?'

She sits back and slips her hands into her pockets. 'You won't like it.'

I shrug.

'For me, showing emotion is showing weakness. I realise not everyone operates like that, and I don't expect them to. But I have always believed that to be true.'

What must she think of me?

'Benny thinks I feel nothing because I show nothing,' she says, reaching a hand down to stroke Lucian as he pads into the room and curls around the leg of her chair. 'But I do. I just haven't got the words.' She puts a hand to her chest.

I look down and see that – without realising – I have clasped my hands, resting them on the table just like she had hers. And when I speak, I take on her same, cautious, measured tone.

'I was a wreck when Glyn died,' I say. 'I couldn't have done what you are doing. I couldn't have returned to work. I didn't understand why he would have wanted to leave us. That question kept me awake all night and plagued me all day.'

Alice cups her chin in her hand, leaning on the table. 'He . . . ?' I can see that she understands what he did.

I nod. 'Kane was only nine.'

'I had no idea.'

'Afterwards, a long time afterwards, I realised there had been signs. He stopped doing the things he enjoyed. He was much quieter. I knew he was unhappy, but I didn't do anything about it. It went on for months . . . I should have asked him what was wrong.'

'Of course.' Alice was smiling at me, a sad smile.

'Of course?'

'Ever since then, you try to fix everyone else's problems.'

'I don't do that.' But I do, I know I do.

'That friend you mentioned, when we were driving to Long Lartin.'

'Kim.'

'Sending her job descriptions for her husband, taking food

round. And were you already working as a therapist before your husband . . . ?' She doesn't say it, what he did, and I'm glad for that small kindness.

'Even if I wasn't, what would it have to do with Glyn?'

Alice drains her glass. 'You think you didn't do enough to help him.'

I shake my head. 'No, I don't think that's it.' But she's right, isn't she? Alice the robot, the last person I would expect to see so far into my soul.

'It's simple logic, I would say.' She pours herself a third glass and tops mine up. I take a sip, moving the cool mouthful around under my tongue before swallowing. It's fresh and lemony – I was saving this bottle for one of the last evenings Kane and I had together before he went away, to enjoy outside on the patio, in the evening sun.

The only noise in the room for a few minutes comes from Lucian's claws, as he scratches at his cat tree, and we both watch him.

Alice breaks the silence. 'So, who's going to call her?' She points at her phone, still sitting between us on the table.

'You do it.' I push it towards her.

She dials the number. I lay my hands flat on the table, crossing my fingers.

'Hello? Yes, I hope so,' Alice says. 'You have someone there called Cassie . . . I was speaking to her the other night? Could I talk to her again?' She pauses. 'Wonderful, thank you.'

She covers the microphone and whispers to me, 'She's there.'

I give her a thumbs-up, then lift my hand to my mouth and start biting my nails.

'Hi, Cassie.' Alice leans forward, resting her elbows on the table. 'We were speaking the other day. You came to see me at work, at the library?'

She nods, listening to Cassie speak.

288

If Cassie won't help, what will we do then? I stand, still working at my thumbnail with my teeth, and walk a few steps to the bookcase Glyn built many years ago. There's a frame sitting on the top shelf, my favourite photo of Kane, taken only last year. I remove my hand from my mouth and trace my fingers around his face, rest my thumb on his smiling lips, and close my eyes. *Please help us.*

'And that's why I'm calling,' Alice says. 'We've spoken to Kane's solicitor and it would be unlikely to go to court if you'd only agree to speak to the police.'

I turn back to the table, pick up my wine glass and tip most of its contents into my mouth, not pausing this time to savour the taste.

'No, it was his mother who spoke to him. But he assures us—'

Alice drums her fingers on the table.

'Yes, I know you don't want to speak to them either . . . But an innocent boy is going to go to prison. Are you sure you can't . . . ?'

I catch her eye for a moment before she looks away.

'No. Court is unlikely. No trial, no cross-examination . . . Yes, Kane's mum – I've got her here.' She pauses, looking at me, and points at the phone. I nod. 'Yes,' she says. 'I'll pass you over.'

She hands me the phone. My hand is shaking as I put it to my ear. 'Hello?'

'I don't want you to think I don't care about your son,' Cassie says. She sounds so much younger than I had imagined, with a soft Northern Irish accent, which I hadn't expected either.

'Oh, love. I know that.' Of course, I had been thinking that very thing. But now, speaking to her, I can hear the fear in her voice. I run my hand along the rainforest mural wall as I pace up and down the room. 'But he's my little boy. Do you have kids?'

She doesn't answer immediately. 'A son. He's eight.'

'They're lovely at that age. Kane was obsessed with his bike; the minute he came in from school he wanted to go out on it.' I pick up the photo frame on the bookcase and look again at Kane's face, remembering one summer's afternoon, watching him cycling round to the shop to buy ice creams as payment for the friends he'd enlisted to act out skits in the back garden, which he'd filmed with Glyn's camcorder.

'With Daniel it's all about his scooter,' Cassie says quietly.

'I bet he spends all his time trying to learn new tricks?'

Cassie laughs. 'And explaining to me, in detail, exactly how to do them.'

'Kane spent weeks perfecting his wheelies. I always encouraged him but I'd watch through my fingers. I was terrified he'd fall off and break his arm.' I pause, putting the photograph back down. 'He still goes everywhere on his bike. And I'm still scared every time he leaves the house that he's going to be knocked off or something. You never stop worrying about them.'

There's silence on the other end of the line.

'Cassie?'

'If I go ahead with this, what do I do? Show up at the police station?'

I widen my eyes as I look at Alice, flapping my free hand in a fanning motion by my face. I try to keep the excitement out of my voice. 'I can arrange for you to speak to Kane's solicitor first, and then you might need to speak to the police later. That's what he said.'

'I'll do it.'

'You're sure?' I squeeze my eyes shut.

'Let me give you my number,' Cassie says, 'before I change my mind. Your solicitor can call me.'

'Thank you, thank you so much.' I wish I could be with her right now, to give her a hug.

I write down her number on a scrap of paper on the bookcase as she relays it over the phone.

'I've got to go,' she says. 'There're calls coming in.'

'I really am so grateful, thank you.'

'Good luck.'

'Goodbye,' I say, but she's gone.

I pass the phone to Alice, letting out a long breath. 'Do you think she'll stick to her word?'

'Personally, I don't understand anyone who does not do as they say they will, but that's by the by.' She stands up and pats my shoulder. 'Yes, I believe she'll do it.'

'Then we've really got a chance. They could let him out.' I lift my near-empty wine glass from the table and hold it up. 'I couldn't have done this without you.'

Alice smiles, lifting her glass to meet mine, but the expression doesn't reach her eyes. I immediately feel guilty. How can I expect her to celebrate?

'I think there's something else we ought to try to do,' she says, 'to make the case as solid as possible.'

I knock back the dregs from my glass. 'Go on.'

'We should get Kane to retract his statement.'

I slump down into my chair, tipping my head back.

'He won't talk to me. And why would he take my advice? It's my fault he's ended up in there.'

'That's the most ridiculous thing I've heard you say, and that's saying something.'

I can't help but smile. 'I told him I wanted to meet his boyfriend. That's why he put pressure on Benny to come out to Lou that night.'

'And I came this close to having an abortion. It doesn't make Lou's death any more my fault than it is yours.' Alice pauses, looking out of the window at the wildflower bed. 'We are not to blame, Indigo.'

I run my finger around the rim of the wine glass. I'm not sure I agree with her. 'Still, he won't let me call him or visit him.'

'Maybe.' Alice pulls out her chair and lowers herself into it, without taking her eyes off the window. Her body is completely still as she sits there, and her eyes are staring past the flowers, as if they can see through the white render on the wall at something in the distance. 'But I'm seeing him on Thursday.'

Alice

19th September

Alice neatly rolled the sleeves of her shirt, looking at the door after every perfectly equal fold. Margaret and Priya were laying biscuits out on a plate to one side of the room, having a quietly murmured conversation. Alice had sat in her bolted-down chair as soon as they showed her in, and she wouldn't get out of it until she had seen this through. Noises filtered in from the corridor – snatched sentences from conversations, the clatter of keys. Each time a new set of footsteps approached, Alice sat up a little straighter. She hadn't let her spine curve towards the back of the seat in the ten minutes since she had been here. She had heard that tall women sometimes hunched their shoulders so as to appear less imposing, but Alice's mother had brought her up to hold her head high and her spine straight, and, anyway, why should she be ashamed of an aspect of her physical appearance which she had no control over?

She thought of Indigo, and what she would be doing if she was here. Indigo wouldn't be sitting down, Alice could be sure of that. She would be flapping about the room like a trapped butterfly, desperate to escape but unwilling or unable to accept the help from a kindly meant shepherding hand. Indigo would not have managed to remain patient, like Alice had, for the last ten minutes. Indigo would have ended up making Alice nervous, too; even just thinking about her made Alice re-evaluate her sleeves, unroll them and rebutton the cuffs. It was best that she wasn't there. Indigo would have been expecting Alice to have a softly, softly approach – so she would have been in for a shock.

More footsteps approached, but instead of carrying on past the door, they slowed and stopped. Alice fiddled with the button on her cuff, twisting and twisting until the cotton felt like it might snap.

The door opened, and three people walked in. She had met two of them – the offender manager, a short, stocky man called Brian; and Pete, a prison officer who thought he was God's gift and wore a disgustingly strong aftershave. In between them was a pale-skinned, scared-looking, thin boy, dressed in a blue T-shirt and jeans which both looked too big for his frame. He was nothing like the photos she had seen of him on Facebook and in Indigo's house, nothing like the boy she remembered on her doorstep. She recalled how repelled she had been by his nose ring, and was surprised to find it didn't bother her in the same way today, although it looked even more out of place against his pinched features.

He didn't look at her as he sat in the chair on the other side of the table.

Margaret spoke first. 'Morning, Kane.'

He nodded, not even looking at her. He was digging his fingernails into his forearm and staring at a smudged mark on the table top.

'This is Miss Hyde, Lou's mother,' Margaret said.

He looked at Alice now, slowly, as if it was incredibly painful to lift his head. She had never seen such sad, grey eyes.

'Please, you can call me Alice,' she said, still twisting the button in her fingers.

He blinked, and lowered his eyes again. Alice hadn't expected this urge that was flooding her to get up and put her arms around him.

'And this is Kane Owen.'

Alice gripped the sides of her chair to keep herself sitting down, felt a tacky lump of chewing gum wedged under one edge and pulled her hand away.

'I'm going to go over the ground rules before we get started,' Margaret said. 'Please let each other speak, and stay seated.' She checked off each rule on the fingers of her left hand. 'Respect what each other says – that means no rolling your eyes or making faces, no calling each other liars. Okay?'

Alice nodded and Kane coughed, still staring downwards. How were they going to have a conversation? She couldn't imagine him saying more than a couple of words to her.

'Now, I'm going to recap how this will all pan out.' Margaret lay the palms of her hands on the table. 'You will both get a chance to speak and ask questions. I will guide you through it all; you don't need to remember whose turn it is or anything like that. If you're both ready to start . . . ?'

'Yes.' Alice's voice sounded loud, too eager.

Kane looked at Margaret and tried to say something, but it came out as a croak. He cleared his throat. 'Ready.' In profile he looked a lot like Indigo. They had the same nose and cheekbones.

'Kane, would you like to start us off?' Margaret asked. 'Talk about the night of the seventeenth of August. No questions at this stage, please, Alice.'

Priya, sitting to the side of the room, clicked the end of her pen and held it poised at the top of a pad of paper on the table, ready to take notes. Margaret sat back in her chair. Alice crossed and uncrossed her legs. They all looked at Kane.

He coughed. 'We'd been out drinking. Me, Lou, Benny.' As he spoke Benny's name, he rubbed his hand against his chest, as if trying to wipe something away. 'Some other people.' He looked at Margaret and she nodded. 'I'd been watching these parkour videos, people climbing up buildings, jumping between them, that kind of thing. I was thinking of shooting something similar, trying to put my own spin on it.' He paused. 'It was my idea to climb the side of the car park. I'm sorry.'

He forced his head up again to look at Alice and met her eye. 'It was my fault.'

How could the police have thought this boy was capable of killing someone?

'Go on,' Margaret murmured.

'It was only me and Lou who did it; he had been really competitive with me all evening. He said the last one up would have to buy the winner a kebab.' He kept his head lifted now, shifting his gaze between Alice, Margaret and Priya's pen, scribbling on her pad of paper. 'We climbed to the third level. It wasn't that hard. Lou made it look really easy, he was so quick.' He coughed again.

'Do you want some water?' Margaret asked. Kane nodded, and Priya got up to fill a plastic cup. He took a sip and set it down on the table, running his finger up and down the ridges on its side.

'When we got to the third storey, Benny was there, with . . . another friend.' He didn't know that she knew about Wilko, he was still protecting him. 'But we'd all had a fair bit to drink, and yeah. Then we were arguing, me and Lou. And then he hit me, and I landed one on him, too. Benny wasn't doing anything; he was trying to break it up.' He looked at Alice, concern in his eyes. 'Benny didn't do anything wrong. It was nothing to do with him.'

'I know.' It was Alice's turn to stare at the smudge on the table between them, and she began scratching at it with her thumbnail. That he cared about Benny was clear; she could see it in his face when he talked about him, the way some of the tension disappeared from his features. 'And he's told me, by the way. About you two.'

'He has?' Confusion passed over his face.

Alice smiled at him. 'Yes.'

'But why would he . . . ?' He shook his head. 'I thought it was all over. I messed up, fighting with Lou. Benny was so angry with me.'

'I think you two need to talk.'

He sat back in his chair and chewed his cheek.

Margaret stepped in. 'Shall we get back to the events of that night? Kane, you were saying that you and Lou had hit each other?'

Kane blinked. 'It was Benny who somehow managed to calm it all down. He has this way, you know?'

Alice nodded, tracing her finger in the shape of a small 'B' on the table.

'He went to get something to help clean us up. But me and Lou, we . . . we got into it again.'

Alice looked up. Kane's voice had changed; the way he was talking was more stilted all of a sudden.

He looked her in the eye. 'And then I pushed him.' He pursed his lips, as though he was holding his breath.

'You didn't.' Alice felt the eyes of everyone in the room on her.

Margaret leaned forward and put her hand out, as if she could press Alice's words down and away. 'Alice, remember the ground rules, please. Let Kane finish.'

Alice didn't look away from him. A blush had risen in his face that wasn't there before.

'Kane? Would you like to continue?' Margaret leaned back into her chair once more.

'After that, I leaned over the edge.' Kane watched Alice warily. 'I could see him, lying on the road, and I panicked. I ran away. I'm sorry. I should have stayed to help Benny.'

'You didn't push him, though, did you? I know that, you know that.' Alice kept her voice level.

Margaret shot her hand out again. Alice had not told her and Priya about what she planned to say, and she sensed their rising panic that the situation was not going to remain under their control. 'Alice, please, I must—'

'But I want to know why you said you did it,' Alice said, ignoring her. 'You owe me the truth.'

Kane dug his nails into his arm again. 'I did push him,' he said quietly. Margaret and Priya exchanged looks.

Alice blinked slowly, formed both hands into fists and pressed them into the table top.

'I've spent most of the last month thinking my son was murdered, when he wasn't.' She spoke more quietly now, but with more force.

'I pushed him,' Kane repeated in a whisper, his eyes wide.

Over at the side of the room, Brian and Pete shifted in their chairs.

Alice went on, letting anger loose into her words, thumping her fists on to the table. 'The funeral has been delayed because of the police investigation. All of this could have been avoided.'

'Alice, really, this isn't how we discussed this conference panning out. I think perhaps we should take a short—'

Alice glared at Margaret. Could she not see what Alice was getting at? She was still looking at her when Kane spoke, and she saw the shock in the other woman's eyes as he did.

'I may as well have pushed him,' he said. There was a lightness in his voice that hadn't been there before.

The room fell silent around him. Alice closed her eyes, a bitter taste in her mouth from all the angry words she had forced herself to say. They had been worth it. It had worked.

'Listen to me,' she said. 'I've spoken to someone who saw it all happen. Someone I believe. Someone who has no agenda, who doesn't care about ticking a box and closing a case. And she says you did not push my son.'

Margaret leaned forward again. 'Alice, I really must stop you there.' She pinched the bridge of her nose, resting her elbow on the table. 'I am obliged to remind you both that if you say any-thing that is different to the evidence then I am going to have to disclose this to the police. Do you both understand?'

'Yes.' Alice was impatient. Any interruption now could pre-vent her from getting what she needed from Kane. Sure enough, he looked terrified, even more colour draining from his skin as she watched.

'Kane, look at me.' Alice ducked her head to get into his line of sight. 'This has gone on long enough. You need to tell the truth. Why did you confess to the police, if you didn't do it?'

Kane crossed his arms. 'It was my fault. They asked me if I was responsible for Lou's death. I was. They asked me if he fell because of me. He did. They asked me a hundred different ways. They said, "You hit him and he fell."'

'And you just agreed with them? You could end up spending most of your life in cesspits like this, Kane. I don't understand why you didn't tell them the truth.'

'I tried. They . . . they knew about the fight before I went in there, that Lou had been punched, before he fell. I didn't realise they'd know that, they caught me off guard. I'd hit him . . . but that was earlier, before . . .'

Alice left him to a moment of silence, hoping he would keep talking.

'I can't even remember it clearly now. I was standing really close to him when he went over. I was really drunk. Like, really drunk. Maybe I did give him a shove? That's what he said, that detective. "You were wasted, weren't you? Are you sure you're remembering it all correctly?"'

'But you didn't do it; you know that now, don't you? You believe me about the woman who saw Lou fall?'

He shrugged.

'Kane,' Margaret cut in, then looked at Alice. 'Can I ask some-thing here?'

Alice nodded.

'Where was your solicitor when this was going on?'

'I didn't have one. They told me I could, but it would take a long time to get one. I thought it'd be less trouble if I took up less of their time.'

Margaret drew in a sharp breath through her teeth then sat back again.

'It should all be on the tape,' Kane said. 'When they started recording the interview again, they said I had the right to a solicitor and was refusing my right to have one – something like that.' He paused. 'At one point they brought this file out and put it in front of me.' He looked ahead at the table, as if seeing the file there. 'They asked me about my dad, said this was the file they had on him. I told them that he hanged himself when I was a kid. They said it must have been hard for me. They asked if it had made me angry.'

Next to her, Alice could see Margaret shaking her head.

'I said, of course it made me angry. That he had left us. Left his responsibilities. Then they asked me, "What about you? Are you the kind of person who accepts when he is responsible for something?"' He was picking up pace now, the words flowing fast, and his face becoming more animated. 'I didn't know what to say to that. They didn't give me time to answer, they just said, "It was your fault that Louis Durand died, wasn't it?"'

'And what did you say?' Alice asked quietly.

'Yes. I said yes.' Kane fiddled with his nose ring.

'And you've believed that,' Alice said. 'All this time you've been on remand?'

'Sometimes. Not always. I couldn't get my head straight, not in these places they've locked me up in. Other times, I've been thinking, even if I didn't actually push him, I was responsible.'

'What do you mean?' Alice asked.

'I told you, it was my idea to climb up there in the first place.'

'That doesn't mean you have to go to prison for murder.'

'After Benny left to get us ice, Lou jumped up on the wall. But all of a sudden, he seemed really, really pissed. I guess because he didn't usually drink.'

'He didn't drink?'

'Not much, no.' Kane looked uncomfortable.

Something Harry Wilkinson had said came back to her. *Always just a half for himself.* She'd assumed that Lou would be a big drinker. But then, there were the full bottles of vodka in his wardrobe, too. She scratched at her scalp, trying to make sense of what Kane was saying.

'It might have been the punch I landed, getting to his head.'

'But why? Why didn't he drink? Don't you all?'

Kane squirmed in his seat again. 'He . . . he told me once that he'd seen what alcohol . . . what alcohol can do to people.' He looked across the room at Priya's pen, still moving across the page. 'He said he didn't want to end up depressed, with no friends.'

Alice felt the skin on her chest burning, rising up to her neck.

'Go on, Kane,' Margaret said.

'He said he was going to climb another level. I asked him, what are you doing? I told him—' Kane hit the table with the side of his hand. 'I told him to stop being so stupid, and he said, "Why? It was your idea." '

Alice could hear Lou's voice saying the words. She could see his expression, the way he would have cocked his head.

'I told him it was too high. I told him he was going to hurt himself, but he just laughed. The last thing I said to him . . .' He trailed off, his voice breaking.

'Go on,' Alice said.

'I told him to get down. He said, "You've got it all wrong. There's no such thing as too high – life's all about the thrill." And then, he . . . he moved and he slipped and then he was gone. It happened so quickly.'

'Slipped?'

'Yes. That's how I remember it. He . . . kind of, lost his footing.'

He hadn't jumped. Lou hadn't committed suicide. Alice felt light-headed and pressed her hands between her thighs under the table to try to ground herself. *I knew you wouldn't do that.*

For a few moments, the only sound in the room was Priya's pen on her paper.

Good, thought Alice. *Make sure you get all this down.*

'One more question,' Alice said. 'I know Harry Wilkinson was there. What went on with him and Lou that night?'

'Wilko?' Kane looked up at her. 'I'm not sure. Something happened, but I don't know what. Honestly. We saw him getting out of a car and he cornered me afterwards, telling me to keep my mouth shut. I told him I had no idea what he meant.'

Alice looked him in the eye. She believed him.

'But that had nothing to do with Lou falling. It was me. If it wasn't for me, he wouldn't have climbed in the first place, he wouldn't have been in that mood. He wouldn't have got up on that wall.'

'It wasn't your fault.' Alice reached across the table, trying to get hold of his arm, but he ignored her hands and her words.

'You shouldn't be trying to help me, not after what I said about you.'

Alice stood up.

'Please, Alice, take a seat. The ground rules,' Margaret said. Alice sighed. Surely by now the ground rules were irrelevant? After everything that had been said here? But she sat back down.

Kane had his head in his hands, his fingernails now digging into his forehead.

'Kane, listen to me.' She reached across again and tapped the table in front of him. 'I forgive you.' Another tap. 'Lou forgives you.' Another tap. 'Now you need to forgive yourself.'

As she said it, she suddenly knew she needed to say it to herself as much as to him.

'Kane, you really should tell your solicitor everything you have said here,' Margaret said. 'I think we should call it a day, if you are both happy to leave it there? Priya and I are going to write up an outcome agreement, saying that you will tell your solicitor the truth, and then we will get you both to sign it. Okay?'

Alice nodded without taking her eyes off Kane, whose head was still in his hands.

'Kane?' Margaret said.

'Okay,' he said, his voice muffled behind his palms.

'You can get up now, if you want. Help yourselves to biscuits.' Margaret and Priya stood and moved to another table at the side of the room, murmuring between them and getting forms out of a folder.

Alice moved round to Kane's side of the table, and as she did so he dropped his hands from his face and got up, slowly. They stood a metre apart, looking at each other, before Alice stepped forward and held out her arms.

He fell into them and she hugged him tight, feeling the wetness from his silent tears soaking through her shirt at the shoulder.

She held him like that for several minutes, giving him the hug she wished she could give Lou.

Indigo

8th October

I've brought a notepad and pen with me this time, to write down everything they say. In case this is the beginning, rather than the end, of Kane's ordeal. Having him at home for the last two weeks has made my heart so full I could hardly breathe; but being back here in court, I'm faced with the terrifying reality – they could rip him away from me again.

He's in the dock, looking immeasurably smarter and brighter than he was when he was last in there, two weeks ago. That day, he should have been sentenced – but instead, we were in the Crown Court to have his case reopened. He looked exhausted and broken then; today he stands straighter. He's had a shave, and I've managed to get some food down him so his cheeks don't look so hollow. If I was painting a portrait, I'd use a reddish base for his face, some purples; if I'd been painting him as we sat here last time I'd have needed greys and blues. Once we'd got home after the judge had bailed him, I'd expected that, like me, he would struggle to sleep, but he's been knocked out every night, exhausted, he says, after the weeks in uncomfortable prison bunks and noisy cell blocks. I have crept into his room each night, as I did when he was a small child. Only this time, I don't have the excuse of going to check that he is still underneath his duvet, or that he still has his beloved but grubby toy dog Blue within reach. For fourteen nights I have softly opened his door, tiptoed in and stood by his bed, watching the rise and fall of his chest as he slept, sometimes for up to an hour. How could I tear myself away, when I don't know if I will ever have the chance to do it again?

I can't stop my left leg bouncing up and down behind the wooden panel at the front of the public gallery. Only a few feet away from me, that smarmy detective DC Brailsford is sitting with a colleague, behind the prosecution barrister. Even the sight of the back of his head, the reddish hair flicking up in all directions, makes my chest rise and fall more rapidly with angry breaths. *Focus on your senses,* I instruct myself. *Calm down.* I pick up my pen, feeling its weight and coolness against my skin, and write: *Exclude the interview.* Listening to the drag and click of the ballpoint as I pull it across the paper, I doodle around those words, replicating the wood I am resting on, sketching the lines of the grain and a knot formed of steadily growing circles. My breathing slows and I look around for something else to draw, casting my eyes up to the high ceilings and large frosted windows. They make the room feel much airier than the dreary Magistrates' Court. Or maybe it's me that is lighter, more hopeful?

Before we came into court this morning, Clive took Kane and me into an interview room. Clive's a different man since Alice went to Long Lartin. His cool disinterest has gone – now he is flustered, he is anxious and, best of all, he is trying. He won't say it, but he knows he's let Kane down, and it turns out he is a decent enough man to want to fix it. As we sat around a table in the small room, he told us that Kane was looking at a couple of options.

'I'm hoping they will agree that your police interview can be excluded,' Clive said. 'But if they don't, you'll be going to trial.'

Kane nodded. Once the restorative justice people had reported back to the police, Clive had recruited a young barrister called Ed Cohen who had met with the Crown Prosecution Service to tell them he wanted Kane's guilty plea cancelled. That's how we'd ended up getting the case reopened, but we knew that the success we'd had at the end of last month had only been a small one – Kane had been bailed while the prosecution worked out what they wanted to do next.

We all sat in silence for a moment.

'But remember,' Clive said, 'we have a great deal in our favour. If I were them, I wouldn't be taking it to trial. We've got Cassie Simpson, Benoît Durand's original witness statement saying his brother threw the first punch, Louis' mother supporting us, and, perhaps most importantly, let's not forget the fact that the police shouldn't really have got a confession out of you without a solicitor present.' He shifted in his seat and pulled a handkerchief out of his pocket to blot his forehead. 'Obviously it goes without saying that I wish I had pushed that more at the time. With hindsight I would have acted differently on your behalf, but then you were so adamant about your guilt . . .'

Kane looked at me quickly before speaking. I knew what the look meant: don't react, Mum. He was well aware of how I felt about Clive's handling of the case. I clamped my jaw shut and fixed my gaze on my yellow bracelet.

'It's not your fault,' Kane said. 'I didn't make your job easy.'

'Well, then. Let's keep our fingers crossed. Ed's with the CPS now, seeing if he can talk them round. We'll see him in court.'

When we had emerged from the interview room, Alice and Benny were waiting for us in the busy corridor outside court ten, and now they are sitting next to me in the public gallery. I met Alice's father, David, at the last court hearing, and his presence in the row behind me today is reassuring – an occasional pat on the shoulder; a whisper of, 'It'll all be fine.' It makes me miss Lily. She knows everything now, and she wanted to come here, but Dawn put her foot down – 'She's not strong enough,' she said. And for once, I had to admit that she was right. But if she wasn't healthy enough now, was she ever going to recover to the point where she could travel again? Neither Lily nor I was able to voice the fear in both of our minds when we spoke on the phone a few days ago. What if we didn't get the outcome we wanted today? Would Kane ever see his grandmother again?

I can't think like that.

He *will* be coming home today. A spray of daffodils has emerged from the top of the curling lines I have doodled, and a magpie perches on the other end of it, its beak pulling at the twigs of a nest. My own nest will be empty in just a matter of weeks, touch wood – I tap the barrier in front of me. I can't believe I was so scared about him going to university. I knew nothing then of what really losing him would feel like. If he can only get through this, I will be glad to pack him off. I promise you, Universe. I will be fine on my own. Just let him walk free.

Benny leans over my arm, looking at my drawings. I have just drawn a second magpie, this one soaring in flight. 'They're just scribbles,' I say.

He leans closer. 'Beautiful scribbles. Especially this.' He taps the flying bird.

'Thank you, they're nothing.'

'All rise.' The court clerk's loud announcement makes me jump and I drop my pen as I stand.

Benny bends down to pick it up after Judge Lafferty has entered the court and sat down. *Thank you*, I mouth at Benny as we take our seats again. The judge spreads his papers on the table in front of him and pushes his glasses up his nose. For all his seriousness – I didn't see him smile once during the last hearing – he looks like a pleasant and, more importantly, fair man. He slides a hand over the red and purple stripes running down the front of his black robes, and I turn a page in my book, ready to take notes.

All is well. All is well. All is well.

A man sitting in front of the judge, also wearing official-looking clothes, lifts his head towards the back of the court. 'Are you Kane Owen?'

I turn to see Kane reply, 'Yes.'

'Thank you, you may sit down.'

'So, Mr Cohen.' Judge Lafferty lays his hands on the table and fixes Ed with his glare. 'Are we going to hear your application regarding the defendant's police interview?'

Ed stands up as the judge addresses him. 'Your honour, I believe my learned friend has something to say on this matter.' He gestures towards the prosecution barrister, who slowly rises to her feet. 'We had a chance to discuss the case before coming into court, your honour.'

Even at this distance, across the court, I see Judge Lafferty's eyebrows arch. 'I see. Miss Madekwe? Would you care to enlighten the court?'

She clears her throat. 'Your honour,' she says, bowing her head, 'we do not seek to oppose the defence's application. In fact, we offer no evidence in this case.'

'I see.'

Benny leans towards me. 'What does that mean?' he whispers.

'They're dropping the case.' I grab his hand.

Kane is free. We did it. I look over at him in the dock, but he doesn't let me catch his eye. He looks panicked, as though he isn't breathing. He is staring at the judge, his hands gripping the glass barrier in front of him.

The judge addresses the prosecution barrister. 'Miss Madekwe, if I may, I would rather like to suggest that you pass on a – how shall I put this? – a recommendation, that's what we'll say. Would you be so good as to pass on a *recommendation* to your colleagues at Avon and Somerset Police?' He peers past her, at DC Brailsford and his sidekick.

'Your honour.' Miss Madekwe dips her chin to her chest, her expression grim.

'Perhaps it would be prudent, in future, to ensure that a murder suspect has his or her lawyer with them before they are encouraged to confess to the crime. Don't you agree?'

Miss Madekwe nods. 'I will pass your recommendation on, your honour.'

DC Brailsford shifts awkwardly in his seat.

'Excellent. Mr Owen, you are free to go.' Judge Lafferty claps his hands together. 'Is that everything?' he asks his clerk. 'May I go for my lunch?'

Is that it?

I glare at DC Brailsford's broad shoulders. Shouldn't he be punished in some way? He and his colleagues could have ruined my son's life.

As Judge Lafferty leaves I switch my attention to Kane in the dock, my heart pounding in anticipation of taking him home – for good, this time – so I don't notice as Alice's father steps around the front row of seats in the gallery and launches himself towards the two police officers. For a brief moment, consisting of equal measures of horror and delight, I think he's going to hit one of them. When they turn around to face him, I can see that they have the same thought.

'Which one of you was in charge?' He spits out the words. His hands are twitching at his side.

'Dad! Don't.'

DC Brailsford looks up at Alice as she calls after her father, pushing past Benny and I as she does so.

'Which one?' David asks.

'I was in charge of the investigation, sir.' DC Brailsford squares up to him, but despite his towering height he looks sheepish and only meets his eye for a second.

The whole courtroom has fallen silent and everyone is

watching. Nobody steps in to tell Alice's father to back off – I'd like to think it's because most of them agree that these shoddy detectives have it coming to them.

'You manipulated that lad.'

'Sir, I was—'

'You manipulated him into confessing to a crime he did not commit.'

Alice reaches her father and puts a hand on his elbow, trying to pull him away. 'This isn't going to change anything.'

'You left me thinking my grandson had been murdered. She . . .' He shook his arm out of Alice's grip and jabbed a finger against her shoulder. 'She thought her son had been murdered.'

'I realise this must be—'

'And that poor woman there,' David said, pointing back at me, 'was told her son was a killer.'

I look over at Kane again. The court usher is standing at the gate to the dock, keys dangling from her hand, poised to open it, but she is staring at David. I meet Kane's eyes, and shake my head. *I never believed it.*

Benny has slipped past me now, and in my peripheral vision I'm aware of him helping Alice to pull David away. My eyes remain locked on my son's. *I always knew.*

'. . . don't know how in God's name you're immune from punishment . . .' David is saying, as they drag him back to the public gallery. 'My grandson and that lad, that poor lad in there, are twice the men you'll ever be . . .'

And now Alice is hushing him, he is calming down, the police detectives are being led out by Miss Madekwe, and the mutters and murmurs are beginning again around the rest of the court. But still I can't look away from Kane. He's coming home. We'll have Sunday dinners together and watch movies and talk without being watched over by prison guards. The usher snaps back into action as if someone had pressed her pause button for the last two minutes and unlocks the gate to the dock.

Kane steps out and walks towards us.

As I pull him into my arms, Alice slips past, head bowed, making for the door, holding her father's hand.

For her, there'll be no Sunday dinners. No movies. No more talking.

There's no ruling that will bring Lou back to her.

Alice

22nd October

Alice stood in her underwear in what was once Lou's bedroom. She stared at the black shift dress hanging from the handle of the wardrobe, the matching court shoes on the floor below it. When she had last worn it, to bury her Uncle George, Lou had told her she should wear dresses more often. She must have blushed, because he immediately clarified his comment. 'You know, just for a change from the monotonous trouser and shirt combo,' he'd said.

She lifted her wrist and checked the time. Ten o'clock. The hanger holding the dress clattered against the door as she opened the wardrobe. She pulled out the two bottles of her Żubrówka that Lou had hidden in there and a pair of oil-stained blue overalls. As she put them on, she fished some fine sandpaper out of Lou's tool bag. She put it in her pocket, along with his needle file, which she kept on his bedside table overnight.

Alice had already made her decision: today was as good a day as any to stop. She crouched on the floor, reaching her arm as far under the bed as it would go, pulling out the Black Cow. There wasn't much left – maybe a quarter of a bottle. She clutched it to her chest, along with the two bottles of Żubrówka from Lou's wardrobe, and went into her old bedroom. Dragging a stool over to her wardrobe, she climbed on top of it, opened the top cupboard, and pulled out an unopened bottle from the back, stashed behind boxes of old clothes. Four down, one to go.

But first, she needed something from the loft. She picked up a bag from the chair in her room and stuffed the bottles inside, slinging it over her shoulder before opening the loft hatch. Climbing the ladder, she felt suddenly dizzy, and rested her forehead against a rung for a moment before forcing herself to continue.

She pulled out a couple of small brushes from a plastic box neatly labelled: 'Painting Equipment'. With them safely stowed in her pocket, she opened the skylight and was hit by a draught of clean, cool air. She inhaled slowly, leaning out over the roof. She'd been planning to take the bottles down to the sink, but this could work too. One by one, she took them out of her bag and poured their contents out of the window, the clear liquid trickling down the roof tiles into the gutter.

As she listened to the vodka running down the drainpipe, she looked beyond the edge of the roof and into the garden. There it was, still – the Tiger.

Lou was always with her, even at work. He was the student sitting upstairs at the library, bent over his laptop and textbooks. He was the boy who ran into the children's area with his chubby little legs. He was the difficult customer who treated her with disdain. He was the blur of a passer-by who walked past the library's huge front windows, in the golden October sun.

And at home, she didn't even have work to act as a brief respite. No minutes of peace while she engrossed herself in a supervisors' meeting or in a particularly complicated invoice. Here, she saw the bike every time she looked out of the window, and saw him hovering in every corner of the house. And it was so quiet and empty now. Benny had left for university not long after Kane's release. But one evening a couple of weeks ago, he had surprised her when she returned from work. The house had been tidy. As she had taken off her shoes in the hallway, the smell of raw garlic and onion had stung her nostrils. When she'd stepped into the kitchen, she had been hit by a waft of fried chorizo.

'What's all this?'

Benny had been stirring a pan on the hob, his face red and beaded with sweat. 'Chicken stew. It'll be about twenty minutes.' He clapped his hands together. 'While that's cooking, let me get you a drink.'

'Hang on. What do you want?' Alice had laughed. 'Money? A new car?'

Benny lifted a bottle of white wine out of the fridge and poured three glasses. Who was the third one for?

'No,' Benny said, taking a sip from one glass and passing her another. 'It's your brains I'm after. And your free time.'

Alice frowned.

'You'll see.' He walked towards the French windows, which were wide open, calling over his shoulder, 'Come on.'

'Wait, let me get my shoes.'

'You don't need any. Come on, just get out here.' He had lifted his wine glass towards her, his body perfectly framed by the doorway.

Alice had never been one for photo albums packed with pictures of the boys, but if she could have taken one of him in that moment, she would have done. She closed her eyes now and remembered it: the way the sun had shone through the glass and threw a small patch of light on to his T-shirt, the way his dark eyelashes had brushed together softly as he blinked, the way he had smiled at her as though he enjoyed her company.

The memory dissolved and she reached for the handle of the loft skylight to pull it shut. She hid the bottles behind a couple of half-used cans of white emulsion. She'd put them out for recycling later, once Benny had gone.

As she made her way downstairs and through the hallway, her

father emerged from the living room, dressed in a black suit and tie. He looked at what she was wearing, but didn't say anything – instead, he turned and softly closed the living-room door behind him. She heard Benny say something on the other side.

The two of them had become close since Lou's death. She knew from her father that Benny had called him several times from Exeter, 'just for a chat'.

That's who the third glass of wine had been for, that evening.

Following Benny out on to the patio, she had paused. It was the first time she had been out there for a long time. She had forced herself to look up at the prison wall, ready for the familiar gloom to fill her heart, but even after several seconds of staring at it, the darkness hadn't come. She'd been struck, instead, by the beautiful earthy redness of it, and the way the sun caught the very top line of bricks, glinting through the razor wire. Had Lou ever looked up at the wall and thought this?

Then she had seen her father, on the lawn by the Tiger.

She glanced at Benny, but he wasn't looking her way; he was handing his grandfather his wine. Next to them, the bike was uncovered, the tarp neatly folded on the grass. Lying to the other side of it was Lou's duffel bag full of tools and a small stool from the living room with the Haynes manual lying open on top of it.

Alice couldn't explain the rising panic she had felt as she walked across the grass towards them. 'You think we should get rid of it?'

'Get rid? No.' Benny put an arm around her.

Her father had pointed at her. 'You two are going to fix it up, Ali.'

Alice turned under Benny's arm to look at him, without pulling away. 'You don't know anything about bikes.' She rested her head against his shoulder, studying the Tiger.

'But you do,' he said, kissing her head.

Her body stiffened. 'I do not.'

315

'That's not what Pops says. He says you were always watching him in the workshop. Helping him out, even.'

She looked at her father, who grinned at her, and tilted her head back to look at the sky. She should be cross with him for telling Benny things about her that she hadn't wanted shared. But instead of anger, what she felt was regret. As the blush bloomed in her cheeks, she pressed her cold wine glass against them. She had always been his little assistant, it was true. And not always so little – she had only stopped when she moved out of her parents' home to live with Étienne, to buy this house together. She never went back to his workshop, and she never started doing any of her own restoration work.

Her father had set his glass down on the open manual and bent to pick something else up out of the long grass. He'd handed her a folded pile of blue material, and she had stepped away from Benny to take it from him, using her free hand to shake it out.

'Overalls.' She had held them up, looking at her father with amusement. 'But I thought you and Lou didn't approve?'

On a chair in the kitchen, Benny's smart black shoes sat on top of a piece of newspaper next to her father's, gleaming in the light from the window. Lou would have told them not to bother, he'd have snatched the pot of polish out of their hands, hidden the brush. He'd probably have told them all to wear trainers, if he could.

In fact, Alice thought as she walked through into the utility room, hadn't he worn his scruffy green Converse to Uncle George's funeral? Why could she find it funny now, but at the time feel his rebelliousness was a personal attack on her?

The Żubrówka behind the casserole dishes was long-finished, but there was one final bottle secreted in the utility room's cleaning cupboard. This had two-thirds left in it. Alice lifted it down from its hiding place, unscrewed the cap and brought it to her mouth, pausing with the glass rim of the bottle against her lips. She licked the ridges of the thread, closed her eyes, then screwed the lid back on and headed out through the back door into the garden.

It was a cool but beautiful morning, which was just as well – she couldn't be doing with a hot funeral. All that standing up, shaking hands, talking to people, sweaty and uncomfortable. That was the only blessing of this day being so delayed by the police investigation – at least they'd avoided the final throes of summer. She stopped outside the back door, slipped her gardening trainers on and walked across the grass to the Tiger.

She set the bottle on the lawn and untied the toggle at the far end of the tarp, before gently pulling it off and setting it aside. Lou would be happy with her progress; the bike had new, shiny black tyres now and the brakes were no longer covered in rust. Squatting next to the engine, she leaned over to pick up her bottle and unscrewed the lid again. She dribbled a little of the vodka over the engine fins and then set about rubbing it in with one of her paintbrushes, dissolving any traces of oil and dirt.

When they'd stood out here in the garden with their glasses of wine, all of their eyes trained on the bike, she'd asked her father, 'Did Lou know – about me helping in your workshop?'

He had nodded, taking a sip of his drink. 'I told them both a while ago.'

'Before he got this?'

'It would have been, yes.'

Lou had never mentioned it to her. 'I don't know, Benny,' she had said. 'I don't think your brother would appreciate me messing with his pride and joy.' She had sat back in the grass, bringing her own glass to her mouth for the first time. But as the liquid touched her lips, she heard Kane's voice. *He told me once that he'd seen what alcohol can do to people.* Kane knew, and she knew, that Lou had been talking about her. The blush returned to her cheeks. She wished Lou had asked her about the bottles he had found – so she could have told him that she had it all under control. She wasn't like the drunkards who smashed their bottles outside the library entrance every other night. A bit of high-quality vodka each evening, to ease away the day didn't mean she had a problem. But even as she thought those things, she let the glass fall from her mouth without tasting its contents.

'He loved you, Mum. He wanted to make you proud. I know he didn't always . . .'

Alice had flattened a patch of the lawn and stood her glass on it, before brushing off her knees and standing up. 'You don't need to say that.'

But she knew what he said was true; she felt it as she touched each part of the Tiger. She had been surprised to find the knowledge within her, and still was. Since when had she known?

Alice wiped her hand down her overalls. As she scrubbed away with the brush, she muttered to herself. She had notes in her rucksack upstairs, ready to use if she needed them later. But she knew it all by heart.

She was pleased with how Lou's eulogy would open: by making the funeral attendees feel awkward, just as he would have liked it. She imagined standing up in front of her gathered audience. 'Lou would not want all this fuss,' she said, her elbow aching already from the effort of brushing the dirty metal. 'How do I know this? Because he was not only my son but also a version of myself.' She poured a little more alcohol over the fins to rinse them, then used some paper towel from her pocket to dry them off. They already looked better – the aluminium was gleaming. 'I wish I'd realised that when he was still alive.' She rocked back on to her heels and rubbed her arm. 'Lou was the most—'

'Leave it out here, it'll be totally safe.' Benny's voice loudly interrupted her, and she looked over her shoulder at him. He was wheeling a bicycle out of the back door and propping it up against the wall, followed by Indigo.

They both noticed her at the same time. Indigo lifted a hand to wave, but Benny's jaw dropped when he saw her.

'Jesus, Mum. Why aren't you dressed yet?' He looked smart in his suit, though his tie wasn't quite straight. 'The car is coming in . . .' He looked at his watch. 'Five minutes.'

'I am ready, I just need to change into my dress, wash my hands. I'll come inside in a minute.'

'One minute, max.'

'I promise.'

Benny shook his head and went back into the house, where Alice could hear him talking to Kane.

She turned back to Lou's bike, smiling at Indigo as she did so. She took the needle file out of her pocket, wrapped it in the piece of sandpaper, and slid it between two of the engine fins, rubbing gently at a patch of oxidised aluminium. She wasn't sure if it would work, but if it did, she could give it all a proper clean when she had more time tomorrow.

Indigo sat on the lawn, spreading her long flowing blue skirt around her, watching Alice work on the engine. More than a minute passed and neither of them spoke. Alice thought Indigo might try to chivvy her along too, but she didn't. She leaned back and stretched her legs out as if they had all the time in the world.

'We're not going anywhere without you,' she said eventually. 'But you are going to have to get it over and done with at some point.'

'I'm not nervous, if that's what you're suggesting,' Alice said, instantly cross with herself for speaking so quickly. 'I'm sure the car will be late. I'll change in a moment.'

'Why not go like that?'

Alice laughed, looking down at her overalls. 'Clearly you don't know me very well.'

'I don't know about that.' Indigo picked a few blades of grass. 'I have a pretty good idea of what makes you tick, I'd say.'

Not many people would presume to say that about Alice, she knew. Her father, maybe? And Lou, she had come to think, had known her better than she realised. Indigo's intentions were kind, but there was no way she could have gained a grasp of the essence of her in just a few months. 'Tell me something about myself that I haven't told you, then.'

Indigo sat up and tapped her fingers on her knees. 'You . . .' She smiled as she thought of something. 'You wouldn't have forgiven me if I had lied to you like you did to me.'

Alice pulled the file out and ran a finger along the edge of the fin to inspect its smoothness. Much better. 'No,' she said, looking up at Indigo. 'And yet, here you are: the only person who offered to come in the car with us today.'

'Here I am.' Indigo pushed herself to her feet and held out a hand to Alice. 'Now go inside and get ready.'

Alice pocketed her file and paintbrush, took Indigo's hand and heaved her body up. Instead of letting go of her fingers, she clenched her own tighter around them, and Indigo squeezed back until Alice's bones ached. They stood like this for a minute or two, neither of them speaking, simply standing side by side; breathing, listening, watching.

She would leave the bike uncovered. One afternoon of air wouldn't hurt it. Slipping her hand out of Indigo's, she rested it on the leather of the Tiger's seat. This would be her next task: ripping off the black gaffer tape that was only just holding the seam, before sewing it back together so it held faster and firmer than ever before.

Acknowledgements

Thank you.

For giving me precious writing time (as well as much-needed love, laughs and support): Matt Hawthorne, my mum and dad, Sascha Bishop. For inspiring me to work hard in that time and to ensure every minute away from you counted: my little whirlwind, Gwen. For keeping me company as I wrote: Bobby – as this book came slowly to life, so did you.

For your wisdom, encouragement and belief: Liz Foley, Peter Straus, Jade Chandler. Thank you also to the incredible teams at Harvill Secker and Rogers, Coleridge & White, who have worked so hard for me.

For reading: Alison Powell, Jen Faulkner, Jen Leggo, Rachel Buckler, Clare Liggins, Beth Jones, Rhianna Cranstone, Vicki Mathias, Lucy King, Paddy Edwards. Many of you gave up time that you didn't really have to fit in with my deadlines, and I'm so grateful.

For sharing your knowledge or contacts: Liz Cass, Alexa Stephenson, Jenny Tallentire, Tony Heydon, Dan Evans, John Long, Andy Jack, Kate Hook, Tony Walker, Tracey Wintle, Steve Ledsham, Geoff Bennett, Sam Clark, Ana McLaughlin. Thanks is also due to the following authors who helped me so much by sharing insights into their former or day jobs: Anne Corlett, Ruth Mancini, Tony Kent, Polly Ho-Yen, Noelle Holten – please go and check out their books. For answering random specific questions by text: my amazing friends. I'm looking at you, Tom Aspinwall, Chris Allen, Luke Hanna, Sophie Riddell, Rachel Profit, to name but a few. Any inaccuracies or improbabilities are my own fault entirely.

For being so open with your painful memories, thank you to all the mothers who helped me understand Alice and Indigo: Vi Donovan of the Chris Donovan Trust, and the women who I spoke to through Affect – a charity supporting the families and friends of prisoners.

And finally, to YOU, for reading – this book or my debut novel, or both. To the bloggers, the reviewers, with a special mention to @LiteraryElf on Twitter – seeing your posts recommending my first book while I wrote my second spurred me on hugely. To anyone who left a review or messaged me saying you were looking forward to the next one – you kept me going when it got tough! Thank you, thank you, thank you. These pages full of words are yours, not mine.